PRAISE FOR GRACE GREENE
AND THE EMERALD ISLE, NC SERIES NOVELS

Beach Rental

DOUBLE WINNER IN THE 2012 GDRWA BOOKSELLERS BEST AWARD

FINALIST IN THE 2012 GAYLE WILSON AWARD OF EXCELLENCE

FINALIST IN THE 2012 PUBLISHED MAGGIE AWARD FOR EXCELLENCE

"No author can come close to capturing the awe-inspiring essence of the North Carolina coast like Greene. Her debut novel seamlessly combines hope, love and faith, like the female equivalent of Nicholas Sparks. Her writing is meticulous and so finely detailed you'll hear the gulls overhead and the waves crashing onto shore. Grab a hanky, bury your toes in the sand and get ready to be swept away with this unforgettable beach read." —*RT Book Reviews 4.5 stars TOP PICK*

Beach Winds

FINALIST IN THE 2014 OKRWA INTERNATIONAL DIGITAL AWARDS

FINALIST IN THE 2014 WISRA WRITE TOUCH READERS' AWARD

"Greene's follow up to Beach Rental is exquisitely written with lots of emotion and tugging on the heartstrings. Returning to Emerald Isle is like a warm reunion with an old friend and readers will be inspired by the captivating story where we get to meet new characters and reconnect with a few familiar faces, too. The author's perfect prose highlights family relationships which we may find similar to our own and will have you dreaming of strolling along the shore to rediscover yourself in no time at all. This novel will have one wondering about faith, hope and courage and you may be lucky enough to gain all three by the time Beach Winds last page is read." —*RT Book Reviews 4.5 stars TOP PICK*

Grab a book and a comfy reading spot,
and get away with a good read.

Thank you for choosing BEACH WEDDING.

Grace Greene

BEACH WEDDING

THE EMERALD ISLE, NC STORIES SERIES
NOVEL #3

It's always a good time for a love story
and a trip to the beach.

BY GRACE GREENE

BEACH WEDDING

BY

GRACE GREENE

The Emerald Isle, NC Stories Series ~ Novel #3

Kersey Creek Books
P.O. Box 6054
Ashland, VA 23005

Cover Design by Grace Greene

Hardcover Release: September 2020
ISBN-13: 978-1-7328785-3-2
Trade Paperback Release: November 2017
ISBN-13: 978-0-9968756-4-6
Digital Release: November 2017
ISBN-13: 978-0-9968756-5-3

DEDICATION

This book is dedicated to the friends and family who inspired it, who were there at the beginning with Beach Rental, and who have continued to inspire and encourage me, including readers like Cora, and my aunt and uncle, Sallie and Ronnie Smiley. Aunt Sallie and Uncle Ronnie introduced me and my family to Emerald Isle. Without that introduction, I wonder whether this series would have happened? I'm so glad it did. It has been the best beach trip ever. Thanks!

ACKNOWLEDGEMENTS

Special thanks to my first readers, Amy, Amy, Terry and Jill for their fortitude and dedication to getting this book right.

My loving gratitude to my husband, my biggest fan and supporter, and I thank God for directing my steps.

BOOKS BY GRACE GREENE

Emerald Isle, North Carolina Stories Series

Beach Rental
Beach Winds
Beach Wedding
"Beach Towel" (A Short Story)
Beach Christmas *(Christmas Novella)*
Beach Walk *(Christmas Novella)*
Clair *(Beach Brides Novella Series)*

Virginia Country Roads Novels

Kincaid's Hope
A Stranger in Wynnedower
Cub Creek (Book One)
Leaving Cub Creek (Book Two)

Stand-Alone Cub Creek Novels

The Happiness In Between
The Memory of Butterflies
A Light Last Seen

Wildflower House Novels

Wildflower Heart
Wildflower Hope
Wildflower Christmas *(A Wildflower House Novella)*

www.GraceGreene.com

BEACH WEDDING

Along the Outer Banks of North Carolina and the Crystal Coast ~ from Front Street Gallery in Beaufort, NC, to the beaches of Emerald Isle and across Bogue Sound to Morehead City...

Maia Donovan watched her friends find true love and dreamed of her own happy-ever-after, but wishes and reality don't always match up.

When Maia met Joel Sandeford, she thought he might be worth the risk of another broken heart. But she's hesitant. Joel lives out of town and always seems to be working. Maia, too, works long hours and spends most of her time managing an art gallery and souvenir shop on Front Street in Beaufort. She fears the distance and their work ethics may spell disaster.

Both Joel and Maia have assumptions and memories from their pasts that make living fully in the present a challenge.

Maia doesn't realize the biggest obstacle to her happily-ever-after may be herself, and the memories she's hiding in her heart—that part of her heart that still belongs to her first true love.

If Maia can't resolve her fears and give up those old feelings, then finding her happily-ever-after may become an impossible dream

BEACH WEDDING

Chapter One

Benjamin Daniel Bradshaw, Jr., known to everyone as Danny, turned a year old on April 23. He was surrounded by loved ones and well-wishers, and lots of colorfully wrapped presents.

Maia forced herself to smile. She refused to cry. She was standing with the other guests in the large living room of the Winters' home, and tears had no place at this celebration.

Everyone was chatting and watching as Juli, seated on the floor next to her son, showed him how to tear the pretty paper. Esther was nearby listing each gift and giver for the thank you notes that Juli would send later in the week. The smell of expensive leather and gleam of well-polished wood mixed with the sweet scent of cake and icing and a multitude of balloons. All the parts worked together to infuse the overall scene with cheerful good will.

Maia stood with the wood and glass railing at her back. Behind her, the main floor was open to the level below and a two-story window-wall allowed an unbroken, expansive view of the sweep of the green lawn and of Bogue Sound beyond, but Maia wasn't interested in the view, or even in the other guests. Her attention was focused on Danny.

Ben wasn't there, of course, but these people had known him well. They were trying to make the birthday fun for his son. Part of the effort seemed to require that no one mention him—Danny's deceased father. It made her sad.

This was the usual birthday party for a beloved one-year-old. Danny was the center of attention, and generally oblivious to the adults. Maia thought that was a good thing. His attention was on the presents, his mama, and ten-year-old Megan—the only other child there.

Danny's fine brown hair was flyaway after encounters with the balloons and static electricity. Light, shining through his feathery hair, created a halo effect. As each gift was opened, he wanted to stop, free the toy from its packaging and play with it. He protested when he was denied, but there were many gifts and they had to keep moving. Danny was also fascinated with Megan. When she spoke to him gently and offered another present, Danny was willing to be distracted.

Every time Maia saw his dark eyes, she was reminded of Ben's warm brown ones. Like his father's, Danny's eyes were the color of toffee. He hadn't inherited his mother's deep blue eyes, though his brown hair had her strong reddish tint.

Megan devoted her attention to Danny. He returned her adoration with drools and chortles—cuteness personified. Maia's dad, Robert Donovan, a retired soldier, said God made infants and toddlers cute so people would put up with the drools and tantrums. She smiled thinking that he'd never seemed particularly bothered by his own grandchildren's more challenging moments. But that wasn't now. This was Danny's party—a family and friend event for Juli and Luke's family and friends. Maia fit under the friend category.

Luke offered Juli his hand and she rose to her feet, surrendering the present-opening responsibility to Megan. Juli and Luke settled on a love seat nearby to watch, probably hoping to breathe for a moment before moving on to the cake cutting. The cake was displayed on the dining room table with Danny's highchair, festooned with bows and curly ribbons, pulled up close.

When cake time arrived, Danny picked delicately at his slice and everyone laughed politely. He was not only brilliant and cute beyond description, but also a very neat eater.

Luke gently smeared Danny's cheeks with a few stripes of chocolate frosting for the all-important photo. Something pinched in Maia's heart—a sharp pain gone in an instant. Phones clicked, cameras snapped, and everyone laughed. Maia tried to laugh, too, but finally moved away, withdrawing from the scene before she lost control.

Juli found her on the back deck. The deck was two levels above the lawn with a breathtaking panorama of Bogue Sound through the Carolina pines. Maia clutched the railing and stared straight ahead as she pretended to admire the view. A boat was tied up to the small dock in the water. Squirrels dashed up the tree trunks and along the pine boughs. The breeze promised another fine beach season ahead. There was plenty for Maia to be gazing at and musing over, but she could only see a blurry, fractured scene through the thin lens of tears obscuring her vision, tears that she refused to give in to. So far, so good. If she started crying she might not be able to stop.

Juli touched Maia's shoulder. "Are you okay?"

Maia turned away, but Juli had already spied the red eyes and wet lashes. She slid her arms around Maia and gave her a big hug.

Painful memories rolled over Maia, almost enough to knock her down. Juli's hug made it worse. She, Maia, should've been comforting Juli, Ben's widow, instead of Juli comforting her.

Maia tried. "I'm sorry for getting weepy. The party is lovely." But the sorrowful words spilled out anyway, "I wish Ben was here."

Juli tightened her hug. "He is here, Maia. Ben is here with us. I feel him."

Platitudes. Maia wanted to shake off Juli's hug and reject her words. The strength of her reaction surprised her.

She said, "No, he isn't. I wish he was. His son is turning one and Ben isn't here. He never held him, never even met him. It's not fair."

Juli sighed. It was a warm sound, but soft and barely audible. Juli released her and Maia stepped back to see her friend's face.

"He is here," Juli insisted. She placed a hand over her heart. "Here, and also in our memories. I feel him nearby."

Clearly, Juli was determined to believe it. Maia wished she could, too.

"You have Luke," she said, not expecting to hear herself say those words aloud. She pressed her lips together before she could say more, but she didn't miss the momentary flash of hurt on Juli's face. It was quickly gone and Juli's expression returned to one of gentleness.

"I do, and I'm grateful." Juli touched Maia's arm. "I should get back inside. Can we meet up this week? Maybe over lunch? It's been too long. I apologize for that. Between Danny and trying to find time for my art...and then there's Frannie."

Juli's smile was gentle again, polite, but Maia detected trouble in it. She regretted her part in that trouble.

Maia tried to lighten the mood. "It's not every day a grown woman finds out she has a sister." Despite her effort, the words fell flat. She added, "I know Brian had to work, but I thought Frannie would be here."

"She had other commitments. Have you heard anything from Joel?"

Joel Sandeford? Maia didn't want to talk about him. She shrugged and uttered a curt, "No." Wanting to soften her answer, she added, "Frannie may have. She's his friend, after all."

"Oh." Juli's face showed surprise, then she frowned slightly. "Let's get together. Just you and me. We'll catch up. We're long overdue."

Maia nodded. Just now, she wasn't sure how much catching up with Juli she could handle.

"And soon," Juli added. "The summer tourist season will be in full swing in a few, short weeks."

Juli hooked her arm in Maia's. "Ready to go back inside?"

"I have to leave anyway. The gallery, you know. Do I need to give Megan a ride home?"

Juli paused at the door. "No. Brian's planning to drop by and get her after he's done at the marina. If he's held up in Atlantic Beach, Luke or I will take her."

Still at the door, Juli said, "I hope you're going to have more help at the gallery this season. You need more time for yourself, Maia. There's more to life than work. You know Luke supports you in that."

Her words fell on Maia's ears like yet more platitudes. Empty words. Polite expressions.

Maia believed that Juli was sincere, but there was a wide gulf between sincerity and actuality.

Back inside the house, if anyone noticed her reddened eyes, they said nothing. No one asked if she was okay, or upset, or needed help. Perhaps they assumed Juli had already attended to that, and doubtless they were relieved. Or they were respectful of her privacy. Either way, it isolated her. Despite knowing many of these people, Maia felt very alone.

Anna Barbour was over by the fireplace. Her long gray hair looked elegant, her light blue eyes flashed with wit and her posture was impeccable as always. Anna, a senior and a widow, was laughing and chatting with other guests, some of whom were her art students. Anna was a client of the gallery. Maia could easily move into that group and join the conversation. But she didn't.

Danny toddled toward Maia, finding his way around the forest of people's legs, then holding out his arms and calling out, "My!" It was his baby version of her name. "My-My," he said, as he reached her.

Maia knelt and extended her arms. Danny managed those last steps hastily, high-stepping in his excitement and nearly pitched forward. She grabbed him up, kissing his soft cheek—he tasted of cake—and congratulated him on his courage and brilliance as people laughed and applauded.

Ben's child.

Danny smelled of sugar and spice and chocolate...from the cake, of course.

He shoved several small fingers into his mouth. It was his sleepy-time signal. Maia looked over at Juli who had settled back into the crook of Luke's arm.

Maia felt like she was the only one still missing Ben. She knew it wasn't true, but even for her, as a daily kind of experience, the sharpness of his loss had eased. It would continue to diminish. Maia felt both glad and guilty. The truth was that such pain couldn't be sustained indefinitely without killing the host. Ben wouldn't thank her for harboring grief. She knew that. She knew also that the pain was sharp today because reality brought the truth home hard—Ben was gone. His absence was final. And life went on.

Danny's delayed naptime caught up with him. He rubbed his eyes and buried his face in her neck. Juli walked over. Maia leaned him toward his mom and he was received into her arms. He fell into his mama's hug with the absolute trust of a one-year-old who never doubted his mother would catch him, would welcome him and solve his sorrows. As mother and son vanished down the hallway, Danny called out a sleepy, "Bye-Bye."

He was happy to be leaving the party.

Me, too, Maia thought.

She retrieved her purse. She'd left her sweater in the car. This time of year, late April, it was still possible to get chilly in the evening and she hadn't known how late she'd stay. As it was, it was barely mid-afternoon. But she'd been prepared because that was her way. Prepared and reliable. Everyone said so. And don't forget helpful and cheerful. Practical. Sometimes she felt like the words were stenciled on her, front and back, and that people had stopped looking deeper to see what really lived inside her. These days that felt like a good thing. She wasn't at her best lately. She understood her sadness about today and Ben, but in general she had fewer woes than most and much to be thankful for, and yet....

She didn't understand what was wrong with her.

Luke saw her leaving. He held the door for her and walked out with her.

"Thanks for coming," he said.

14

"Of course. Wouldn't have missed it for the world."

Luke was handsome with lean good looks and amazing cheekbones. Dark hair, dark eyes, he was a mix of no-nonsense business and athleticism. He kept a pair of running shoes under his desk at the gallery. Maia knew that wasn't by chance. Those running shoes were a symbol of where he wanted to be. Boating. Jogging on the beach. But duties must be attended to first. Luke could've posed for a billboard ad for success and stability. Maia knew those traits were a big part of what had drawn Juli to him. Did Juli recognize that? Probably not. People didn't usually see themselves clearly. For Juli, the biggest draw was about being loved and being able to trust that love. And about security. Given Juli's rough childhood, Maia couldn't blame her.

Everyone had secrets and private motives—not necessarily bad motives, but rather unspoken needs that were often hidden even from themselves.

She hugged Luke and thanked him for the fun. "I'll see you at the gallery? When? We have numbers to review."

Luke frowned. "Nothing urgent?"

"No, I would've told you immediately if that were the case. This is the usual recap but with those other figures you asked me to add in. It can wait until you want to see it."

"Good. Thanks." He tapped his fingers on the roof of the car. "You're not headed back to work now, are you?"

"Why not?"

"Why not?" he echoed. "Because it's a beautiful day. Take advantage of it." He opened the car door for her. "Doesn't Brendan have the gallery covered today?"

"He does. But it's April. It's that time of year. Business is already picking up."

"You've been preparing all winter." He fixed his dark gaze on hers. "Why don't you take some time away?"

"Seriously?" She almost laughed, but it wouldn't have been a pleasant sound. What was this about? Was he belittling her dedication? Her concerns about the business?

"Maia, you look like you're about to rip my head off."

Her immediate response was to say, no, all was well, but she didn't give those words voice. She looked aside to rephrase the words in her head before speaking them aloud.

"We're in good shape for the tourist season. And, yes, Brendan is doing well, but he can only do so much, especially when he's working alone."

"We need to find you more help."

"For now, we're good. Lora Carter is coming back. She's been gone a few years, but we'll get her on board in time for the summer business."

His frown lingered.

Irked, she added, "If you have any issues with how I'm managing the gallery, I wish you'd say it plainly."

"You know better."

She nodded. "I do. At least, I thought I did." She pressed her hand to her forehead. "I'm sorry. I don't know what's wrong with me. I feel...touchy."

"You're right about speaking plainly. I'll tell you what's on my mind. Memorial Day weekend is only a month away. You've got the gallery as ready as it's going to be. Brendan is doing well and gaining confidence because of you. You. Your hard work. If something happens to you...if you get sick or whatever because you're working too hard.... Well, that's my nightmare. I can't afford to lose you because you burn out or wear yourself down."

He placed his hands on her shoulders. "We're friends, Maia. I depend on you. This will be a slow week, at least until Friday when the weekenders roll into town. I'll be in and out of the office this week, too, so I'll back up Brendan. The weather is perfect. Take these days off while you can. Get away and have some fun before the craziness starts in earnest."

"Go away to have fun? I love the gallery. It's where I want to be."

"I know that." He stepped back and opened the car door wide.

"Seriously, Maia, when you get to the gallery, take a moment. Stand inside and look around, then ask yourself if I'm right." He smiled a thin, but kind smile. "Go away somewhere. Laugh and breathe. Forget work for a few days. Come back on Friday." He lowered his voice. "I promise the gallery will still be there."

After a quiet pause during which the furrow between his brows deepened, he smiled. This wasn't a kind, polite smile. This was a "Luke" smile. These were rare and lit up his eyes, his whole face, and made the recipient feel like the worthiest person on earth.

"Be Maia," he said. "Go be Maia Donovan for a few days and forget the rest."

"We'll see," she said. "I'll consider what you've said." She climbed into the car.

He closed the door firmly and stepped back.

As Maia settled in, fastened the seatbelt and checked the mirrors, she pushed doubt away. Luke had something on his mind—she didn't know what—but they both knew she ran Front Street Gallery exceptionally well. Luke owned it, but she was its heart and soul.

She wasn't a robot. She might get sick or whatever. That was true for anyone. Luke could replace her. But he might as well change the gallery name or knock down the old restored building altogether because without her, it wouldn't be the same place for anyone. Whatever else she might not know, she knew that for certain sure.

With a satisfied grunt, she pressed her foot to the accelerator.

She drove up the long half-circle driveway to the street, used her signal and checked both ways before pulling out.

It was all well and fine for Luke to say, "Go somewhere. Laugh and breathe." He had Juli and Danny, plus his boat and jogging sneakers and the other stuff he enjoyed for recreation. If she went away, unless it was to see her parents or to church, she went alone. Not that she minded being alone—it was just a fact of her life.

She'd never felt the lack before—the failure to cultivate hobbies and such. It hadn't been a conscious decision along the road of her life. She'd just taken one step after another and honestly, she couldn't look back and see that she'd ever put a foot wrong. She was where she belonged.

All of this was on her mind as she drove east on Emerald Drive and it became Atlantic Avenue, and then she crossed the bridge from Atlantic Beach to Morehead City. She turned east on Arendell Street as usual, but then, instead of keeping straight and taking the next bridge over to Beaufort, she turned north on 20th Street, and drove the few short blocks to the cemetery—to visit Ben.

CRLSO

Maia walked past the low brick walls of Bay View cemetery and followed the narrow asphalt road between the graves on foot. She'd parked on the street not wanting to block anyone else who might be driving through. This was a huge cemetery, and it was likely that someone might want to drive past. In fact, it was a good thing she knew exactly where to go, otherwise she could wander for days looking for a specific grave.

Old graves were mixed with new here. Family plots were neatly contained within well-marked, bordered squares. Most of the headstones, even the old mossy ones, were neatly in line and upright. The grass was a trim, green carpet. This large, sedate cemetery was very different from the historic graveyard in Beaufort where the tourists took tours.

It was appropriate that this cemetery was quiet, orderly and respectable because this was where Ben had been laid to rest.

Maia walked past the veteran's memorial with the flag waving high overhead, then followed the walkway between the historic cedars. How old were they? She had no idea, but they lined this area of the cemetery with massive dignity.

Just past the headstones, one topped by a sleeping infant and the other by a lamb, Maia turned and headed toward a shady clump of trees overarching a white-painted iron loveseat.

The breeze ruffled the pine boughs high overhead. It was inland, but not by much, and the nearby bay was peeking between the trees and the fresh scent of ocean salt was still in the air. It mixed with the cedars and other smaller trees, but it also mingled with the smells of asphalt, commerce and city. Beyond Morehead City and business, lay Bogue Sound and the island where Emerald Isle, Atlantic Beach, and other small towns lined up along the main road. The ocean was out of sight from here, but ever-present, as with everywhere you might wander in coastal Carolina.

This was the place Ben had wanted to be buried. Ben's family, his sister Adela and his cousin Luke, had honored his wishes. He was laid here, alongside his parents, just over a year and a half ago. It felt like a lifetime. It felt like yesterday.

Maia always kept new cemetery flowers in a cardboard box in the back of her car. This time, she selected lilies and a few sprigs of lavender for a splash of color, then carried them to the Bradshaw plot. She knew the way well and thought she could've walked right to it with her eyes closed.

Mr. and Mrs. Bradshaw were long gone. She'd never known them. Ben's first wife, Deborah, was buried here, too, in an adjacent plot, the Driver family plot, such that except for the intervening walkway, the two were all-but buried beside each other. Maybe that was appropriate. Maia hadn't known Deborah. By the time Maia had arrived at Front Street Gallery seeking a job, Deborah had already died tragically, and Ben was grieving.

Grief. Old and new. Too much of it.

Grief and love—the glue that bound together the string of memories each person carried—were both important. Each had their place and needed to be respected.

Maia hadn't known how to breach the emotional wall of Ben's grieving, or even whether she should try. Back then, she decided his grief should be honored and that it would pass in time. She understood patience. Now, ironically, she was still waiting for her own to lift. In truth, she didn't know how to let Ben go.

After arranging the flowers and snipping and tweaking the grass that wanted to grow awry, Maia rested her hand on the headstone.

With a sigh, she sat on the bench.

She looked around. She was alone. She looked again at the headstone, at the dappled shade moving across the granite.

"Hi, Ben. It's a beautiful day today. It's Danny's birthday. You wouldn't believe how big he's grown; how smart he is. He's walking already. He's a delightful child." She ran out of words as her eyes stung and her throat grew thick. She pressed the back of her hand against her eyes to stop the tears that wanted to flow. She drew in a long, ragged breath. When she had her emotions back under control, she began again.

"He looks like you, Ben. His eyes, his hair. And he's such a neat eater." She tried to laugh but it sounded perilously close to a sob. She shook it off. "Esther made the cake. Luke had to put frosting on his face for the photo. Chocolate. That cake was delicious. Esther is magical with all things food. And, apparently, your son is a chocolate lover, too."

Maia sighed. "You should have seen him, Ben. I saw your determination in him, but also your warmth. He and Megan were so cute together...."

Chapter Two

Maia returned to her car and drove east, toward Beaufort.

The Front Street Gallery in Beaufort, named for the street on which it stood, was Maia's second home. In many ways, it had become her primary residence, at least in terms of time spent there.

The gallery occupied a renovated Victorian home set a little farther back from Front Street than the main block of shops. It faced the stores and restaurants that fronted on the boardwalk and the water. Part of the marina was in sight to the left. The yachts and sailboats, and all manner of sea craft, bobbed there in the deep blue water. The open square gave a view of the boardwalk and strolling tourists. Blocked from sight by intervening buildings, was the dock where the tourists lined up for boat trips to Shackleford Banks, a world-class shelling beach. Beyond Front Street and the boardwalk, waterways like Taylor's Creek and Beaufort Inlet glimmered and sparkled in the sunlight, and beyond them lay the Atlantic, less playful and more intense. Beyond the ocean? The rest of the world.

She thought about it as she drove across the bridges to Beaufort, and she laughed. She wasn't a sailor by any means, or even much of a traveler. This—sailing on four rubber tires over the bridges with the water far below—was about as close to watersports as she usually got.

Maia spent most of her time in the gallery. The main floor was the showroom, with a small office for Luke and a breakroom. The upper floor was filled with backup stock and unused displays, but she had a cozy corner set up with an old, threadbare divan for those rare moments when she craved solitude and had coverage for the sales floor.

The breakroom was at the back of the main floor with a door that exited into the alley where a couple of parking spaces were available for those who worked here. The breakroom was fitted with a small stove and fridge, and plenty of table space. From that room, Maia could listen for the bell over the customer door or sit where she could keep an eye on that door and the sales floor while eating lunch. In fact, many of her friends had shared lunch, or hot cocoa, with her over the years sitting right in these chairs.

Maia ran her fingers along the well-worn Formica table, thinking that this room was, for her, the heart of gallery.

She walked through to the main sales floor. Brendan was dusting. No customers were in view.

"Hey, Maia. How was the party?"

She couldn't help smiling at Brendan. He was barely twenty, and an attractive young man, tall and lanky. He didn't always remember to take his shirts from the dryer before they wrinkled, but he was holding a feather duster and wielding it carefully and conscientiously around the knick-knacks, just as she'd trained him.

Brendan was a local boy. He'd graduated high school, but didn't have the support or funds to go to college. He'd said he didn't want to anyway. He wanted to stay in Beaufort. And, truly, being local, he was especially helpful to the tourists with directions and information about area activities. Despite his shirts tending to wrinkle and him being too thin to keep the tails tucked in neatly, he'd become a true asset to the gallery.

"The party was good. Danny is a sweetheart. Lonely for him, maybe, with mostly adults there."

"Yeah, but my nephew turned one last November and they don't really play with other kids, you know? They need someone to show them the ropes."

Maia nodded. "He'll learn." She walked to the counter where the customer transactions were handled. "Everything going okay?"

"We had a few people...sunny Sunday afternoon and all that...but it's dropped off."

From the large, plate glass display window at the front of the shop, Maia often enjoyed watching the activity on Front Street and the businesses on the docks at the water's edge. With spring, life was returning to the town. Soon it would be crazy-busy. Maia loved that time, seeing the regular or returning customers, the random shoppers, and her special clients. The stock that surrounded her here were reminders of family and friends. She knew the artists personally. Her friend, Anna Barbour, had painted those seascapes. Ted Sims had carved that driftwood with reliefs of birds and fishes. Even the shell creatures, googly-eyed and merry, meant something special to her. They delighted children and had tickled the funny bones of more than a few adults. They were the last ones that Margie, with her talent and whimsy, would ever create.

Maia was tied to this gallery in many ways. The knot was intricate and secure, and welcome.

Brendan had resumed dusting and it was Luke's voice she was hearing in her head now. He was right. They were in good shape for the beginning of the season. She'd been doing this a long time, a decade, so they should be.

They were only open for a few hours on Sunday afternoons during the off-season and they closed early. Four o'clock wasn't that far away.

As much as she loved the gallery, suddenly the silence—marked only by the small noises Brendan made as he moved the merchandise to dust under each item—overwhelmed her and the walls seemed to close in.

She walked past him and out the door.

A few scraps of paper littered the grassy area between the gallery and the public sidewalk. She gathered it automatically, then crossed the street to the trashcan on the far side where she disposed of the paper. The boats in the marina slips caught her attention. Their owners sailed them or carried sport fishermen out for the day. As the warm season advanced, the activity would increase to crazy-busy.

Every year, it was the same. With the arrival of spring, the people, and the merchants, too, kicked off the slow rhythm of winter and felt life stirring more strongly.

Was that the source of her problem? Restlessness? Spring fever?

She'd been doing this job for ten years. It had been her first job out of college. She'd never expected to stay here this long.

A decade ago, freshly home from college graduation, and with a few interviews complete, but with the results still pending and nothing certain, she'd seen the ad in the paper. Different town. Close to home, but not too close. And on the shore. That was a nice bonus. She'd dropped by to check it out.

It seemed more of a retail opportunity than a job suited for her art history degree. It was a small gallery in a small tourist town. No, she'd never viewed it as a place to stay indefinitely, but rather as something to do while waiting for a career-type job to be offered.

So, ten years ago she'd liked what she'd seen and called the number in the ad and set up an interview. She remembered arriving for that interview and standing on the steps at the front of the gallery, thinking this view was hard to beat. Then she walked inside and met Ben and Luke.

The rest was history. A decade's worth.

Back in the present, the spring breeze swept across the water bringing the chill of the Atlantic, fresh from winter, with it. She shivered and wished for her sweater. Yet she continued to stand facing the sound, the marina, the boats, and she could almost believe if she turned around and stared hard enough, or maybe squinted to view it through her lashes, she could see them as they'd been back then—ten years younger and full of plans.

Time moved on and things changed, often despite logic and in defiance of good sense, even to the detriment of what was already close to perfect.

Today the sky was blue, yet she felt socked in by a bad mood, as if an emotional fog had rolled in across the harbor to the shore and blanketed her. This was unlike her normal upbeat demeanor. She tried to shake it off by thinking better thoughts. Happier thoughts. For the first time in her life, she couldn't find any. She was fresh out of joy.

Luke had suggested going away for a few days, right? Maybe she did need time to recharge.

She took her phone from her pocket. She hesitated to call Cathy. Her older sister was very intuitive, including when it came to reading nuances in the voices of her loved ones, so Maia texted, "Anyone at the cove this week?"

She slid the phone into her pocket, crossed the street and returned to the gallery.

"Hi, Brendan. Anything I need to take care of over the next few days? Give attention to?"

"Nope."

"Good to hear. I'm taking some days off."

He stared at her. "What's wrong? Are you sick?"

"Sick? No, I'm fine. Luke said he'd back you up while I'm gone. You don't have anything happening this week that would interfere with you being here every day?"

"No. It's all good. No worries."

"I won't be far. Less than an hour away. You can call me if there's a problem."

"Now's a good time to get away. Before the holiday weekend."

She nodded. "That's what I was thinking."

"Have fun."

She was proud he was confident. The assistants that preceded him had come and gone. She never would've guessed Brendan would be the one who stayed.

"Lora may drop by this week. She's not starting work yet, but feel free to talk gallery process with her, if she asks. We've made a few changes since she left."

Maia sensed uncertainty in his posture.

"She knows you'll be in charge. She and I discussed it."

He relaxed, and pride showed in his face. "She was good with that?"

25

"Of course, she was. She'll only be here part time and likely temporary. You're my in-charge person. I trust your judgement, including knowing when to call on me or Luke for decisions or backup." Maia waited to gauge his reaction and was satisfied.

"I'll get moving. Are you sure you're good?"

Brendan gave her a pretend salute. "Yes, ma'am."

"I'll be in touch. Call me if you need me. I'm serious."

By the time she was in her car, she had her sister's answering text: "No one. It's all yours."

Maia intended to pack and get an early start in the morning. She liked to be properly prepared and outfitted. But once back at the apartment, a second-floor flat in one of the many old houses that lined the streets of Beaufort, she realized packing would only take moments. This trip was only to please herself. She could take whatever, no special requirements or plans. She went through the kitchen raiding the cabinets and fridge, grabbed a few changes of clothing and her personal pillows, and tossed them into the back of the car.

Next stop Bridle Cove.

Chapter Three

Bridle Cove was a world away from the pounding waves and the wide oceanfront beaches of the Outer Banks.

At the ocean, the waves crashed onto shore, the seabirds skimmed the water hunting for food, gulls scavenged, and sandpipers danced away from the foamy ends of the incoming tide and left their twiggy footprints in the wet sand. At the ocean, the wildlife dodge fishermen, kite flyers, swimmers and shell-seekers.

It was different at Bridle Cove. The gulls might visit if someone brought food out to the narrow strip of sandy beach, a person could sunbathe there if they really wanted to, and if the dock were in proper condition, you could even tie up your boat, but such activities were rare at Bridle Cove.

The cove was situated in that area near where the Neuse River met the South River. In Merrimon township the roads ended at the water or circled back to the one main drag that led in and out of the peninsula.

Bridle Cove had a narrow area of sandy beach, a quarter-moon, formed and sheltered by the shoreline, the lay of the land, the grasses and bushes that anchored the banks along with a few trees. The trees offered pockets of shade until one reached the thicker woods a few yards inland. Here the birds still left their marks, but it was also a quiet haven with a feeling of timelessness, as if long undisturbed by man. That wasn't technically true, though one could say it was less disturbed, certainly. Here, along this inland waterway, the shoreline curved trapping and protecting a sliver of sand and offering a pocket of peace.

Boats traveled the water, but there were no crowds, no pounding waves, no cars. The old dock was small and disreputable, so no sensible boat owner would tie his craft up here. The next storm could take the rickety assemblage of sticks away, put it out of its misery. It seemed to be waiting for just such an event.

Maia was normally busy and efficient. But time passed differently here, and her internal pace slowed to match it. She wasn't much of a swimmer, not a surfer or fisherman, and she had no patience for sunbathing. When she wanted to get away, this private hideaway where nothing was happening suited her fine.

Cathy's husband owned it when they married. The property had been in his family for some years. Marshall and Cathy had spent a lot of time out here during those first years together, and often hosted family and friends. Maia had a sweet memory of Marshall telling her about the name, Bridle Cove. Long ago owners had kept horses here. Back in the trees there were still the remains of the stable. The bridle paths had become foot trails over the years and most had vanished altogether now. Something about the idea of horseback riding along the South River and the Neuse appealed to the romantic in Maia. She could imagine riding those horses along the paths that bordered the rivers and the marshes. As time had moved on, the properties along the water had been broken up and developed. The shoreline paths were first interrupted into shorter segments, some were fenced off entirely, and the horses had gone. Maybe had even been forgotten, except for a few old timers.

Marshall had died unexpectedly and much too early from a heart ailment. Cathy and their two children were devastated by grief. Even after they began to move forward again, trying to find a new life, Cathy couldn't bring herself to sell Bridle Cove, nor was she willing to relive the memories by staying there. Occasionally, she rented the property out, but over time it deteriorated. Houses needed people. Empty, nature fought to reclaim them. Maia suspected that, perhaps subconsciously, Cathy was deliberately allowing it to disintegrate. At any rate, it wasn't within walking distance of the ocean, the dock couldn't tolerate the weight of a person, much less secure a boat, and the house and amenities didn't qualify as a hot property like vacationers sought in Hatteras, Atlantic Beach or Emerald Isle, or even Beaufort. But Maia loved it.

The house was a small bungalow-type built around 1920 with the basic living room, kitchen and two bedrooms, but on a tall foundation in case of flooding. The house exterior was old and peeling, but thus far it was still sound. The best parts of the house were the view of the rivers confluence from the screened porch, and the live oaks and pines that sheltered the whole works.

If Maia could've bought the property from her sister, she would've. Her bank account couldn't stretch that far and even if she could manage the rent for her apartment in Beaufort plus a mortgage for Bridle Cove, her budget could never cover the repairs and upkeep, too.

The light was failing as she drove up the road to Merrimon. She no longer felt like she was about to drive off the end of the world, but she never lost that feeling of being watchful for oncoming traffic or animals in the road, because, here on this two-lane road, once you were out of the Beaufort area, there was nowhere to go except into the deep, wet ditches on either side. So, she was careful, but then she always was. Careful and practical.

When she entered the town area, there were houses and other roads and that eerie, end-of-the-world feeling, eased. Then, before you totally ran out of road, the dirt road leading into Bridle Cove came up on the left. She exited the car and unlatched the metal gate, pushed it aside and then drove up the short road to the house.

She parked her car and sighed with a smile. She was back at Bridle Cove. And safely. In time for sunset and the house was still standing.

Always a good thing, she joked silently.

She unlocked the front door and flipped on the light switch, giving a small whoop of joy. She felt that surge of joy and relief each time she found the power was working. There were lots of trees out here, and rodents were always happy to chew through the lines. But this time, it was all good. She carried her clothing and food in while the twilight still lingered, then locked the door behind her. Tomorrow would arrive on its own.

CRSO

Maia greeted the solitary, peaceful morning at Bridle Cove from the porch.

Beyond the shrubby growth overtaking the shoreline and the old dock, the water moved freely. The thin, dry grasses that thrived in the marshy areas where the water joined the land, rustled in the early morning breeze. She loved the sights and sounds that were part of the early stirrings of the day. She stood on the porch in the same cotton shorts and t-shirt she'd slept in and stared at the changing color of the morning sky as it brightened with dawn.

The grass on the lawn below was still dark and doubtless wet with dew. Shaggy, too. A neighbor was paid to keep it cut, so it wasn't quite a jungle. Not yet. But green stuff grew fast here in eastern Carolina.

Barefooted, Maia descended the many steps to the ground. She crossed the wet grass to where it ended, changing to white, fine-grained earth that sloped down to the water's edge. There, it became coarser. Sandier. The gentle slope looked as if boats had been launched from here long ago. No tire ruts, so very long ago. But the result was a lovely, wide area of soft, fine sand that formed a quarter-moon sliver of beach framed by the tall grasses.

The cove was different from the ocean. Juli had once told her that the ocean is. *IS.* It didn't think, it didn't care. It simply existed in a mindless state, performing to the laws of nature. Several weeks after they'd lost Ben, Maia had asked Juli how she could bear to continue living at Ben's house in Emerald Isle, *Sea Green Glory*, with the ocean as a constant reminder? Living, in fact, on that same stretch of beach when Ben had run into the ocean and perished?

Juli responded that it was pointless to curse the ocean for the loss of a loved one because the ocean does what the ocean does. For the ocean, there was no truth or motive beyond that simple existence. Blame gave no value.

Maia thought that was true of nature, and of time, too. People might try to hold it back—time or nature—to keep what their hearts most desired, and might even succeed for a while, but no one could stop it cold. Even a long-lived life lasted only a moment in the span of time on earth.

There was no heart, no mercy, in time or nature.

Maia had concluded that life was equally blind and heartless. It was the essence of life, perhaps, without the intervention of God or angels or divinity, at its most basic. Whatever life brought to them, people were left to deal with.

A struggle was happening in her heart and head. Faith had always been her strength and her foundation. She'd always been sure of things, and confident of the things she wasn't sure of because she was content to trust to God for the future. Same with love. She'd been content to wait on that, sure that someday it would be there for her. But things didn't always work out as one hoped.

Somewhere along the way, things began to change inside her. It had been a slow, sneaky change.

A rustic swing had been hung from the branch of a live oak tree such that it was almost over the water. The seat was a flat board and ropes, knotted in the board, took the place of chains. Maia tugged on the ropes, always wondering if it would still hold her. She sat gently, carefully, testing her weight, before relaxing. She wrapped her arms around the rope, clasping her hands together, but she didn't swing. She wouldn't tempt fate that far.

Swinging or not, it was a good spot to sit and ponder things both great and small.

Yesterday haunted her. A baby's first birthday. A joyous

occasion. A beloved child. Danny was delightful. Ben was gone, but love remained. Including the love she'd felt for him, but had never expressed.

Juli had found happiness following loss. She could, too.

What about Joel? She liked him. A lot. And she'd believed Joel returned her feelings.

If he did, then he had an absent way of showing it.

She'd met him through Frannie.

Frannie and Joel had known each other for many years. He'd followed her from Raleigh to Emerald Isle, thinking they might be more than friends, only to lose her to Brian. Juli already had Luke. That left Maia and Joel as the two spares amid happy couples. As the unattached parties, they'd gravitated toward each other, but she didn't believe their attraction was only about convenience.

She felt like she'd known Joel for a long time, but that was time, again, like nature, playing games and wreaking havoc in the lives of people. She'd met Joel in February and they'd gone on one date in March. Their chemistry had felt natural to her. Then he'd left. Two phone calls since, and that was it. And those phone conversations had seemed more like reluctant courtesy calls, awkward and polite, than that of boyfriend-girlfriend.

He'd said he had to travel overseas for his father's business. She hadn't thought too much about it at first, but then days turned to weeks. It was three weeks since she'd last heard from him.

If he'd changed his mind about wanting to see her, she wished he'd had the guts to just say it. At this point, if he called again, she might refuse to answer.

Her example of marriage was her parents. Their union was proof that love could endure for years. She wasn't willing to settle for less. Maybe the attraction between her and Joel had been a matter of convenience, the convenient attraction of proximity. If so, then it was good if he'd truly moved on.

She stared at her left hand, at the bare fingers. Only a few months ago, back in early December, her last single friend from college had called. Amelie was only single because she'd already divorced her first husband and was starting on the second go-around. While Maia knew better than to compare her life and choices with Amelie's, still she couldn't avoid it entirely.

Amelie was planning her next wedding and wanted Maia's promise to be a part of it. To participate. "A beach wedding, this time," Amelie had said. And, of course, Maia must be part of the bridal party. A bridesmaid, yet again. Another opportunity to fit into someone else's idea of what represented a perfect bridesmaid's gown. And she'd be going alone because she was the only one of her old group of college friends without a husband, or at least a fiancé.

"When is the wedding?" Maia had asked.

"Oh, not for ages," Amelie said. "Not 'til September. Late September. I want to find the best venue, the best beach and have lots of time to make sure everything is perfect. This marriage is going to be a keeper."

Amelie's words echoed in Maia's brain. ...*want to make sure everything is perfect*... A keeper marriage? Sounded like a warning that Amelie might be a diva-bride, even the second time around.

I'd rather skip it.

Maia had tried to shrug off her annoyance. After all, who knew what might happen between December and September?

The sad truth was: Not much had happened. It was April now—four months since that call. Nothing in Maia's life had changed, nor showed signs of doing so. As for Amelie, her wedding plans seemed to be progressing, but Maia had managed to plead work obligations and allowed the other bridal attendants to take the major roles in the planning.

She wasn't up for any kind of wedding. Certainly not a beach wedding.

Maia saw an old penny beside her foot. She reached down and scooped it up along with a handful of sand. The grains of sand fell between her fingers, returning to and reclaimed by the beach. The penny remained.

It was dark and rough. The date was 1953. Who knew how long it had hidden here? Twenty years or a day?

There was more to life than a husband. Maia knew that. "Better no one than the wrong one," her mom used to say. Mom had stopped saying it a couple of years ago when Maia hit thirty. Maybe she thought her younger daughter had taken her admonition too closely to heart.

On that day back in December, after offering Amelie suitable congratulations and assuring she'd help, Maia had disconnected and stared at the phone. What was she feeling? Not jealousy, surely. Just some sort of odd, in-between emotion she couldn't pin down. In the gallery's lost and found drawer was a fake, but convincing, diamond ring. Either a customer or a former employee had lost it, but no one had come looking for it. Maia confirmed it was fake at the time and thus it made sense that no one had bothered. The ring had banged around in the drawer with the usual unclaimed debris for a long time. That day, after disconnecting from Amelie, she'd found the ring in the drawer and drawn it onto her finger.

That day in December, she'd stared at her hand, and at the ring. What difference did this bit of jewelry make? Where was the magic? What was the difference between a beringed or a ringless finger? She'd always been content, a happy person—happy with her life even if she'd endured a few heartaches along the way.

Before she could slide the ring off and toss it back into the drawer, the gallery door had opened, setting the bell to jingling. She'd looked up and seen Kelli, and with her, a young man, a stranger, carrying a box of shell creatures. The shell creatures were Margie's specialty, except Margie was deceased now and Kelli was hoping to sell the last of Margie's creations. Maia was more than happy to oblige on behalf of the gallery. If Luke had objected…well, he wouldn't and didn't. They both knew Kelli needed the cash and Margie would want her to have it. The shell creatures moved slowly off-season, but sold well as novelty souvenirs in tourist season.

Something had happened in Maia when Kelli spotted the ring on her finger.

A cheap ring with a fake diamond and no groom, or even a fake proposal, attached to it. Meaningless.

Yet when Kelli asked her about it, had taken her hand and admired the ring, Maia hadn't been able to say it was nothing. The truth had lodged in her throat.

After Kelli and her friend were gone, Maia removed the ring quickly, distastefully, as if leaving it on her finger might tempt her to continue the charade. Perhaps save the ring to wear at Amelie's wedding? None of the people likely to attend the wedding would know she was inventing a fiancé. She could make up a story about business preventing him from attending the wedding. Who would know the difference? Amelie was an old college friend who lived in the Midwest. None of those likely to attend the wedding knew about Maia's current life. They weren't connected with her family or close friends here.

But it would be a lie.

Maia shuddered, embarrassed. She would never do anything so dishonest. She was shocked she'd even had the thought.

She'd put that silly incident out of her brain until now. Why did the memory return at this moment and make her feel even more lonely and futile?

Because that was life. It could be just as cruel in its mindlessness as nature. And that's why, she reminded herself, one put one's hope and faith in God, and not in things of this earth.

She knew the words, but she felt an emptiness—a hollow spot where the connection should be.

Across the water, on the shore across the South River, opposite Bridle Cove, a few houses peeked out from among the greenery, but they seemed barely there compared to the water, the sky and the trees. The scene was a good reminder that as problems went, hers were small, no more than one tiny piece of the whole. This dissatisfied lull she was experiencing would pass.

She closed her eyes, soaking in the smells and sounds, and spoke a quiet prayer. She didn't know what she was praying for. She already had so much, was very blessed, and it seemed selfish to feel she lacked something, so she simply asked for help—whatever might help her to shake this omnipresent dissatisfaction.

Maia stood. On impulse, she tossed the penny back into the river as if into a wishing fountain. She had no wish to send with it, except perhaps to wish for a wish.

She brushed the sand from her hands. She'd rushed down here even before fixing her coffee or tea, wanting to see the colors of dawn and suck in the peace like a lifeline. It must've worked to some extent because now she was thirsty and hungry, and ready to do nothing useful or practical for four days.

It was a tough job, but she could manage it.

ငွ၆ာ

Maia stood at the closet door. Cathy had books, jigsaw puzzles and old games stashed here in a small closet that had begun life as a coat closet. Someone had added shelves long ago. Books and board games, old and well-used, were stacked relatively neatly. They'd probably belonged to Marshall's family, maybe even to him as a child. It was reassuring to see the old hardbacks and the worn, curled pages of the paperbacks. She hadn't thought about what she'd do for amusement during this stay, being alone with no obligations.

She used to enjoy reading, but most of her time was spent at the gallery. On slow days when the work was caught up, she might manage to read a chapter of a romance or thriller, but the reality was that she seldom cracked the cover of a book these days.

Because the house was isolated, mostly empty and surrounded by water and untamed green growth, Maia made a circuit through the house, kicking the couch, shaking the beds and checking for any evidence of mouse leavings in the dark corners. She found none and sighed in relief.

On the exterior, some of the gutters were losing their grip on the house and one of the shutters was hanging at an angle. She made a list for Cathy. She always did. Not that Cathy did much with it.

After scrambling a couple of eggs and fixing toast and iced tea, Maia scoured the yard for fallen branches and tossed them into a pile away from the house. She wouldn't attempt physically difficult work on her own, but clearing away the bits and pieces soothed her. Irony, right? Well, nature couldn't be controlled, but to some extent it could be managed. She swept the porches, front and back, and trimmed the bushes near the house. At lunchtime, she wasn't hungry, but she was pleasantly tired.

Cathy kept the fabric part of the hammock stored under the bed in the back bedroom. It was heavy canvas. Maia carried it out to the grassy side yard where the shade was deepest and dropped it onto the grass while she pulled the hammock frame from the shed. Before the growth around the dock area had gotten out of hand, there'd been a view from this spot. Now the view was mostly obscured unless you were up on the porch, but you could lie in the hammock and feel that delightful breeze and hear the water, and that made it worth the effort.

Maia hooked the hammock to the frame, then went back inside to grab a couple of novels and a bottle of water.

The most challenging part was to climb into the hammock and get comfortably settled without tipping it to the side and being dumped. Maia moved carefully, books and water secured by one arm, and managed the boarding process quite well, congratulating herself.

She settled into the hammock center with her water bottle and the books. Which to read? Both appeared to be romances.

One was a thick, dog-eared paperback called *Castle Cloud*. Judging by its worn cover and the browned paper edges, it was decades old. The other was a thin hardcover called *Sweet's Folly*. She'd try one and if it didn't grab her at the opening, she'd move on to the other.

Both books stayed unopened. Birds warbled, and squirrels scampered through the trees. The wind sighed in the branches over her head and gently rocked the hammock. It rocked and soothed her thoughts of engaged and married friends. Of frustrations and disappointments.

The sense that time was passing her by seemed almost laughable because there was only one time here...just the here and now.

Her painted toenails at the opposite end of the hammock mesmerized her and before she knew it....

CREO

Maia was startled awake, her arms flailing. The hammock dipped radically to the side. The books and her water bottle went flying. Her frantic movements would've flipped the hammock all the way over but for the hands that rushed to grab it. Juli's hands. She stood there, her expression almost as alarmed as Maia felt.

"What—what—" was all Maia seemed able to say.

Juli kept her hands on the hammock to steady it, "I'm sorry I disturbed you. I'm very sorry. I did try to call."

"How—how did you—"

"I tried to call you. When you didn't answer, I was worried."

Still gripping the edges of the hammock, Maia looked around, confused.

She sat up carefully, moving her legs over the side until her feet hit grass. She ran her hands through her short dark hair.

"How long have you been here? I must've been dreaming. It was about someone sneaking up on me, watching me." She looked around. "There's only you?"

"Only me," Juli said.

"How did you find me?"

Suddenly, fear struck her. "Is Danny okay? Luke? The gallery? Is something wrong?" Now she was all the way up, on her feet, her heart racing. "Tell me what's wrong."

"I'm sorry, so sorry, Maia. Truly. I shouldn't have bothered you. I didn't think it through before driving up here."

Maia put a hand on Juli's arm. "Tell me now. What's wrong?"

"Nothing's wrong. I've disturbed you for no good reason." Juli clasped her hands in front of her. "You seemed troubled yesterday and I couldn't reach you and I went by the gallery and Brendan said you'd gone away but he didn't know where. I called Brian and he suggested you might have come here. He said you loved coming out here. To the cove, he said. "Go see for yourself. You'll love it," he said. He gave me directions."

She shook her head. "I've never been out this way. Didn't even know the town of Merrimon existed. Honestly, that stretch of road…it seemed almost like passing through a different world."

"I know. I've driven it. Why are you here?"

"We were worried, Maia. No one could reach you."

"Worried? I haven't been gone twenty-four hours." Juli's words made no sense to Maia. "The gallery is okay, then?"

"Oh, yes. Brendan is managing well, and Luke is staying in touch with him. Everything, everyone, is fine."

"But people were trying to call me?"

Juli shrugged. "Well, me. I was trying to call you. Others may have."

"Because I was in a mood yesterday?"

"Yes, but to be honest, you've been in a mood for a while."

Maia frowned. "And for that you drove up here?" She shook her head. "I don't understand."

She picked up the water bottle. Juli retrieved the books.

"I had some things I wanted to chat with you about, too. We are long overdue for that lunch we keep talking about." Juli seemed to be trying to establish a sense of normality. "You looked like you were sleeping. I approached quietly and whispered your name, just in case you weren't really asleep. I didn't want to scare you, but then I did anyway."

Maia couldn't shake the dream fog. She stared at Juli, but Juli was gazing up at the branches of the Carolina pines overhead and at the ancient live oaks in both the open area of the yard and in the edges of the forested area.

"It's beautiful out here, Maia. I can see why you love it." Juli did a quick scan of the unkempt lawn. "Not very far from Beaufort, is it? Yet it's private. So quiet."

She sighed. "And I've disturbed your peace. I'm sorry."

Juli handed the books to Maia. "I'll leave now. Right away. Please accept my apology and forgive me for intruding."

"Whoa. Just a minute. You did disturb me. You can't just leave and expect me to accept that. What did you want to talk about?"

"Nothing important."

Juli stood there, her expression uncertain. She looked okay. Dressed casually, but nicely, in black capris, a white cotton top, and comfy sandals. Nothing that indicated any urgency.

Maia said, "I know you. There's something on your mind. Why did you call me in the first place?"

"To check on you."

"Right. Lovely." Maia was still annoyed and very cranky from the sudden waking. "Now tell me why you called."

"It's nothing. I'm embarrassed that I've intruded this way, for nothing, really."

"Where's Danny?"

"He's with Luke's parents today."

"And everyone is okay?"

"Yes."

"Then let's make lunch. I'm hungry." She paused and fixed her eyes on Juli's. "And I expect a better explanation from you. One that I can believe."

She walked to the back door and waited on the porch.

"Come inside."

CR&D

Maia tried not to see it through Juli's eyes—the shabbiness, the yellowed paint on the walls. The kitchen floor was clean. Or clean enough. When linoleum was this old, it was bound to be permanently stained and marked. But there were no dirty dishes in the sink and nothing was growing fur in the fridge. At the beach house, this river-beach house, clean was important, but no one earned bonus points for shiny surfaces. Most of the outward shine had worn off years ago, anyway, but the inner shine was here for anyone who was willing to look deeper.

"Tea? Iced or hot? There's instant coffee, if that's what you prefer." She held the jar and eyed the expiration date. It was worn and hard to read. "Better skip the coffee. Is iced tea okay? It's not sweet. I'm trying to swear off sugar."

"Unsweet tea is fine."

Maia pulled out drinking glasses. Old glassware. A generation or two ago, it had been cheap glass. It was well-used, scratched and clouded, for sure. She had that feeling again, that odd shiver of time suspended. No one disputed that the house at Bridle Cove was old. They'd all watched it grow shabby over the years. When had it gone from shabby-comfy to shabby-is-a-mouse-living-in-the-sofa? It needed money and the will to drag it out of the past and bring it back into a useful present.

Cathy didn't have that kind of money. If she did, she wouldn't invest it here. She had two children to think of. Maia felt a moment of panic, thankfully interrupted by Juli asking, "Did I see a lemon in the fridge?"

"Sure. I grabbed a bunch of stuff from my apartment because I never know what I'll find out here. Sorry about the coffee."

"Tea is fine. Lemon makes it perfect."

Maia sliced the lemon and put it in a dish. She found some crackers. Within their "sell by" date because she'd brought these with her too. She put the tea, lemon and crackers on the table. She sat and faced Juli.

"Tell me."

"Tell you what?"

"Don't be evasive."

"I'm not." Juli looked away, staring at the floor and then the walls.

Maia followed her eyes. There were stains on the wall beneath the windowsill. Moisture stains. Old, but not active. Someone should've wiped those off.

Suddenly, she was angry. She was being forced to see things as they were. She wanted to see the Bridle Cove she enjoyed, see it as it existed in her head despite its imperfections.

"Look," Maia said, "I know it's not new. It's old and reliable. It's peaceful. I don't need fancy."

"What?"

The look in Juli's eyes was distant, almost haunted. It chilled Maia. She touched Juli's hand. Her friend seemed to snap out of it. Her chin lifted. She found a small smile to share.

"I'm sorry," Juli said again.

"No more apologies. Let's get past the unannounced visit. I should be glad someone cared enough to track me down, except I haven't been gone all that long, nor ignored my phone all that long, so I'm guessing that's just an excuse?"

Juli sighed and clasped her hands. "Remember I said it had been too long since we'd chatted? I meant that. Seeing you, but not as your usual self yesterday, stayed on my mind. It's true that I called because you were on my mind and when I didn't get you last night or this morning...when I didn't even get a reply to my messages, I was worried."

Maia stopped and breathed for a moment, needing to calm herself. The after-effects of the sudden, shocking waking, lingered. "I'm glad all's well with Brendan and the gallery, and everyone else. Now tell me, what's on your mind?"

"Oh, Maia. It's nothing. I don't know why it's troubling me."

"Please just say it."

"It's Frannie."

"Frannie?"

Juli shook her head. "Well, not so much Frannie as...Frances Cooke." She whispered half-under her breath. "Frances Ann Cooke."

"Your mother."

This time the shrug was hugely exaggerated, almost like someone trying to rid themselves of a recurring pain in the neck.

"Our mother. Yes. Frannie wants to go find her grave."

"Okay." Maia kept her tone non-committal.

"Okay, yes, she can do as she wants. The problem is she wants me to go with her."

"The private investigator Frannie hired found out where she's buried, right? What's the issue?"

"Remember, he said there's not even a headstone or marker. There's nothing to see. No reason to go. Why does she want to?" Juli's words almost ended on a gasp.

Maia touched Juli's hand again and then jumped up from her chair and put an arm around her friend's shoulder.

"It's not unreasonable, Juli. I can understand why she might want to. After all, the drama with her mother—Laurel, that is—is very fresh and recent for her. The idea of a birth mother she never knew is bound to be intriguing. And a sister she never knew—you. It's natural that she wants you to go with her. Like bonding. You knew Frances. You are Frannie's only living connection to a woman she never knew."

Juli gave a painful little laugh. "Because she's hoping to find memories to cherish? She won't find those because I'm along. She won't find those anyway."

"But she doesn't understand that yet. Have you tried explaining how it was to her?" Maia stopped abruptly seeing Juli cringe. "Is it truly so hard for you? I know you don't have good memories of that time...the time before the authorities took you away from Frances."

Juli didn't answer. Instead, she focused on some distant point.

Maia added softly, "For you, the present is where your life is, and it's a good life."

Juli nodded. "The best."

"The past is in the past and you'd rather keep it there."

"Exactly."

"But Frannie...not that she wants to return to the past, but she's working through everything that happened, all that she has discovered."

Maia paused to see Juli's reaction. There was none. Juli was in control again. Her expression was politely impassive. In a soft, encouraging tone, Maia continued, "I could offer to go with her, but it wouldn't be the same as making the journey with her sister."

"I don't want to go. I have a full life. I don't want to re-live ancient history."

"Then don't." Maia shrugged. "Don't go."

"But Frannie...."

Maia said harshly, "What about Frannie? She's an adult. Let her deal with her own issues. Why is that your problem?"

Juli looked briefly shocked, then she slapped the table.

"Oh, I see what you're doing. Very clever and not at all funny. You're playing devil's advocate, is that right? Saying the opposite to make me conclude I'm wrong? Am I being unreasonable? Don't I have the right to decide what to allow in my life?"

"Of course. Though...."

"What?"

"Often what we don't want to face, is what we need to face the most. Who said that? Someone much smarter than me, I'm sure, and they probably said it better, but the meaning is clear."

Juli stood abruptly, pressing her hands to her cheeks. "I found out just over a month ago that I have a sister. An older sister. That my mother, whom I hardly remember, died soon after she abandoned me. That she's been dead in an unmarked grave for a quarter of a century and I never missed her. Not one day. I never regretted not seeing her or hearing from her. I was glad to be safe and warm and with a full stomach." She pressed her hands over her eyes and held them there for a few moments before pulling them away and staring with dark, painful eyes at Maia. "Does that make me a monster? Truly? I think it might, Maia. Am I no better than the woman who neglected me and abandoned me?"

Maia grabbed Juli's hands. "Is this what brought you here today?"

She closed her eyes and drew in a deep breath. "That, among

other things. I can't talk to Luke about this. I've tried, and he tries, but he doesn't understand. He tells me that I'm not an awful person and I have every right to feel the way I do and to stop worrying about it."

"He's right. But I'd ask you this—what does your gut say? Your heart? If your heart agreed with your brain, then I don't think you'd be so distressed."

Juli looked away, withdrawing her hands from Maia's, and sitting again. She stared at her open hands.

"I'm supposed to be drawing and painting today. When I asked Luke's mother if she'd take Danny for the day, I thought I was going to Beaufort to do some sketches of the town. That was the plan. Or so I told myself. I dropped in to the gallery thinking I'd say a quick hello to you first, and see if you were feeling better. Now I wonder if I was lying to myself? Thinking only of myself. What kind of person have I become?"

"I think you are torturing yourself for nothing. You aren't perfect. You never will be. But you know who your friends are. The people who love you, who know how wonderful you are, but who will also tell you the truth when you need to hear it. I think that if you face this thing you'll know there was never anything to fear, not in the present." She sipped her tea. "Sadness, yes. Perhaps even reconciliation to some degree."

An unexpected idea flowed into Maia's head as if the cosmos has sent it special delivery.

"I wonder if, when you really think about it, if you'll find Frances Cooke, and what happened in the past, isn't truly the problem?"

"What do you mean?"

Maia chose her words carefully. "Your mother let you down. For whatever reason, she wasn't the mother she should've been."

"Yes."

"I'm thinking of you and Frannie—a sister you hardly know— and the two of you travelling in a car together for hours, visiting the grave of a woman, your mother, that you barely remember. A woman Frannie never knew at all. It's bound to be emotional. Intensely personal."

As Maia spoke she watched Juli's eyes widen, assuming a look of near-fear. She added, "You've always been very self-reliant."

"I had to be. I learned to trust, thanks to Ben, and now Luke. I depend on him, I admit it. I'm not as independent as I was when I was on my own."

"Maybe you're afraid you'll let Frannie down? That whatever she needs from you, you won't be able to deliver or might not want to provide?"

Maia reached out again, placing her hand over Juli's.

"Don't answer. I'm just thinking out loud anyway. You'll figure it out fine without me. Let's stretch our legs. I want to show you around the place. Bridle Cove. Not really a cove...though now that I think of it, I'm not totally sure what a cove is. Do you know?"

Juli shook her head, no, her face blank.

"It doesn't matter. Come along." She took Juli's hand. "I'll show you around."

"I should get home."

"You mean you don't want a tour? It's a beautiful place. Run-down, but special to me."

"Well, sure. Of course."

As Maia had expected, Juli's innate courtesy had stepped in to help her. Honestly, Maia didn't know what to do for her, what to say that she hadn't already said? Mostly, her goal was to get Juli's mind off her troubles for a few minutes. Maia had planted a thought or two that Juli would need to digest slowly. For now, Juli needed to decompress. But she'd better decompress quickly because there wasn't much to see here.

"Finish your tea," Maia said.

"Oh? Oh." Juli picked up the glass and drained it.

"This way." Maia gestured toward the front door. "We'll go out to the porch."

As they walked through the living room, Maia gestured around the room. "It's not fancy, but it's cozy. No cable TV, but there's always the closet."

She'd left the closet door open. Juli paused and peeked in at the books and games. She stared for a few, long moments, then without remark, she moved past. She pushed the screen door wide and went out to the porch.

The porch was painted, and much of the paint was peeling. The gingerbread fretwork framing the porch posts and roof was mostly intact. Once upon a time, the trim had been painted a sunshine yellow. Now it was cracked and chipping. Everything needed a good sanding and paint job. Maia placed her hand flat against the post by the steps, feeling the temper of the house, so to speak, and almost in apology for the neglect. She wondered if she might be able to persuade Cathy to fund at least the sanding and painting? Perhaps if she, Maia, contributed?

"I would press Cathy to do more, but I'm afraid the reality of repairs and expenses might be the straw that pushes her over the edge to sell." She smiled. "Sorry, I think I've scrambled some metaphors together, but you get the idea."

"Cathy. Your sister, right?"

"Yes, my older sister. You've never met her?"

"I haven't met any of your family except for Brian."

Maia considered. "I guess that's true. You're all sort of mixed together in my mind. All my people. I forget you don't actually know each other. We'll have to fix that soon. You'll see how crazy and chaotic it is to be part of a large family."

Juli shrugged. "One of the families I lived with was large. It was fun, but then I was very young. Children are more flexible, I think. Cruel sometimes, too, but at least you knew where you stood."

"You've never talked much about the foster families you grew up in except in very general terms. I'm glad they weren't mean, and it worked out, but you haven't kept in touch with any of them, right? Never really bonded with them."

"It was all good. Not great, but not bad either."

"That's more than some can say, I guess, whether of foster or birth families."

Maia heard and saw the tension ease from Juli as they safely dismissed her history with platitudes. Platitudes again. She pushed away from the post she was leaning against.

"Let's walk down to the beach."

Maia set off down the gentle slope with Juli alongside. They walked onto the soft, white dirt of the driveway and followed it as it widened into a beach at the water's edge.

The sunlight flickered on the surface of the water and even through the leaves of trees on shore, dappling both the water and the sand. They stood beneath the twisted oaks and the pines and it all worked together to create a special place, a safe place. A place to be.

Juli didn't speak. Maia didn't expect her to. She waited as Juli moved closer to the edge, to gaze up the waterway and then down the other way. She looked overhead and down at her feet.

Maia didn't create art, she managed a gallery. But she was pretty sure Juli was taking in the details, composing a painting in her head. For Maia, it was the touch of the breeze, the smell of the water and greenery, and the sounds all around. For Juli, it was probably strongly visual. It was on the tip of Maia's tongue to say, "You should paint this," but she wouldn't because art didn't work that way. Creativity and its byproducts needed time to come into their own, each to seek its own birth and to find maturity. Plus, Juli had a streak of contrariness to her personality.

Juli stared to her left. "What's down that way?" She turned to face the right. "And in that direction, upriver?"

"It's the remains of an old bridle path."

She looked confused. "Bridal path?"

"A long time ago, the people here kept horses. The trail went for miles along the water's edge and wound through the forest and marshes. Time changed that. The horses were taken away and the properties were broken up."

Juli started laughing. Maia was almost shocked. She hadn't heard Juli laugh like that in....maybe ever. She leaned against a tree, practically gasping for air, as she tried to regain control.

"I was envisioning brides out here hiking along the trails in their lacey veils and satin gowns, their veils catching in the sticker bushes," she said between whoops of laughter. She finished with some hiccups. "I know why I misunderstood, but I don't know why it seems hilarious."

Maybe you were just overdue for a good laugh, Maia thought. She said aloud, "You thought I was calling this place, Bridal Cove? A-L as opposed to L-E?"

Juli nodded, pressing the back of her hands to her eyes. Her cheeks were wet with tears. "Thank you, Maia."

Juli threw her arms around her friend and hugged. "I needed that laugh. I didn't even know I needed it. I was busy being caught up in worry. I forgot to have fun. To laugh."

They went back up the slope to the yard and the house.

"I'm going to get out of your hair now. I'm going to let you enjoy your days off."

"That's fine. It was okay that you came out here, and I'm glad you're feeling better, but Juli, nothing has changed. What about Frannie and her quest?"

"Her quest?" She gave a tired chuckle and shook her head. "A quest. I suppose that's what it is." She shrugged. "Who am I to deny someone's quest? Seriously, I don't know what I'll do, but I'll consider it. I've survived worse, right? Maybe I've built this up bigger in my head than it deserves."

"Probably. You might discover you like having a sister. Give her a chance."

They stared at each other for a long minute before Juli said, "I already have a sister. You are my friend but also the closest thing to a sister I've ever had."

Her words hurt Maia. They were touching words, of course, but they caused a strange tightness in her chest as she forced out an answer. "I'm honored, Juli. Thank you. And I agree, but there's more to it. You've been through a lot, but you've received some amazing gifts of love because of you, of who you are...because of the person you are. No one should ever decide that what they have is enough. There are some things that should multiply, and they can only grow by being received and accepted. Among those things are love and sharing."

"You were always kind to me, Maia. Kind to a stranger. When asked to help me—Ben and me with our marriage, our wedding—you were there, never questioning or complaining. You made me feel welcome."

"It was nothing. A dress." Maia looked away. "Not a big deal."

"You were there after Ben's death, helping me when I was lost."

Maia had no response to that. She stood quietly as they watched the broad swathe of water and the birds swooping past.

Juli added, "I owe you much more than I can ever repay. Sometimes kindness comes when we least expect it, when we've done nothing to earn it, and we must simply accept it because we need it and it's there, but don't ever think I didn't appreciate you and what you did for me. I still do."

Juli cast a last look around at the house, the yard, stared perhaps a few seconds longer back at the narrow beach.

"Thank you, again, Maia." She paused. "By the way, those shorts look great on you. I'm accustomed to seeing you dressed up for work. Both styles suit you, but I like seeing you here and relaxed. You should play more often."

Juli drove away. Maia sat on the porch chair. Play more often? The advice ticked her off.

She'd been very relaxed until Juli had disturbed her under the guise of worrying about her, but it had really been because she was upset about something. Something? Upset because her newly-found sister wanted the two of them to go together to visit their mother's grave?

It seemed a natural desire to Maia. It was an opportunity to pay one's respects from the vantage-point of adults who have more understanding. Curiosity, too, from Frannie, was natural considering the circumstances. Plus, this was a chance for the two women to spend time together getting to know each other as sisters.

Where was the downside? There was a possibility they might discover they couldn't stand each other, she supposed. If so, they could avoid spending time together going forward. Not much of a downside considering what they might gain.

Maia acknowledged that she couldn't really understand how they felt about all this. She had a sister, Cathy, but she'd always had Cathy. Cathy was as much a part of her life as Mom and Dad. Come to think of it, the mom and dad thing hadn't worked out well for Frannie or Juli either.

Juli had been self-reliant and proud of it. Maia believed that's how Juli had survived her childhood so well. Frannie's background was very different, but no happier. Despite living comfortably, Frannie felt unloved after her father died because her relationship with her mother, Laurel, had always been difficult.

Thinking of it that way, Maia was grateful she wouldn't be in the car with Juli and Frannie on that road trip, if it ever happened. She, herself, had had a very different growing-up experience with loving parents and a large, supportive family.

Juli and Luke were a perfect match. Each brought to their marriage what the other needed. Maia didn't think they were conscious of it. But it was obvious to any objective viewer who knew them well.

And then there was Maia's brother, Brian. He and Frannie hardly knew each other. Both were intense people. Brian was heedless and Frannie was touchy. The atmosphere around them was always super-charged. At times, Maia was uneasy around them. It likely made Juli nervous, too. She and Juli had more equable temperaments.

Yeah, considering all that, Maia didn't want to be on the road trip with them. It was bound to be bumpy.

Hearts, and what brought people together, seemed like a mystery. Brian and Frannie seemed to thrive on the energy they created, whereas Luke and Juli had blissfully their gifts of emotional centering and stability.

And what about her? Maia. Everyone's friend. The gal everybody could count on.

What had happened with her and Joel? First Ben, and then Joel, and to be honest, a few guys in between who didn't work out either. Those in-betweeners had showed up so briefly in her dating life they hardly counted.

Was it her? Or just bad luck? Joel was different. They hadn't known each other long, but they'd clicked. Despite all common sense, she felt something for him and had allowed that happy hope to bloom.

She looked at her hand. She remembered him holding her hand and how it had felt. That day at the Denman house, *Captain's Walk*, when Frannie had fallen into the waves and Joel had pulled her out... After she'd changed and rejoined them in the living room, when Frannie had approached the sofa, Joel had slipped over closer to her, Maia, moving to make sure no one, including Frannie, sat between them. Later, Brian had encouraged Maia, telling her not to assume Joel would know she was interested in him. To tell him.

Tell him? Just like that? Well, she hadn't been too aggressive—that wasn't her style—but she'd made sure her interest showed when they were in each other's company, and when they'd gone out to dinner that one time.

They'd had fun and lots of conversation. Not loud or brash, but companionable and smart. Witty. And when he'd taken her home, she'd waited at the door to make sure he knew he was welcome to kiss her goodnight. He'd leaned down and as his arms went around her she'd put hers around him, and she'd kissed him back. Nothing too outrageous. After all, it was early yet in their relationship and she didn't want to give him unintended expectations. This was a first date, after all, but she'd tingled clear down to her toes and they'd both been more than a little flushed when he stepped away.

They were adults. Not kids. She'd almost invited him up for coffee. Would he expect more? This relationship, if it was a relationship, felt too new and her better judgement warned her away from that.

Again, failed expectations. Broken hearts.

It was important to take time to get to know each other. He'd called the next day sounding friendly, but she hadn't felt the warm connection she'd experienced in person. It was almost a relief when he said he was going overseas on business and would be in touch. She was glad of the opportunity to put a brake on things for a short while and give herself a chance to think before losing her heart altogether.

Their phone calls had been less than stellar. It felt like someone was holding back, guarding their heart or their ego. She didn't know which or who, and here she was now. Alone.

But alone at Bridle Cove.

And that was perfectly fine with her.

Mostly.

Chapter Four

B eaufort streets were old. Blackbeard had passed through here. A walk in the cemetery, The Old Burying Ground, told many tales of centuries gone by—at least since 1724. The houses were likewise old, but quaintly so, and many were picturesque and impressive.

Beaufort streets were new. A thriving community of year-round residents, day-trippers and vacationers who breathed and spoke and made the present real.

She wasn't originally from Beaufort and had never lived here before taking the job at Front Street Gallery, but it felt like home. It was her home.

Maia never grew bored with walking the streets of Beaufort and she strolled along them often, cherishing the feeling of time past and time present converging—with time, like a ribbon, drawn out, unwinding from an infinite spool. She saw that image in her head. The ribbons were colorful and fresh as they unwound from the spool, but inevitably they tended to tangle and fade as they were pulled farther from the source, eventually creating a heap of what had gone before, a mess in which anyone who cared to pick through the pile of yesterdays could find any number of interesting things and make of them what they would. What they deduced might or might not be the truth.

No one had ever labeled Maia a dreamer or a philosopher. Everyone said she was a responsible, reliable person of business and service. And that was true. But it wasn't the whole truth.

Bridle Cove was still fresh in her memory as she drove up the street passing the familiar homes and buildings. She maneuvered into a parking space on the street in front of her upstairs apartment. There were two spots behind the building, but she tried to leave those for her downstairs neighbors. The two-story building was on a street near the county building and only a few short blocks from Front Street. As she gathered her belongings from the car, she caught whiffs of the lingering scent of the water and trees, and even the old house out there at the cove.

Or maybe it was wishful thinking.

It was past time for lunch. She should've stopped at the grocery store on her way back into town. No matter. If she hadn't left enough food here, at the apartment, to put together a meal, she'd walk a couple of blocks down to the restaurants. Her downstairs neighbor Fay was sitting on the porch with her baby. Maia grabbed her bag from the back seat and juggled it in her arms with the rest of her stuff, hoping to carry it all to the porch in one trip.

Fay waved and then gently held baby Allie's hand and waved it in Maia's direction. Alice, AKA Allie, was six months old with flawless skin and fluffy golden curls. She grinned at her mother's larger, long-fingered adult hand waving her own small chubby hand as if it were a game, but mostly she was focused on how best to drag her mommy's hand to her mouth and chew on it. Teething. Drool. Lots of it. Fay laughed, and Allie chortled.

Maia set the bags down and paused on her way to the door to touch the baby-soft cheek. Allie grabbed for her hand. Before the infant could fasten on it, Maia smoothly pulled it away. Her hands weren't clean enough to serve as Allie's teether.

Fay was younger than Maia by almost a decade. Still in her early twenties, she had long, straight, light red hair, and Allie had inherited her mama's coloring and complexion. Fay's hubby, Reggie, adored her and their sweet child. Fay leaned forward to speak to Maia, but then had to redirect her attention to grab her long hair out of Allie's grasping reach.

Hair rescued, Fay asked, "Did you have a nice time?"

Maia nodded. "I did. I always enjoy spending time at the cove, even for short trips. Which, is good, I guess, since short trips are all I can manage." She gave a polite laugh to show she wasn't complaining.

"Too bad you can't get away for longer."

"No, truly. I'm not complaining. I have a great life. No complaints."

"Why don't you join me and Allie for lunch? We were about to go inside."

"Thanks, but no. Laundry to do, and all that good stuff. It's back to work for me, tomorrow."

Fay smiled and was about to respond when she was distracted by a long thread of drool planting itself on her sleeve. Maia gathered her bags again and continued inside but set them on the floor at the foot of the stairs.

For ten years, she'd been going up and down these stairs. Today she was going to give in and do it in two trips. Maybe three.

After getting everything up the stairs, Maia tossed her clothing in the laundry and had a quick bite to eat. She told herself she wasn't going to the gallery. Not until tomorrow. Today, she was still officially on vacation.

Of course, she might walk by. Not go inside or anything. Just peek in to check and make sure Brendan was doing okay.

☙❧

She arrived at work early on Friday, unlocking the front door and flipping the sign to open. She reached up, standing on her toes, to tap the bell and hear it jingle. It was an announcement—*I'm back and I'm ready*.

She smiled. As good as it was to get away, it was always fabulous to be back.

Fridays tended to be busy in late April, especially afternoons. But fair was fair. She offered Brendan the day off.

"No, thanks," he said. "I can use the hours. Besides, I have tomorrow off. Unless you need me."

"Luke will back me up tomorrow. Go have fun."

"You can call me if you need me to come in. It's okay."

She beamed at him. She was proud of him. Almost like a mom. Or maybe more like an older sister.

"You're doing very well, Brendan. I want you to know I've noticed, and that Luke and I both appreciate you."

He flushed slightly, his cheeks pinking up. She smiled and looked away.

Maia said, "Lora officially starts next week. Between us, we'll have her up to speed in no time." She cast him a sidelong glance.

"She came by. You said she might."

"And?"

"She's nice. Reminds me of my aunt."

"Any worries?"

He shrugged. "We'll do okay."

"Glad to hear it, but if you have doubts or any concerns as you go along, don't wait until it's a big problem before you say something to me. Seriously."

Brendan smiled. "Yes, ma'am." As he turned away, he stopped suddenly. "I almost forgot. A package came for you."

Receiving packages weren't remarkable at a business. Maia looked at him, wondering.

He'd ducked below the counter, then stood again, holding a small box wrapped in brown paper. She accepted it and held it, checking the address. It was hand-written in a controlled, neat print.

"Why didn't you open it?" Maia asked.

"It looked personal. It has your name on it, not the gallery name."

True, she thought. "It does have a personal look, but it might be for the gallery."

"You could open it and find out. Do you need scissors or a box cutter?"

She gave Brendan a long look, ignoring his suggestion to open it.

"Who delivered it?"

"Mailman."

"Of course." Maia took another look at the stamps, and then the lettering again. The stamps were postmarked. "It's from New York, but no return address."

"I noticed that." He shrugged. "At any rate, it was sitting here with the rest of the mail a couple of days ago when I came back from lunch. Luke was covering for me. He left it all stacked together on the counter. I put the mail in the office."

She looked up again. "I'll open it later."

He looked a bit disappointed and maybe a little mystified.

The box was small enough to sit on her outstretched palm. It was lightweight. She kept her fingers on the box and didn't tear the wrapping.

Why? Inside she smiled, a little embarrassed, but didn't show it on the outside, to Brendan.

Because, for all that she was practical, the romantic in her was tickled to be holding a mysterious box from a big city, a city that she'd never seen. It seemed almost exotic and the contents could be anything. Well, anything small. Like the unscratched lottery ticket— all things were possible until you scratched it, or the numbers were drawn or whatever. And small packages often contained wonderful gifts.

"Aren't you curious? My mom would be. She'd already have it open. Unless it's something you were expecting, and you already know what it is?" His expression changed. "Hey, I'm sorry. It's none of my business. Unless it is my business, gallery business, that is, and then you'll let me know, right?"

She tried to sound casual. "I don't think it's anything special. Thanks, Brendan." She nodded toward the open door to Luke's office. "I'll be in there for a while going through the mail. Just yell if you need me."

⊗

Maia sat at Luke's desk. The light from the window behind her filtered in from the narrow passageway between the buildings and into the room. It fell onto the desk where the box was set.

How long had it been since she'd received an unexpected gift?

It held potential. If she opened it, and if it was cheap or ordinary—perhaps nothing more than a promotional, gimmicky type of gift…. Well, that was likely the case.

Maia smiled. She was being silly, of course. But that was her choice. She could be silly if she wanted to.

In the end, she picked up the box and carefully worked the paper loose to avoid tearing it. She pulled the paper free slowly and drew the whole process out deliciously. Meanwhile, the voice grew in her head and reminded her that it would be something pointless, an advertising trinket, and she would have a good laugh at herself for thinking that the ordinary might actually be precious.

There was no return address on the package or inside the wrappings.

A white cardboard box, a dressy one, came out of the shipping box. She lifted the lid from the white box and pulled out a square of cottony fill.

A necklace. White gold. With a pendant. A key. The key was also gold with little sparkly stones embedded in it.

She removed the suede-like card that secured the necklace in place in the box and looked beneath it. Nothing. No clues under the base of the box either.

Who sent it?

With great care, she removed the delicate gold chain from the slots on the card and held the necklace up. The same light that had highlighted the box on the desk, now glittered as it touched the gleaming metal and the inset stones flashed white and blue. For all the world, they looked like diamonds.

This was costume jewelry, and someone was promoting something, or maybe she'd won a prize for something. Maybe.

The key must have significance.

She repacked the card and cotton into the white box, and slipped the necklace and pendant in with it.

A mystery. Costume jewelry or not, it was lovely. She'd wear it. But she'd really like to know who'd sent it and why. There must be someone she needed to thank.

Briefly, Joel flitted through her mind.

Would he? Might he have sent it? Why no card?

Memory lane grabbed her and whooshed her back into the past as she remembered something that had happened after Ben had died. Christmas gifts had arrived at the gallery—for Juli. Ben had ordered them before his death, long before Christmas, and no one had known, thus no one had cancelled the order.

Maia felt the air leave her lungs and she sat down again.

This instance was different, surely. At least, different in that the necklace hadn't come from Ben. That would be impossible. But Luke… Brendan said Luke had left it with the mail. Could Luke have intended it for Juli? As in symbolically giving her the key to his heart?

No. The package was addressed to her, Maia.

Then it hit her. Juli and Luke had married soon after Danny was born. Danny had just had his birthday. They had an anniversary coming. Their first anniversary.

Yes, this was Juli's gift.

Did Luke have it sent to the gallery, so he could surprise Juli? He'd probably meant to warn her but forgot—as Ben had forgotten to tell her Christmas presents would be arriving at the gallery for Juli.

Luke had wrapped Ben's gifts for Juli. And, in Ben's memory, he'd tiptoed onto the porch of *Sea Green Glory* to leave them discreetly by Juli's door. Maia had teased him about that. He'd said he was only carrying out Ben's wishes. He hadn't put a "from" card in those presents either. He'd said it would make Juli sad to know they were from Ben, but Ben had wanted her to have them, so it was better for her to wonder and think they'd come from a friend or admirer.

The whole idea deflated her, but it made sense. That's why there was no card and no name in the box. Because Luke was going to get the box from Maia and give the necklace to Juli.

Sweet. Nice for Juli.

Maia shivered, her eyes stinging.

She bit her lip and emptied the box again. This time, she repacked it with extra care, restringing the necklace on the card and making sure the pendant hung as it should. She put the lid back on the box and rewrapped the paper around it as well as she could, but clearly it had been opened. There was no disguising that.

She put the box and shipping paper in the top right-hand desk drawer. Luke's drawer. By the time he thought to ask about it, or she decided to mention it, she would've accepted her disappointment and be ready to move on. No one would know the difference.

Except her. Because of those lovely few minutes before she'd scratched the ticket.

It didn't matter. She could be happy for Juli and Luke.

When she stepped out of the office, she realized she'd forgotten Brendan was in the showroom.

He looked the question at her and waited.

"What?" she asked. "The box?" She shrugged ever so slightly. "It wasn't for me. It's a gift Luke ordered for Juli. I put it in his desk drawer for him."

"Oh. Okay." He smiled. "Well, mystery solved."

Indeed. The mystery was solved, and Maia didn't figure into the answer. It felt like the story of her life.

Chapter Five

Maia opened the gallery on Saturday morning at ten a.m. Luke arrived at noon. He stopped to offer a quick hello and asked, "How are you?" But he wasn't chatty. Hardly slowing for a response, he went straight to his office.

Maia thought about the package in the drawer. She turned, thinking she should tell him it was there, but his office door was already closed.

Later, then.

She went about her own duties, including taking a call from a customer who'd commissioned one of Anna's delightfully dramatic windowpane sets. Shortly before noon, Luke opened the door and called out, "I'll be here for about an hour longer. Why don't you go grab lunch? I'll listen for the bell and you can eat in peace."

Maia looked toward the front and the plate glass window. Front Street was quiet. "I'll take you up on that. It's a gorgeous day. I think I'll take my sandwich out to the bench. Sure, you're good?"

Luke nodded. "I'll leave the office door open, so I can hear the bell." He went back into the office.

She could tell him about the package.

Luke seemed especially quiet today. She wasn't intimidated. They'd known each other too long. But she decided to let it be. He would've found the box by now and would know what it was for. What more was there to say?

She exited the front door and walked across the street to the wooden bench at the marina. The weather was perfect. The sky was blue. A few visitors wandered along the sidewalk. Some were going into the restaurants. Some to gift shops. To her left, over at the marina, a handful of people were talking to one of the charter boat captains.

Maia arranged her lunch bag, her sandwich and her drink beside her. The gulls called overhead and a few loitered nearby, eying her as she tugged the sandwich from the plastic bag. She wanted to toss them a hunk of bread, but she knew better.

The gulls alerted to more promising prospects—a family with young children who were dropping crumbs. The gulls deserted her for them, all except one forlorn looking fellow, but even he positioned himself midway, hoping for something and not sure where his best interests lay.

She laughed softly and watched white, puffy clouds sail by as she sipped iced tea. Joel was on her mind again. Probably the fault of Luke and the necklace. For a few moments, she'd had a crazy idea that the gift might've come from him, intended for her, before reality had struck.

Joel. She recalled that one, true dinner date they'd shared. The easy conversation. The goodnight kiss. How she remembered the kiss... She sighed deeply and tried to push the memory away. But her attention drifted and when a sweet breeze caressed her cheek, she again recalled the feel of Joel's arms around her, his lips on hers.

Stupid to remember. It was old news.

Luke called out, "Maia? You okay?"

She jumped up from the bench, feeling like she'd been caught in an embarrassing indiscretion. She brushed her fingers against her lips even as she felt relief knowing Luke, smart though he was, as a guy would never pick up on the mysteries and secrets within that gesture.

Luke had crossed Front Street and was looking amused. "I called your name a couple of times. You didn't hear me."

She gave him a broad smile as she walked over to him and they crossed the street together.

"Has it been an hour already?" she asked.

"Just," he said. "You look relaxed. Those days off did you some good."

She almost laughed. "I'm sure. I'm glad to be back though, and to be here."

Luke held the door open for her. "I have an appointment. If you've got things covered, I'll be on my way."

"I'm good."

Luke said, "Talk to you later."

"Okay. Tell Juli I said hello." She waited a moment to see if Luke would say something about Juli's gift, but he didn't.

The afternoon was surprisingly busy and lucrative. Several customers made purchases. Lora dropped by. Maia could see she was eager to get back on board.

"You'll start on Monday, then? I hope you won't miss the grandchildren too much?"

Lora said, "I'm settled back in my old house. I'm glad I rented it out instead of selling it. The children are wonderful, but they're starting school now and while I don't mind helping out around the house, it wasn't what I wanted to do all day."

"Oh," Maia said, not sure how to respond.

Lora laughed. "Not that my son and his wife expected me to clean. But I'm used to be being busy." She lowered her voice as if they might be listening. "I was ready for my own time again, too. If anything happens and I'm needed, I'll be there to help, but right now, I'm ready for a little change, and I surely did miss Beaufort."

"And we're glad to have you back. Sounds like good timing all around."

"See you Monday morning, Maia. I'm looking forward to it."

The door closed, and the bell jingled. Maia was smiling. She could feel the season building. She was eager for this. The tourists. The energy. The annoyances and the joys were equally welcomed by her. She was made to walk this gallery floor. She belonged here, welcoming folks and chatting with them and steering them to the purchases that matched their needs and wants. She had a knack for it, probably all the stronger for enjoying it. But by the time she flipped the sign to "Closed" that afternoon and locked the door, she felt done for the day.

And she'd hardly thought of Joel at all.

Which thought, brought him back to mind, and the necklace, too. She should've mentioned it to Luke. Made sure he'd found it.

No. She wasn't his secretary or anything. She managed the gallery. She would handle her personal business and others could take care of theirs. Including Luke and Juli and Frannie. Instead of complaining to Maia, Juli needed to face any worries she had with Frannie head-on.

Maia would stay focused on forward motion, positive interaction and the business of selling works of art she loved. This feeling of dissatisfaction would eventually pass.

Luke didn't understand that this gallery was her life. Her joy.

He loved the gallery, too, or used to back when he and Ben were partners and shared the running of their businesses. The loss of Ben, personally tragic, of course, also put the businesses solely on his shoulders. Ultimately, he'd sold one of the galleries, keeping only this one and the one in Charleston, and had scaled back on other business interests. Hiring good people wasn't the same as working with your best friend and cousin, someone you trusted totally. Besides, Luke was at heart an outdoors guy, not someone who thrived within four walls and a roof.

Maia picked up her tote bag. She let herself out the back door, jiggling it to make sure the lock caught. The late afternoon light was still plenty bright, but the day had a winding down feeling. She walked along the alley to the sidewalk on the side street. She took her time. No rush. She was headed home to an empty apartment. She loved her flat, but it wasn't going anywhere. This day was. It would soon become yesterday, and she wanted to enjoy what was left of it.

She knew the route well, including the cracks in the sidewalk, and hardly even needed to watch where she was putting her feet. As she turned onto her street, she saw someone sitting on the porch.

A tree blocked much of her view. Fay? Not Fay. She could tell that much. Reggie?

She didn't think so.

Still unable to see who it was, she walked closer. Now the view was clearer. She glimpsed jeans-clad legs between the porch rails, and a sandy-haired head.

Maia ran the remaining distance. Before she got to the steps, she called out, "Brian? Is everyone okay?"

Her brother stood. He looked well. His hair, usually short, looked a little longer, as if he'd missed a cut. His light blue eyes, his smile, took on a teasing look. His cotton shirt was untucked, and his jeans were worn thin on the knees. He leaned against the railing as she came up the steps.

"No need for alarm. Is it that unusual for me to show up at your place?"

She glared. "Yes, it is, and you know it."

"My fault. You're right. But I'm here now. And yes, as far as I know, everyone is fine."

"Mom and Dad? Megan?"

"Yep. They're all good." He gave her an odd grin. "Maybe you should ask about Frannie?"

"Frannie? Is something wrong with her? Is she sick?" Maia climbed the steps to the porch. She knew Frannie, of course, and some of her personal history. But Frannie was a very private person, and she and Brian were focused on each other, not always in a cheerful way.

Maia asked, "Is there a problem with her Uncle Will? Or more problems with Frannie's mother?"

"Laurel's not really her mother."

"Laurel married Frannie's father when Frannie was a toddler, right? As I understand it, she adopted her."

"Technicality."

"More than a technicality. It means she is legally her mother. All mothers and daughters, regardless of how they came to the relationship, can have problems."

"There's more to it in this case. This isn't a spat. I've told you some of it."

Maia sighed. "It's sad, I agree. Considering all that's happened with them, I guess any idea of a reconciliation is a moot point." Maia gestured at the rockers. "Want to visit out here or come upstairs?"

"Here's good. I can't stay long."

"You never can." She grimaced. "Sorry. Didn't mean to let those words loose. Forget I said them. I'm just glad to see you." She sat. "You look good. You're moving well. Your leg is better."

He moved his leg, patting the denim with his hand, as if to demonstrate that it was good as new. "Probably due to the weather being milder, warmer."

"And due to Frannie making you take better care of yourself?"

Brian grinned. He said, "Speaking of which...."

She felt a chill despite the warm weather and his cheeriness. She considered getting her sweater out of the tote.

"Well, don't you want to know?" He persisted. "You're usually curious."

"Gosh, it got chilly suddenly, didn't it?"

Brian leaned forward, his smile now tentative. "What's wrong, sis?"

"Wrong? Nothing, of course." She pulled the sweater over her shoulders.

"Are you worried?"

She frowned and shook her head. "Me? What would I be worried about?"

"Because you know things. You're intuitive. You know what I am about to say, and you don't want to hear it. Why?"

Maia shrugged. "I... I want happiness for you, Brian. You are such a good brother, a good man. The last few years have been challenging for you, with your marriage to Diane, the divorce, and then the accident. I'm your sister. I'm allowed to worry."

"I love her, Maia. I want to spend my life with her."

Maia shook her head. "Don't you think it's too soon? For both of you?"

"When is too soon? I don't know. Sometimes I think it's riskier to wait and maybe lose something, someone, important."

"How long have you known each other? Three months? Maybe closer to four, but a lot has happened in each of your own lives. You hardly know each other and you're both emotionally vulnerable." Maia tried to show love and kindness on her face and in her tone. "Don't take this wrong, but it seems like you two are always at odds, picking at each other. Almost every time I see you together, one of you is annoyed or huffy or something. Is that a good basis, a solid foundation, for a marriage?"

"An engagement first. It's not like we're getting married tomorrow. Frannie is less certain. She'll want a longer engagement."

"Uncertain? About marriage?"

"About everything." He shook his head. "She doesn't trust easily, including not trusting her own judgement. If I can convince her it's smart to marry me, she'll probably still insist on a long engagement. We both have baggage. We'll work it out together. And then there's Megan. Frannie is a great influence on her. Megan adores her, and she adores Megan. I adore them both. We make a good team, the three of us."

Maia rapped her fingers on the chair arm. "I hope Diane sees it that way and doesn't complicate that rosy picture you're painting." She cringed, hardly believing such harsh, cynical words were coming from her mouth. She hurried to apologize. "I'm sorry, Brian. You don't need me telling you how to live."

He nodded, "You're right about that, but you're also right that Diane is likely to cause trouble. That won't stop, ever, unless she dies or falls in love, moves away, and forgets me. Even then, she might want Megan to go with her. What am I supposed to do? Put my life on hold?"

His elbows rested on his thighs and his hands were held half-open and palms up as if he expected an answer, a solution, to fill them. Maia wished she had a good one to offer. She regretted, too, interfering back when he and Diane had been approaching divorce. Her well-intentioned interference was something he'd resented and been angry about for a long time. And now it felt as if….

"Why are you asking me anyway? You haven't wanted my opinion in a long time. Maybe you have doubts of your own?"

Brian pulled his hands back as he sat straightened, the relaxed posture gone. "I have doubts. I might always have doubts. But I didn't come to ask for your opinion. I came to tell you what I planned. Sort of a head's up. I know it's quick. I didn't want...well, I wanted you to know it was on my mind and give you a chance to get used to the idea."

He stood. She did, too. He gave her a hug, released her, and said, "I'd better get going."

Maia was speechless. Her mind went blank. She couldn't think of an acceptable response. As he went down the steps, she saw his motorcycle parked on the far side of the street. She followed and stood on the sidewalk while, across the street, Brian settled on his bike.

As he was about to strap on his helmet, he looked at her and repeated, "I have doubts, and probably always will. Doubts and reasonable caution aren't necessarily a bad thing, but nobody is promised tomorrow, Maia. A person can have doubts and still move forward with their life."

Maia stood, her body almost paralyzed, but her brain was running hard and fast. Her brain knew he was right, at least in part. Perfection was unlikely, but surely it was better to be closer to perfect before taking such huge life-changing steps? Was that the definition of courage? Or was that foolhardiness? Doubts were doubts and shouldn't be dismissed without considering what might be prompting them and whether the concerns were valid.

She was worried for her brother. The last thing he needed was one more heartbreak.

He'd come to tell her what he was planning. She'd dumped on the idea.

Some great sister she was.

And yet, standing here on the sidewalk with Brian already gone on his way—her hand belatedly raised in a weak wave—would she call him back if she could? Take her cautionary words back?

She groaned. What she'd said was harsh but true. Had Brian told their parents? They'd met Frannie once. Mom had said she was sweet. What else could she say? Frannie was many things, and a lot of them good, but she certainly wasn't sweet. Mom was trying to be accepting. Dad hadn't said much at all. Only that Brian was a grown man and, for that matter, Frannie was an adult, too. And then he'd gone back to whatever he was doing at the time. Her dad wasn't a guy who chewed stuff over. He didn't speculate.

Had Brian told them already? No, Mom would've called if Brian had even hinted about engagement or marriage.

Well, no mistake about it, she'd said her piece and that was that. Now she'd follow her dad's lead and leave it to Brian to handle as he thought best with the rest of the family.

"Maia?"

Fay.

Maia came back to the steps.

"You okay? I thought I heard voices. I thought maybe Reggie was home."

"That was my brother you heard."

"Brian? I wish I'd stepped out sooner. I've only met him once. We don't see much of your family here."

Maia shrugged. "No, I visit them mostly." It felt a little odd, but Fay was right. She didn't invite many people over. She was single, a working person. Not much time for partying and when there was time, it was more convenient and comfortable to be at her parents' larger home.

"I'd better get back inside. Allie will be waking any time now."

"I need to go, too. I'm just getting in from work."

Fay laughed softly. "You always look like you've been doing

your thing, but not necessarily working. I mean, I know you are, but you never come dragging in like my dad and mom, or even Reggie. One look and you can tell they've been at work all day. I never see that with you. Everyone should be so lucky."

She smiled, opened the front door and let Maia in ahead of her before moving to her own door.

"Join us for supper, why don't you? We'll be eating as soon as Reggie comes home."

"Thanks, but not tonight. Can I take a raincheck?"

"Sure." Fay gave a quick wave and went inside.

Chapter Six

Brian must've proposed to Frannie on Saturday evening because Sunday afternoon, Mom called Maia.

Maia was at the gallery when she saw her mom's photo pop up on the cell phone. She checked the time and knew what this call was about. Had to be. The newly engaged couple had probably barely made it out the door before Mom started dialing.

She answered, saying, "Mom, can you hold for a minute?" She excused herself to Brendan, waving the phone and saying, "I need to step outside for this call."

Maia left, descending the steps and crossing the street at a quick clip. Like running away? It was an odd thought. She had the phone with her and there was no running away from this news or the conversation.

She put the phone back to her ear. "Hey, Mom. Thanks for holding. What's up?"

Mom asked, "Did you hear?"

"Hear what?" But she knew, of course.

"Brian. He already told you, didn't he?"

Maia sighed, but quietly. "Is this about Frannie?"

"He did tell you, and you said nothing to me."

"It was his news, and his right to share it."

"Which he did. He and Frannie both. They came together, and they just left here. An engagement. But it's too quick. They haven't been dating very long at all."

"It's an engagement, Mom. Probably a long one. They'll have some time. From what Brian said, they won't rush to take their vows. Anything could happen before that."

"Well." Mom made a noise that sounded like a cross between a sigh and a grunt. "Frankly, Maia, I don't know what's worse. Worrying over a quick engagement or saying congratulations and thinking there's time yet for them to reconsider and break up."

"It's not our worry or our decision, Mom. I know you'll worry anyway, but Brian and Frannie are adults. They'll make their own decisions, take the risks and all that. They could use our support. They'll have enough doubts without us adding to them."

"But Maia, when two people are in love, just starting out and planning a life together, should there be many doubts? Isn't that an indication that it's not such a good idea?"

"They're adults. They've been burned before. Doubts seem reasonable and normal to me."

"You sound very cool about this. I'm surprised, really. But then, you know Frannie much better than I do. Should I feel reassured?"

"Of course."

"Well, alright. I'll remember that both are in their early thirties and they already have experience with life. I'll put a smile on my face, and in my heart, and let them get on with their future. I'll do my part and plan the party."

This time Maia had to bite her lip to hold in the sigh. She closed her eyes, then slowly reopened them and released her poor lip. Calmly, she said, "Great. Don't go overboard. You know Brian won't like that. I don't think Frannie likes a lot of attention either."

"I understand. But remember we've already decided they are adults and can deal with adult decisions. That works both ways. If they are adults, then they can deal with what comes as a consequence of their decision—an engagement party. Are there any dates that are totally out for you? Cathy's open for the next few weeks. I know that much."

"I'm open, too. Evenings are best for me, of course. Don't do a surprise party. They wouldn't like that."

"Who should we invite?"

Maia looked around, trying to think of some way to end this conversation. Normally, she enjoyed chatting with her mom—except for when there were things to be chewed over. Her mom like to twist it this way and that, to consider how it might work, should work, and how it might go wrong. Maia wanted to resolve issues and move on. Action items, please, she thought.

"Maia? You there?"

"I am. I was thinking about your question. Just family, don't you think?"

"Well, yes, of course we'll have family, but I don't know them all. Frannie's sister, Juli, should be included, right?"

A quick intake of breath. "You're right. They are sisters. Of course, she and Luke should be included."

"Heaven knows. Discovering a sister nearly three decades after the fact? Better late than never I guess."

"Mom. That sounds…."

"Oh, I don't mean anything by it, goodness sakes. It's just so…unexpected."

Mom had a bunch of sisters. Happily, they got along fine.

"What about Frannie's mother? Her name is Laurel, right? Laurel Denman? Related to that Will Denman you've spoken of? By marriage, right?"

"Sure. Yes. Laurel was married to Will Denman's nephew. Frannie is Will's great-niece." She refused to get into all those relationship twists and turns.

"Okay."

There was a pause as Mom made notes. Maia heard the scratching of her mother's pencil and the crackle of note paper through the receiver. She was well-acquainted with her mother's habits.

Mom said, "I've added Laurel to the invite list. What about Will Denman?"

"Yes. He was her father's uncle. He's a gallery customer. But he's in a rehab and confined to a wheelchair. You should send him an invite, but I don't see him being able to attend. As for Laurel, don't put her on the list yet." Maia stammered. "I don't know...there's some bad feelings between her and Frannie right now."

"But she's her mother."

"Frannie only recently learned the truth about Juli and Laurel's part in that. Frannie and Laurel have been at odds for years, as I understand it. It blew up."

"I can't not invite her mother."

"It's complicated. Ask Frannie how she wants to handle it. My guess is Laurel's not welcome."

"I can't imagine not inviting someone's mom. Although, now that I think of it, your cousin Sissie's husband's mom was outrageous. Just outrageous. A diva. I remember thinking they would've done much better to have left her at home. Maybe sent her on an all-inclusive trip to somewhere exotic and held the party while she was out of town." Mom laughed. "I know that sounds devious, but you just don't know...."

"I remember you telling me about that. I hear they're doing okay now, right? Their marriage is good and even the mother-in-law is cooperating. Didn't you tell me that?"

"True. Having that sweet grandbaby helped mend a lot of ill will. Which just supports what I was saying about NOT leaving her out. As you suggested, though, we'll get Frannie to approve the guest list."

Mom continued, "Cathy will bring her boyfriend. What about you? Plan on bringing along a plus one for yourself."

"A plus one? Please, Mom. This is a family shindig, right?"

"Of course. That's fine. Do whatever you think best. I was just hoping to see who you're dating these days."

"I'm not dating anyone right now."

"Their loss, then. The right one will be along soon, sweetheart." She added, "I'll get some dates from Brian, run them by the others, and let you know when. Need to get it done before the college

75

graduations hit and then the younger kids are out of school and everyone's taking off on vacation. You know how summers are. I'm thinking weekend after next."

"What?" But Mom was gone. Disconnected.

In two weeks? Well, if anyone could do it, Mom could.

Cathy must be serious about the new guy if she was bringing him to a family gathering. She wanted to be happy for Cathy. And she was, but she felt a little isolated. She, Cathy and Brian were the singles among the larger Donovan clan. Brian was now off that list and Cathy might be leaving it, too.

Happily married people wanted other people to be married—happily, of course.

Bridle Cove. If Cathy decided to remarry, would she decide it was time to sell the property?

Maia stood. Her fingers hurt from gripping her phone too tightly. She relaxed them.

She didn't move to return to the gallery. She watched a group of tourists walk by. They were carrying buckets and wearing hats as they headed down the boardwalk toward the dock where the boats took folks out to Shackleford Banks.

They'd better hang onto those hats, she thought. Once Hank had that boat revved up and roaring across the water, those hats would go airborne.

Should she talk to a bank? See what might be possible?

A waste of time—that's what it would be.

She could stretch to cover most of the down payment, but it would take all her savings and she'd never be able to afford loan payments on top of her usual living expenses. She'd be paying for her apartment and for Bridle Cove. It was impractical.

She wouldn't be able to take care of the property any better than Cathy seemed able to. What her heart wanted didn't jive with reality.

Maybe Cathy wouldn't sell it. Maybe she and her new hubby would choose to invest in it and renew it. It could go on as it had, perhaps even better. That was the best solution because ownership for her, Maia, was out of the question. There were too many strikes against it.

CRSO

That evening, with Mom's voice and words still playing in her head—no one could ever doubt Irene Donovan's love and devotion to her family—Maia cooked up a light supper and then watched TV before preparing for bed.

She stood at the sink as she washed her face and brushed her teeth. The mirror was unavoidable, as was her image looking back at her. There were fine lines now at the corner of her eyes. Very fine lines. Barely-there lines. But a forecast of more to come. Smile lines, her mother called them. Laugh lines, but not necessarily a laughing matter. However, her complexion was good, and her eyes were clear and bright. She smiled to reassure herself that youth was still on her side and saw those lines reappear again.

She sighed. Her twenties were behind her. She'd had so many hopes. Not all of them had worked out, but she'd accomplished a lot and had much to be grateful for. A job she loved, for one thing. But recently, satisfying employment didn't seem enough. If she managed to quash her present general discontent, she would once again be able to enjoy running the gallery and serving the customers.

The decades might change, but not her life. Her life remained as it had.

Was contentment enough?

As concerned as she was about Brian and Frannie rushing into an engagement, she also had a certain amount of admiration for them—for their willingness to take a chance. Sometimes it paid off. Sometimes it hurt. But she thought it was romantic in a crazy kind of way, for those who were willing to take the risk.

Maia sighed again, turned off the light in the bathroom, and crossed the dark bedroom to the living room. Wide pocket doors separated the two rooms and she'd left them open such that the outside light spilled in. In this old, renovated house, the front windows were tall and wide. The light from the outside washed across the floor of the living room and into the bedroom. It touched the soft candlewick bedspread and faded out near the pillows. The light filtered in from the streetlight outside, aided by the moon and stars, and the reflection off the water. She couldn't see the water from here, but still it altered, enhanced, the quality of the light for a wide area.

She pushed aside the lace curtains and observed the night. All was silent. No movement. The starlight and streetlights also brushed the asphalt surface of the road, the cars parked along the road, and even the roofs of the houses that lined the road. The porches of the houses were hidden within the deeper shadows cast by the moon. It lent them a temporary mystery even though she knew the landscape of each porch. The Witherspoon's porch with a red rocker and old-fashioned glider. Or Fay's porch—her porch, too—with a box of toys. Maia could imagine how those toys would change over time, from rattles and teethers, to stuffed animals, to dolls and trucks, to games and bikes, as baby Allie grew.

At this hour, everyone was inside. A few windows were lit. The overall aspect cried of emptiness. The quiet used to look like peace to her. The change troubled her because she knew the atmosphere of emptiness, loneliness, was rooted in her own perception.

Below on the street, a lone figure came walking. An unknown figure who didn't tarry, but Maia had a fleeting thought of Romeo seeking his Juliet. She, Maia, no Juliet, could open the window and step over the low casement onto the small balcony. It wasn't really intended to serve as a balcony but was just a flattish area on top of the porch roof. Maia's balcony, unlike Juliet's, was only a suggestion of a balcony, nothing that a true Romeo would stay below and call up to his sweetheart.

She released the lace panels and the curtains fell back into place as her phone rang. She picked it up from the coffee table. It was late for calls, but Mom might still be fretting over some aspect of the engagement or party.

"Hello."

"Maia?"

Joel's voice. Joel. *Now what?*

"Maia?"

"I'm here. It's me."

"Did I call at a bad time? It's probably too late. I'm sorry."

She wanted to yell, "Too late? No joke. Why didn't you call sooner?" But instead, muffling her anger, she said, "No, not a bad time."

There was a tiny silence, then he said, "I'm glad." He cleared his throat. "Business kept me busy, but of course, you already know I've been travelling. I'd like to see you. Are you free tomorrow?"

"Tomorrow? Monday? I have to work."

"We could go out to lunch."

"I'm assuming you're coming from Raleigh? That's a long way to drive for lunch." She tried to hold them back, but the words burst out anyway. "I thought you'd decided to... to write Beaufort off."

"Beaufort?" He paused. "I called while I was travelling. We spoke on the phone." Another pause. "I'm not coming from Raleigh. I'm driving down from Richmond, stopping by Beaufort on the way home."

"Are you just getting back to the states?"

"Yes. I told you I'd call when I got back, right?"

"I guess you did. I didn't realize you'd be gone so long."

"Neither did I. It's a long story and a boring one. The important thing is that I'm back and I'd like to see you."

"Beaufort is definitely not on the way from Richmond to Raleigh."

"I don't mind. Do you? Is this bad timing?"

She breathed, trying to reorient her thinking. "No, it's fine. Are you staying over tomorrow? Do you need a hotel? There are some bed and breakfasts in Beaufort. I could reserve you a room."

"I'll have to continue on to Raleigh after. I just wanted to see you and speak to you in person."

Suddenly, he sounded awkward. Not like a businessman at all. Mentally, she compared him to Ben and Luke. He fell short, on the phone, that is. Not smooth or easy in conversation.

Perhaps because she was silent too long, he added, "We don't do well on the phone. Have you noticed?" He paused, then added, "It's different when we're together in person."

He was right. It was different between them in person. Or had been.

"I'll come to the gallery?"

"Sure, I'll be there."

As she was about to disconnect, she heard her name.

"Maia?" Joel said.

"Yes?"

"I'm looking forward to it, to seeing you again. I'll try to arrive around lunchtime."

His voice, slightly rough, but warm with sincerity, touched her heart. She smiled for no good reason. She was alone here, after all. No one could see her foolish grin.

"Drive carefully, Joel."

After they disconnected, Maia continued holding the phone for a few minutes. Joel was a puzzle. She didn't really know all that much about him. Only about as much as hanging out in a group and one real date could tell her. But she'd thought they were close to something. Then, after he left, it seemed to fizzle out.

But he was back now, and he'd called as he'd said he would. It just seemed to Maia that a person who was really interested in another person would call more often. The other thing he'd said was also true. They weren't great on the phone. Maybe, for Joel, calling without a specific reason seemed...what? Pushy? Despite his apparent success in business, there a shyness about him.

He was a nice guy. Sometimes a guy could be too nice, or the chemistry didn't work. Or the guy thought she was too nice. Not mysterious or intriguing or sexy enough. And he moved on. She'd been there, done that.

Was that the problem with Joel? Could two nice people—courteous, ordinary people—have romance and excitement? Because that's what she wanted. She wanted love and companionship, but she also had dreams of adventure and romance with the right person—someone she could love and respect and have fun with.

The gallery…. Satisfaction, yes, but it was hard to find much adventure there. And romance? Well, that had almost happened more than once. It had taken more than one disappointment over love to cast her into this gloom of discontent.

But Joel was coming to see her. She was curious enough to look forward to it. He was driving hours out of his way to see her for a few minutes. Even if they managed to stretch it into a longer visit, it was still out of his way. Plus, she'd be at work. Should she try to get part of the day off? Or coverage for lunch?

How was she supposed to know? Would she feel that attraction she remembered when they are back together again? Would he? Or had the whole thing blown over before it could develop into something worth the bother?

Apparently, despite his absence, it hadn't blown over for Joel since he was coming out of his way to see her.

And maybe, it hadn't blown over for her either since she was giving it all this thought while wearing a smile she felt down to her toes.

Chapter Seven

Joel Sandeford had never been so glad to be back in the States. There was a time, not long ago, when he'd loved traveling, even for work. It had felt more like play than work, and the future felt wide open and full of opportunity. But that was before his father's company became his sole responsibility.

He'd checked out of the hotel in Richmond this morning. After a good night's sleep, he was ready for the drive. He could've caught a connecting flight from Dulles to Charlotte yesterday, instead of to Richmond. It would've made for a shorter trip back to Raleigh. But he'd flown that route deliberately, and had stayed overnight in a motel on the south side of town to be rested and fresh for today. He was taking that detour to Beaufort, and he wanted to time his arrival for about lunchtime.

He wanted to see Maia.

Traffic demanded his attention until he'd cleared the Richmond metro area. At that point, his mind was free to wander, and to wonder how he'd gotten into this situation. And how he could get out of it.

Life had slipped up on him. Other than the death of his mother when he was young, his life had been pleasant. Sometimes lonely, but he'd always had plenty of whatever he wanted or needed. He'd had a few good friends over the years and the approval of his teachers and his father. His father, Gerald Sandeford, worked a lot, but except for when he had to travel out to California or overseas for Sandeford Corp, he was always there for Joel. As a teenager, Joel had worked in the family business each summer, and by the time he finished grad school, joining the family business fulltime had been expected. It had been as natural as breathing in those first years. He'd never been afraid of hard work and long hours, and he loved a challenge. But some part of him must've viewed it as temporary and it took a little longer for the rest of his brain to get the message.

He didn't know exactly what he wanted to do with his accumulated education and business experience. Something different, though. Not just to switch to another company that made a different variety of widget but looked the same otherwise, day after day. Same office décor, same endless paperwork, with even the employees and co-workers beginning to look alike. He'd kept his eyes open, not actively seeking, but keeping his eyes open, sure he'd take the leap when the right opportunity presented itself.

Everything changed late last year when his father fell sick. His father, who'd never faltered, suddenly was fatigued and lightheaded, and then one day, his heart nearly stopped. He was lucky. He was home and near medical facilities and specialists in Raleigh. The pacemaker put his heart back on track. But it had been scary. Facing one's mortality always was.

In December, while his father was being treated and recovering, Joel assumed a larger role in the business. It made sense that he would. His father jokingly called it a promotion when they were at the Denman house having dinner with Frannie and her mother, Laurel, in early February.

That evening at the Denman house, without warning, Frannie had abruptly left the dinner table. He and his father remained at the table, sitting and staring, while Laurel excused herself to chase after her daughter. Joel and she had been discussing childhood memories, specifically her sixteenth birthday party. Had he said something wrong?

He'd mentioned her father. He knew she still missed him. She'd lost her father shortly after that birthday.

He'd folded his napkin and placed it on the table next to his plate, concerned. Had he been callous? Bringing those memories back to her? He'd lost his own mother. He knew how that felt. But it had been years ago for both of them. Surely, she'd accepted the loss and could manage it by now. Still, he felt badly, as if the emotional distress, the dinner disruption, was his fault.

Laurel had returned. Frannie hadn't. It was just as well, Joel had thought, because his father was looking tired.

His father had gone out to the car, but Laurel detained Joel. She'd said, "Please forgive her manners. She has feelings for you, Joel. Don't tell her I said so. She'd never forgive me. She's driving back to Emerald Isle tonight to her uncle's house...."

He'd been polite to Laurel, but he'd had commitments to his father and the job. Plus, he had difficulty believing Frannie was in love with him, so he hadn't rushed to follow her.

Was he callous? Insensitive?

He liked Frannie. They'd been friends for years. He wouldn't hurt her for the world.

She could be very intense. At one time, he'd thought that piece of her personality was intriguing, and he'd admired her style. Maybe she'd thought he was interested in her romantically.

Maybe Laurel was right. He owed Frannie, as a longtime friend, a chance for her, and for him, too, to see if there was anything to pursue between them. Since his father was doing much better, and Joel was badly in need of time away, he'd finally followed Frannie to Emerald Isle.

Late February. He remembered how cold it had been, but interspersed with those rare sunny, warm days that the beach sometimes gifted almost as a tease. A tease? Despite her good intentions, Laurel had been wrong. Whatever was bothering Frannie, it wasn't unrequited love from good old Joel.

Nice guy Joel.

They said nice guys finished last. It might be true, but it's who he was. Women liked him, and he enjoyed their company. But his closer relationships had never worked out. He was never sure whether

84

they liked him or his money better.

But he didn't blame the women. After all, those relationships had followed a pattern and he was the only constant. Had he fallen for them too easily? Had he pursued too eagerly? Yet, each time the relationship faltered and then failed, he'd only felt regret. As if for an opportunity lost. As if this woman might have been the ONE, the love he was hoping for, and he was sorry it hadn't worked out. But he hadn't felt like a man with a broken heart.

While he was relieved he hadn't hurt Frannie unknowingly, it was a little embarrassing to have followed her to Emerald Isle, even inviting himself along to a party, only to realize he was making a pest of himself, for no good reason. They went to the get-together together, but he knew she'd brought him along for cover. If she needed an excuse to leave early, she had him, her out-of-town friend, Joel.

A get-together, Frannie had said. Just friends. At Luke Winters' house on Crescent Lane.

He'd met Maia.

For the first time in his life, he'd been more than nice—he'd been shy. It was a crazy feeling to encounter at thirty-two. He recognized the why of it. It was about more than attraction. There was a spark, almost like the pilot light on a gas stove. Suddenly, he was awake. His heart was aware. And he felt an odd hope, too, because this time he cared about it working out. He wanted to know her better and for her to know him. He wanted her to look at him and smile and mean it.

Maia had greeted them when he and Frannie had arrived at that get-together. There were the usual greetings. She'd used a friendly saying, "The more, the merrier." Throughout the evening, he kept hearing her words, The More, The Merrier, as if they were in caps. Stupid words. Stupid reaction on his part.

He didn't need More, but he wanted Merry. And Maia.

While she'd been speaking, he'd been busy taking in her flashing eyes, the short dark curls that framed her forehead and cheeks, her dimples…the petite build that made the taller, slimmer women look bland and a dime-a-dozen.

Maybe if he took it slow, got to know her, and gave her the chance to know him, then maybe....

She hadn't embarrassed him by calling out his awkward silence. Instead, she'd brought him into the group of friends as smoothly as...the more, the merrier.

He watched the interactions and noted that she was friendly with Brian, but then figured out Brian was her brother. She joked with Luke, too, but then he realized Luke was married to a quiet, naturally elegant woman named Juli and they had a baby. Maia was friendly with everyone, more of a host than the Winters who actually lived there. No one laughed the way she did. No one seemed to have her heart.

His own quickened.

After that get-together, he'd asked Frannie point-blank if there was a possibility of anything happening between them. She'd said no. He was careful not to show how grateful he was. Now that he had no worries about hurting Frannie, he could focus on finding opportunities to spend time with Maia.

He'd hung around for a while, from late February and into March. He had come to know them all—Maia, Brian, Luke and Juli. Frannie's friends, yes, but instinctively, he knew they could be his friends, too. He'd found himself reluctant to go back to Raleigh, reluctant to leave his mini vacation. It was as if he was getting a fresh breath of air, the first in a long time, perhaps the first in years.

For the first time, when he thought about the family rental in Hatteras, he wondered what it might be like to live at the beach instead of catching a day here and there, between the demands of business and occupation by renters. Really live there. But as tempting as it might seem, the getting away from it all, he knew it wouldn't satisfy him for long. Because he was about business. He enjoyed doing business. He just wasn't sure what kind of business.

He was missing balance. That was it. And because he could choose anything to do, sick father considerations aside, he'd never chosen anything. He'd followed the expected path.

But he didn't have to. As soon as his father was back to one hundred percent, Joel could make his own move. Direct the course of his life, himself.

Was it Maia? Was it these people? Was it simply the ocean air getting into the nooks and crannies of his brain and blowing out the old, accepted, dusty expectations?

In March, he'd found the nerve to ask her out. He hadn't sweated a date invite like that in a long time. They'd gone to dinner. It was typical first date. They were both awkward but hadn't let that stop them from laughing at themselves and having fun. Then he'd gone home because his father said he had news and needed to have a face-to-face conversation.

Joel thought his father had received more bad news about his health. Maybe he was sick again. His dad's voice had sounded off, but not like when he was sick. He'd been much better when Joel left. So, no, Joel didn't think his father was seriously ill again. But what? Joel always did a lot of thinking. His head was always full of thoughts. Perhaps because he'd had that solitary childhood.

Back in March, as he'd left Emerald Isle to return to Raleigh, his brain was full of how he'd approach the subject of a change with his father. In his head, the arguments and counter-arguments about his participation in the future of Sandeford Corp had alternated with high-flung, emotional appeals about happiness and fulfillment. Because now he knew that while he might not know exactly what he wanted for his life, he knew it wasn't what he'd been doing for the past several years.

"Dad?" he called out as he entered the house. His voice rang through the large foyer and the rooms that opened onto it. "Dad?" he called again, not yelling, but just calling out as he walked down the hall to the office suite.

Laurel Denman had greeted him at the door.

Joel frowned. "Is he okay? Where's my father?"

"I'm in the office," his dad said. The chair squeaked slightly as he rose. He walked around the desk to where Joel and Laurel were standing. "I'm glad you're here, son."

Joel's first thought was, "He looks good, thank goodness." His second was, "Why is Laurel Denman here?"

His father said, "Laurel, thanks so much for coming over."

His father's words were innocent enough, but Laurel reached up and touched his cheek. Such a light gesture, but potentially, it said much. Joel frowned.

Laurel smiled at him. "I'll leave you two alone. I know you have much to discuss." She paused before leaving. "Call me, Gerald."

She patted Joel's sleeve as she walked past. "I hope Frannie is well? I presume you saw her?"

"I did. She's fine." Some unexpected energy made him reckless. He said, "She has a boyfriend. Not me. A guy named Brian."

Laurel's eyebrows lifted to convey her surprise. Her lips assumed a polite, thin, non-committal smile. Joel thought her eyes looked cold.

"Well, dear," she said, "I still have hope. I think you and Frannie would make a perfect match."

With that, Laurel moved past him and went through the door. Not even a goodbye. Just her blonde hair and silk suit moving down the hallway and then gone. That was okay with Joel, but it felt odd. The word, portent, popped into his head. It sent a shiver down his spine.

"Dad?"

His father gave him the usual one-armed hug and patted him on the back. Like Joel was eighteen again and about to get the family business speech before leaving for college.

"Have a seat, Joel." He gestured toward a stuffed chair, but instead of going behind the desk, he took the chair's twin and settled in. "I'm glad to see you."

"You said that. You're making me worry."

Gerald drew in a deep sigh and released it slowly. Joel noted that he hadn't winced at the chest movement, and his color stayed good. Joel relaxed.

"I hope you've always understood how proud I am of you."

Joel nodded. "Yes." Had that changed somehow? *Portent.* Again, that word. And another word echoed. One he'd already thought of. *Change.* "I have some things I want to discuss with you, too."

His father smiled. "Certainly." He shifted in is seat. "If you don't mind, I'll go first. It feels awkward to say what I need to tell you, so I'd like to get it over with."

"Of course." Somehow Joel knew that every argument he'd rehearsed on the trip here was suddenly pointless. It was in the air all around them. He fought the urge to get up and walk out, to prevent his father from saying whatever it was he had on his mind. "If it's your health...."

"I'm in love, son. Joel, after all these years without your mother, I never expected to meet that person, the right woman, one with whom I wanted to spend my remaining years."

The words burst from Joel unplanned, "What? Not Laurel!"

Gerald laughed. It was a hearty, belly laugh. It reassured Joel both in terms of Laurel and also in terms of how his father was doing. That laughter was intense and seemed not to cause him any harm.

"I'm sorry, Joel." He pulled out a handkerchief and dabbed his eyes and then his nose. He sniffled. "No, not Laurel. She's been a good friend over the years, and I appreciated her attention when I was struggling with the loss of your mother long ago and recently, with my health issues, but no."

The next, obvious question, Joel didn't ask aloud. He waited.

"Her name is Sharon. You've met her."

Joel frowned, thinking. He shook his head. "No, dad. I can't think of anyone I know named Sharon."

He smiled broadly, grinning beyond Joel, at the doorway. He held out his hand as he stood. "Son, you remember Sharon."

Joel turned to look. "The nurse?" She was standing there smiling, but she wasn't in uniform. They'd hired her as a private nurse when dad was in the hospital and then in rehab. She'd accompanied him home, to ease the transition and so he wouldn't be alone with Joel travelling—the travelling his father would otherwise have done. Other than those first days at the hospital before he'd had to take on the business single-handed, Joel hadn't spent much time around her. He'd expected her to vanish when the job was done. She was still here.

"Your nurse?" he said, but this time aloud.

Sharon stepped into the room and took Gerald's hand. "I know this is a surprise, Joel. I hope you'll give me us a chance to show you how much this means to us."

His tires hit the rumble strips on the side of the road.

Suddenly, he was back in the present, and a good thing it was, too. His attention had drifted along with that recollection. He'd set the car on cruise control and the traffic had been light south of Petersburg and now he was in North Carolina. Back home in NC and just passing Halifax.

Amazing. Driving while preoccupied was almost like time travel. He'd hardly been on the road and now here he was, miles along. Yeah, it was great as long as inattention didn't get himself and others killed.

Just south of Rocky Mount, he exited onto 64 east. There, he pulled into a service station parking lot and got out to stretch his legs and call Maia.

Maia. Would she be glad to see him? They'd hit it off before, when they'd first met and went out on their date, but there'd been this gap since. It was due to life, including business and personal. Life had to be dealt with. When he'd called from Europe, she'd seemed less…friendly? Less enthusiastic? Less warm. More guarded. It was hard to know what to expect this time, thus he wanted to see her in-person. See for himself.

He reminded himself that he needed to keep things cool for now. Too much was up in the air with his father and the business. He didn't want to set expectations with her he couldn't make good on. So, he'd play it friendly and cool.

Face it, Joel, this visit is really for you. Not just about Maia. Because….

Because I want to know, need to know, if what I thought I found here on the coast is real. Not something that seems desirable now because I don't like the current state, or where it has me...trapped.

Trapped meant no way out. That didn't really apply to him. Maybe for the moment, but not forever.

Trapped. Maybe that's how it had been for his father?

Back on that day, more than a month ago, when his father had said, "I need to tell you something...I'm in love," Joel had leaned toward his father, and had spoken gently, earnestly. "Dad, you were very sick. It happens...people develop attachments for their doctor or nurse. It will pass."

His father smiled. "I don't think so, but it's more than that. Please listen. I took over this business from my father. I grew it and tended it, for myself, for our family, for our employees, knowing that one day I would hand it over to you. That day is here."

"Dad, I—"

"Seriously, Joel. I'm turning it over to you. You make the decisions now. I have total confidence in you." He nodded at his son, "The attorney is drawing up the documents to remove me from the businesses, so that you'll be clear to make any decisions you wish."

"Dad. I worked this business with you, because it was important to you. On my own—"

"You're a grown man, Joel. It's time. Sharon and I are going to the Caribbean. She loves the sun and the turquoise seas. We're going to get married." "Dad—"

"No worries. We'll have a pre-nup. Sharon has no interest in the company."

Neither do I, Joel thought. *Not like this.*

But how did you tell your father, who'd given his life to the company, who'd nearly died such a short time before, that you didn't want what he and his father had devoted their lives to?

He told himself they could talk this out. It might take a few hours, or a few days, but they could make sense of this. Joel walked outside. Sharon followed. She came to stand beside him.

She said calmly, "A brush with death, that sudden, in-your-face awareness of one's mortality, makes people rethink their lives. It brings a certain clarity to their thinking. That's what has happened to your father."

They had stopped on the steps overlooking the back gardens. His mother's gardens, though his father had paid to keep them trimmed and fertilized for more years than his mother had tended them. He said, "And when he confronted his mortality, you just happened to be there."

"I was hired to be there."

"You weren't hired to take advantage of his weakness."

"I don't think I did. I've been a nurse for many years and it hasn't happened before. This is different. This is real. But, Joel, I want you to know I won't marry your father without your blessing."

Nice words. Cool words. But were they sincere?

Next thing he knew he was neck-deep in the business again, and Alice, his father's administrative assistant was purchasing airline tickets and making hotel reservations. Suddenly a month and more of his life had vanished, into a series of yesterdays and tomorrows with no respect for the day itself.

It had been late March when he'd gone on the dinner date with Maia, had left her to return to his father, and then learned of the change about to force itself into his life. And now, the calendar was flipping from April to May.

He wanted to see Maia. Beyond that, he wanted to test the memory of his time with her, to determine if it was truly as he remembered. To understand whether it had all been a mirage.

That time he'd spent with her, and in Emerald Isle and Beaufort…it might have been no more real or solid as the past thirty plus years of his life now seemed. He needed to know.

He needed to feel the ground steady beneath his feet again.

Chapter Eight

That Monday morning, Maia dressed with extra care, choosing a blouse that brought out her eyes, or so she'd been told, and applied more makeup than usual. Not enough to look like she'd tried especially hard, but understated, she assured herself, to enhance her natural beauty. At that thought—enhancing her natural beauty—she broke into laughter and tossed the mascara into her makeup basket on the bathroom vanity. Then, the appropriateness of the word, vanity, made her laugh again.

She hadn't felt this upbeat in a while. The silliest things seemed to be tickling her funny bone. It felt good.

She expected Joel to arrive at the gallery around lunch time. Of course, no one could control the traffic, and the time was uncertain. Even so, she found herself checking her face, her clothing, and looking out the plate glass window at Front Street. A customer came in and Maia was glad of the distraction. As it turned out, he was an artist, recently moved to the area, who was inquiring about displaying his work.

"No promises, of course. Bring in some pictures of your work and I'll make sure the gallery owner gets a look." She pointed at the walls. "As you can see we're pretty full, but we like to highlight local artists, so yes, drop off some pictures and information and we'll see."

The man thanked her. She sensed he would like to have discussed other things. Perhaps to tell her how much he loved the area? Or maybe to ask the best place to buy art supplies in the area. Or he might be interested in local groups for creative types or maybe for poodle fans. Who knew? Maia didn't. She didn't seem to be operating with the full quota of brain cells because half of her brain was busy keeping an eye on the window and the street outside.

The man apologized for keeping her and left. She felt terrible, but not badly enough to invite him back in to continue chatting. She didn't even recall his name.

Disgusted with herself and her selfish, superficial preoccupation, she resolved to focus on business, but as she passed the display window, she caught sight of her reflection again. She paused to smooth her hair and re-tuck her silk shirt into her slacks. Should she have worn a skirt?

She groaned. She had to get past this foolishness.

It was late morning when Maia heard the smooth rumble of a motorcycle, and then heard it go suddenly silent. She went to the window. Brian and Frannie were standing on the sidewalk in front of the gallery. Brian's helmet was already off and Frannie was fussing with hers. The chin strap seemed to be giving her a problem, and Brian paused to help her. It was a sweet scene. He was attentive as his fingers wrapped around hers and then efficiently released the buckle. All four of their hands lifted the helmet from her head, freeing Frannie, and the sun shot bright flashes of reddish light through her long, straight fine hair. It reminded Maia of Juli's hair. Frannie and Juli shared sapphire-blue eyes, too. Not surprisingly, they looked like sisters. In normal indoor lighting, their hair was more brown than red, but when the sun came out, the highlights did, too.

That hair, those eyes—the unusual similarity in their features and in their physical builds had made Maia wonder right from the start. It was too coincidental. The similarities had kept picking at her until the truth finally came out, a truth that no living person had known except for Will Denman, Frannie's great uncle.

It occurred to Maia, that Will Denman was Juli's great uncle, too. Both women had the same birth parents, but had known nothing of each other until recently. It seemed almost impossible until one saw how DNA was being used to unite family members who were lost or unknown. Those TV shows were popular these days. The credit here didn't go to DNA comparison or science, but to an old man, Will Denman, who stumbled upon the evidence, but then had a stroke that prevented him from telling what he knew. He'd left clues, though, that Frannie had happened upon.

Truth, as always, sought to be known.

Finding one's family had its shocking aspects, in part because the idea of the relationship was very new to everyone involved, which was probably the greatest cause of Juli's unease. Some stuff was hard to deal with when it was new and needed time to be assimilated, to mellow and be understood.

If the degree of red in one's hair could truly be associated with temperament, then it was a truer fit for Frannie than Juli. But then Juli would've learned to rein in any temper she might have had in favor of getting along, to be able to get along in foster homes and to support herself. Frannie had never had any need to worry about the roof over her head or about earning a living.

The bell over the door jingled and Brian said, "Maia, hey there."

Brian stopped and held the door open for Frannie.

Slim, trim, and long-limbed elegant in white capris and a peachy-orange silky top, Frannie looked ready for a fancy barbecue function instead of like someone who'd just climbed off the back of a motorcycle. Even her hair was hardly mussed. But that cool exterior was usually at odds with what was going on inside Frannie, and even now, as Maia met her eyes, she noted uncertainty.

If Frannie did feel uncertain then perhaps she might be wondering what Maia and the other members of the Donovan clan thought about the sudden engagement. On the other hand, if Frannie were head over heels in love shouldn't she be walking on air and glowing like the sun? Her last thought would be to worry about what others were thinking. Maia was sure she, herself, would be beyond excited if....

Brian said, "Hey, Maia. I hope we're not interrupting."

She remembered her manners and opened her arms wide to hug Frannie.

"Congratulations. That's not what one says to the bride-to-be, right? But I'm saying it anyway. Congratulations to the two of you for finding love."

Frannie looked surprised. Her perfectly-shaped eyebrows lifted slightly as if she suspected hidden meanings in Maia's words. She asked, "I know it's quick. I'm sure it was unexpected."

Before Maia could answer, Brian threw an arm around each of them. "Frannie and I want to treat you to lunch to celebrate, right?"

Frannie hesitated and, again, Maia saw doubt in her eyes.

Maia said, "I'd love to, one day soon, but I can't today."

"Come on, Maia."

"I'm sorry, I'm alone here." She didn't want to mention Joel.

"Flip the sign. We'll make it a short lunch."

Frannie elbowed him. "We'll try again another day. There's no rush." She ended with a look at Maia.

Her expression seemed odd, strange, almost pleading. But why? Frannie brushed at some tiny speck on her blouse and Maia caught the flash of light from the ring on her hand.

She gulped. Her own reaction troubled her, as did her reluctance to gush and congratulate. But she did it anyway, forcing herself forward to grasp Frannie's hand. She tried to sound eager.

"Can I see? Oh, that's gorgeous!" And it was. The diamond was round and flashing brilliantly and set off by the pear-shaped sapphires on each side. "Brian, did you pick this out? This ring is exquisite."

Brian's cheeks reddened. He shrugged but with a pleased smile on his face. "I have good taste. Don't act so surprised."

A quick glance at Frannie's face suggested she agreed with Maia's assessment of the ring. If Frannie liked the ring and loved Brian, then what was the problem?

Jokingly, Maia said, "Brian's expertise is in boats and marinas. The ultimate blend of business with play. Not jewelry." She smiled at the newly engaged couple. "But you did well, Brian. I'm impressed."

The bell over the door sounded. Maia dropped Frannie's hand and looked up.

"Sorry, you two. Business calls."

A customer entered. If Maia smiled more brightly than usual as she moved away from the Brian and Frannie to welcome the customer, it was due to gratitude that the needs of business provided an intervention of sorts. Sad, but she wasn't up to a celebratory, spur of the moment lunch with the happy couple.

The customer had only a quick question which Maia answered and then the customer was gone. Now what? She turned back to Brian and Frannie, apologizing. "Brendan is out today and you can see this is difficult timing."

Brian said, "We could bring something in?"

Maia shook her head. "Too many interruptions. You two go along and we'll try again soon." She smiled her best smile, but couldn't shake the feeling that she was being rude and selfish.

Frannie asked, "Mind if I use the ladies' room?"

"Not at all. It's right through there." She pointed toward the breakroom.

"Thanks."

As soon as Frannie had left the room, Brian dropped his voice and said, "What do you think? How did Mom sound?"

"Sound?"

"About the engagement."

"She's excited. She is looking forward to getting to know Frannie better, introducing her to the family and all that. She's planning the engagement party."

"Seriously?"

"Well, you know Mom. It's a big life event, right? She had some concerns, but she seemed very positive."

"Listen, I was hoping you'd do me a favor."

The lowered voice warned her she might not like the request. She responded less warmly. "What do you need?"

"It's Frannie. I'm not sure what's wrong. I don't understand women. I thought she might talk to you about whatever is on her mind."

They heard the door hinges squeak in the breakroom and Frannie was back with them. Maia was glad to be spared having to answer Brian.

Maia said, "By the way, have you two set a date for the wedding?" She waited and then added, "People will ask, you know, at the engagement party, if not before."

Brian jumped into the conversation. "We're still working dates, but there's no reason we can't move forward with the details. It'll be that much easier when we know the date." He lowered his voice. "Of course, as far as I'm concerned we could just go to the courthouse and get it done. All that other stuff is for you girls. But whatever Frannie wants, is fine by me. If she wants fancy, then fancy it will be."

Maia, annoyed on Frannie's behalf, glanced at her brother's fiancé. But instead of the cold gaze from a few minutes before, Frannie's face now wore a loving look as she gazed at Brian. Frannie had a million moods and every one of them was in earnest while it was the uppermost. For the life of her, Maia didn't understand Frannie and Brian as a couple. Such volatility made Maia uneasy. Yet, there were times she liked Frannie very much. She had to trust that Brian knew what he was doing. Clearly, he'd made his choice and committed his heart.

"What about Megan? How does she feel about her dad remarrying?"

"She adores Frannie."

Frannie said, "I adore her, too. I think, though, that it's awkward for her with her mom."

"Diane doesn't want me, and I more than return the feeling."

Frannie's hand slipped across the distance between them and rested on Brian's arm.

"I don't want to deal with her either. But Diane has a way of complicating things."

Brian said, "That's my problem. I'll handle it."

He spoke in such a way that all conversation ceased for a few moments. Finally, Maia cleared her throat, then asked, "What do you have in mind for the wedding? The gown? Flowers? Are you looking locally or back in Raleigh? What about the wedding location?"

"We haven't decided," Frannie said.

Maia thought she caught a warning note in her voice. Or maybe just surprise at Maia's ill-breeding. As she should. The woman was barely engaged and already the in-laws were pushing in.

Brian said, "I told Frannie to set up some time with you to go look at dresses and all that stuff. She knows everyone around here, shopping and all that, and could be helpful."

Again, an awkward silence.

Maia struggled to break the stalemate. She was losing patience with this. Intrigue had never intrigued her, and she had no interest in dancing to the tune of anyone's emotional storms. Besides, more questions would just prolong the conversation, and—she cast a look out the window—just now she had other things on her mind.

She said, "We need to get together with Juli. Go out to lunch and talk. We can exchange ideas and then you, Frannie, can tell us what you want us to do. Or if you have it handled otherwise, or just aren't ready to make decisions, that's fine, too." She hoped she'd left enough wiggle room in there for Frannie not to feel cornered, and she hoped Frannie understood what she was trying to do: Offer help without forcing it on her.

Those unsettling currents between her brother and his fiancé were enough to give anyone heartburn.

"Remember to call Mom. She wants the two of you to approve the guest list. Better speak now or be happy with how it ends up."

Frannie's dark blue eyes grew larger and Maia realized Frannie was afraid...no, afraid was too strong a work—more like wary. Of their dear, sweet mom, Irene? Or of mothers in general?

Juli's worry—the one she'd expressed about Frannie's quest—suddenly popped into Maia's head and almost popped out of her mouth, but she kept her lips together. That issue was between Juli and

Frannie. After the impulse to speak the words was safely passed, Maia forced a smile. Brian and Frannie had stopped on their way out to admire the shell creatures on the round display table.

She wanted to be happy for Brian. For Frannie, too. And then there was her sweet niece Megan. Lots of folks could be hurt if this relationship didn't sort itself out well.

Brian should've waited. He shouldn't have rushed the engagement. But that was Brian. All or nothing with him. She felt a twinge of sympathy for Frannie. She'd help her if she could, and if that's what Frannie wanted. Maybe Frannie hadn't realized what she was getting into when she'd said, "Yes." And maybe that was a good reason for a girl to have caution and take her time before making a commitment.

Maia was facing the window as Joel crossed Front Street and approached the steps. She glanced at Brian and Frannie. Frannie was also looking toward the front of the building and had clearly spied him. Frannie walked to the door to greet Joel as he pushed it open.

"Joel. Hi," Surprise was obvious in Frannie's voice. So was pleasure. "Good to see you."

Brian frowned. "Yeah. Good to see you, Joel. What brings you to Beaufort?

"Unsweet."

She smiled. "Me, too."

She called in the order, they chatted about his trip for a few minutes, and then Joel went across Front Street and down a few shops to pick it up. While he was gone, Maia pulled out paper plates, napkins and utensils.

No more worry allowed. Enjoy this. It's lunch. A nice opportunity to get to know Joel better.

Hopefully it would stay quiet in the gallery, at least enough for them to spend time together without too many interruptions.

He returned, and they sorted out the food. As they sat down at the table to eat, Maia held up her hand and pointed to her bare ring finger. "Did you notice Frannie's hand?"

"No."

"They became engaged this weekend." She watched Joel's face. How did he feel about Frannie and Brian? Did he still care for her? It would be natural enough, she told herself.

Joel said, "This seems quick. What do you think?"

"Same as you. Maybe I shouldn't say this. We haven't been seeing each other for very long.... We are seeing each other, right?"

"Yes. This an official date as far as I'm concerned."

"Well, I don't know about you, but I've never been lucky in love, so I don't know if I can judge well in the abstract. As for Brian, I know that when he sets his mind on something, he can be determined. It doesn't do to stand in his way unless you feel very strongly about it." She shook her head. "I know. I tried to mix in with his personal life when he and Diane, his first wife, were having problems, and I didn't help despite good intentions and he had trouble forgiving me."

"You meant well. As for this, it seems he knows what—who—he wants. He knows he's lucky to have found that special someone and he isn't willing to risk losing her."

Maia listened and considered. "Maybe. For Brian. But then there's Frannie. You know her better than I do. How do you feel about her and Brian?"

"I wish them both the greatest happiness possible."

"It doesn't bother you?"

He frowned. "Why would it?"

"No reason." She believed him. Apparently, Joel harbored no lingering feelings for, or regrets about, Frannie. Reassured, Maia said, "My parents were, are, lucky in love. You lost your mom, right? You mentioned your dad is a widower?"

"When I was a teenager. In fact, at one time I thought Laurel and my father might get closer. They're friends and both lost their partners. It seemed like it might happen, but it didn't. Not sure why it didn't, but I'm glad."

"Why? I imagine your father was lonely on his own."

"Do you know Laurel Denman?"

The corner of Joel's mouth quirked up as if he didn't want to smile or grimace, but couldn't resist giving into it a little. She only knew what Brian had said about Laurel. She suspected he and Joel would agree on that subject.

Joel said, "I hope you'll join me for dinner on Friday evening."

Maia, surprised, was silent for a moment.

Joel said, "Maybe seven p.m.? That gives you a few minutes to catch your breath after closing the gallery and before rushing out to eat, but we could meet earlier or later depending on what works for you."

She shook her head. "Whatever time is best for you. Where would you like to go?" Since she was local, she was prepared to suggest a few places. "Did you want to stay in Beaufort? We can go into Morehead City or Atlantic Beach or—"

"I'll make reservations someplace special."

"Are you sure, Joel? You'll be coming from Raleigh, right? This is a lot of driving back and forth."

"It's worth every mile."

"If you're sure. It just seems...."

"Maia."

"What?"

He smiled. "You're spending too much time worrying over this."

"I'm not worried," she said, quick to respond.

"Trust me. This is what I want to do. These days I travel. Too much. But at least, I'm staying in North Carolina this week." He smiled reassuringly. "As for our date, it's something special. Trust me on this?"

"Of course." Her brain threatened to start racing again. She was used to planning, being the one in charge, not a passive participant. She took a deep breath. "You don't talk much about what you do. You mentioned something about import-export once, or maybe it was about supply chains, but it was vague."

Some of the happiness left Joel's face. She noticed his jaw tensed.

"I'm sorry. Should I not ask?" If that was the case, then she had more to worry about than she'd thought.

"No. Asking is fine. Explaining is something else."

He continued, "It's a business with lots of moving pieces. That's how my grandfather and father built it, as if they had to have their hands on every step of the supply chain. That's not to say they were entirely wrong, and it may have been a more valid method back when granddad had it running well. My father built on it, but was reluctant to change much. True, it's a challenge if you have to work with many different entities to sell, produce and ship, but having ownership in those various entities can be a nightmare of intricacies, at least for what is essentially a family business."

"What are you producing? What is your product?"

He sighed. "Specialty products that support other products across a variety of manufacturing fields. It's more about the equipment than the end-product. Much of that is offshored now, which, in part, accounts for the travelling, and unimaginably complicates the accounting. At the very least, I'd like to sell or close parts of the chain, but there are people to worry about, decisions to make, and well, my father isn't as engaged as he used to be. He was sick."

"I'm sorry."

"He'd had a heart issue before my last visit." He smiled. "In fact, that was my first and only visit, wasn't it?"

Maia added her smile to his and nodded.

"He was already recovering back then and he's doing well. But in the meantime, it fell to me to do both our jobs."

"You seem sad when you speak of it."

"I'm immersed in it these days, I'd rather speak about almost anything else."

Maia was happy to oblige. "Let's talk about our date, then. What should I wear?"

His face lit up again. "You are beautiful in everything."

"Thank you, but that's not terribly helpful. Jeans? Dress? I don't want to walk into a nice restaurant dressed for a clambake."

"You don't need to worry about what anyone else is wearing. If it helps, I'll be wearing slacks and there will be a tablecloth and candles."

Was it his words? The phrasing? Or the teasing expression on his face? He amused her. The amusement pushed the questions away.

"That's very helpful, yes."

"What time shall I pick you up? What would be most convenient for you?"

"How about six-thirty?" She gathered their trash. "Do you know where my apartment is? Because, even though I always seem to be at the gallery, I don't live here."

"I know your address. No worries." He glanced at the time on his phone. "For now, I'd better get moving." He picked up the trash and put it into the trashcan before turning back to her to say goodbye.

Maia thought his posture, the way his arms moved, indicated an imminent hug, and she was willing. When his arms went around her, he also planted a gentle kiss on her cheek. "See you on Friday," he said.

The bell over the door jingled as he exited. She watched him walk down the steps, the sidewalk, and across the street toward the marina parking lot. She was intrigued, puzzled, disturbed by things left unsaid, especially now that he was on his way back to Raleigh and she was alone to fret over unanswered questions.

"It's dinner, Maia. That's all." She paused in front of a metallic wall hanging with one highly polished component that acted almost as well as a mirror. She tucked a short lock of hair behind her ear absentmindedly while observing her reflection.

"It's a meal. With a friend. Give your mind-overdrive a breather."

But there was also fear. She didn't want her heart to be broken again. She didn't want to hurt anyone else either by letting him think there was more to "them" than there was. Yet, how could they find out whether there was a "them" without giving it a try?

She thought of Frannie and Brian rushing their relationship, jumping into an engagement when they'd only known each other a few short months. No wonder Frannie was reluctant to discuss the details. Brian would rush her right to the altar.

She was grateful that she and Joel were a different sort, less driven by their impulses. What was the saying? Marry in haste; repent in leisure. She believed that was true. On the other hand, the idea of being swept off one's feet had a certain appeal.

After a while she realized she was back at the display window and staring out at the street. How long had she been standing here?

She slapped the wall and returned to work. She was over thirty, a woman with responsibilities and too mature, too practical, for all this daydreaming.

Chapter Ten

Joel almost stopped the car. He was tempted to turn around and drive back to Beaufort. Sitting at the breakroom table, discussing his work, he'd sensed an opportunity to tell Maia about his father, the reality of his father's plans, his father's desire to marry the nurse—all of it—no matter how personally embarrassing it was, but he hadn't, of course.

He'd sensed a certain doubt in her that seemed directed at his long absence. He'd wanted to tell her about how his world had changed since he'd seen her back in March. But he couldn't bring himself to go into that kind of detail. So, he'd let the moment pass.

Instead, he'd cited the sudden, increased work burden, but without all the rest of it. Regarding all the rest, speaking it aloud was almost like confirming it was not only true, but immutable. He hadn't hit that point yet. He still believed that things in his life would right themselves again and he could resume finding his own path.

The truth was, he and Maia hardly knew each other. Entrusting another person with such personal family details, telling his father's news…. It would be like exposing his family…his father…to derision. So, he kept driving. Raleigh waited at the end of this trip.

Joel sighed. He had to figure this out. Hopefully, when he reached home, he'd find a happier story this time, one with a better outcome for him, and when he returned to Maia on Friday, the madness of the last few months would be behind him.

Friday evening—anticipating that made him smile. He would do something special. He had a business acquaintance who owned the perfect spot for a romantic evening and was happy to accommodate Joel's request.

He looked down, surprised by the speedometer reading. Adrenaline, maybe? Because he was thinking of his father? Or of Maia and their coming date?

Joel backed his foot off the accelerator and let the cruise control do its job. Driving faster wouldn't get him to Friday sooner. He looked at his phone. He could call his father now. Find out how things were.

Or not. He was only about an hour away from finding out in person.

Chapter Eleven

Each day that week, Maia expected Joel to call and cancel. She, herself, thought of reasons to cancel, but none of them made sense.

When flowers were delivered on Wednesday, she hesitated to open the card. The card was on a holder half-buried in the middle of the pink tea roses and baby's breath and deep purple carnations. She knew this would be an apology. An expression of Joel's regret for the need to call off or postpone Friday's upcoming date.

It wasn't. It was a polite note saying, "I look forward to seeing you Friday evening. Joel."

They were lovely flowers. It had been awhile since she'd received flowers for any reason. She took them home with her and added water to the vase, then situated it where she'd most appreciate the bouquet, on the coffee table.

That started a fresh round of worry. The flowers were lovely, the message was polite, but it felt a little overwhelming. What sort of expectations was Joel setting? For her? For himself?

Every night that week she chose what she'd wear for their date, then changed her mind. She drew the line at shopping for something new. She wasn't that pathetic. She had plenty of nice clothing. She didn't need to shop to please a date, certainly one who wasn't worried in the least about what she was wearing and who'd said she looked beautiful in everything.

But standing in front of the full-length mirror brought doubts. She was short, but reasonably fit—but also a lover of chocolate, and curvy courtesy of genetics. She'd always envied the slim, sleek lines of some women, and their slim, sleek hair, too, for that matter. She plucked at her short dark hair. It had just enough natural curl to give it body. Should she get it trimmed?

No, and again, no. This was just dinner. A second date. Well, really a third date if you counted the one before Joel went missing.

Not fair, Maia. She knew he was gone on business for most of that time. He'd told her before he left. And he had called while he was gone. But he hadn't kept calling.

Now he was back again. Counting that date and their lunch in the break room, this would be their third date.

Just roll with it. Don't try to control it or over-analyze it. See where it goes.

CRSO

Friday arrived. Maia left work a little early and went home to freshen up. At precisely six-thirty p.m. her doorbell rang. She grabbed her purse and went down to greet Joel.

He asked her to be patient as he drove. She tried. She knew the streets in Beaufort well, and she knew pretty much all of the secondary roads in the area outside of town. At first, she was mildly curious, but more focused on Joel himself than on where they were going. He was wearing slacks, as he'd said, and a nice shirt, but no suit jacket. Suit jackets were generally rare at beachy locations, so that was reasonable. Yet it gave her no clues as to where he was taking her. As they left the town behind, her curiosity grew. It wasn't as if there were lots of dining opportunities out this way.

"Joel…." She wanted to ask. Perhaps he'd taken a wrong turn.

"Almost there. A little more patience."

He turned soon after. He turned east onto a wide, nicely paved driveway that wound through the trees. She thought she saw a roof off to the left, but they continued past.

This was private property. Were they having dinner at someone's house?

"Joel?"

He smiled. The road descended, and Maia glimpsed water in-between the trees. The North River, of course. She hadn't been this way since that trip with Juli out to Amanda Barlow's house. Long ago now.

Candles. There were so many that even in the early twilight—well in advance of the full dark—she could see them glowing and flickering out on the railing of the deck. Someone's deck. There was a small, dark building off to the side. It was a small house, not much more than a cabin. Ahead of them, at the shoreline, a wooden walkway led to the large octagonal deck perched out over the water. Adjoining it was a large boathouse. Impossible to tell whether the small house, or the boathouse, were vacant or not. Lights were strung along the walkway and all the way out to and around the deck area.

Joel took her hand as she climbed out of the car, and assisted her up the steps to the walkway. Together they walked out over the water, their way lit by those small white lights. They glowed at a low level, a soft light that didn't overwhelm the candles, but complemented them, giving them an exotic look.

There was a table, too. Its white cloth gleamed, but the candles weren't lit there, not yet, and two chairs were politely drawn up. She paused and glanced at Joel. He took her hand again and drew her over to the railing. The last of the day's light was fading and despite the candlelight, the first stars appeared overhead. The moon was hanging above the trees on the far shore. As she watched, lights like little stars began to pop on in the dark on that far side. She looked left and right but saw no other lights brightening this side of the water.

"It's beautiful. Is this someone's home?" The small house on shore looked too simple to be the residence attached to this fancy deck and boat house.

At the table, Joel picked up a carafe. In her world, they called it a pitcher...maybe a fancy pitcher, but here tonight, carafe sounded right. Maia suppressed a tiny giggle.

"Iced tea?"

Maia laughed. "You know who you're with, don't you?"

He smiled and poured the iced tea into a wine goblet, set the pitcher down and crossed back to her. He extended the glass and she accepted it. He had his own and it was iced tea, too.

"This place belongs to a business acquaintance. He gave me permission to use it. I couldn't find anywhere else special enough for this date, for you, for us, for tonight."

"So, you created your own place on a borrowed deck?" She wasn't sure how she felt about that. For some reason, it troubled her. Seemed to break unwritten rules. "Somehow the house doesn't fit right with all this." She waved her hands at the walk, the fancy deck, the lights....

"Well, it's a cottage...the family uses it down here by the water, but their residence is back on the other side of those trees. We drove past it on the way."

"Oh."

"They're on a trip. We have privacy here. No worries about interruptions."

Or food, she thought, but kept it to herself.

Joel smiled again. "We'll eat soon," he said, as if reading her mind. "How about some music?"

She looked around half-expecting at this point, at this surprising point, to see a string quartet, but no, Joel stepped into the boat house, apparently unlocked, and left the door open. She waited.

Music began to swirl softly in the twilight.

Joel emerged from the boathouse. "I thought something unobtrusive...maybe light and jazzy...would be good." He hit the arrow as if selecting stations and they passed in a blur. "Call out if you hear something you like." He stopped on an instrumental tune. "Good enough?"

"It's fine," she said.

She stood beside him at the railing. In the near dark, she heard the splash as a fish jumped. She turned to smile at him, to thank him for all the effort he'd taken when the next tune started and an older melody, one she recognized from one of her favorite movies. The tune wasn't originally from the movie, but she preferred this interpretation to the original big band rendition. This was a slow, languid version of *Moondance*, perfect for a southern, candlelit night.

"May I?"

"Delighted, sir."

Joel's arm went around her back. His hand took hers, and, seamlessly, by unspoken but mutual consent, they danced. She relaxed into the movement.

As the song came to a finish, Joel said, "There's something I want to say to you. Just listen, okay?" She stared into his eyes and nodded.

Another song began. Another slow tune. She didn't recognize it, but moved along with him to its rhythm.

"I don't know a good way to say this, so I'll just say it simply," he said. "Nice guys, right? You know what they say? They finish last." He touched her cheek, then her chin. "That's okay. I am who I am." He dropped his hand and placed it against her lower back as he paused and dipped her slightly backward. For only a fraction of a second, her body, her balance, was at the mercy of his arms, and then he brought her upright again and spun in a turn.

Somehow in Joel's arms, Maia's feet found the right steps. She wasn't much of a dancer, she knew. She was impressed by his skill, not merely at dancing, but in leading. It didn't seem to occur to Joel that Maia couldn't keep up or might crush his toes with her shoes.

Was a response required to what he'd said? She wanted to focus on the dance and the music. The spell.

He resumed speaking. Now his face was close to her hair, his breath on her ear. "One thing I learned from prior, well, from when I was younger and thought I was in love, is that a person should want to be pursued; otherwise the attention from the pursuer is just annoying. A nuisance."

One more spin and then Joel paused and pulled her more closely into his arms until he couldn't pull her closer and she was pressed against his chest. She looked up at his face.

"Do you want to be pursued, Maia? By me?" He waited, his blue eyes warm and somber at the same time. "I'm not asking for any kind of commitment or even for permission. Just honesty."

"I enjoy your company." Had she whispered the words? Said them loud enough? Her heart was thudding. There was only thin fabric between them. He must surely feel her heart through his shirt.

Perhaps that was sufficient response.

The music continued in the background, but they stood, still pressed together, his hand clasping hers, his other hand on her back.

"I think there's something special between us. I'd like to find out. But only if you feel the same."

She nodded and somehow noticed the stars had popped out into the sky and that the breeze from the sound was as pure, as fresh as she'd ever smelled before. The night and the air embraced her, embracing them both.

"I do," she said.

She smiled and expected him to do the same, but instead, his jaw tightened. The planes of his face seemed to harden. He was going to kiss her. She wanted him to kiss her. But instead, he took a step back, dropped his hand from behind her back and with his hand still clasping hers, he moved that hand and somehow, she spun with it. Gracefully. When she faced him again, he took her hand in both of his and raised it to his lips and pressed his kiss there, to the back of her hand. She was still staring and wondering at this unexpected dance, when he gestured toward the table.

Someone had lit the candles on the table. They, and the other candles and crossover lights, competed with the moon and starlight—no, not competed, but rather complemented the cooler lights of the universe above with the warmer lights arrayed below them on earth. The flickering reflections in the crystal goblets and vase was surrounded by the backdrop of the shimmering night lights dappling the gently moving night water.

Waiters were there. Dressed in crisp white. They were standing near the table, not quite at attention, but almost.

Where had they come from?

Joel let her to the table and held her chair as she was seated, then took his own seat.

The waiters' movements were practiced and almost unobtrusive as they opened the gleaming serving dishes on a rolling cart. Even the cart had its own tablecloth. They filled plates. No words. No eye contact. Just service. And then they took their cart and were gone.

Maia's back was to the crossover. She didn't watch their departure, but she heard the cart rolling away and eventually a vehicle started and drove away. By then, she'd already tasted the wine and was eyeing the plate of food. The world had once again come down to just the two of them, Maia and Joel. And a lovely meal on the table between them.

"You like beef, I recall. And I ordered the same salad we had for lunch. That seemed a safe choice?"

"This smells unbelievable and looks delicious."

"Please, start eating while it's still warm."

"Joel…this is amazing. I don't even know what to say."

He gave her a pleased look. "I'm glad. We're lucky the weather's fine."

They ate, and they conversed. As they moved from the entrée to dessert, Joel asked, "Did you get the gift I sent?"

Maia looked up at him with her fork poised over the chocolate cheesecake with dark chocolate dribble over it. She went briefly blank. "Gift?"

"I had it sent to the gallery. I wasn't sure of your address."

"Gift," she breathed. "That was from you?"

He looked confused.

"A box arrived. A small box. Addressed to me. But there wasn't a card inside. I thought…" She felt her face burning.

"I'm sorry. I did wonder if it might be from you, but then…" She shook her head. "I hadn't heard from you in a while." She shrugged.

"I thought it must be for someone else."

"From someone else?" he asked, his voice small.

"*For*—for someone else. I thought Luke had ordered it for Juli as a surprise. For their anniversary," she added, and then groaned.

She couldn't read his face. She tried hard, but she couldn't, so she waited.

"Your first thought, your instinct, was right." He touched her hand. "I'm sorry there wasn't a card. I had the jeweler mail it. I'm sure it was an oversight."

Dang it. Her eyes were stinging. She didn't want to cry. Didn't even know why she should cry.

Maia said, "You hadn't called in a while. I thought maybe you wouldn't."

He nodded. "I was busy, but it wasn't just that. Our phone conversations...they aren't the same as being with you in person. They are...."

"Unsatisfactory."

"Agreed. I wasn't entirely certain that you *wanted* to hear from me."

"Why didn't you mention it when you came to lunch?"

He hesitated before responding. "I didn't want to put you on the spot...in case you didn't want it."

"Not want it? It's beautiful."

"That's not what I mean. I mean, in case you didn't want it from me. I thought you'd say something, but you didn't. It wasn't until after I left that it occurred to me you might not have received it." He smiled, but sadly. "I don't think guys are supposed to say this, but my heart's been bruised once or twice."

"Not broken?"

"No, only roughed-up a little. What about you?"

"I'd say we're well-matched."

He touched her hand, picking it up and turning it over to examine and trace the lines on her palm. "I foresee a bright future for both of us."

She tingled from her scalp to her toes.

A small voice in her head spoke to her heart, saying, "Take it slow. Long distance romances don't work out. Be careful." She ignored it.

CRED

After Joel's declaration, their conversation had been the usual—what do you enjoy? What do you like? Even a few stronger opinions and more than one amusing anecdote. She assured him that the necklace was safe.

"I put it in Luke's desk drawer. He never said anything. I assumed because I thought he knew what it was about. He either never saw it, or thought it was mine."

When Joel drove her home, he drove down Front Street. Somehow, Maia knew exactly what he had in mind. She didn't speak. She could hardly breathe.

"Do you have the key with you?" he asked.

"I do."

He parked behind the gallery. The night was moonlit, but the shadows cast back here were dark and the low pole light cast just enough.

They went inside together, not bothering to turn on the light until they entered Luke's office where Maia switched on his desk lamp.

Suddenly worried, her palms almost sweaty, Maia opened the drawer.

The box was there, undisturbed.

Joel retrieved it. Solemnly, he opened the box, pulled out the white gift box and removed the necklace. The key pendant, including its sparkly stones, seemed to come alive in the light.

She turned her back to Joel. Pressing her hand over her heart, she tried to breathe while his fingers brushed the nape of her neck as he fastened the catch on the chain. She was certain those fingers lingered longer than they needed to. She, herself, didn't move. The moment drew out until finally she had to. She simply had to. She turned to show Joel the necklace, feeling a sudden need to giggle, as he most certainly already knew what the necklace looked like.

But not on *her*. He hadn't seen it on her. He reached toward her, toward the necklace, and touched the pendant.

"Why a key?" she asked.

He smiled. "It will sound corny. I hope you'll forgive me for not being more...whatever. But all I could think of was that almost from the moment I met you, you owned the key to my heart."

"Corny? Not at all."

The practical person in her wanted to tell him he shouldn't have spent so much, that it was too expensive a gift for a third date. Purchased even before the third date.

He took her hand. He lifted it to his lips and kissed it.

"Corny yet?" he asked.

She had no words, but stepped into his arms and kissed him back.

He drove her home after that. She was in such a daze, she hardly remembered. Had she locked the gallery? Probably. Had she kissed him again when he escorted her to the porch? Definitely. Had she invited him up?

No. She'd considered it. She was tempted. She was afraid of getting in too deep, too fast. She wasn't a casual sort of person. Old fashioned? Okay. She was. Cautious? Yes, that too. Corny? Yeah. They shared that, for sure.

Then he'd mentioned about helping his father with the business, about driving home, about another trip coming up. About coming back to see her as soon as he could.

"You travel all the time."

"In my opinion, it's not a sleek operation, it's a hodgepodge. The business grew over time but without long-term planning, and the result is that the holdings are scattered here and there."

Maia pulled him over to the railing, away from the windows. She didn't want them to disturb Fay and her family.

"Are you still having to cover for your father? I'm sorry, I really should ask about your father. Is he still recovering well?"

He shook his head. "He has recovered. It was very serious, and during his recovery, he…well, he discovered he wants to change the course of his life."

"What does that mean?"

"He wants to remarry. Leave the business."

"Oh. I see."

"It's worrisome and inconvenient, that's for sure."

She cringed a little. "I understand worry, but inconvenient? Really?"

"You're right. That didn't come out sounding as it was meant. But it's the truth, Maia. Just now, I wanted to be working on my own life. Instead, seems like I'm more firmly trapped in his. One he no longer wants. Makes it harder for me to make my own choices."

She let him leave with a kiss and a wave. But long after he was gone, the memories lingered with her. That small voice had tried to return, warning her about risking her heart.

Hush, she told that pesky voice. Raleigh isn't a world away. But it was more than long distance, right? There was a lot going on in his personal life, too. She didn't quite understand, but she found his remark about his father's desires being inconvenient, to be a little off-putting.

Actually…maybe he was unhappy with his father's preoccupation and the resulting travel because he, Joel, had strong feelings for her. He wanted to spend more time with her.

She liked that explanation.

CRƎD

Maia went to work on Saturday morning feeling both special and conflicted. The romantic glow of their date had lingered and followed her home, and had sweetened her dreams.

Despite herself, Maia spun slowly in the open floor space of the gallery and then leaned back against the customer counter, one hand on her neck, the pendant under her fingers, and then her hands on her shoulders, remembering the feel of Joel's arms around her. The candlelight. The delicious food. The stars above them. She hadn't imagined that Joel had so much romance in him.

And again, despite herself, she acknowledged that, for her, romance meant a lot. As for practicality, she had plenty of that already. She needed a complement—that special someone who could complement her innate practicality and also add in the romance she craved.

She wanted to tell someone about Joel, about the date, about how she might be falling for Joel. Juli? She'd be the most likely confidante, but these days Juli had troubled undercurrents of her own. Troubled waters, of a sort. Maybe it was the reality of having a husband and child, as well as the addition of an unexpected sister.

Maia wasn't ready to share her thoughts about Joel with her mother or sister yet.

It was too new and felt too tender. And too early.

The last thing she wanted to do was to tell anyone, and then have to tell them all over again when it fell apart. For now, she'd to keep it to herself.

The flowers arrived at noon. A charming bouquet of daisies and tall purple things with a few red roses intermixed. She tipped the delivery man and he left. She leaned into them, drawing in the scent, then pulled the card free.

"To Maia, Thanks for a wonderful evening. Here's wishing for many more. Joel."

Chapter Twelve

Maia visited Ben on Sunday afternoon. A couple of weeks had passed since Danny's birthday and her last visit. She'd been busy. But someone needed to tend the grave, to bring flowers, to keep things—including memories of him—fresh.

She didn't mind. She felt useful. And, strangely, she felt heard. As if being here made a difference to someone. Did Juli come here? Did she wonder about the flowers decorating the grave when she did? Surely, she must.

Maia didn't blame her for not being here more often. Juli had Luke and Danny to take care of. Her life was focused on the present.

Thinking of loss and cemeteries, of keeping memories fresh, reminded Maia of what Juli had said about Frannie wanting to find their mother's grave.

Frannie had never known Frances, the woman who'd given birth to her. Frances had been married to Frannie's father, Edward Denman, and then, after Frannie was born, she'd run away. Mental or emotional illness? Post-partum issues? Or maybe it was substance or addiction problems? No one knew. But whatever had troubled Frances had driven her back and forth from the Denman home until Juli was conceived, and then she'd run away again, with her husband none the wiser about the second child yet to be born.

Maia believed that Frances, the mother, had tried to take good care of Juli, otherwise why would she have kept her with her? Unless it was some sort of revenge against her estranged husband…but that made no sense since said husband had no idea that the second baby existed. In the meantime, Edward had obtained a divorce and then married his second wife, Laurel. Frannie had been very young when all that was going on she didn't even remember a time when Laurel hadn't been there. Frannie had believed Laurel was her birth mother for nearly thirty years.

Recently, Juli had told Maia, "Frannie said that one day while she was at school, first grade maybe, Frances brought me with her to the house. She wanted to leave me there with my father. I don't remember any of it. I was too young. Frannie said Laurel turned us away. Laurel told Frannie only when Frannie pushed so hard that Laurel spit it all out in anger."

Maia couldn't conceive of the jealousy or insecurity that would have driven Laurel Denman to such a cruel action.

Frannie had discovered all this only a couple of months ago.

Julie confided to Maia that she had trouble believing the story Frannie told her, but she'd come to accept that the sad tale was probably true. Juli hadn't seen her mother since she was five when she was taken away by social services and put into foster care. Juli had been happy to forget the woman, her own mother, who'd neglected her so badly.

Laurel had told Frannie the tragic story in anger. Frannie had told Juli because she had a right to the information. Juli had confided to Maia. And Maia?

Well, here she was at Ben's grave.

"Ben, you introduced me to Juli, but you never had the chance to meet Frannie. You would like her. Brian certainly does."

"This has been hard on Juli. I don't blame her for not wanting to rehash all that history. I don't blame Frannie either for wanting to know about Frances. Frankly, I don't understand how finding that grave will help anyone?"

The irony of saying that to Ben, as she sat at his graveside, wasn't lost on her, but she kept talking anyway.

"I can't help her, Ben. Juli has to figure this out for herself.

Frannie, too, I guess."

There by Ben's grave, her hand covered Joel's pendant, pressing it to her chest. "As for me, I suppose the answer is the same. No one can figure out what I should do, except me."

Was Ben listening? She hoped he wasn't here. She hoped he was in heaven and living eternally, except for that tiny part of him that she carried in her heart—right about where the pendant now rested. Time and living would resolve it, erode those memories, even as they were already doing.

Thoughts of Juli kept intruding. Juli and Frannie, and Frannie's right to want to know about the woman who gave birth to her. It was Juli's right to not want to resurrect old unhappy memories. But how wrong it was for Juli to withhold whatever she remembered, to keep it to herself. It struck Maia as unhealthy, not really a matter of right or wrong. And while Joel and Ben might be her business, none of the rest was. It was between Juli and Frannie, and the two of them would have to work it out.

"Ben. I wanted to tell you about Juli and Frannie. About how what should be good can get very complicated. And I have. But guess what, I want to tell you about Joel, too." Saying his name struck a tiny chord, a small twinge in her heart. It felt good.

The squirrels scampered. The breeze stirred. Maia looked at the light playing among the tree branches and said, "I don't think I mentioned him to you before. He came to town with Frannie…rather, following Frannie, back in late February."

CRED

Joel called that evening. Those feelings from their date rolled back in, a very sweet memory, when she answered his call.

"Just wanted to say hello," he said.

"Hello, then." She laughed. "No troubles on the road, I hope."

"Not at all."

"I'm glad you called. I wanted to thank you again for a lovely evening."

"My pleasure."

"And the gift. I'm wearing it now."

There was a long silence, then Joel said, "I'm glad you like it. Thank you for wearing it."

"It's beautiful." She followed his lead, but she was a little disappointed. This careful conversation was a long way from the romance of their date.

"How are things at home? Your father?"

After a pause, Joel said, "He's well. Nothing else has changed."

Was it his words or the tone of his voice? Maia felt shut down, as if a door had been closed.

He asked, "Did you have a good day?"

"I did." She hesitated, then said, "I visited an old friend."

"Nice. Anyone I know?"

She was sorry she'd said it. The statement was misleading. How could you tell a guy you were dating that you'd been to visit a man's grave...one whom you'd loved. She closed that line of conversation.

"Maia? Are you there? Did I lose you?"

She gasped. "Sorry, no, I'm here. I was thinking. I almost forgot to tell you. Mom is planning the engagement party for next Sunday afternoon. A week from today. You are welcome to join us."

"A party? For Frannie and Brian, right? Are you sure?"

"Of course, I'm sure. It's mostly just family. We have a lot of it. I warn you it will be noisy. Also, be prepared that some may make assumptions about you and me."

"Ah. Well, I deal with corporate types you know. I'm pretty tough. I can probably deal with matchmaking relatives."

She kind of wished he'd said they *should* make assumptions.

"Seriously," she said. "I'd understand if you'd rather not or if it's too last-minute."

"I'd like to."

"Really? Okay, then. I'll let you know what time."

They disconnected. She sat on the sofa and stared at her phone.

She closed her eyes and tried to visualize their date, the candles and the dancing and the food. Not to mention the stars above and reflecting in the waters below. She recalled the scents, the warmth of his embrace.

She put the phone on the coffee table and went to stand at the window. It was a deep night, a night where stars proliferated in the sky and families sat around their kitchen tables. Parents were fussing at their kids to hurry up and finish their homework. Soon, the pet owners would be taking the dogs out one last time before locking up for a night's sleep. None of that was happening here.

She had much to be grateful for. But she had it alone.

Better no one than the wrong one? She still agreed with that. She didn't mind going the extra mile, trying harder. But what if it failed and she couldn't hold onto him?

The other "but" was what if the right one was in front of her and she wasn't brave enough to take a chance on him, risking it all in the face of possible failure and heartbreak?

That was a lot to ask of anyone.

Chapter Thirteen

Joel stared at his phone. An engagement party? With Maia's family. The Donovan's.

He'd grown up in a big house with few people. He vaguely remembered grandparents. His parents had no siblings, so he had no aunts or uncles.

He grown up as only child with good manners. He was generally logical and courteous. Yet, when around groups of people where he wasn't in control of the facility...rather, the social occasion...he felt awkward and tended to be withdrawn. Sometimes people viewed that as cold or arrogant. He wasn't.

But he was curious about Maia's family.

What about Frannie? He knew her background, her insecurities. How would she manage in a group setting where everyone knew everyone, except her? Where she, Frannie, would be the center of attention? It might help her to see a familiar, friendly face. He didn't mind being that for Frannie, though for him, that face would be Maia's.

Joel smiled. He leaned back in his desk chair and propped his feet up on a nearby ottoman.

They'd had a wonderful date on Friday evening. It had been worth the effort he'd put into it. The favor he'd called in for the deck. Arranging the caterer and waiters. The lighting.

So much for holding back and keeping it low-key. Maybe he was more of a romantic than he knew.

Thinking of romance…his father and the nurse. Sounded like a cliché. When he'd returned from Beaufort, they'd been making plans. Instead of finding out that everything had been set right, and life was back on track, he'd found brochures and samples spread across the dining room table.

It was a huge, highly polished table that they rarely used except for when his father had hosted bright and glittering dinners. There'd been conversations across that table, both witty and boring, with business connections, local philanthropists and other friends, and laughter and occasional hot-tempered words.

Now it was a display table. When he first saw the array of pamphlets, he'd moved a few steps around the table, staring down at assorted brochures advertising for Caribbean cruises and sandy, sun-drenched beaches, and turquoise waters. And what was this? Here was a sampling of luxury yacht-type cruises around Spain and the south of France. Brochures about destination weddings.

Suddenly angry, he swept all of them, including the glossy pics of wedding cakes and floral arrangement, from the table and sent them flying.

Was he angry or jealous?

His anger swiftly changed to remorse.

Where, in fact, was his father? Where was Sharon? He didn't doubt they'd return soon enough. And then what?

"Joel?"

It was a woman's voice. He spun around. "What are you doing here?"

"I saw your car driving past. I thought…well, the door was unlocked. No one answered. I hope you don't mind. I want to speak with you. I'm concerned about your father."

"Not Frannie?"

She pressed her lips together and her eyes suddenly glistened. "She and I are…on a break, I guess you could say. I think you know that."

He did know. He was embarrassed to have given into the impulse to say those words, to be hurtful.

Laurel added, "For more than a month now, in fact. But I have hope." She looked directly at Joel and ignored the tear wanting to fall down her cheek. "One must always have hope when it comes to the people we love."

She dabbed gently at her lashes with the back of one gracefully crooked finger. She smiled bravely through her sorrow.

"I understand," he said.

Laurel moved into the dining room and eyed the colorful papers and booklets in disorder on the table and on the floor where they'd landed. She bent at the knees, keeping her back straight—very ladylike—and secured one of the pamphlets on the floor.

In one graceful motion, she stood. After a quick look at the booklet, she made a sour expression, briefly there and quickly gone, and tossed it onto the table.

"She's tricked him, you know." Laurel shook her head slowly, her face sad. "He isn't the first person who's been taken in by someone who was supposed to have their best interests at heart…someone he depended on. It's a natural human response and I don't blame him. But I worry for him."

Joel was skilled at negotiation and in reading faces across a business table, but going one on one with Laurel Denman, even knowing what he did about her, was almost beyond him. Maybe because he'd known her all his life, but courtesy had the uppermost hand in this encounter. He'd been the child of a friend, she'd been the distinguished, well-mannered mother of his friend.

"You told me Frannie had feelings for me. You encouraged me to follow her. She didn't. She never did. Never felt anything for me beyond friendship."

Laurel held up her hand. "I'm sure she had feelings. But by the time you followed, she'd met Brian Donovan." She shrugged delicately. "Is your father here? I was hoping to talk some sense into him." She moved with slow steps around the table. "You may not know this, but at one time I thought he and I had a future."

At least one reason to be grateful for Sharon.

"If the two of us work together, Joel, we could save him. Help him be himself again."

"You should leave, Laurel."

"Joel. Be sensible. We want the same thing. I can help you have your father back. With your help, I—we can get him free of this mess he's in now. She'll break his heart—after she takes everything he has."

"Maybe. But that won't be your problem, Laurel. That will be my problem. My father's problem. But not yours. It never was and never will be."

Chapter Fourteen

Maia drove over to Jacksonville and spent the night at her parents' home.

A decade had passed since she'd officially left her parent's home. Her old room had become a combination guest room and craft room. Her old bed, her dresser, shared the space with a cabinet brimming with craft materials. It was small room, seemed even smaller now, but it was neat. Always neat. Both of her parents were organized. Her dad was a retired marine and his passion for orderliness and self-control had hardly relaxed. As for her mom, she was naturally orderly and diligent.

Maia had stayed overnight so that she could attend early service with her parents at their church…the church from her youth. They'd returned home after the early service ready to jump into finishing up the party prep.

Upstairs, Maia changed her clothing, switching from her dress to a worn pair of jeans. Before the party started, she would change yet again to a cute silky top and the long, but casual skirt she wanted to wear. The dress code was lax. Everyone would be wearing different things. She could've kept the jeans on, or simply worn her church clothes, but she was mindful that Joel would be here.

Was she dressing up for Joel? Yes.

By the time she returned downstairs, Mom had the oven heating and was arranging the table pad on the surface of the dining room table. Maia helped her float the tablecloth atop the heat-proof, vinyl pad. She was still smoothing the folds of the cloth as Mom added the centerpiece and candles and began arranging the serving dishes.

Mom asked, "How are things with you and Joel?" She paused and when Maia didn't jump into the conversation, she added, "He sounds like a nice man and a good catch."

"He's not a fish, Mom." Maia shifted the candles and the other items. "And you've never met him."

"Brian has spoken of him, as have you." She made an impatient noise. "Stop tweaking. Not everything has to be lined up perfectly, darling daughter. What's wrong with you?"

"Nothing." She shrugged. "I don't know."

Mom stayed silent.

"We've been on a couple of dates. It might work out. Time will tell."

"That sounds cryptic, but interesting."

"Please don't make assumptions."

"Would you have preferred not to invite him?"

How could she tell her mother that she was worried about exposing Joel to her family—or perhaps vice versa. Exposing them to him. His background was very different. "Of course, not. He's friends with our little group, especially Frannie."

"Is that it? Does your mood have something to do with Frannie?" Again, a pause, and when Maia didn't answer, her mother rushed to say, "Is there a problem with her and Brian? Or just her? We hardly know her, after all."

Maia cringed inwardly at the sudden worry evident in her mother's voice, and even in her face and her eyes. She shook her head. "No, not that I know of." Which, of course, did nothing, in tone or words, to allay her mother's worries for Brian.

Maia put her hands on her mother's arms and spoke calmly, "Seriously. As far as I know they are happy and eager to spend their lives together."

Mom sighed. "That's how it was with Diane, too. I remember. You know how your brother is. He gets his mind made up and then he's so stubborn."

"Well, then Frannie may be the perfect match for him."

"Really? Why do you say that?"

"Well, because Brian wants to run things. He steamrolls over wishy-washy people. He and Diane were bound to implode. He was seeing with his eyes. Diane was pretty and blonde, and he loved her energy, but he wasn't seeing with his brain, else he would've known that they'd never be on the same page about anything. Brian doesn't like to fight for the sake of fighting. Diane was all about drama. Frannie is different. She and Brian pick at each other a lot, but I think that's just their way of getting to know each other. Of negotiating." Better them than her, Maia thought.

"But they're getting married. They should already know each other."

"Is that how it was for you and dad? Did you know each other well?"

Mom frowned. "No matter how much you think you know someone, you never do. It's a lifelong effort."

"Really? Then there's no point in worrying about Brian and Frannie. They aren't kids. They've made mistakes and learned from them. And learned from their successes, too. They make a dynamo couple, and both have Megan's wellbeing at heart."

Had she painted the picture too ideally? With pigments that would fail and degrade much too quickly when exposed to the bright light of the sun? If so, then oh well. Her magic ball wasn't working well these days. She could only wish the couple the best, and having Mom worry over her children wouldn't help anyone.

Cathy walked through the wide opening from the living room to the dining room and gave them both a hug. "We're running out of time. Don't waste it worrying or trying to borrow trouble. This party, this celebration, is for Frannie and Brian. I'm looking forward to meeting her."

Cathy stopped at the table, gave it a look, then rearranged the candles.

"That's better," she said and clapped her hands once, lightly. "Now, let's finish up. Don will be here with the kids any time now and you know Aunt Mags and Uncle Paul will arrive early. They always do."

Mom added, "They'll be coming straight from church. And hungry. As for Joel, I'm looking forward to meeting him."

Maia almost warned her mom not to interfere, but then bit her lip. Mom would have her hands full with the party. No need to hurt her feelings by warning her to be careful around Joel. As for Brian, he was a big boy. This wasn't his first go-round and he could figure it out on his own—and would prefer to.

Cathy moved swiftly across the living room to the front window. "Here he is now. The kids will be delighted to see you, Maia. It's been ages."

Maia moved to stand beside her. " I'm looking forward to meeting Don."

Cathy couldn't hide the slight flush on her cheeks. "Be nice. Don't tease."

"Me?" Maia laughed.

"You and Brian are so alike. He promised, too."

She hugged Cathy. "Don't worry. We'll be good."

Her sister's flushed cheeks and bright eyes made her own heart warm, and Maia was relieved that Don seemed to be a nice guy, judging by voice and appearance, if one could judge by those things.

"Don, this my younger sister, Maia."

Don shook Maia's hand and Mom called into the foyer, "Good to see you, Don," and the kids came through, finding their ways around the adults' legs, sparing quick hugs for Aunt Maia and rushed to hug their grandmother. The addition of these three increased the noise level beyond proportion. Maia just laughed, and Cathy leaned into Don and his arm went around her. Comfortably. They seemed to move in unison—the movements not identical but attuned.

That was it, Maia thought to herself. They were attuned.

Suddenly Aunt Mags was there with Uncle Paul close behind as if he'd catch her if she missed her step on the stairs. Maia didn't doubt he'd try. But who'd catch him?

She stepped past Don and grasped Mags' arm and helped her over the threshold.

"Well, hello, Maia dear." Aunt Mags grabbed Maia and held her close for a minute, then released her to reach back for Uncle Paul.

Beyond her uncle's shoulder, Maia caught a glimpse of Luke's car. She hugged her uncle, bid him welcome, and stepped past to welcome Juli and Luke and to give Danny his own peck on the cheek. She was making over him when some older cousins pulled up, parked, and tumbled out of their vehicle. Vivi waved—she was Brian's age—and her youngest brother. Some carried presents, some didn't, but the crowd and the noise grew.

They were all back inside the house and Cathy was fussing at a child who'd poked a finger into the cake icing for a taste, and Mom asked loudly if anyone had seen Dad, and Vivi's loud laughter bounced off the walls. The near-chaotic good will fed on itself. The shoes had ended up along the wall near the door—a neat lineup disintegrating as someone's toddler checked inside each shoe before tossing the footwear aside.

"What on earth?"

Vivi said, "Lynette's little one is checking for cell phones. He found one in someone's shoe. I took it away, but he's determined...that's what being two is all about."

Maia was straightening the shoes, matching them back up with their mates, when suddenly the room went silent. She looked up expecting to see Brian and Frannie and wondering why everyone wasn't rushing toward them to wish them love and happiness?

Joel was there, standing just inside the open doorway, not more than a foot or two away. What was that expression on his face?

Maia recognized the "looking" look. The one where a person expects to see a special someone and stops on the threshold to scan the room. And whose face, when he spies that special someone, lights up and a smile breaks out. And you, Maia told herself, object of the looker, the recipient of that smile, knows without doubt that YOU have been SEEN and that the sight of you has made that person's world right again.

It was a heady feeling.

Joel held out his hand, extending it to her and for that moment, everything and everyone else seemed to dim, if not actually to vanish. She took his hand and rose to her feet fluidly. She put her other hand on his arm and said, "Just smile. I'll introduce you."

He blinked. "There are a lot of cars out there. At least I had no doubt as to which house."

She turned to face the room—her aunts, uncles, cousins and cousins of cousins, and even a few unrelated but close-as-family friends—and said, "Everyone, this is Joel. Joel, these lovely people are my family and friends." She smiled brightly. "Excuse us both. We are wanted in the kitchen right away."

She almost got him out of the foyer, but Aunt Mags waylaid them and insisted on greeting him. She cast an extra look at Maia's empty ring finger, and then the storm door squeaked, and dad entered.

"Hello, everybody. The kids are almost here." Dad saw Maia standing there with a stranger beside her. A stranger, a guy, whose arm was firmly in her grasp.

He walked over and held out his hand, saying, "You must be Joel. We've heard a lot about you."

Chapter Fifteen

D ad's hair was heavily peppered with gray, but his posture was as straight as when he was active military. His manner and voice hadn't eased one iota, except for when dealing with the younger grandkids, and then he was calm and gentle. When he'd retired, he'd traded in his uniform for a golf shirt, non-uniform khaki slacks, and leather loafers. Maia thought that if you squinted you might notice the posture and silhouette and not realize his uniform was a civilian one now.

"Where have you been, Dad? Mom was asking for you."

He shook Joel's hand and released it.

"Good to meet you, sir," Joel said.

"Pleasure." He looked straight into Joel's face, into his eyes. Nodded slightly and briefly, then said, "We'll talk later. Sounds like Mrs. Donovan needs me, and the newly engaged couple will be arriving at any moment. Maia, will you let everyone know to be ready and in position?" He moved past them into the kitchen.

Two children quick-stepped through the foyer—they knew better than to run in the house with Grandpa Donovan around—and bumped into Joel. Maia tightened her grip on Joel's arm. One of her cousins was laughing loudly and another was carrying a charging cable like a divining rod looking for an electrical outlet, while his mother, cousin Kay, was fussing at him to put the phone away.

Maia announced in a loud voice, "Everyone. Head's up! Brian and Frannie will be here any moment. Everybody get ready."

She didn't tell them how to get ready. She didn't really care. It would work out. She pulled Joel through the kitchen, out the back door and onto the screened porch.

She heard her dad call out, "Don't be long. They're almost here."

"Okay, Dad." She closed the door. The cooler air, the quiet, hit her and she breathed deeply. Then laughed.

She said, "I'm sorry. I tried to warn you."

"About what? What's wrong?"

She groaned and waved toward the house. "All that. Chaos. Nice and fairly well-controlled, considering. I should've prepared you better. It's crazy and loud."

"It's wonderful. Not what I'm used to, true. But that doesn't mean it won't be fun or that I won't enjoy myself. If there are any actual dangers, let me know."

"Danger?"

"Sure. Landmines. Anyone I should avoid? Topics to tiptoe around? Or what?"

"No, no danger. As for landmines, I guess there are always those, but we're family and people get over those things. Besides, you're a guest. You'll get the benefit of the doubt. I just didn't want to overwhelm you with the extended clan."

"I'm a grown man. I can handle anything that's likely to happen inside your childhood home. These people love you, right?"

"Yes, but—"

"Then we're good. Don't worry about me."

Suddenly applause, augmented by hoots and yells, broke out. The sound traveled right through the closed door to the porch.

"They're here," Maia said.

Joel reached for the doorknob. "Let's go in and join in the congratulations."

"Sure. Lead the way."

He surprised her then by stealing a quick kiss, then giving her a grin, saying, "I'm pretty tough. I can handle the crowd." Then he gently escorted her back into the house.

Later, she told herself it was the crush. People, noise, kids running around, folks raising their voices to be heard over the general babble—all fun, but instead of feeling at one with it, as she had used to without giving it a thought, now she felt a bit on the outside. As if she wished she had an excuse to leave early. Wished she could say, "Sorry, but I have to get to work."

And she couldn't blame it on Joel.

Joel had gone straight over to Frannie and Brian. He'd shaken Brian's hand, put his arms around Frannie and she hugged him back warmly. Not surprising. After all, they knew each other well and neither knew anyone else here, Brian and Maia aside.

Her mother had the kitchen running like well-oiled machinery and interacted with the guests in her usual deft manner. Even Dad was looking pleasant and relaxed, spending time with the guests in groups and individually.

At one point, Maia brought a basket of fresh bread to the table, a table that was harder to reach because Brian and Frannie were holding court nearby and people, including Luke, Juli and Joel, were gathered in a group with them or standing near enough to participate in the conversation.

She asked Juli, "Where's Danny?"

Juli and the others looked up in surprise. The truth was she felt a bit panicky.

Juli said, "He's with Megan, back in the bedroom." She frowned. "Should I check on him?"

Maia forced a smile. "I'm sure he's fine. I'll go take a look." She went quickly, before Juli could decide to go look for herself.

As Juli had said, Danny was fine. He was happily playing on a scatter rug with Megan in Maia's old bedroom. They were playing quietly with another child, safe from the feet of distracted guests. They were happy and peaceful in their quiet pocket of play and blocks and cars. As much as her arms ached to pick up Danny, to press her face against his neck and take in that baby smell, Maia knew it would be selfish to disturb them for her own comfort... And what comfort

139

was that? What inside her needed to be comforted?

Brian's laughter boomed. Maia turned and saw he'd taken a seat right at the dining room table despite it being set up as the buffet. No matter, though, most everyone had filled their plates already. Folks were coming back now for seconds and thirds, but they had to reach across Brian for the food, and most were getting in congratulations while they were refilling their plates.

Brian had his hand on Frannie's shoulder and she looked relaxed as she laughed in unison with him, their faces equally joyful. Mom was standing in the kitchen doorway and Maia read relief in her face. Juli and Luke were sitting at the table, too, and Joel was right there with them. Cathy and Don were standing, leaning into each other, nearby, against the sideboard.

Maia felt outside. She couldn't help it. She wanted to be in that chummy, conversational bubble of friends. They were her friends. And these people were her family. What was wrong with her? The party was going great. Everyone was getting along. A few people had departed early, and the crush was improving.

She thought of Ben. Ben was missing. He would've loved to have taken part in this. No one had loved his family and friends more than Ben.

Yet, if he were here, it would be different. She could visualize Ben in Luke's place. Luke would be there but sitting a bit apart. Luke was always a bit apart. It was his relationship with Juli that made him at ease with the group. Almost as if Juli had tamed Luke... No, tamed wasn't the right word. Even Juli wasn't naturally at ease with others. But the two of them together created a new entity—a couple that were easy together and easy with others.

Maybe if Juli had met Luke first, before Ben....

No. It would've been like oil and water. Without Juli having loved Ben first, learning to trust and have faith, to discover confidence in herself and finding the power to dream, Juli and Luke wouldn't have had a chance.

"You're standing here shaking your head and looking gloomy.

Not gloomy. Pensive, I guess. What's up, baby girl?"

"Daddy." She leaned against his arm. "Just tired, I guess. Nothing's wrong."

"No worries about your brother and his fiancé?"

"Not a bit." And she wouldn't say it if she did. "I was thinking about the ones who aren't here. The missing loved ones."

He patted her hand. "That's life. From beginning to end. Some go before us, some after. And no one can control any of it no matter how hard we try."

A familiar, querulous, voice rose over the others. Aunt Mags' voice. "Well, she should be. She was named after me, of course."

Dad said, "Here we go. She's off and running now." He gave his daughter a gentle push. "You'd better get in there, Maia."

Maia moved in the wide opening between the living room and the dining room.

Her aunt pointed at her. "And here she comes now."

Joel asked, just as Aunt Mags intended, "She's named after you?"

"She is. Named after the sisters, but I'm listed first."

Mom said, "Because you're the eldest."

Mags laughed, "And I'm here. You notice I made the trip."

Dad said, "You have the benefits of longevity and being local, Mags." He raised his glass of iced tea in a toast. "And we have the benefit of your company."

Juli spoke. "But the name... If Maia is named after you...but you're called Mags. I assumed your name was Margaret."

Mags stood taller, her thin frame straightening as she took the floor, demanding their attention. Maia had seen this before. All of them had, except the newcomers, so this little speech would be a reminder for most, and for a few, a matter of Mags imparting information.

"Margaret, Iva Lee, Ashley, and Irene," Mags intoned as if carving the words into stone. She stopped, and no one spoke.

Satisfied, she added, "Me and my sisters. I am the eldest, by a lot, some might say, and without children of my own. Our baby sister," she pointed at Mom, "named her baby after all of us." She grunted. "I think she chose to do that so none of her sisters would feel left out, but our baby, Maia, and I have always been especially close." She walked over to Maia and planted a kiss on her cheek. "Today we're here celebrating with my nephew Brian and his lovely bride-to-be, Frances...Frannie. Sorry, dear. I'll get it straight soon. And we wish them the best of all things. The best of life and love together. And I look around this room and see my many nieces and nephews with their wonderful spouses and I can hardly wait for the day I'm here to celebrate my namesake's engagement."

Mom made a noise. "Mags...."

Mags shook her head. "I'm not speaking out of turn or saying anything I ought not, but just what my heart is calling on me to express." She looked around. "Paul? Where'd you get to?"

"I'm here." He moved into the room holding a cup of punch, apparently having been hanging out in the kitchen.

"Well, tell everyone 'so long'. My hip is hurting and it's time to go. Can you find my cane?"

Maia said, "I'm so sorry. Let me help you to a chair."

"You can help me over to where little miss Megan and those darling little ones are playing. I'd like to get some proper goodbyes before we leave."

Maia heard the fatigue in her voice. As the eldest of the sisters, she was in her seventies. Generally energetic, her right hip had been giving her trouble in recent years and sometimes took a toll on her energy.

When they were away from the dining room table, Mags whispered to her, "I didn't mean to embarrass you, sweetie. Hope I didn't. I wanted to make it clear to your young man that I have expectations. If he's not the one, then he needs to move on so the right one will know you're available."

Maia groaned, sounding a lot like Mags herself. She said, "That was embarrassing."

"Nonsense, and I'm not sorry. I'm not getting any younger. I like the looks of your Joel, but then I'm not the one thinking of marrying him."

They sat on the now empty sofa.

"I like him, but we're a long way from any possibility of marriage. We've only been on three dates. Maybe four, if family events count."

Mags gave her a funny look. "Keeping a tally, are you? Did I tell you about how I met your Uncle Paul? We look old now, but once we were young and it was romantic, let me tell you. Everyone needs romance. Make sure you have that. As much as I'd like to see you married while I'm still alive and able to attend the festivities, don't settle for less than romance."

Maia smiled. "I'll remember that."

"Megan, come say goodbye to Aunt Mags. I'll go find the other children."

Maia left Megan, with Danny clinging to her leg, hugging Mags and went to find Cathy's kids. They were out in the back yard. She shooed them inside to bid Aunt Mags and Uncle Paul goodbye. They rushed in and as she stood aside to let them pass, she backed directly into a tall, warm body.

Joel.

"Sorry," she mumbled.

"I'm not. This is the closest we've been since I arrived. Shall we step outside for a minute?"

"Well, Mags is about to leave."

"Only for a minute. Plus, you did say goodbye."

He ushered her out so skillfully that she hardly knew they were on the porch and he was already pulling the door closed behind them, but somehow keeping her close.

"I'm sorry," she said.

He shook his head. "Don't apologize. For anything."

She opened her mouth to say she was sorry again, but then stopped herself.

Joel said, "I had a wonderful time. As long as I didn't embarrass you in some way, then it's all good. I would like to have spent more time with you, but I understood you were helping your mother and helping your parents host the party.

"I enjoyed meeting your family but what I really want is to spend more time with you. We had that dinner. We both enjoyed it, but I still don't know you, not like I'd like to. I don't know what you—Maia—likes to do. I want to meet Margaret-Iva Lee-Ashley-Irene." He grinned. "Sorry, I couldn't resist."

He put his hands on her shoulders and slid them down her arms. "You. Maia Donovan. Tell me her secrets. Tell me what she dreams of. What she thinks about."

"I can do that. Except for maybe the secrets part." She teased with a smile.

"Excellent. I'll work on learning those secrets."

He was going to kiss her. The slight inclining of his body, his face, the tightening of his hands on her arms...but then the back door slammed, and Cathy's kids came barreling out and pushed them aside and ruining the moment.

"Come with me. Let's go somewhere. Even for a walk."

She smiled but with regret. "I need to stay and help mom with the cleanup."

"And I'm supposed to be back in Raleigh tonight for an early meeting in the morning."

"I'm sorry."

"I am, too. But I'll be back. I'll call you tomorrow. We'll plan something."

She nodded, but felt the disappointment trying to edge in. Long distance dating combined with work responsibilities and family needs.

"You sighed."

"I guess I did. I didn't mean to."

"You were thinking about long-distance as a problem."

"It's that obvious? Well, long-distance is, isn't it? And working. Everyone works, but working the hours we do, combined with the travel reality, is a challenge."

"It's inconvenient, I'll admit that." He communicated more with his eyes. "In the meantime, let's take it a step at a time. Check your schedule and I'll call you tomorrow."

 CR&SO

The crowd had thinned considerably when they returned inside. Some of the younger cousins were eager to get on to more exciting pastimes than family get-togethers. The older ones were feeling the early morning rising for church and the afternoon nap they'd missed. Many were continuing their visits in the cooler, fresher air in the front yard.

Maia saw Frannie standing alone and instantly felt guilty. She'd neglected her. This was a party for her, Frannie, and so folks could get to know her and her, them, and Maia had spent the party going from one person to the next, from one task to the next. Then Juli moved into view and Maia realized the two women had been chatting and were now moving together as they walked toward the front door.

Joel spoke from behind, "Where should I put these?"

He was holding serving dishes.

"I'll take them. Truly. No need for you to clean up."

"I'll put them on the counter."

"Thanks." Maia paused. "And Joel?"

"Yes?"

"Thanks for coming. I'm glad you did."

"Me, too."

"Have a safe trip back to Raleigh, but come back and see me soon."

"I will."

Those words were quietly exchanged, and sincere. Maia felt that and held the sound of his voice in her head for a long moment, wanting to recall it later.

She walked him out to his car. Brian and Luke were chatting over by Mom's A-frame swing. Luke cast a quick glance her way. It was a

145

good reminder. As much as she would've liked to hold Joel's hand as they walked to his car or to wrap her arms around him when he paused before getting into it, she was acutely aware of the family and friends also emerging from the house, and she kept her distance, as well as her hands, to herself. Gossip, even well-meaning, gossip, could get out of hand so easily. She didn't want to spend her time in days to come responding to questions about her and Joel. About "were they or weren't they"? About managing relationships or "catching" a guy and wrangling him into marriage.

Better no one than the wrong one.

What about Joel? Right one? Wrong one? He seemed very right, except for the distance problem. Why was there a distance problem? She'd never move inland. His family and business were in Raleigh. She couldn't expect him to leave his whole life behind for her if she wasn't willing to do the same.

Brian joined her as Joel's car disappeared around the curve. Maia looked back but didn't see Luke or anyone else.

"How'd she do?" he asked.

She? Maia raised her eyebrows. "You mean Frannie?"

"Sure. She isn't used to such crowds, and most of them strangers."

"She did fine. Everyone loved her."

He glowed a bit. "Good. That's what I thought."

"Does it matter to you?"

He shrugged. "It matters in terms of Frannie's happiness. She never had much family, not a quantity of loud friendly family, that is, like we're used to. This is new to her."

"She has Juli now. Sisters. There should be enough joy in that to get her a long way."

Brian nodded, but didn't agree or disagree or anything. Not even a grunt. That was unlike him.

She looked at his face closely. "Are you still worrying about Frannie and the engagement? Why? I didn't see anything other than happiness in her at the party. No doubt in sight."

Brian shrugged. "I think you're right, but I was thinking that lunch with friends would be a good experience, like a bonding experience, right? If the three of you gals went out to lunch, made plans to shop for gowns and flowers and all that stuff. Make Frannie feel like she belongs. Like she has support."

Something about his phrasing made Maia feel rather small, second-best or third-rate, and even a little jealous. She'd been through a lot of this with a lot of her friends over the years, and more recently with Juli. Now with Frannie?

She shivered, shocked at where those dark thoughts had taken her.

"You cold, sis? Sick?"

"No, I'm fine. Just a sudden chill. Already gone."

"Mom would say a ghost just walked over your grave."

"Mom might and it makes no sense and never did. I don't have a grave."

"I'm pretty sure Mom would get angry if she heard you saying that. She'd fuss at you for tempting fate."

"Well, don't tell her, for heaven's sake. What's wrong with you, Brian?"

"With me? I'm just asking a favor. For me. For Frannie. For the family."

"Frannie's a big girl. If she wants help, she'll tell me. I don't want to invite myself into her business without any signs that she'd like help."

Brian looked down at her. He stared at her face. Suddenly, Maia felt like some of the unhappy thoughts plaguing her these days were perhaps beginning to show. Like early wrinkles.

Deep breath, Maia, she told herself. She visualized that path at Bridle Cove, at the shimmery light floating just about the sparkling waters....

"Maia? Are you alright?"

"I'm fine," she snapped. She shook her head. "Okay."

"Okay what?" Brian sounded hesitant.

"I'll set it up. What about Mom and Cathy?"

"Mom and Cathy? You mean they might want to come?"

"You aren't stupid. Don't act like you are. You can't be surprised. If this is about wedding planning, they'll want to be included. This isn't your first marriage."

"You're right. I wasn't thinking."

Maia crossed her arms, then uncrossed them. "We'll start with lunch. Just us three. Friendly. Not a wedding thing. I'll see how it goes before committing to more." She gave Brian a hard look. "You need to keep in mind that this is Frannie's business. Frannie's wedding. She may or may not want help from me and I won't push myself into her business."

Brian grinned and gave her a hug. "You're the best."

She wanted to smack him and remind him that he'd given her the silent treatment for months after she'd interfered with him and Diane. He'd treated the rest of the family almost as badly. He'd been in pain from the motorcycle accident that had injured his leg, and so angry over Diane and the divorce that he had no patience with or understanding available for anyone else. Now it suited him for her to interfere. This time she didn't want to.

But she would. Because this was about more than her. This was about the people she cared for. Even if she didn't feel the desire to help, she knew how to pretend. And maybe, just maybe, pretending would bring some of that old feeling back.

Besides, if things went well with Joel, and so far, it was looking very good, she'd love to do all this with them for her own wedding. For now, the reality of it hovered in the air just beyond her reach. But she could see it, and it was a promise of sorts. And if things worked out with Joel, it was a goal that was attainable.

Chapter Sixteen

Maia and Juli arrived at the same time. The restaurant was next to the marina and had outside dining. They asked for a table in a shady area and settled in. Before Frannie joined them, Juli said in a low voice, "Don't mention what I told you about going to see our mother, okay?"

Maia nodded. "Of course not. That's between you two."

Frannie joined them and Maia tried to avoid sore points and sensibilities. While were reading the menus, and discussing what to order, the mood was easy, but once those tasks were done, it became more difficult. It was hard not to mention the things that were uppermost in one's mind. Plus, she was dealing with additional brain acrobatics as she went back and forth between wanting to mention Joel and their wonderful date, versus keeping her personal business to herself. When a person offered their information, they were inviting comments and remarks. And no matter how sincerely others promised not to repeat the info to anyone, it almost always happened anyway.

Maia learned long ago that if you told someone your secret, you were, despite all promises of confidentiality, ultimately inviting them and the world into your personal business. She wasn't ready for that, not with her feelings for Joel, so Maia danced around that subject, in addition to mentions of mothers and unmarked graves. As they waited for their food, it seemed to Maia there were several elephants at the table with them—elephants that they all pretended not to notice. It was safer to focus on wedding-related topics.

"There are some bridal shops in the area, but you'll find a much better selection in Raleigh, I'm sure. How fancy a wedding were you considering?" Maia pasted a congenial, no-pressure look on her face, but it felt fake.

Frannie said, "Plenty of time to think it through. By the way, I was surprised to see Joel come into the gallery. Pleasantly surprised." She glanced at Juli. "He was there to see Maia."

Juli made a noise expressing some degree of interest. Maia threw her a hard look.

"We're just getting to know each other." She pressed her lips together, determined not to mention dancing on the dock by candlelight and starlight.

Frannie looked at her face, then stared at her plate and all but refused to speak. Maia could hardly blame her.

Juli was no help. She had retreated behind a pleasant mask, a smile, but wary of the uneasy crosscurrents.

Between Juli's misleading composure and Frannie's avoidance, Maia felt caught in the middle, awkward, and even dishonest. Why did Brian push this on her? This was Brian's fault. Or hers, for giving in to him.

Somewhere between salads and the main dishes, she sighed loudly in frustration, not bothering to hide it. Juli sat up straighter and her eyes lost their dreamy look. Frannie's face lost all expression. Maia fixed her gaze on Frannie.

"Tell me, do you want to marry Brian?"

Her face was suddenly a shifting landscape of emotion. She raised her hands as if an explanation was coming, but instead, she said, "Of course, I do. Why do you ask?"

"Then is it me? You just don't want to discuss it with me? I assure you I can understand that. I won't hold honesty against you. Just tell me."

Juli nudged Maia's foot. She tried to ignore it, then it pressed into her shin and she cast a quick look at Juli. Juli gave her a hard look back, a look with cold steel in it.

"I'm sorry," Maia said. "I'm sorry for pressing. Ordinarily, I would've waited for you to say you were ready for, or even wanted, my help. But today, when I mention it, you keep changing the subject."

"And you can't let it go?"

Maia took a moment to breathe. To compose herself. "I can. I don't want to keep after you about a wedding if you're regretting accepting his proposal." She shrugged. "He is my brother."

Frannie rearranged the salt and pepper shakers before saying, "I do want to marry him."

"I thought maybe everything had happened too quickly. A whirlwind and all that." Maia smiled at Juli to reassure her that she hadn't lost her mind or manners, then turned back to Frannie. "So, what's the problem?"

She shrugged.

Maia waited. She had to wait. She couldn't bring herself to push again.

Frannie said, "It seems too quick." She shook her head and hastened to add, "I don't mean too soon about knowing I love Brian. It's not that at all. But a wedding? A wedding. Why is he in such a rush? Do you know?"

Maia shook her head slowly.

"I don't mind discussing wedding possibilities, but I don't want to rush it. Once I start making decisions, I feel as though Brian will take that as a sign to move even faster. He can be…pushy. But why is he pushy about this? Why is he in such a hurry?"

Maia knew why. Brian was afraid Frannie would change her mind. Get cold feet, maybe. That he might lose her somehow. Or drive him crazy worrying about it. But she didn't say all that aloud. Instead, Maia said, "Have you asked him?"

Frannie moved her hands back onto the table, and sure enough the fingers were entwined. "I have. He said he was afraid I'd change my mind."

"And?"

Juli leaned forward. "It's normal to have doubts, don't you think?"

"I suppose. But...."

"But what?"

"This is going to sound foolish."

Maia waited.

"I don't know where to start. Once I start, I know Brian will rush me. But I really don't know what I want. Big or small. Fancy or beachy? I suppose we should get married in Raleigh, that's where I'm from, but Brian's life, family and friends are here. I don't have family there anymore." Frannie pressed her fingers, the nails perfectly manicured, against her temples.

They stopped speaking as the waitress removed the salad plates and delivered the main course. Maia was thinking, though, and she found it interesting that Frannie was concerned about being rushed more than anything else. And she was right about Brian. Maybe Frannie needed to practice telling Brian to back off. Maia had barely tasted her salmon when Juli spoke.

"Is it Laurel?"

Juli's voice was soft and low, yet the words seemed to hit Frannie with force.

Frannie responded, her own voice on the edge of brittle, a gunslinger's voice that responded with its own question, yet dared anyone to answer. "Is what Laurel? What about her?"

Juli didn't respond. She raised her eyebrows but kept the focus on Frannie.

Frannie looked from Juli to Maia and much of the hard edge in her voice softened. "Sorry about that, Juli. Honestly, what about her?"

Maia glanced over at Juli who said, "If you two hadn't broken ties, I'm sure she would've been helping you with the planning."

Frannie pursed up her lips as if tasting something sour. "I'm sure she would've been, but she knows better than to intrude in my life again. Ever again."

"You don't need her for planning," Maia said coolly. "You know what you like."

Frannie stared.

Maia continued, "For anything you want to discuss, you have Juli and me." After a short pause, she added, "If you want us."

"I...." Frannie stopped and cleared her throat. "I hadn't really thought of it that way, just felt at an impasse, but you might be right. I never did anything that Laurel didn't weigh in on, didn't try to control. Is it possible my subconscious is expecting her to step on stage at any moment?" She clutched her hands. "Or am I unable to make my own decisions?" Her voice quavered on those last words.

"Enough of that." Maia spoke firmly. Both Juli and Frannie looked surprised. "Enough of that self-defeating talk. You know that's not you. It's not true. It's just her voice you're channeling—Laurel's voice." She leaned forward. "Which, since we're laying this all out on the table here, I'll ask now. What should I call her when we're speaking of her? Your mother? Your stepmother? Mrs. Denman? I don't know but I'm not comfortable referring to her as Laurel. We've never even met, and she doesn't sound like someone I'd want for a friend."

"She's out of my life. No need to call her anything." Frannie crossed her arms. "I had a mother even though I never met her. And Laurel...well, she married my father and pretended she was my mother, but she wasn't. She was never a loving mother."

As Frannie spoke, Juli's expression clouded and she stared toward the water at a yacht at anchor, as if she'd never seen such an odd and unusual sight before.

Maia said, "It's not fair, but we don't get to choose our mothers. Some of us get lucky. Some don't."

Frannie eyed Juli and even glanced toward the water, at the white sails shining in the mid-day sun. As she turned back to the table, Maia caught her disappointed frown.

"What you say is true," Frannie said. "But when we get to be a certain age, we are responsible for our own choices, regardless of what brought us to that point."

Juli spoke, surprising them. "You make it sound easy, but you can't always control where fate puts you. Or where the future leads you."

"Are you okay?" Frannie asked.

"I'm fine," Juli said. "But I've been there, done that. All I know is that you have to consider your actions and where you'd like them to lead. Preparing and planning is fine, but, in the end, you can only live the day you're in, in the best way you can. Doing much beyond that is wasting your time." She checked the time on her phone. "I'm sorry. I need to fly. Esther will need to leave soon. I don't want to take advantage of her kindness."

She rose, and they all stood and shared hugs. Juli took her purse and as she walked away, Maia thought she caught a certain lightness in her step. No doubt Juli was happy *not* to be stuck in this conversation.

Frannie said, "What did she mean? Is she saying I shouldn't plan my wedding, after all? I'm confused."

Maia shook her head. "I have no clue."

"Well, I should be going too, I—"

Maia turned to Frannie and said, "No, you don't. Now that Juli's gone, you and I are going to have a real talk.".

Chapter Seventeen

"Let's walk?" Maia asked.

"Sure." Frannie answered, but there was a warning note in her voice.

When Maia handed the waitress a credit card, Frannie picked up her purse, saying, "I'll take care of that."

Maia laughed. "No worries. Brian is paying this bill."

"Brian?" Frannie looked confused.

"This was his idea, so it's his treat." Maia swept right past the look of hurt on Frannie's face. "Don't get me wrong. It was a good idea. I wanted to talk to you about all this, but I didn't have the nerve to push myself on you and into your wedding plans…or no wedding plans, for that matter…without encouragement from you. But Brian kept after me and I'm glad he did."

Frannie rubbed her forehead, then pressed the fingers of both hands to her temples. "I'm confused. I don't understand. Has Brian been going behind my back?"

"Not like that at all. I assure you." Maia smiled and gave Frannie a hug. She'd better move fast before Frannie decided she was angry at Brian and started questioning whether she could trust any of them.

"Let's forget moms, Frannie. Brian and all the rest, too." By then she had Frannie on the boardwalk and walking.

Frannie said, "I think I should be offended, maybe."

"Don't be. It's a waste of energy. And try not to let on to Brian that I told on him?"

"Why?"

Maia couldn't help laughing. "Let's let him think his plan succeeded, else we won't have any peace. I wish I had a man who loved me so much that he's willing to be an idiot for fear of losing me." She touched Frannie's arm. "Do yourself a favor and don't try to make sense of it. Just accept it as sincere and well-meant."

"From Brian or from you?"

Instead of answering, Maia laughed again. Finally, Frannie laughed a little, too.

Maia chose that slightly more relaxed moment to interject, "Do you want a beach wedding or not?"

Frannie stumbled. "What?"

"Everyone does, right?"

Frannie made a rude noise. Maia giggled.

"I already told you I don't know."

"Well, we know you're going to have a wedding at some point. Let's consider. Just for possibilities. Not really planning, okay?"

Frannie didn't answer at all.

Maia resumed, "Beach or not a beach?"

She said, "I don't see the appeal. Beaches are lovely for barefoot walks when the weather is good, but for a wedding?"

"People do it all the time. Pay a lot of money for it, in fact."

"But you can't count on the weather. It could be rainy or windy. Everyone will get sand in their eyes and an ocean gale will destroy our hair."

"Really?"

Frannie shrugged. "I guess you're more comfortable with the beach, being around it so much. Same with Brian." She paused. "Do you know what he wants? Does he want to be married at the beach?"

Maia took a mental step back. "What did he say?"

"He says whatever I want is what he wants. Totally unhelpful. In fact, maybe...."

She broke off with a shudder, a tiny shudder that Maia would've missed if she hadn't been focused on her.

"Maybe what?"

"Nothing...but maybe he has doubts. Maybe it's his way of delaying...."

Maia laughed. The sound was rude and loud, and the breeze picked it up and swirled it in the air around them. A couple down by the boats turned their way and she laughed again.

Frannie looked sheepish, but also annoyed. "What's so funny? You think I'm wrong?"

"Brian doesn't care about the "where or how" because he only cares about the goal—marrying you. Go to the ocean. Hike to a peak in the Smokies. A church. A justice of the peace. Dressed up or naked. Brian only cares about the end goal. He wants to marry you. He's a straight-line kind of guy. Surely you've noticed that."

Frannie was smiling, a small shy-looking smile.

"Well?"

"I was just envisioning what you said."

"Really?" Maia's almost laughed again.

Frannie groaned. "Oh, stop it. You are such a tease. Brian is, too. You two are so alike. It's hard to know when you're joking. Sometimes it takes a moment to figure it out."

Alike? She and Brian? Maia laughed and Frannie probably assumed they were laughing at the same thing. They were, sort of. They were laughing at the silliness of people.

Finally, Maia asked, "What do you want to do? Put all this on the back burner? Discuss it, but keep it at a slower pace? I can tell you aren't ready to run to the altar."

After a long silent moment, Frannie said, "What I said about Brian is true, about him rushing me if I show any sign of moving forward with the plans, but maybe it is also about Laurel. Maybe I'm having trouble moving forward while she's...out of my life, of course...but maybe it's not that simple?"

Now she sounded sad, almost despairing.

"That might be it."

"Sometimes the past gets in the way, doesn't it?"

Maia said, "That's true, but is she really in the past? I mean, I know you have that past between you, but...."

"I thought I was done with her." Frannie made a small noise. It sounded suspiciously like annoyance.

Maia said, "I'll apologize properly now. For pushing in. For being so abrupt. I wanted to get it all out on the table, to understand where you stood and to make sure you know that I'm available to help, or not, as you want."

"I appreciate that."

Frannie sighed. "Okay, so here's a question for you. What's up with you and Joel? You two make a lovely couple. Perfect for each other, I'd say. And don't think you can ask about my life and my plans and not allow me to return the favor."

Maia shrugged. "We went out again and it was fun. We had a great time. The engagement party was fun, too. Joel was a good sport, especially with Mags."

"Joel is always a good sport." She smiled. "You have feelings for him."

"Yes."

"Then what's the problem?"

"Is there a problem?" Maia snapped back. Then she nodded. "There is. "The distance. He travels a lot for work, and he works a lot. So do I, for that matter."

"That won't go on forever."

"Won't it?"

"People do manage with long distance relationships."

Maia shook her head. "I don't think I'm one of those people. I want a guy who's with me. Not always on the road. And yet...."

Frannie frowned, but only slightly, and then she shook her head and said, "It's never simple, is it?"

"Love?"

"Love. Caring. Anything worth having. Sometimes it takes effort, sometimes a lot more. The risk is always there."

"But how do you know?"

"Know what?"

In a small voice, Maia said, "How do you know when it's worth fighting for? Worth taking the risk?"

Frannie put her hand on Maia's. Her hand was cool, and her fingers were long and slim. "I don't think it's as clear as an equation or a balance sheet. You must trust your heart. Trust yourself."

"And volunteer for hurt?" The words sounded rough, almost painful. Maia was shocked at herself. "I've been hurt before." The words faded, growing smaller as they were spoken.

"Me, too, Maia."

"Are you worried about you and Brian?"

"Oddly, no. Everything seems right with Brian, even when we're fussing at each other." She sighed. "I trust him. His anger is never ugly. Never dark."

Maia grasped the railing and leaned against it. "You're right about that."

"Try to trust Joel, too. You can, you know. It might work out. It might not. But love stories deserve the opportunity to play out in case they have a happy ending."

"You sound like a romantic."

"I think I am."

"Brian is, too."

Frannie smiled. "He is, isn't he?" She shrugged. "Raleigh's not a bad place, you know."

"I'm sure."

"But it's not home, right? I'm not a beach person. Brian loves it. I don't think he'd agree to live anywhere else. Certainly not inland."

Frannie placed her hand on Maia's. "It's early days for you and Joel. Give yourselves time. A chance."

"Give ourselves time? Are you kidding me?" Maia asked.

Then they both laughed.

Maia said, "One last thing. About your mother...."

"Forget Laurel."

"Not that one. The other one. Frances."

Frannie stood taller and answered with a curt, "Okay?"

"You want to go visit her grave, I hear."

She nodded.

"You should. Just go."

Frannie looked blank, but carefully so.

"Tell Juli you're going. Tell her when you're going and what time to be ready if she wants to go along."

"What?"

"She might not show up, but my guess is she will. She seems gentle...genteel...but she's tough, and you're asking her to take a trip into a past that she's worked her whole life to forget. Hard to blame her for dragging her heels."

Maia added, "If you push her, she might refuse. Probably will." She shook her head and shrugged. "Who knows for sure? But that's my advice. Don't push her, don't discuss it or try to persuade her, just tell her, give her a smile or a hug, and then walk away. Then do it. She'll either go or she won't."

Frannie said, "I understand she has bad memories, but she was so young when she was taken away from Frances. How much can she remember? Very little, right? Surely, she could bring herself to share those few memories with me."

"No, you misunderstand. It wasn't just the memories from when she was five or younger. This is about those, yes, but also about the next years...the years of foster families, of not feeling wanted or appreciated, of not having the benefit of a stable education and college...all the things that most of us take for granted."

Maia stared at that boat again. "Part of what helped her succeed is her interior toughness. It shuts out what she chooses not to deal with. She's happy now. She feels loved and appreciated. Why would she want to risk tainting all that with a trip down a difficult memory lane?"

"Do you think she resents me for having the advantages she didn't?"

"No, I'm sure not. She's not an envious or jealous person, but she's an arranger, and when she has the bits and pieces of her life, and everything impacting her life, in order, she'll work to keep it that way."

"I'll give it more thought. Perhaps you're right. I need to reconsider how I approach it with her."

"I hope she'll go."

Frannie nodded. "Thank you, Maia."

She looked surprised. "For what?"

"For talking to me about all this."

"My pleasure."

"More than that, thank you for talking to me like an adult, like a friend."

"Well, you are. On both counts. And soon to be a sister." She smiled. "I hope you're ready to join our gang. It can get a little crazy...but let me assure you that everyone has a good heart. Every sibling, aunt and uncle and cousin. Never second-guess their intentions even if their manner or actions seem unexpected or thoughtless. Always give them the benefit of the doubt. You won't regret it."

"I'll remember that."

"I meant to ask sooner... How's your Uncle Will? Will he be able to return to home any time soon?"

Frannie sighed. "Brian and I have been working on making his house handicap accessible, but it may be wasted effort. He tries to work hard at the physical therapy, but every step forward leads to a step or two back. His overall condition is fragile. I worry about another stroke."

"And the doctors?"

"They say about the same. If he is able to return home, he'll need skilled nursing care. He's never going to live on his own again. If that's the case, then day trips home may be the answer. Or is it better to encourage him to hope for recovery?"

Maia said, "You have to be honest with him. In the end, it's his choice as to how he wants to view it, right?"

"Yes. I wouldn't do anything that he didn't approve of."

They knew, though, that was true only in terms of Will Denman staying stable. He was fragile. His condition could change. He might lose the ability to make those decisions and then it would be on Frannie.

Maia cast a sidelong look at Frannie, wondering if she would be able to make the transition to full responsibility for Will's life? But there was Brian, of course. He was a longtime friend of Will Denman. In fact, if not for that relationship, Brian would never have been over at the house and he and Frannie would never have met. If something did happen regarding Will's condition, Frannie would consider the details, but Brian would push the decision, always with Will's best interest in mind.

"You and Brian make an excellent partnership. Your strengths complement each other."

Frannie stared. "Do you really think so?"

Maia nodded.

Frannie agreed. "I think so, too. I truly do. I guess there's no question then, except for the where and how of the wedding. Frankly, I don't care about that either. I feel as though I should care, but I don't. I'm like Brian in that regard, at least as far as the venue question goes."

"Then elope. Don't torture yourself with the details. Just go. Just do it." She paused, then added firmly, "But take us with you. Mom and Dad, too. And Cathy and the kids."

Frannie lifted her face to the salty breeze, closed her eyes, drew in a cleansing breath, and laughed. It was a freeing sound and Maia joined in.

Suddenly, Maia grabbed Frannie's arm. Frannie stared, surprised.

Maia said, "I know what she was saying. Juli? Remember what she said as she was leaving?"

"About not planning for the wedding?"

Maia shook her head. "No. Or rather yes. What she meant was it's all well and fine to plan and prepare, but only if it doesn't interfere with living today. Meaning, don't drive yourself so crazy worrying over what's ahead, that you miss enjoying today."

"Really? That's what she was saying?"

"That's what I'm going with. And I think she's right."

"Maia, thanks for helping me talk through this. I'm not going to worry. I'll know when I have the right answer. And Laurel? I'm not sure about that, but I need to figure it out. I don't want to bring her, or any negativity connected to her, into our marriage. I'll resolve that first."

"I suspect that when you're ready to move forward with a big life event like getting married, you'll discover she is truly no longer a consideration in your life anyway."

⋘⋙

Maia called Brian that night. "Frannie is fine. Give her time to decide what she wants and don't bug her or us. You'll have to be patient."

After she hung up, Maia sat out on the front porch enjoying the evening air and thinking about Joel. She had the nagging idea that she'd preached to Frannie was advice that she should apply to herself.

The door creaked. Fay stepped out onto the porch.

"Are you okay? You're out here late." She looked around curiously. "Don't you want the light on?"

"No. The light will draw bugs. It's peaceful like this and there's plenty of light from the street. The air is nice this evening. Is Allie asleep?"

"Yes, thank goodness. She's getting very active. It's wearing me out. By the end of the day..." She sat on the edge of the seat, carefully, not wanting it to squeak. "Reggie should be home soon. He had to work late tonight."

"You have a lovely family, Fay."

She smiled. The lights from nearby porches touched her cheek and profile.

"When you fell in love with Reggie.... I mean when you really knew it was love, did you have doubts?"

Fay's expression went from a momentary blankness to a soft smile.

"None. Except for when I did. Which was at least every day." She laughed, but softly. "Plus, our parents weren't thrilled. They said we were too young."

"But you committed to each other anyway."

"Sometimes I think being young works in your favor. You don't believe bad things will happen. Even when you do get worried that you made a mistake, it goes away as soon as you hear his voice or see him walking in the door. That's how it works for me and Reggie anyway."

"But it's harder when you're older?"

"I think it must be. My mom and older sister kept warning me about things...stuff that had happened to them and to their friends and to their manicurists." She smiled. "It didn't feel as if it applied to me and Reggie. But for them? They worry about all that. And yet, my sister is getting married. One more time. After all those love-horror stories, she's taking another chance."

Maia grinned, but a bit sadly. "It doesn't always work out."

"No, but it never can if you don't give it a chance." She stood and looked past Maia, to the street. Her face lit up. "There he is."

Maia felt the energy around them change as Fay greeted Reggie.

"Hey, Maia." He looked at Fay. "I guess our girl's asleep?"

"I'm keeping supper warm for us. Come on in while it's quiet," she said to him as they hugged. "See you later, Maia."

The porch floor creaked, the door closed softly, and she was alone again—just a gal and her thoughts.

Was Fay right? Doubts were normal. She'd said that about Frannie and Brian.

She thought of Ben and of what had never been. Would she have done anything differently if given the chance of a do-over? How might it have worked out if she'd been less respectful of his grief and more aggressive about her feelings? If he'd known how she felt....

It was too late with Ben, but Joel was here now. She was too young to throw in the towel, right? Surely, she had heart enough left to risk one more try? Surely, the risk was worth the potential reward?.

Chapter Eighteen

"Morning, Maia."

"Good morning, Brendan." Maia walked into the gallery and did a visual once-over of the sales floor as she walked past him to the sales counter.

Brendan shook his dark hair out of his eyes and tried to re-tuck his shirt in his pants. He was thin, and the tucked-in shirts never cooperated. Maia appreciated that he tried.

"You look nice," she said to reassure him.

"Thanks. You look good, too."

"Thanks back at you."

Her phone rang. They each reached for their phones, but it was hers and the caller was Joel. Maia said, "I'm going to step outside for a moment."

He nodded.

As she opened the door, the bell sounded overhead and the fresh air, just off the water, rushed in. It felt like spring. Today, it smelled like early spring to her even though Memorial Day weekend was nearly here.

"Joel?"

"Hi. Are you at work? Is this a good time to talk?"

"Perfect. Brendan's covering the gallery. I'm walking across Front Street at this very moment to sit on the bench while we talk, so don't end the call too quickly," she teased.

"Wish I was there with you. Tell me what you see."

"It's spring here, Joel. I mean, I know it's been spring for a while now but somehow today is a perfect spring day. The breeze is gentle, the marina is filling up with boats. Birds are chirping in the tree that's opposite the gallery. There's room on the bench here, right next to me." She patted the seat.

"Beats my meeting this morning. I'm sorry to say I have to travel again. I was hoping to see you before I fly out, but it won't work."

"Where are you going?"

"Staying stateside this trip. California. You should go with me sometimes."

The suggestion startled her into a stuttering response. "Well, there's work, you know." And many other reasons why she wouldn't take off across the country, or even over the Atlantic, with a guy she thought she liked a lot but had only been on three dates with. Unless the engagement party counted as a date.... But none of that needed to be said at this point.

"I'll be back in North Carolina on Thursday or Friday. Can I see you then?"

"I'll be here. Just let me know when."

After a short goodbye, Maia hit "end" and stared at the phone. Short and sweet. There were things she could've said. Might've said.

It was hard to know how fast or slow to go. She wished she could see ahead and know whether they had a future, or whether it would drift away.

What was it her grandmother used to say? If wishes were horses.... Wishing was fine, but it didn't mean you could get what you wanted. Unless you were willing to work at it. Even then there was no guarantee of happiness.

As she stood musing, she saw Lora arrive. Maia crossed the street and went up the steps. Lora was already inside and standing near the customer counter where Brendan was packaging some items for shipment.

"Hi, Lora," she said. "It's good to see you. We can certainly use your help."

"Hi, Maia." Lora was neatly dressed in slacks and a silk blouse. Her posture was perfect, and her hair was threaded with gray. "I'm glad business is going well. It's good to be back."

"It's getting busier all the time. That's a good thing, of course, but we all have personal lives that deserve attention."

Brendan gave her a surprised look.

She added, "Well, let's put it this way—if we don't, then we should have. There's more to life than work."

CR&SO

Maia had said those confident words to Brendan and Lora, and had meant them, but that old devil, doubt, wasn't done with her. The reality of jobs and homes and personal economics began to worm its way back into her thoughts. As the morning wore on toward lunch, she heard Brendan say, "Hey, look what I found."

She did look and saw he was holding a small photo scrapbook, the kind people make online after uploading their picture files.

Pictures. A digital scrapbook of pictures from over the years. Maia had put it together, a history of the gallery, a couple of years ago, intending to give copies as keepsakes to Ben and Luke, but hadn't given them after all. She must've stashed that proof copy under a stack of dusty forms and forgotten to take it home.

Small wonder she'd decided to hold off on sharing the photo book, and small wonder that she'd lost track of it. Because it had all happened at about the time Ben told them he was sick. Cancer and Juli had come onto the scene.

She cringed inwardly. The thought had sprung into her brain that way, but it wasn't something anyone could blame Juli for. It was just life or fate or whatever.

But she'd lost the desire to share the book. The timing seemed all wrong.

Now Maia flipped it open again to the first pages. They were glossy white, and the first part showed black and white photos that someone, probably Ben's parents or grandparents had kept from the early days of the gallery. There was a grainy photo of the original house before it was a gallery and before the plate glass window had been installed where smaller windows had been.

Suddenly wistful, Maia wanted to take a closer look at these memories, but not here. She checked the clock. It was nearly noon. Maybe the breakroom?

No, Lora was sitting in the breakroom filling out forms.

"Brendan," she spoke softly. "I'm going to take my lunch upstairs. Yell if you need me."

She grabbed her lunch from the fridge.

"You okay, Maia?"

"Just the beginnings of a headache. I'll be fine. How's it going with those?" She nodded toward the paperwork.

"Almost done."

"When you're finished, see Brendan. If you have any questions, check with him. I'm taking a break."

The stairs to the top level creaked slightly as Maia held the rail and made her way up. She walked between the stacked boxes to the old divan she'd placed by the front window. The green-purple flowered brocaded fabric was worn in areas down to the bare threads. She fluffed the sofa pillows with their old-fashioned tassels to dislodge the dust that had settled on them. It was warmish up here because it didn't get the full benefit of the AC, but it was do-able.

She cracked open the window beside the divan to cut the mustiness of the air and settled on the divan. She arranged her lunch on the table, kicked off her shoes, tucked her legs up beside her, then opened the book.

Most of the pictures showed the early days of the modern era, the beginning of the twentieth century, for Beaufort and Front Street. Back then, Ben and Luke's great-great-grandparents had purchased this house. The elder Mr. Bradshaw had stocked the downstairs with shoes and hats, and his family had lived on the second floor. One of the small black and white photos showed a tall man standing stiffly, proudly, on the sidewalk in front of the house, holding his cane as if anchoring the moment in time. Within a couple of decades, shoe leather had given way to an art gallery. How had that change come about? It seemed a risky, dynamic shift to her. Was the family together in the decision? Or had there been strife? She understood it had happened after that elder Bradshaw's death. She guessed there was either resistance, or respect, involved. The color pictures were faded, many copied from the old Polaroid Instamatics mid-century. Some of those had continued to degrade, but they were preserved here, scanned for use in this book.

Here was a photo with Ben and Luke as boys, each standing with their parents, with his grandparents posed on the topmost step behind them all. Both boys were easily recognizable. Handsome boys, whose smiles said, "Hurry, take the photo, we have adventures waiting."

Ben's brown eyes were the warmest, most loving eyes she'd ever seen. His eyes had drawn her in the day they met and had kept her here near him.

Joel was similar, but different. He had nice eyes, too, and she loved his smile. He was also a good dancer. In fact, good enough that he made her feel reasonably good, too. That was saying something.

He had a fun sense of humor and a romantic streak. She touched the key pendant. He was often thoughtful.

Why did she feel distance between them? More than a physical distance, there was a feel of things unsaid.

Well, she didn't blurt out everything about her life, either, so she could hardly blame him for that.

Time would resolve some of it, but she wanted, needed someone here. So, again, she was back to worrying over the geography when that was probably the least important obstacle.

She wasn't getting any younger. The biological clock was ticking. Maybe she wasn't destined for children of her own. Maybe she was fated to be 'Auntie Maia' and save her hugs and kisses for other people's children.

If so, then so be. But meanwhile, there was Joel and she was looking forward to seeing him again.

Chapter Nineteen

On Thursday, Lora left mid-afternoon and Brendan left shortly after. Maia was going through the forms and receipts below the counter and tidying the clutter when Joel called.

"I'm driving back from Richmond and I'd like to see you."

She teased, "Beaufort isn't exactly on the way from Richmond to Raleigh."

Joel laughed. "Sounds like a conversation we've already had. I'll be there in an hour or so. Want to join me for supper?"

"Love to. Today's my day to close the gallery, so you know where to find me. Come to the back door."

"Soon, then." He sounded pleased.

They disconnected. Maia went to the door to turn the sign and cut off the lights. It was mid-May and was staying light later now. She could see her way around without a problem. She flipped the switch for the exterior light out back in case it took Joel a little longer to get here than expected. Then she carried the day's receipts into the office.

Maia closed the office blinds and switched on the desk lamp.

She sat and sorted the receipts. Not many people wrote checks any more. It was mostly credit cards and cash. Two of the dollar bills were seriously crumpled having come straight from the pocket of a child who'd bought one of Margie's shell creatures.

Maia chuckled as she banded and wrapped the receipts and knelt to put them in the safe. Those shell creatures seemed to have tiny personalities. They were quirky and borderline tacky, but each one seemed to cry for his own name. When she'd said that in jest, the kid had told her this one's name was Bernard.

Bernard. What kind of name was that for a googly-eyed shell creature?

When she stood, intending to walk around the desk, on the wall in front of her were the pictures. She was seeing them for maybe the gazillionth time. Funny how, if you saw something almost every day, you almost ceased to see it at all. And then one day, it was there, boom, right in front of you and almost speaking to you.

This picture was one she'd included in that photo book. Here was Luke's dad and Ben's dad. Brothers. Wearing waders and looking more like fisherman than gallery owners. Rakish. Grinning. Luke's father, Mr. Winters, was a gem. Ben's father had died before she came to Beaufort. A decade ago, she'd applied for the job because she needed one and she loved the idea of working with the waterfront mere steps away, and in a gallery. Beauty inside and out. She'd come for the job, and though she loved the gallery, she'd stayed for Ben.

Next to it was a photo of Ben and Luke with Anna, a local artist and everyone's friend. She was a seller here, and also a patron of the arts throughout the area. She lived over on Emerald Isle. As did Luke and Juli, of course.

She touched her finger to Ben's face. In this picture, His hair looked darker than Luke's. His build was a little more substantial, not as lean as Luke, and with softer features. Luke was certainly an attractive man, but he didn't have Ben's toffee-brown eyes or Ben's warmth and kindness. Maia had fallen for Ben. But he'd been grieving, and she was respectful. As each year slipped past she thought they were getting closer, that one day, Ben would put his broken heart aside, would see her as more than a friend. As a desirable woman. As a woman he loved and wanted to spend the rest of his life with. And she was willing to wait.

Maia took the photo from the wall and carried it over to the desk. She sat again. Here in the office. Luke's office. But she remembered when it had been Ben who was here every day. Ben with whom she'd shared the gallery management.

She set the frame on the desk blotter and leaned back in the chair.

She remembered the day that Ben had come into work with a different air about him, a special, burning light in his eyes and suppressed, barely contained excitement in his voice. Things had been very tense since he'd announced he was sick. They'd known he wasn't well. He'd been struggling with a cold he couldn't seem to shake. He was in his late thirties and had always been active and healthy, so he'd put off going to the doctor, but it had taken hold of his chest and after constant nagging from her and Luke, finally he went to the doctor. In that relatively short time, even before they knew how bad it could get, Luke was already having to shift his focus from the other, out-of-town galleries, to this one.

The doctor diagnosed pneumonia. It was a serious ailment, but with the right medicine, Ben responded well. It was the unexpected, that which was unconnected to the pneumonia, that the doctor also found and that, when diagnosed, had changed his life. Their lives. Pancreatic cancer. Seeing a dear friend, someone you loved, walking and talking and recovering, yet knowing they were dying, was inconceivable. She remembered the arguments, too. The pressure to get treatment. At one point, Luke had angrily accused Ben of wanting to die. He hadn't meant it. Ben knew that and so did she. And then the dreadful quiet encompassed them all wherein nothing could be discussed because no one was allowed to discuss the only thing on their minds.

They almost didn't go to the Hammonds' party. The Hammonds held an annual gala at their fancy estate to entertain friends and business associates. Ben said he was going. He was still weak from the bout of pneumonia. They argued with him, but he was determined, so they went, the three of them, Ben, Luke and Maia. Ben met Juli there. Their meeting was by chance and the others didn't know about Juli that evening—only that Ben went home early having left a message for them not to worry.

So, when Ben came into the gallery that day, bright and more energized than she'd seen in ages, she'd responded in kind. The bell over the door jingled and he was already across the room and to the counter before the door was halfway closed. Her skin tingled, her heart raced. He stopped abruptly in front of her and placed his hands flat against the glass top.

"Maia. I've met someone."

The smile was still on her face, frozen there. She felt it. But Ben, he was so happy that he didn't notice her shock and that freakish grin on her face which hadn't gotten the message that she wasn't the one who had made this day special.

She touched the glass again over Ben's face, then dropped her face onto her arms on the desktop.

"Maia," he'd said, "I need your help."

She wanted to say 'of course' but her mouth continued to gape. Ben kept speaking, his words soaring past her.

"Luke isn't going to like it. I don't care. I'm going to marry her."

Chapter Twenty

Her paralysis had broken, and her smile faltered. Her hands waved frantically as if to call him back to reality. He raised his own hand and she captured it, clasping his hand in her own, not giving a thought to the temerity.

"Calm down, Ben."

" I am amazingly calm and clear-headed. More so than in years."

It hit her, hard and rough and with utter clarity, that he was on an emotional rebound. He'd only just found out about...about...being sick. She didn't want to think of it. Of course, he didn't. either He'd do anything, seize on anything, for a distraction.

Firmly, she said, "That's right. Calm down. Take a deep breath and then tell me what's going on." She kept her hands securely on top of his hand, trapping it against the counter.

He put his free hand on top of hers. She bit her lip. That look in his eyes—

He said, "I have to move quickly before she changes her mind."

"What?"

"Before she talks herself out of it."

What have you done, Ben? Those were the words that slammed around in her brain. But she kept them inside because it wasn't in her to kill, or to even dim, that bright light in his eyes. The first joy she'd seen in him since his diagnosis…and prognosis.

And she'd helped him. God help her. Yes, she'd helped him even though Luke was angry, and her own heart was breaking. When she was a child, she'd witnessed safety glass fracturing in a sliding door, and that spidery, spreading, crumbling break was no more than a roadmap of her devastated heart.

"The wedding is in four days."

"You want me to…to do what?" Her head was spinning. "Four days? What are you talking about?" This was impossible. A sick joke.

"I'm making the arrangements myself, but she needs a dress."

Maia stared. Ben's eyes. Ben's forehead. The curve of his lips...but now they were smiling, and his eyes were shining. She felt her own spirits rise again. Then reminded herself his joy wasn't for her. It was about another woman.

"Who is she?"

"You don't know her."

They all knew the same people. She waited.

"I met her a couple of days ago."

That touched off the fuse. "What? What?" Deep breath. "Just met her? Where?" She tried not to grit her teeth too obviously. Someone was taking advantage of Ben. Grown man or not, men were mostly saps at heart, especially Ben. Women could be... And she was confused now. Throwing women under the bus because Ben....

"Tell me."

"I—" Ben stopped. Then started again. "I know this sounds crazy and that's why I was so glad to see you here. No one else could possibly understand. You see the best in everyone, Maia, and you're a romantic at heart. No one else is going to understand how I feel. I need to share it. Can you imagine…." He shook his head.

"I have it all handled except she needs a dress. We'll have a beach wedding, but nothing fancy and we'll be barefoot. What do you think?"

"What size?"

"Size?" He looked blank.

"You don't know her dress size. Of course, you don't." Maia shook off his hands and walked around the counter and stopped in the middle of the sales floor. She turned in a slow circle. When she stopped, she asked, "Is she taller than me? Wider? Skinnier?"

Ben stared at her, approaching slowly, step by step, his eyes narrowing as he focused on her face, then her torso, and finally her legs. She couldn't help it. Despite reality and despite her breaking heart, she felt an answering tingling sensation in her legs and chest.

His hands moved as if measuring as he came closer. He stopped. "This much taller, I think."

He moved his hands again. "Narrower? Maybe?" He shook his head. "I don't know. About your size. Maybe a couple of inches taller than you?"

In the end, Juli was the girl's name and she was more than a couple of inches taller—Maia was petite—and more than a couple of inches 'narrower' too, especially in the hips and waist. But not knowing ahead of time, Maia had chosen a 'forgiving' cut of dress that allowed for guessing. And a blue dress. Not white. Not even ivory. A bit spiteful, but who would know?

It was something borrowed, something blue, right? She didn't accept repayment for the dress, so Juli, the bride, was covered on both counts.

When Ben saw the dress, he paused. Quickly, feeling petty, she smiled broadly and said, "Borrowed and blue!"

But that wasn't Ben's concern. Instead, he slid his arms around Maia's waist and pulled her close. It was the most amazing hug she'd ever experienced in her life from the most amazing man she'd ever known. He released her slowly and stepped back. He kissed her cheek. "You and Juli are going to be wonderful friends, I know it."

Swift, ripping pain brought her back to the present, to where her face rested on her arms on Luke's desk. Back then it had been Ben's desk and she'd believed that ultimately, she and Ben would spend their lives together. But it was never going to happen. She knew it for sure that day. It hurt—back then and again today, even two years later. Maia pressed her arms over her head and cried.

The back-door buzzer sounded. Maia suddenly recalled where she was. Why she was here. She'd been counting the receipts and had morphed into this tearful trip down memory lane. She brushed at her eyes and smiled broadly hoping to clear the after effects of the tears from her expression.

"Coming!" she called out.

The lighting was dim. She let Joel in knowing she had a moment or two to compose herself before he got a good look at her face and eyes.

"You sound like you have a cold. Are you okay?"

"I am. I'm fine." She avoided looking at him and turned away, putting a little breeziness in her tone. "I'm almost done with closing up. Why don't you have a seat and I'll be ready to leave in a few minutes."

She glimpsed disappointment on his face and realized her welcome had probably seemed cool. But she was still trying to hide the ravages of the crying. She headed to the office and the desk. Joel followed.

The large framed photograph squarely on the middle of the desk, lying atop the receipts, stood out. Joel picked it up.

"What's this?"

She shrugged. "A photo from the old days...."

He touched the glass over Ben's face and Maia stiffened.

She said, "That's Ben."

"It's wet. Just a drop." He seemed bemused, but then he looked more closely at her face. "You've been crying. Your eyes are red."

Maia shook it off. She didn't want to discuss Ben with Joel. With anyone, really.

"No, it's just allergies. Not a big deal." She took the picture from Joel and hung it back on the wall. "It was crooked and when I tried to straighten it, it came off the wall." She gave it a gentle tug. "Seems secure enough now."

They went to dinner, but that feeling of the past hovering over her plagued Maia. She couldn't shake the mood. It didn't help that Joel seemed preoccupied, too. Back at the gallery, she'd shooed his concern away with harmless lies. Well, it hadn't really been his business anyway, had it? More than that, if things worked out between them, one day she probably would tell him about Ben, but now? It was too soon to talk about former loves, even loves that didn't work out.

She tried to put a more cheerful look on her face. "How was your trip?"

"Fine. It was okay."

"You do travel a lot."

"My father...his focus isn't on business these days."

Maia asked, "I hope he's well?"

Joel made a noise. Not a happy sounding one. "Maybe too well."

They exited into the alley and Maia checked that the door was locked. "Where's your car?"

"I parked over by your apartment. It was a nice evening. I thought you might enjoy the walk?"

She smiled, genuinely pleased. "I'd love to."

As they strolled down the alley toward the street, Joel said, "He thinks he's in love. Maybe it's a mid-life crisis kind of thing. Or maybe it's a reaction to facing one's mortality, as Sharon said." He shrugged. "I don't know."

The streetlights were popping on. Maia slipped her arm into the crook of his. He smiled down at her and she gave his arm a squeeze.

"Maybe he really is in love?"

"Maybe."

"You sound annoyed."

"Well, he's paying less attention to business and leaving most of it to me. That translates into me being able to spend less time with you."

She liked the way he'd wrapped his complaint up in a compliment to her. She wanted to offer encouragement, but the best she could come up with was, "I'm sure it will work out."

After that, they walked in silence. She sensed a sadness in him and knew it must stem from what was going on with his father. Other than offer a sympathetic ear, there was nothing she could do. She was willing to listen, but it was up to him to unburden himself. So, they walked in silence, but a companionable one. They took the long way, her arm in his, walking quietly together past the church and the old cemetery and along the open area of the town complex before ending up in front of her home. They stood on the sidewalk. The air was still warm but pleasant. The occasional noises along the street—the slam of a door, a dog's bark—gave it a homey feel. The lights were on in Fay's apartment and they saw her, holding her daughter as she closed the blinds. Did she notice them outside? Maia didn't think so.

Impulsively, Maia stepped up on tiptoe and kissed Joel. He gave her a close look. What was he seeking in her eyes? She didn't know, but regardless, he responded with his own kiss, more insistent and lingering. His lips, his posture—his intent seemed to be focused on more than she understood.

When he stepped back, he said, "I have business in the area tomorrow. Mind if I hang around and pick you up after closing tomorrow? We'll grab some dinner."

"Lots of restaurant food," she mused, her voice husky. She was surprised to realize she was nearly breathless from his kiss. "Maybe I should try cooking?"

"At your apartment?"

"At my apartment. I have a working stove."

"Well, that's good." He paused. "Why don't I pick up salad and steak. I'll bring the food, and we'll cook together."

She smiled. "Deal."

Chapter Twenty-One

Maia's mood was upbeat. Dinner with Joel—and she suspected it would be a lot of fun cooking with Joel. She wasn't much of a cook, nothing like her mom and sister, but even she could handle salad and steak, so she shouldn't embarrass herself in front of Joel.

"Maia?"

She was in the break room, grabbing a cup of tea. Iced tea in an insulated cup with a lid. No spills welcome in the gallery, thank you very much.

"I'm in the breakroom, Juli," she answered. "Would you like some tea?"

"No, thanks."

Maia walked into the main room of the gallery and welcomed Juli with a smile.

"You look cheerful," Juli said.

"I am. Might as well be, right?" She tried to subdue her anticipation over dinner with Joel. Should she tell Juli? Not yet.

Brendan said, "I'm leaving now."

"See you tomorrow."

Juli said, "Bye Brendan." She continued staring, then with a smile, she turned to Maia. "I knew something was missing."

"What?"

"The bell. It didn't ring. It's not there."

Maia picked up a bell, a different bell with a different hanger, and said, "Changing it out for the season."

This bell chain was decorated with shells. Maia shook it as if to prove it would do the job.

"Cute," Juli said.

"I meant to have Brendan hang it. I'll get him to do it tomorrow."

"How's it going with Lora?" Juli asked.

"It's nice to have better coverage and I'm already familiar with her strengths and weaknesses. That helps. No surprises. At least, no potentially unpleasant ones." She walked to the display window and watched Brendan disappear down the sidewalk. "I'd be hurting without Brendan. I've really come to depend upon him." She turned back to Juli, "What brings you here?"

Juli lifted a large, loosely wrapped package. It was about the size of a sixteen by twenty canvas. Maia's eyes widened.

"What do you have there?"

Her friend suddenly seemed diffident. Uncertain. A bit flushed. "I like this very much. You've been wanting something new from me, right?"

"Absolutely right."

"I wanted your opinion on whether this one would be right for the gallery?"

Maia was genuinely excited. "What a day," she said. "A new piece from you and Joel's coming to pick me up for a date after the gallery closes." Oops. The words had just slipped out.

"Really? Didn't you say he took you out yesterday? Is he still in town?"

Maia smiled. "Yes, and yes."

"It's going well with Joel?"

"I think so."

Juli set the package back on the floor, leaning it against the side of the counter. She hugged Maia impulsively. "I'm so glad. You deserve the best, Maia. I hope that's Joel. I like him."

"You don't know him all that well, do you?"

Juli hesitated, then said, "Not really. He's been to see Luke a few times. Business."

Something unpleasant stirred in Maia.

"Business?"

"Yes, I think he's interested in the gallery business. Something like that."

She, Maia, was in the gallery business. She was spending time with Joel and kissing him… But he was also meeting with Luke and this was something Juli and Luke knew about, but not her? There was evasiveness evident in Juli's tone when she mentioned that bit about the gallery business. As if she immediately regretted disclosing it. Juli wasn't a liar, but she preferred to avoid unpleasantness. It made Maia uneasy. She felt…omitted. Once again, she was left out of something potentially important—something that was critically important to her life. At the same time, a small, sane voice in her head told her to relax, that she was making something out of nothing.

"Dinner again?" Juli said it in a teasing way, smiling.

Maia read the truth in her eyes. Juli had recognized the shift in the quality of the air between them. The tension. She was trying to restore the earlier good mood.

Maia tried, too, but her response sounded forced. "Yes."

"I'm glad. It's time you put yourself first." She paused. "A long time ago you told me about taking joy in service. It was before Danny was born. Do you remember? Service to family, to friends, even to strangers through your church? And to me. I didn't understand." She smiled at Maia. "You made me understand. You and Ben."

"Ben," Maia repeated after Juli. A pain hit her heart at the sound of his name, the memory, especially spoken by Juli at that moment.

Juli leaned against the counter, pressing her hands against the glass. "There is something I wanted to mention to you, something I was thinking about with Ben and Danny. Since we're discussing them now, maybe this is a good time."

Ben and Danny. Sort of a double body-blow. Maia felt it in her heart and head. Even in her stomach. Maybe seeing the pictures earlier, and with so many past associations here in the gallery. And then there was Joel. Too much was happening. She felt almost dizzy with it. And she was seriously annoyed.

"And about Frannie, too," Juli continued. "I'd like to talk to you about Frannie and Brian. That conversation we had about the wedding over lunch was a little painful, didn't you think? I'm worried they are moving too quickly."

Maia felt a flash of pain in her heart, a rush of heat up her body, and she laughed, but it was an ugly laugh. Nothing the least bit nice about it. She rubbed her temples. "Moving too quickly, did you say? You're one to talk."

Juli stopped, her expression changing. "What do you mean?"

"Mean?" Maia uttered a short, harsh laugh. "I'm talking about you and Ben. It was only a matter of days for you two." Her words sounded bitter, but she was distracted by her suddenly stinging eyes. She shifted her fingers to press above her brows, yet the words continued to flow. "You two met and married. Just that quick. Never mind even a short engagement. You were strangers."

Juli pressed her lips together. She looked down and looked aside, as if checking to make sure they were alone. She said, in a low voice, "That was different."

"No joke, it was different." She wanted to stop. A small voice in her head told her to stop. She ignored it. "There was no love involved, not for you. It was a business arrangement."

"Maia…"

"Ben thought he felt something for you. I know that. You accommodated him, and he was so happy."

"Accommodated…" Juli's voice trailed off, then returned stronger. "Maia. Ben and I…that was an unusual arrangement, a different situation."

"And then, conveniently, there was Luke."

"I knew Luke for over a year before he and I married." Her voice cracked. "There was nothing between us while Ben was alive."

Maia made that embarrassing noise again. It was as if her brain and her body were in cahoots, conspiring to betray her, encouraging her mouth to spew old, angry, unspoken words. Yes, sure, while you were married to Ben. That's when you knew Luke. How convenient for the both of you that he died.

But heaven rescued her in the nick of time and those last awful words weren't uttered aloud. They were true in the strictest sense, but they were unfair. It *had* been a different situation. She couldn't credit herself for showing restraint. She seemed to have lost all self-control. Her hands were suddenly in her hair, her fingers pressing against her scalp. She felt like her head was about to explode.

Juli said, slow and carefully, "Maia, are you okay?"

"I loved Ben, Juli. With all my heart. I loved him for years. You didn't love him." *Later*, she thought. You loved him later, but not when he broke my heart for you.

"Maybe we should discuss this when you're calmer." Juli's voice was soft and a little breathless.

Maia's voice rose. "Didn't you hear me? Was I speaking only to myself?"

"I heard you." She moved closer to Maia, but stopped when Maia stepped back. Juli crossed her arms, hugging herself. "You loved him. I don't doubt it."

"He was grieving when I met him. I was beginning to think that he was never going to get over his first wife...and then he met you. You took him. From me."

Juli's mouth opened, then shut again.

"You didn't know me. And you didn't know Ben was mine. You didn't even have to try and take him. It was like I meant nothing to him."

Juli looked dazed, or bemused. "I'm so sorry. I owe you so much. I would never have made it through those dark weeks after Ben died, if not for you."

Maia shook her head and held her hands up in front of her, raised in a defensive posture. "No, it's your fault, but not your fault. He never cared enough about me to spend even his last days with me."

"That's not true," Juli whispered. "He loved you very much. He trusted you, respected you, and valued you."

"But he wasn't *in* love with me. And if he did care about me, even as a friend, surely, he would've known I cared for him. I loved him. How could he not know?"

She waved her arms. "What? I'm not smart enough? Pretty enough? What's wrong with me that he preferred to marry a stranger?" She was slapping the glass top of the counter, she realized. It hurt her palms a little. Mostly, she felt ridiculous. Pointless. As pointless and disposable as she'd felt that day—the day that Ben had told her he'd met the young woman he wanted to marry, and then again, the day she'd stood with them on the beach at their wedding.

Her voice dropped. "And yet, I'm the one who remembers him. The one who cares enough to visit his grave. I bring him flowers and tell him everyone's news. I opened my heart to him years ago. To a man who never wanted it. And I still do. I can't stop." She sniffled and turned toward the counter to search for the tissues. "I understand about Luke, and you have Danny. I'm glad for you and that's how it should be. But Ben will always be first in my heart. Nothing can change that."

She heard the catch in Juli's voice, the gasp. She saw Juli's hands pressed to her chest, and then they moved to her face.

Maia was stricken. She'd gone too far. She'd spewed too much poison, too much resentment. Had known it while she was doing it, and now that it had been vented, sanity was returning. She started away from the counter, wanting to apologize, but Juli turned and fled toward the front door. She hardly paused, almost pretending not to see, to acknowledge Joel, standing at the half-opened door.

He looked stunned. Maia paused as her brain tried to process what her eyes were showing her—how long had he been there? In those long moments, Joel stepped back outside, releasing the door as he did. It swooshed closed.

Frantically searching for the right words, something that would make sense, explain all this embarrassing craziness, Maia rushed to the door. She yanked it open and flew down the steps. He was walking fast and was nearly to his car before she caught up to him.

"Joel, wait, please!" She didn't care who might be around or might hear. Only that Joel should hear, and wait for her. "Let me explain!"

He stopped beside his car. "What do you want?"

His expression was cold. His eyes, hard and glittering like ice, chilled her.

She put her hand on the car door, near his. "I need to talk to you. I don't know how much you heard, but I can explain."

"You don't owe me any explanation. If you owe me anything, it's something you owe yourself more. Truth. I was honest with you when I told you before, I won't play second-best to anyone."

Now she was conscious of eyes on them. Strangers' eyes.

"Joel, please come back into the building with me. Let's talk."

"No. I'm not going back into the gallery. That's done."

His words hurt. Words had such power and were so often wielded like weapons. Like she'd done with Juli? But the power in Joel's words was in the finality with which he said them. He lifted her hand gently from the car door.

"Excuse me," he said, as he opened the door and moved to climb in.

"Please, Joel. Did I mean anything to you or not? If I did, then let me speak now.".

Chapter Twenty-Two

Would anything she said make a difference? She took a deep breath. This required reasonableness.

"Joel, I'm sorry you heard all that unpleasantness. I don't know where it came from and I don't know how much you heard, but it was all old news. Old history, old feelings. Juli and I should've cleared the air long ago. I'm glad it's said now."

"Is Juli glad?"

"She will be. Juli is a very honest person, but a little more reticent than I am." She shook her head. "I'm sorry you heard me say those things. I know how it must have sounded." She tried to laugh politely. "But this had nothing to do with you. You weren't involved with all that back then."

"Back then? Not all that long ago as far as I can see. Two years? Less than that, right? And today, in present time, you're visiting a dead man and unburdening your heart to him?"

"That's not fair."

"Those were your words."

They had to communicate, get this said and get beyond it. She tried to sound matter-of-fact, as if the events were safely in the past.

"Amazing to think of all that has happened since that day, the day that Ben met Juli."

They'd started walking together along the marina. Joel appeared to be listening. He was calm. Courteous. But Maia felt undercurrents shifting between them. Suddenly that image of her reeling in a fish— that's what her mother had said—made her cringe. Her knees weakened. She was grateful for the bench and sat.

But Joel continued past her to a railing where he stopped and stared out across the water. She forced herself to stand again and joined him there.

"We lost Ben," she said. "We gained Danny. Luke and Juli married. Frannie came to *Captain's Walk*. Then you, and we met."

The scene before her glittered through unshed tears. She was determined to keep them unshed. She wouldn't play that false card. The tears would be real, but happening here and now, they felt manipulative. She touched his hand. "I'm glad I met you."

"Maia."

"Yes, Joel?"

"I enjoyed spending time with you. I hope you know that. I have feelings for you. I thought you felt the same. I thought there might be more."

"I do have feelings for you."

Joel cut her off. "Wait. Let me finish." He cleared his throat. "You always seemed to be holding back. I thought it was me. Now I understand."

"Wait a minute. You've been traveling. Working. I understand it isn't by choice. But how are we supposed to build something lasting, a real future, if we're always apart?"

"I was working that out. Sorry I couldn't do it faster. People do, though. They manage despite distances. All over the world. They work stuff out if they care enough." He touched her forearm. "I'm grateful that I overheard. I don't doubt it was painful for both of you, but you're probably right about needing to clear the air. But I'm not in that story. That's you and Juli and Ben." He sighed. "But in our relationship—yours and mine—I can't compete with a dead man."

"That's ridiculous and offensive."

"Is it? How can a person compete with a memory?"

"But everyone does, right? We all have them. As you said, if people care enough, they work it out."

"Maybe it's the difference in kinds of memories...or how deeply they have their hooks into us."

Maia shook her head. "I don't understand."

"It's about being willing to replace them with new memories."

She tried to feel encouraged. He was willing to discuss this with her, but there was a note in his voice she'd heard before with former boyfriends.

He shrugged. "Some memories are a part of us, our lives...but other memories are so much a part of us that they keep us tied to the past." He paused. "Like anchors, they chain us to yesterday."

A chill had been growing in her, beginning in her arms and legs, then heating up as it reached her chest and stomach.

She saw goodbye in his face and heard it in his voice.

"Maia," he said as he turned to face her fully, putting his hands on her shoulders and then moving them up around her neck in a soft, caressing motion until his fingers were in her hair.

He tilted her face up to his and put his lips gently to hers, first testing and finding no resistance, he pressed the kiss home.

She returned his kiss, her heart wanting to soar despite herself. Her arms found their own way around Joel to press against his back and pull him closer.

And then it stopped. Joel moved his face away from hers. She was still lost in the kiss, her eyes closed, and she opened them slowly. She stared into Joel's eyes. They looked sad, grieved.

"I'm not coming back this time. I'm sorry, Maia."

"Because of a memory? A dead man's memory?"

He nodded. "I won't share you with a memory, a ghost, a man who's been dead for two years. I told you before, I won't take second place, and I won't share your heart with him."

Maia whispered, "Is this about sharing my heart? Or about things going on in your own life?"

Joel wrapped his arms around her one more time...one last time...and whispered against her hair. "I'll miss you." Then he dropped his arms and walked briskly, not looking back.

She watched him as he crossed the parking lot, got into his car and drove off.

Stunned, she stumbled into the road nearly falling over the curb because she was still staring after him, expecting to see his car returning. She crossed the street and went up the steps to the gallery door where again she stood, watching and waiting. Finally, she went inside.

Maia stood in the middle of the room surrounded by the tables of souvenirs, the paintings hanging on the walls, the tall sculptures arrayed around the room like silent witnesses. It all looked dark and fuzzy. Meaningless. This was the biggest part of her life and it felt like a cold, alien world.

She walked back to the door, flipped the sign to close, killed the lights and turned the lock. She went to the customer service counter thinking she'd find something useful to do, some mundane task that would reconnect her with reality, with her life, with all the things she enjoyed, but there was no connection. Nothing had meaning.

When strangers came walking down the sidewalk outside, and paused, looking up at the building, she realized she'd been staring out the window. They glanced up at the door.

They couldn't see her from where they were, but if they climbed the steps and stood at the door, they would. Maia stepped away from the counter and into the shadows.

She needed to lie down. If she could just rest and relax for a little while, she'd be better able to think and understand. Make sense of this.

Maia climbed the stairs, feeling half-blind, and holding tight to the railing. She straightened the divan pillows and wrapped the shawl around her torso. She sat and slipped off her shoes. Each movement was deliberate and calm. Before putting her head down—she was desperately tired, of course she was after a day like today, and she needed rest—she took the small frame from the table. Ben.

Who cared? She cared. Yes, she did care about Ben and Juli and Joel. Caring hurt. She was grateful to be so numb because it made the pain seem distant. She tucked Ben's photo into the crook of her arm, near to her heart, thinking I had a chance at true love and I missed it. But was she thinking of Ben or Joel? Or both? Had she missed her opportunity twice?

CREED

Later, when Maia woke, she felt disjointed. Disoriented. Her neck was stiff and there was pain in the side of her chest and her arm screamed for attention. All around her, it was dark. Only weak moonlight lit the room.

Had she fallen? Injured herself? Was that why she was hurting?

And then she remembered. Joel had dumped her.

She sighed, but the sound was ragged. She'd been here before. But this time was different, wasn't it? This time it hurt desperately. It felt like a mortal blow. She knew it wasn't. People survived far worse. She would recover eventually. She always did.

She had a brief flash of memory, of Joel's smile, his kind eyes, his embrace, warm and urgent. She sat up and the frame fell from her grasp. That pain in her side and arm eased now that the frame's sharp, hard corners were no longer digging into her. The frame had fallen to her lap. She picked it up. In the dark, she could hardly see anything, much less Ben's face in the photo. She placed the frame back on the table and began hunting for her abandoned shoes.

Her phone. Where was it? Downstairs? It must be.

She left the lights off and felt her way to the stairs in the dark. She descended to the main gallery floor. There, the plate glass windows let in a flood of moonlight. It bathed the interior with a surreal aspect. On the counter, her phone waited, its screen brightly lit with notifications. The time read 4:10 a.m.

Maia had no interest in returning to the divan upstairs, nor in staying here in this place. She couldn't shake the otherworldly, nighttime eeriness of it. Like an old Twilight Zone movie, or that Stephen King story set in a world that was moving on, leaving only an unpeopled landscape, like an empty stage-set to be destroyed by the agents of time—she didn't want to still be here, miserable, while the world moved on.

If she turned on the lights, this nightmarish fantasy would suspend, but she would be visible from the street, on display to any middle of the night wanderers. A deputy might knock on the door to find out if everything was okay. She wasn't okay. Nothing would make her okay. At least not for a while. For now, she should go home.

She'd traveled this heartbreak road before. She'd make it through this time, too. She had a lot to be grateful for and she'd remember what those things were in a few days when she was feeling better.

After double-checking the front door—yes, it was locked—she turned to leave by way of the breakroom, and saw a package leaning against the counter. She paused.

Had Brendan forgotten to take care of something?

Was she really worrying about this? Always business? Even when she was feeling utterly broken?

Then she remembered Juli stopping by. Had that only been hours ago? She'd lost control, spewed awful words, and ultimately ended whatever was happening between herself and Joel. Who could blame him for moving on?

Enough, Maia.

Juli's package was wrapped in paper with light twine around it. She picked it up. There was surely a better place to put it for safekeeping. But it was lightweight. Not a stretched canvas or even hardboard.

She carried it to the breakroom where she could shut the door and turn on the overhead light. The breakroom had cozy memories for her. Many friends had shared lunches and hot cocoa here with her. Her eyes suddenly burned with unshed tears.

The twine was tied in a bow. She pulled one end and the twine fell away. Thinking of how Juli had taught Danny to unwrap his gifts, Maia slipped her index finger beneath a flap and lifted it.

A thick sheet of watercolor paper was secured between two large, stiff pieces of cardboard. For protection, she saw.

193

Bridle Cove.

Juli had started with light pencil whorls, then moved to splashes of watercolor. Maia bent over the artwork. Yes, that was pastel crayon employed around and integrated with the watercolor and pencil to deepen and solidify the ethereal and the earthly together into one image. The result was delicacy delineated with hints of savagery.

Maia was breathless.

She sat at the table, willing her fragile calm not to crack. She couldn't manage the walk home if she dissolved into tears. Nor could she leave Juli's artwork laying here, exposed and unprotected, on the breakroom table.

The gallery, and its contents, were her responsibility.

She knew where the spare frames were and knew she had one, just the right size, handy. It wouldn't be a polished frame job, but it would serve. It might even be appropriate to the clash of media and technique.

The frame was a deep teal color. Inappropriate, yes, and perfect. She brought it back to the breakroom, along with a gray-smudged, leftover mat she'd found hiding among those frames.

When she was done, she turned on the gallery light long enough to shift some other paintings and wall hangings to clear a space. She wanted to position Juli's work in a prominent place, yet out of the easy reach of dirty fingers. She stepped back checking the placement and the overall impact. Then she went to the counter, pulled out a piece of fine white cardboard used for labeling displays. She wrote on it, trimmed it to size, and then affixed it below Juli's mixed media art.

DISPLAYED COURTESY OF ARTIST, JULI WINTERS
NOT FOR SALE

She let herself out the back door. She had walked to work that morning...no, yesterday morning. Now she'd walk home. The streets were dark and quiet. Soon households would be stirring, families rising, parents preparing for the day. A dog slunk by in the darkness. A cat scooted past with an offended meow.

The streetlights showed her the breaks in the sidewalk and lit her way home, but as she let herself in to the door to her apartment, she noted that the first light of the new day was already blushing on the horizon.

Ready or not, tomorrow had become today. It looked very different than she'd expected such a short time ago.

Chapter Twenty-Three

Coffee. She needed coffee. She wasn't sleepy, so there was no hope she could retreat into the cocoon of blankets on her bed and find peace. But she needed to clear the brain fog, to joggle her senses. Caffeine should work.

Yesterday, and even the memory of waking in the dark and hanging artwork in the wee hours before dawn, seemed cloudy.

She got the hot water going in the shower and stood under it, but the fog couldn't be steamed away. It occurred to her that maybe the fog was a kindness, a buffer from reality. She could allow herself some emotional hiding, some pity-me time, but she wouldn't stay that way. She refused this state. Besides, Joel was wrong. He was wrong to break up with her, and he was wrong to do it the way he had, using Ben as the excuse. He was wrong. Even if he truly believed her heart belonged to...Ben. Ben. She sighed. If Joel did believe that, and if he loved her, then why wouldn't he fight for her?

He didn't know how to fight memories. That's what he'd said. Or had he said he didn't want to bother with fighting memories? Maybe she wasn't worth the effort?

Ben. His eyes and smile were there before her. They warmed her heart. Maybe the fog would lift now. And it did, a little. Ben.

On the other hand, if Joel had broken up with her because she was a cruel, grudge-bearing, anger-harboring harpy—well, she'd have trouble disputing that. He'd witnessed the outburst personally.

Her cruel words lingered with her. Perhaps regret and guilt contributed to her foggy state.

She turned on every light in the apartment. Dawn was in full bloom over the rooftops and a few cars moved along the street. Were they headed to work or to school? Or were they seeking coffee to dispel their own morning fog?

She texted Brendan and Luke notifying them that she wouldn't be in to work today.

They'd question the text. This was unlike her. And Memorial Day weekend was almost here. She texted them again.

"Don't worry. I'm fine. I'll be in touch."

She tried to remember whether it was Brendan or Lora who was scheduled to open the shop that morning, but gave up. Her gray matter wasn't working right.

Never mind. Luke could figure it out.

She wasn't hungry, but she knew warm food would help restore her. Just being out among the living would help. She'd get breakfast at the diner, shake off yesterday and prepare to move forward. Instead, she sat near the window. She told herself she was watching the day begin, that she wasn't watching for any particular person or car. She wasn't watching and waiting for someone who was never coming back.

When her eyes started burning, she shook herself. She could do this. She wouldn't sit here feeling sorry for herself.

ભ୍ୟୁ

If she dined in Beaufort, it was entirely possible that someone she knew would see her and expect a cheery good morning chat. Instead, she drove over the bridge to Morehead City. She hadn't been to the Cox Family Restaurant in a while. The traffic picking up on Arendell St. as the workday came to life. Maia found herself slowing the car as she approached 20th Street and the turnoff to the cemetery. She gave in to the pull.

The grass was damp and there was enough early morning chill in the air to make her glad she had a sweater in the car. She tugged it over her shoulders and walked to Ben's grave.

The flowers still looked good. They should, being plastic. A few droplets of dew clung to the grass near the headstone and sparkled in the new morning light. Maia brushed a fallen leaf from the headstone and then sat on the bench. It was surprisingly cold and damp, but she stayed anyway.

"Ben, so much has happened. I don't know where to start. I miss you. I miss having you to talk to." She stopped abruptly, noticing a woman was moving around a nearby grave. A fresher grave. Maia recognized the actions of tweaking the grass, of smoothing a bit of dirt, of arranging flowers. She didn't know the woman but felt a kinship. Many people had suffered losses. Anyone who had ever loved, had experienced this. She wasn't odd. Joel was wrong.

In the silence, a bird trilled and then she noticed other morning sounds and sat quietly to listen. The woman moved out of sight. Maia closed her eyes wishing she could curl up on this hard bench and rest. When she heard movement behind her, she first thought was of that woman and turned to speak, but it was Juli.

Juli said, "I'm sorry. You usually come on Sundays. Sometimes on Fridays, so I visit on other days. I wasn't expecting to see you here."

Her tone was flat. It matched Maia's emotions.

Juli was dressed in jeans and a cotton top. She was neat enough, but not as put together as she usually was—as Juli usually made sure to be before going out into public.

As if Juli had read her mind, she plucked at her shirt and smoothed the denim of the jeans, saying, "It was early. I woke early, thinking of...well, Ben. You know. After yesterday, I guess."

Maia felt a wall materialize. A shocking, unexpected, invisible wall.

"Mind if I sit with you?" She sat, anyway, not waiting for confirmation.

"You never bring flowers," Maia said.

Juli smiled sadly. "No, there's only room for just so many and your choices are always beautiful."

Maia fought it—the word, No, and the need to push Juli away. Juli didn't come here. This was Maia's place. Her task. She, Maia, had accepted this duty because no one else had. Because she was the one who remembered, the one who cared the most. She wanted to speak, but her breath was coming too fast. She looked away not knowing where to settle her gaze.

She asked, "Are you angry with me?"

"For what? For speaking your heart?"

Maia shook her head, but kept her eyes on the grave.

Juli took Maia's hand in hers and held it loosely. "Why are you here so early?"

Maia said, "I'm sorry. I'll leave and let you visit Ben."

Juli's hand tightened on hers. "Stay," she said.

"I'm allowed to visit his grave. He was my friend before...."

"Before he met me? Yes, he was. He was your friend until the day he died."

Maia blinked. She wanted to yank her hand away. Run.

"I've been wanting to say this to you for a while now. I didn't know how or when. It never seemed to be the right time." She paused. "And yesterday became emotional so quickly. For both of us, Maia." She looked down. "I'm sorry I left so abruptly. I felt overwhelmed. I didn't know what to say that wouldn't make it worse."

Maia felt herself shrinking. Shrinking within herself. She was staring at Ben's headstone again, but her field of vision also seemed to be shrinking, shutting out everything around them.

"I'm sorry I didn't take better care of him," Juli said. "I'm sorry. If I had...if I'd been a better wife, a better friend, he would never had died the way he did."

"What?" The words burst out. "That's ridiculous. His death wasn't your fault. In fact, if he hadn't drowned...."

Juli nodded and rocked their hands gently. "I tell myself that. But

199

sometimes...." She swallowed hard and then continued. "I woke up crying this morning. I didn't know why. Sometimes it just happens that way. Luke was in a hurry, on his way out, and didn't notice. But Danny did. When I picked him up from the crib, he touched my cheek. His fingers were wet. He said, "Danny sorry, mama." And he started crying, too."

Juli pressed one finger to a sinus point in the middle of her forehead and squeezed her eyes shut for a moment, then she resumed, "I said, No, sweetheart, don't cry. Everything is fine. We are fine." She added her other hand to the one she was already holding Maia's with. "And we are. We are fine."

Maia repeated, "We are fine." Suddenly, she asked, "Wait. Luke was on his way out? Where's Danny?"

"Esther has him. She adores him, you know. She was feeding him breakfast when I left. I felt...I felt compelled to come here, especially this morning. I thought maybe I really had lost my mind, but now I understand."

Maia shook her head. "What do you understand? I want to understand. I don't understand anything."

"You've been a blessing to me, Maia. A blessing. My life changed when I met Ben. Through Ben, I met you and I met Luke. I have Danny. I found the power of faith. That faith has made the difference for me."

"I have faith. I have a church and a church family."

"Yes, but that's not what I meant. In order to get what I needed, what I wanted, I had to give up what I prized most—my belief in myself and my self-reliance—to learn. To learn what I didn't even know I needed to learn. It took that for me to understand I don't have to do this life all alone. Even when I lost Ben, I still had the gifts he brought to my life. Sometimes, and this will sound silly, but I almost feel like he put those gifts into my care. To care for in his absence. You are one of those gifts. And I apologize for not being a better friend."

This time Maia successfully pulled her hand free.

"You've been a fine friend. I'm only here because someone needs to care for Ben's grave. Or so I thought." She stood abruptly and noticed Juli's eyes were swimming and one tear slipped down her cheek. "Truly, I don't mind. I do have to go now. Please excuse me."

"Maia," Juli whispered. "One more thing. Something I need to tell you."

Maia paused. She didn't want to, but she had to, right? It was the courteous thing to do, plus Juli seemed distressed.

"One day I asked Ben why he'd chosen to pursue me, to ask me to marry him, to spend his last weeks with me." She paused and took a deep breath. "I asked him "why me" when he had you and others who would willingly have given him companionship? He said it was because you were his friends, that you would, as friends and loved ones do, hover, reminding him he was sick and be hurt all the more by seeing him weaken and going through the long days and nights of losing him."

Juli paused, but Maia didn't move. She knew Juli wasn't finished.

"I didn't tell him, though I knew by then, that you loved him."

Maia protested, "Many people loved Ben. That's how Ben was."

"No, I knew that you were in love with him. Head over heels kind of love. I didn't tell him. I didn't think it was my place. Perhaps I was wrong. But, if I had…"

Maia stood, breaking their handclasp.

"If I had, I was sure he'd feel awkward around you. It would color those last memories you'd have with him."

Maia turned and left. Fled. She moved heedlessly past the headstones and memorials and made it to her car, her refuge. But it wasn't her refuge. There was no comfort here. She gunned the engine and sped out onto the main road never pausing to check for traffic. She skipped going to the restaurant for breakfast. She was in no fit state for public interaction.

Her apartment wasn't a refuge either. She wouldn't go to the gallery. Juli had spouted a lot of words but she hadn't mentioned why Luke was in a hurry. Maia felt sure he'd seen her text and was at the gallery. If somehow, he wasn't, and if the gallery didn't open today, that was okay, too. The world would still turn on its axis until Luke or Brendan stepped up to handle the business.

Maia threw clothing into her duffel bag and tossed toiletries in on top. She had what she needed and other than stopping to gas up, she was heading to Bridle Cove. It wasn't likely to be in use by the family during the work week.

If she texted Cathy and people started talking and speculating, then she'd be too easy to find by well-meaning people, people who should just keep their mouths shut and their thoughts to themselves.

People who should worry about their own lives and leave her alone.

☙❧

Bridle Cove was as shabby-cozy as ever. It welcomed her. She went down to the river, stood on the fine-sand beach and found the expanse of river meeting river as blue and serene as ever. Reassured, she tugged on the rope swing and found it still solid. She sat.

The narrow curve of sandy beach was littered with broken shells and some long grasses that had washed up. She would bring her small rake down here later and tidy it up.

Juli's painting. She couldn't shake the familiar, yet foreign essence of it. Juli had captured the deep mystery of the water, the slash of the sun, and the inherent tidy untidiness of nature. Untidy by human standards, she amended. Yet, over the things they governed—or had some hope of governing—like their choices, people were the untidiest of all.

Gradually, her brain, her heart, grew quiet. The water sang softly as it flowed by. The grasses whispered in the breeze. Maia began to feel her pain ease.

She'd never wanted to inflict her pain on anyone. But she had, and she'd done it with a vengeance. Was she really blaming Juli for her own failure to find love? That was laughable.

Juli wasn't that kind of person either so why had she felt compelled to share that un-charming anecdote about not telling Ben that Maia was in love with him?

How did that change anything? Help anything?

It didn't. She'd said something else, too. About waking up crying in the morning? That it happened sometimes?

Maybe Juli did still grieve. She never really showed it, but it seemed reasonable. And if Juli grieved for a man she'd known for a few months, then how much more would she, Maia, and the other people who'd loved Ben for years, grieve?

Suppose Ben had realized she loved him? Had come to understand he'd hurt her badly by his impulsive act? Would she have wanted him to bear that knowledge on his mind, his heart—especially an act he couldn't undo—as part of his last days? No. He hadn't loved her in the way she'd loved him. That wasn't his fault.

She pressed her hand over her heart.

Love wasn't about justice or common sense. Like nature, time, and all those things people wanted to control and couldn't, love just was. It was what it was.

Unrequited love. It wasn't uncommon. Friendship was common, open to all, and every instance should be cherished.

Juli was right about Ben bringing them together. That was certainly true. Ben had died way before his time, but he had made a difference in the lives of others. Ben would've considered that a life well-lived. And Maia had to agree.

But she felt bleak. And lost. Anger still stirred within her. She wished there was some sort of roadmap that would help her get her head and heart happy again, and her life back on track.

Chapter Twenty-Four

Maia carried the rest of her stuff into the house. The morning was already growing hot and she opened the windows. The screens were sagging but without too many tears. The old rips had been repaired with sewn stitches. It gave the screening an odd, almost artistic effect. Maia wished she had a good camera. She didn't have much skill with photography, but the old windows and patched screens would yield intriguing black and white photos. She could frame them. Hang them in the gallery maybe. Someday.

She wished she hadn't thought of photos. Ben's face. Joel's face. They plagued her, haunting her. Regrets? Anger? She couldn't parse out the individual feelings from among the dizzying morass to figure out what was reasonable and what didn't matter.

Maia plugged in a fan and went through the house fluffing cushions to get rid of dust, and then swept behind the sofa and chair. She ran the dust mop across the floors and pushed it around under the beds. So far, so good. No signs of rodents.

She set up the hammock outside, but couldn't climb aboard. There was still too much turmoil swirling in her. She couldn't relax.

She showered to cool off and ate some peanut butter and crackers, then lay down on the sofa because the air currents were best there. She dozed off and woke several hours later feeling warm and slightly nauseous. Fuzzy.

Her internal clock was totally out of whack. If she wasn't careful her new normal would be waking at three or four am. Not a welcoming hour. The only thing good about being awake at that time was that it was easier to avoid the rest of the world.

She stumbled to the kitchen, splashed water on her face and ate more crackers. She should've planned better for the food situation. She hadn't planned this time and her instincts had failed her. The only real options were the canned goods. She finished up the peanut butter and brewed some too-old coffee. The pickings were very lean.

The old washing machine looked like it still had some life in it, so she took down the cotton curtains in the various rooms and tossed them in to wash. While they were out of the way, she dusted the blinds and washed the windows. Her hair, short though it was, kept falling in her face, tickling her forehead and cheeks. She grew tired of pushing it back, so she tied a strip of fabric around her head like a sweatband.

It was past noon and humid. She was sweaty and grimy in no time. It felt good sweating out all the anger and anxiety. Life's poison. She could feel it being forced out of her body. She could stay here forever. Or wished she could. She'd like to hide here and forget the rest of the world.

She put the kitchen chairs on top of the kitchen table and washed the floor, then went to work sweeping the front and back porches.

As the afternoon wore on, the sweat was running in rivulets down her face and stinging her eyes, she stood in front of the fan with her arms spread wide and felt evaporation work its cooling magic. Maybe it blew away those troubling, nagging faces, too, because nothing and no one seemed to be haunting her for the moment and she was exhausted.

The perspiration dried but she still felt grimy, gritty and disheveled—which she was. She stood at the sink and guzzled a large glass of water and then stumbled out to the hammock where she crashed in the shade of the Carolina pines.

CREO

"Is she okay?"

She heard the whisper. Was it a dream?

"I think so. She looks...."

"Yeah. That's how she looks."

"Shhh. Don't wake her."

Maia kept her eyes closed. She refused to open them. Some of the words floated away but she knew the voices. Juli and Frannie.

Together? Here? That realization was enough to force her eyes open. She looked at them. Juli appeared faintly alarmed, caught in the grip of some flavor of drama or desperation. Frannie was mostly hidden behind Juli.

Juli said, "You're awake."

"Sorry." Frannie spoke in a loud whisper. "We didn't want to disturb you."

Too late now. Maia frowned at Juli.

"Are you okay? You look...."

"I look awful. Is that what you want to say?" Maia struggled to sit up and the hammock swung, ready to dump her.

Juli steadied it. She gripped the hammock and held it. "You look very angry. That's what I was going to say."

Frannie kept her mouth shut this time.

Juli added, "Maybe not angry, but fierce."

"Yes, fierce is a better word," Maia said.

Juli asked, "Have you been cleaning house?"

What did it matter?

Exasperated, Maia said, "Why? Why do you ask? Why are you here?" She swung her legs over the side nearly kicking Juli's arm. Juli continued to hold the hammock steady anyway.

Frannie said, "You look thirsty. I'll get you something to drink." She took off, going straight into the house.

Maia fastened her stare on Juli. "Is this some new routine? I want to be alone and you follow me?"

Her words, her manner was testy, and deliberately so. She offered no welcome. Not this time.

Juli flinched as Maia spoke, but she didn't turn away.

"You can be angry at me all you want. I need your help."

"Ask Frannie for help."

Juli shifted her eyes toward the house as if trying to convey a message.

"You drove here together, right? Looks like you made it okay." Maia started to walk away. "I'm sure you two can manage your lives without me."

"Wait," Juli said, but her voice broke before she could finish saying the word.

"What?" Maia said with irritation, but she waited.

Juli cocked her head back toward the house and spoke low, so low that Maia could hardly hear her.

"What did you say?"

"Keep your voice down."

"I can't hear you."

"It's Brian and Frannie. Something happened."

"Is Brian okay?"

"Yes, I mean he's not injured or anything."

"Okay. Fine. Then they can handle their own issues." Again, she tried to leave Juli. Go somewhere. She had no idea where, but standing here was ridiculous and infuriating.

Juli grabbed her arm. "They've called off the wedding."

"Do what?"

Juli gave an exaggerated shrug. "She won't talk about it. Maybe that's for the best, so please don't mention it. You'll get her upset all over again. It's Brian she needs to talk to. She was all ready to head back to Raleigh. I stopped her. I told her I wanted her to come with me to visit you."

Maia pressed her hands to the sides of her face. Her head was starting to throb. "What? Why?" She massaged her temples. "She should talk to Brian."

"Of course. Exactly. I thought it would be good to delay her, keep her from running away. Give her a chance to calm down and think.

207

Bringing her here was all I could think of."

"What am I supposed to do about it?"

Juli shook her head. "Nothing. In fact, it's good that you look sick. She'll see that we need to stay and help you."

"Help me? Please don't help me. I want to be alone. Tell her to talk to Brian and you go home to your husband and son."

"Maia. We need your help."

Maia closed her eyes and sighed. She was the helper. Everyone came to her to solve whatever. Mostly, she didn't mind. But where was her help when she needed it? And where was her peace?

Now Juli had a hand on each of her arms. She whispered, "Just play along for now, okay? Give me a chance to figure this out?"

Frannie called, "Is she okay? Is she fainting?"

The door slammed, and Frannie joined them at a run. She pushed a wet cloth onto Maia's face, then she put her hands on Maia, too, on her arm and her back, as if supporting her.

"No, I'm fine. Or I would be." Maia tried to disengage and move away, but then they were all moving together toward the porch as if she couldn't manage it under her own power, and she let them control the movement for the moment because it was just easier. This was all too confusing.

A breakup, Juli had said.

She looked at Frannie. "Are you okay?"

Frannie smiled weakly. Her eyes looked worried. "I'm fine. Let's get you inside. We need to get you hydrated and fed."

Get her fed? As if she were an invalid?

Maia sat at the kitchen table. "There's no real food."

Frannie said, "Juli brought some groceries. She was just coming from the grocery store when we ran into each other."

Maia frowned. Something didn't add up here. If she could just get her brain working again, she'd figure it out.

"Be right back with the food." Juli said, then with a strange nod— a nod that said remember what I told you—toward Maia, she went out to the car.

"I don't understand," Maia said, looking at Frannie now. "How did you two come to be here?"

"Juli drove. I was...heading out of town and she persuaded me to delay...and so we drove up here instead."

And that told Maia exactly nothing.

"How's Brian?"

"Fine? You know how he...." She took a deep breath and bit her lip.

Maybe if she'd had more patience, been in a more sensitive mood, Maia could've pulled more details out of Frannie. But she wasn't and didn't try.

"I'm going to grab a shower."

Frannie's expression brightened. "Good idea. As soon as Juli gets back in here, we'll cook up a meal. That will help us all."

Maia grunted wordlessly. This made no sense. Frannie didn't seem devastated by any means. So maybe she hadn't loved Brian after all? Could she have judged them so wrong? What would their mother say?

Suddenly, Maia did feel a surge of thanks that Juli had delayed Frannie's departure. As volatile as Brian and Frannie could be, perhaps a bump or two in the road to the wedding shouldn't surprise anyone.

The small bathroom was stuffy. The tiny window over the tub was stuck fast, having been painted shut many years ago. The hot shower was changed to cool too quickly and was decidedly more refreshing. Cold might be more useful. Maia felt like she needed a shock to wake her, so she could make sense of her current state.

She'd fled here, in part due to Joel and Juli. Juli, as she'd done before, had followed her here because she "needed" help with something. Bah. Maia believed it before, but this time it didn't ring true. False. More likely she come here out of guilt over what she'd said at the cemetery that morning.

Maia cracked the door open to allow the steam to escape the room. Fresh air came in, bringing cooking smells with it. But, gee, the air was hot. No kidding. If she owned Bridle Cove, she would install AC first thing.

She was toweling her hair, planning to leave it wet because it was cooler that way, when she heard a raised voice through the open door. She stopped.

It was Frannie's voice. Maia stepped out into the hallway. Frannie must've gone out to the front porch, perhaps thinking she'd have more privacy, but her voice came right through the screen door and funneled back via the hallway on the breeze.

"No," she said. "I don't care."

After a pause, Frannie resumed, "It's done. There's nothing more to discuss. I don't care, Brian. I don't want to talk about it anymore. Done."

As the call ended, Maia realized she was holding her breath.

She'd been on the verge of thinking that the breakup was nothing more than a ruse, an excuse Juli had manufactured as a reason to barge in. And had drafted Frannie into it with her for some bizarre reason.

She wished it had been a ruse.

Once she'd accepted the reality of Brian and Frannie as an engaged couple, it had felt more and more right. Now, well, if this was true and it must be, then what about Brian? How was he handling it? He could become reckless when upset. Was this something she could ask Frannie about? Maybe it wasn't as dire as it seemed. Maybe with a little help....

Then she remembered how angry Brian had been when she interfered with him and Diane. She'd only wanted to help. Get counseling. Try harder, she'd urged. And the whole mess had grown sourer and uglier. Brian would've done better to trust his first instinct and ignore his sister. But because of Megan, he'd tried. And been so angry ultimately, that he'd avoided Maia and the rest of the family for months.

She paused, the towel still in her hand and pressed against her. She didn't want to go through that again with Brian.

A small voice argued that Brian himself had asked her to help.

But in truth, she knew he only wanted help with moving the wedding plans forward because, in Brian's opinion, Frannie was dragging her heels.

Clearly, that signaled potential for real trouble. And now here it was. Trouble.

Could she ask Frannie? If, for instance, the trouble was resulting from the pressure about deciding the wedding details then, well, that would be okay to ask about, right? Brian himself had pulled her into that.

She mopped at a drip running down her throat. Maybe she could test the water, so to speak. See what she could discover. Juli might have details, too, that she hadn't yet revealed. And then, depending upon what she did or didn't find out, she would call Brian. Not call. Better to speak with him in person.

After all, Brian was her brother. Frannie was potentially her sister by marriage. And then there was Mom. Mom and Dad and everyone—none of them needed to be saddled with the distress of a broken engagement. Heaven knew, they'd only just had the engagement party. There'd be a ton of people who'd be trying to dig out the details if the engagement was broken off, especially so soon.

Here she was, being dragged back into other people's problems. But she was born to help others. The ability to help was ingrained in her even if doing it felt like a nuisance these days. It was like a super power. Hers. She should use those powers to help her brother and Frannie, if she could.

Maia slipped from the hallway into the bedroom where she kept the few clothing items she'd brought. She dressed and fluffed out her damp hair. She followed the aroma of food down the hallway to the kitchen.

She joined Juli and Frannie, and this time, she watched and listened with much keener eyes and ears.

Chapter Twenty-Five

Juli scrambled the eggs while Frannie buttered toast.

"I like breakfast for supper," Maia said, pulling out plates and utensils, but she kept a sharp eye on Frannie. Was there distress or anger in her voice or manner? Any indication of how serious this problem was between Brian and Frannie? It troubled Maia. In the same way that she had expected to see a newly-engaged woman head over heels in love, walking on clouds and flashing her shiny new ring around, she expected a woman on the edge of cancelling that engagement to be distraught.

Frannie was different though. She'd proved that before. She seemed anxious now, but then she often did. There was no hint of tragedy or drama. Every time Frannie caught Maia looking at her, Frannie would avert her gaze or turn away quickly, so that confirmed there was a problem.

She was still wearing the ring, so she hadn't called the engagement off yet, despite what Juli had said.

When they were seated and eating, Maia asked Juli, "You said Danny is with Esther. Is Luke at the gallery today?"

"I believe so."

Maia then turned to Frannie. "And Brian? Is he wondering where you've gone? Or did you tell him before you left?"

No one spoke.

She looked directly at Frannie and said, "I ask because I wouldn't want him to worry or anything."

Frannie shook her head vigorously and then clapped a hand to her face.

Immediately contrite, Maia dropped her fork and went to stand beside Frannie. She leaned down, putting a hand on Frannie's shoulder. "Are you okay? If Brian has done something, tell me. He probably didn't mean anything by it. You know how men are...and Brian is the worst." She put her hand on Frannie's. "Is this a problem that can be worked out?"

The front door slammed. They'd been so focused on the cooking and conversation that they hadn't heard the motorcycle drive up. Good thing it was Brian and not someone dangerous, thought Maia. On the other hand, it was Brian, and he had a temper, though it was mostly bluster, and his face was flushed. From the helmet, she wondered? Or?

He spoke as he walked into the kitchen. "What needs to be worked out? Nothing between us, Fran. Isn't that right?"

Frannie jumped up. "No, but let's step outside and talk."

Maia said, "Don't let him bully you, Frannie. If you want to speak to him, fine. If not, then don't."

Brian didn't even glance Maia's way. He kept his eyes trained on Frannie. "What was up with the phone call? You sounded so strange. Is something wrong?" He paused, cleared his throat, and added, "Do you need my help?"

Frannie sort of melted. Maia was astounded as Frannie's expression changed from anxious to glowing and smiling. Her posture relaxed, and she tilted her head to look at him. She said, her voice soft and warm, "We're good."

"Hold on," Maia said. "What do you mean, you're good? I thought you and Brian were having a crisis?" She drilled her gaze into Frannie and Juli, but Frannie had pressed herself into Brian's arms and they were kissing.

Maia turned to Juli. "What's going on? What is this?"

Juli held up her hands. "I can explain."

"They aren't breaking up?"

Juli shook her head no.

The plan was unravelling—whatever kind of madcap plan it had been. In fact, it hadn't been more than thirty minutes or so since she'd overheard that phone call. Maia turned to Brian and Frannie.

"What are you even doing here, Brian? How did you get here so quickly?"

"Quickly?" he asked, looking over his fiancé's shoulder.

"You were on the phone with her just a short time ago."

"I was coming to pick her up when she called to tell me not to, so I came all the faster, of course."

Frannie put her finger to his lips. "Hush. Let me explain." She stepped away from Brian.

"I'm sorry, Maia. Brian and I are fine. When Juli and I were driving up here we thought...we decided it would be good to have a reason. I mean a reason that didn't involve Joel. We came up with this idea to—"

Juli interrupted. "It's my fault and I'll manage the confession and the explanation."

Frannie looked relieved. Brian looked interested.

"I came because I was worried about you. Frannie and I wanted to distract you and give you something to focus on...instead of...you know."

"Joel."

Brian said, "What's up with Joel?"

Maia closed her eyes and drew in a slow, deep breath. She said, "We broke up. We're done."

Brian harrumphed. "I'm not surprised. He wasn't good enough for you. He's just too...what do you call it? Too polite? Not much of a guy, really."

Maia raised her voice. "Not true, Brian. Joel's a great guy and he's handling a lot of responsibilities and the problem is me." She finished weakly. "I'm the problem, not Joel."

Brian shook his head slowly as he walked over to where she stood. He put his hands on her arms. "You are not the problem. Joel's not good enough for you. If he comes around bothering you, let me know. I'll take care of him."

Maia's eyes opened wide despite her attempt at cool. "No, you will not. I can't believe you'd even talk that way. If Joel and I ever get a second chance—" She broke off.

Brian kept his face grave and stared into her eyes. "So, you'd consider giving him another chance?" He waited. When she didn't respond, he said, "So, then maybe it's not over. Not in a forever kind of way?"

She shook her head. "I don't know, Brian." She touched his cheek. "You did that on purpose, didn't you? Saying those awful things?"

He grinned. "I do mean part of it. If he hurts you, Sis, he'll have me to deal with."

She threw her arms around him and hugged him.

"In the meantime, don't be confusing me and my fiancé. We're good and have plans to make." He released Maia and turned to Frannie. "You ready to go?"

Frannie and Juli exchanged glances.

Juli said, "I'll bring her back to *Captain's Walk* this evening. Or to your house. Whatever."

"Why? I have a helmet for her."

Frannie said to Brian, "Come outside with me. I'll tell you about our plans."

As Brian and Frannie walked out to the porch, Juli turned to Maia. "We're going to New Bern. I hope you'll come with us."

"Was that part of the plan? Where I come from, deliberately false and misleading statements are called lies."

"Lies?" Juli said. "I guess so. I'm sorry about that, but we needed a reason to intrude and we needed a mission to get you involved with. The trip to New Bern seemed a good solution for the mission part, plus you know Frannie's been wanting to do the trip, and we really need you along to help."

"Still manipulating?"

"Again, I'm sorry. I meant well. Don't blame Frannie. It was all my idea. I shouldn't have interfered. I was worried about you."

"After what I said to you at the gallery?"

"I understood about that. I'm glad you got it out. I'm just sorry Joel overheard." She grimaced. "If you think it will help, I'll speak with him myself."

"No, please. No more. Not from you or Frannie or Brian or anyone. This is between Joel and me."

Juli nodded. "I promise. Now will you come with us to visit Frances' grave?"

"It's a trip you and Frannie should make together."

"Together with you. The three of us. Please."

Maia shrugged, tired of fighting. The lethargy of the day was moving back in on her. "Fine, then. Let's go."

"When? I think it's too late today."

"Tomorrow? It's not exactly a long trip. An hour each way, more or less. Let's go first thing in the morning and get it over with."

"Thank you," Juli said.

"Good," Brian said. "You gals go. Get it done so we can get back to business."

"Business?" Frannie asked.

"The business of planning our wedding."

"One thing doesn't have anything to do with the other."

"Great. Let's go choose a cake."

Frannie pushed at Brian's arm. "Enough."

Brian laughed and Frannie's annoyance faded away. Maia saw the silent communication passing between their eyes, and saw their happiness. They didn't need her help. They already had exactly what they needed.

Juli gave Maia a look before they left, one that she understood to say, "We'll be back in the morning. Please don't change your mind."

Honestly, Maia thought. Juli's an adult. She should be able to deal with something this simple.

Maia spoke to Frannie through the open car window.

"Bring whatever info you have from that investigator about where she's buried. I don't remember hearing the name of the cemetery."

Frannie said, "It's in New Bern, he said. He sent a plat, but I can't make sense out of it. There isn't a cemetery name on the plat. It's just a hand-drawing."

"Bring it tomorrow. We'll figure it out."

Chapter Twenty-Six

Juli and Frannie arrived at Bridle Cove mid-morning. Maia had risen early, had enjoyed dawn down by the water, but then suddenly hungry, she ate and showered, and was ready for their road trip early.

She wanted to feel helpful. She didn't, and this reminder that she didn't, felt forced upon her by Juli and Frannie and annoyed her. She felt that resentment especially hard when Juli climbed into the driver's seat and Frannie took the front passenger seat. Maia was left to settle alone into the back seat. Which was fine. Except it wasn't.

"What's the plan?" she asked.

Frannie handed her an envelope. "That odd paper the investigator called a plat is in there. Take a look. The only intelligible words written on it are Harris Garber Road." Her neck was craned around awkwardly as she tried to speak to Maia from the front seat. "I looked on a map and found a Garber Road, but not a Harris Garber Road. I thought maybe we should start by going to a police or fire station and ask them if they've heard of Harris Garber Road. How does that sound?"

Maia shrugged, not really meaning to be rude but it didn't sound like much of a plan to her—no more than what could be accomplished over the phone with a lot less gas and hassle—so she kept her mouth shut and examined the paper. In truth, the "plat" looked like a greatly enlarged portion of something else, though it was clear that some of the markings indicated graves. As Frannie had said, Harris Garber road was written on the paper near the bottom right edge, but faintly, with perhaps additional text being cut off. Again, it looked like a poor photocopy job. She wanted to ask Frannie why she hadn't followed back up with her investigator and asked for a usable copy, but clearly, she hadn't, and they were here now already on the trail, so what was the point?

She moved on to the other document in the envelope. This was Frances Cooke's death certificate. The poor woman had had a short, hard life. She'd given birth to two children she'd never been able to enjoy, had lost them both, one to divorce and the other to social services, and had then died of pneumonia while still in her twenties.

Maia shook her head, feeling the tragedy, the futility of it, and looked away.

The countryside sped by to the rhythm of the tires on the road. Maia stared out the window, but without really seeing anything. It seemed she was spending her life surrounded by cemeteries these days, and by problems that were mostly other people's problems, and that she had no heart for. Despite what Juli had said about her helping others...what was she supposed to do? Turn her back? Lately, she'd caught herself wanting to do that. It wasn't a reaction she was proud of. Being of service should be reward enough. Maia had always believed that. Sometimes you just had to push down your annoyance or fatigue. Even if you weren't feeling it, the action counted. The act was what made a difference in someone's life.

But when you didn't feel it, no matter how worthwhile the good deed, it felt hollow inside.

Maia remembered a conversation she and Juli had had a long time ago, after Ben was gone but before she married Luke. Juli had said she didn't understand people who were always eager to help others. Maia had told her then that she had a heart for service, that she wanted to help others. Mostly, that was true. Lately, it wasn't true. Her heart was confused and otherwise occupied. And it wasn't just about Ben and Joel. Maia hoped that if she kept her dissatisfaction hidden, no one would know. It would be her secret and hopefully, one day her head and heart would be back in sync. One day soon, she prayed.

Maia sighed as they passed one small town after another with miles of woodland in between. It should've been a pretty drive with all this scenery, but there wasn't much conversation coming from the front seat. Maia read the tension in Juli's stiff posture and her fingers clenched around the steering wheel. Frannie was a study in anxiety.

If they'd just talk, Maia thought. No matter what about. The camaraderie they displayed back at Bridle Cove when they were trying to manipulate her had vanished. Maia sat in the back seat and reflected that it served them right, for messing in her business to the point that even Brian was aware (and who might he tell?) and then pressuring her to come along. At this point, Maia could see it was just how things would be until they found Frances Cooke's grave. Maybe it would be better on the return trip home.

Maia took another look at the plat. Harris Garber Road. But if she stared, she could just about see a dash between Harris and Garber. That didn't necessarily mean anything. It could even be just one of those odd dots that sometimes show up on photocopy enlargements, but…. Maia took another look at the death certificate. Harris was the last name of the person reporting the death.

Maia used her phone to search for Garber Road in the New Bern area. She found a promising result, but before she could announce it, Juli spoke.

"Exactly what do you hope to get out of this, Frannie?"

Her tone sounded harsh. Juli must be feeling a lot of stress with this trip, so much that it was forcing its way out. Maia held her breath.

"No expectations," Frannie said. "I'm trying not to overthink it. We don't know what we'll find. But I know we'll be sorry if we don't try."

"Correction. We know what we'll find, or rather, won't find. That private detective you hired said the grave is unmarked. We don't even know why she was here in the New Bern area." Juli coughed. "Are we really just going to ride around chatting with deputies and firefighters, telling strangers over and over about our dirty laundry and what we're doing?"

"Dirty laundry? What dirty laundry? All families have problems.

As for this trip, for today, we'll do the best we can, that's all. One step at a time." After a pause, Frannie added, "Someday I hope you'll be willing to tell me what you recall of your life with our mother."

On that last word, "mother," the car swerved. Frannie exclaimed in surprise. She glanced at Juli who quickly recovered. The car was moving smoothly again, with no harm done, except for the sudden shot of adrenalin they'd all received.

Maia's view of Frannie's profile as she glared at Juli, alarmed her. She thought for a moment that Frannie might full-out accuse Juli of scaring them on purpose. Would Juli have done such a thing? No, Maia knew that, but Frannie might not. In the end, Frannie said nothing but leaned closer to her door and made a show of staring out the window.

Thus far, Maia had tried not to trespass on the heart of this trip. She'd done her part by sitting back here, alone and quiet. No one seemed to appreciate that. Which annoyed her.

They'd dragged her along on a trip where she was as needed as a flat spare tire. As a mediator? Or to keep her busy? To make her feel needed? Which was just another way saying she wasn't needed. That this was some kind of pity invite.

While she respected Juli's bad memories and Frannie's need to know, there were far worse troubles in the world and far worse things for these two gals to worry over in their own lives. At least Frannie and Brian, and the state of their engagement, wasn't one of those things. Maia had never known Juli to be devious and deceitful, and Frannie, for all that she was smart and chic, had no gift for deception, so while respect for honesty had suffered in their little ruse, it was only a bit tarnished. Her own dignity had suffered a bit, too, over being fooled. But she was also grateful. She might worry over her brother and his fiancé and the wisdom of their engagement, but at least their hearts were still whole and intact, and the two were still in love.

The only sound was the hum of the tires on the road surface.

Maia broke the silence. "Why am I here?"

Frannie jumped and Juli stared into the rearview mirror at Maia. "To go with us," she said.

"You don't need me. It would be more effective if you two would discuss this like adults. I thought you were about to, but then you lost control of the car. Do you need someone else to drive?"

"Not fair. It wasn't on purpose. A squirrel ran in front of the car. Didn't you see it?" Juli paused. "Maia, I heard that noise you just made. That snorty noise and acting like you don't believe me. But I've hit squirrels before when I couldn't avoid it. Sometimes they seem suicidal. And the sound of them hitting the tire, or worse, going under the tire with that plunk sound, stays with me."

Frannie said, "I agree. I can't stand that either."

"See?" Juli said, still staring at Maia in the rearview mirror.

"Oh, goody," Maia said. "Something we can all agree on. We swerve for squirrels." And saying that, Maia realized she was shutting down the conversation again, almost as if she intended to, instead of building on the squirrel thing. It was stupid, but at least, they were agreeing on that.

Did she want to shut them down? Maybe she needed to check her own motives. At the very least, her attitude.

"So, I found Garber Road. The one that's mentioned on the map? I don't think it's Harris Garber Road. I think Harris is tacked on there for another reason. I suggest we do this—take the second exit after the Neuse River Bridge and then we'll go a few miles to a place called Garber's Crossroads.

Looks like it's out in the country. Hopefully, there, we'll get more information. Unless, that is, you two really want to visit the policemen and firemen? It's possible it may come to that."

Juli gave her a surprised look via the rearview mirror. Frannie turned back and gave her a quick smile.

"I vote yes," Frannie said.

They stopped at a gas station convenience store at Garber's Crossroads to visit the ladies' restroom and get fresh drinks and information.

Maia said, "There's a mention of a Harris family cemetery on Garber Road, but no address. Ask the clerk. If he's local, he may know of it." She left Juli and Frannie at the counter and walked outside to wait. She pushed a stray hair out of her face and unscrewed the cap from her soda bottle. This day was so messed up. She should've bought a chocolate bar, too. Might as well go bad all the way.

Around her the fields stretched back to where the trees had been left standing. Farming, here. What they grew, she had no idea. Corn was about all she could recognize. Maybe tobacco. Maybe cotton. Gnats swarmed her. She swatted at them as she moved away from the store and closer to the car.

Frannie and Juli joined her. They had funny looks on their faces—a sort of shared look that emphasized their physical similarities—and Maia almost laughed. She stopped. Neither of the women looked amused.

"Any luck?"

Juli said, "Yes, crazy, but your plan worked. That cemetery.... The reason we couldn't find it in the New Bern directory or on the map was because it's a family cemetery."

Maia frowned. "Great. Like those that are off in the middle of a field or in the woods where snakes live, and ticks are looking for a new host? Not to mention spiders. That kind of cemetery?"

"Well, yes," Juli said, "except the man said he was familiar with it...a distant relative or such. He said if that's the one we're looking for, then it's not hard to get to."

Frannie said, "He gave us directions. He suggested we knock on the door of the house first. As a courtesy, he said. And to avoid problems with the dogs." She shook her head. "Maybe this isn't such a good idea, after all. I mean, knocking on strange doors and risking dog attacks...and then we'll probably find out it's not the right cemetery anyway. All for nothing."

"Just a minute," Juli said. "I didn't come all this way to leave without finishing the job."

Maia thought Juli sounded plain ornery. She said, "Juli's right.

You'll get back home and regret letting the prospect of a stranger's door and a dog deter you." Maia waved away a fly before opening the car door. "As Juli said, we didn't come all this way for nothing. As for strangers and dogs, there's three of us so the odds are good that at least one of us will make it out alive."

Frannie gasped. Juli laughed gently.

Maia said, "Let's get this done."

CRSO

They found it easily.

The Harris house was trim, tidy and painted white with a green tin roof. Geraniums and chrysanthemums were planted in the brick-bordered garden, and pines and oaks picturesquely framed the scene.

"It looks like a postcard. It's beautiful. Are you sure it's the right place?"

Juli pointed at an adjoining field. The unkempt field was very different from the house and lot. Nothing had been planted or cultivated here for a while. The weeds were high, but they could make out cinder block walls about thigh-high in the middle of it.

"I see," Frannie said, with doubt heavy in her voice. "Are we going to have to walk through all that?"

Maia said, "Let's knock. There's bound to be a path."

Juli said, "Did your private detective mention any of this? Why wouldn't he say it was a small private cemetery? What did he actually say, Frannie?"

"Just that the grave was unmarked. That Frances died of pneumonia twenty-five years ago and had been living with someone in the area at the time. That was about it." Frannie ran her fingers through her hair, pushing it away from her face. "I don't think the investigator went himself. He's in Raleigh. Someone else may have done the footwork. Maybe the type of cemetery was lost in translation."

Juli said, "Or maybe he got it wrong?"

Frannie stared at her.

Maia asked, "My gut says this is the place. Do either of you know of any family in this area? Cooke or Denman or any other name?"

"No."

"Well, then, maybe you've just discovered some." Maia spread her arms and gestured them forward. "Let's find out."

Chapter Twenty-Seven

An old man answered their knock. He was thick in the middle and his shoulders were rounded forward. He was almost bald and what hair still clung to his scalp was pure white.

Maia guessed that he was alone and lonely because he seemed pleased to see them.

"We're sorry to bother you."

"No bother at all." He placed his hand on his chest, on the red cotton shirt that he wore with his jeans. "Three lovely young women show up on my porch. Not a bit of bother. Are you selling something? Or with a local church group?"

Juli stepped forward, her natural courtesy and a lifetime of dealing with customers and other strangers, carried her smoothly into this man's world.

"No, sir. Might we have a word with you? Perhaps sit on your porch for a minute and explain why we're here?"

"Surely, Miss. Can I get you all something to drink?"

"No, sir. We just had refreshments at the corner store back up the road, so we're fine."

"Johnnie's place? Though I don't guess Johnnie was likely there. He's about as old as me. Are you from around here?" He waved his hand at the swing and a chair, and took the nearest metal chair for himself.

"My name is Juli Winters and this is Frannie Denman and this is Maia Donovan. We are on a bit of a quest today. We are looking for our mother's grave. *Our* mother." She pointed at herself and Frannie. "We were told that she was buried at the Harris Cemetery on Garber Road."

"Well, we have one of those here, but Harris is a fairly popular name."

"We think our mother may be buried here, but we didn't realize it was on private property...a family cemetery."

Frannie added, as if Juli wasn't clear enough, "We only just found that out."

He looked like he was thinking and then he laughed, but in a kind, pleasant way. "Well, then maybe we're kin. Are you related to the Harris's? I'm Ned Harris. Used to be junior 'til my dad died many years ago. I don't recollect you young ladies showing up at the family reunions?" He said it with a quirk to his smile, but with a question in his eyes.

"Not that we know of."

"Then who's your mother and why don't you ladies already know where she's buried?"

"Frances Cooke," Juli said, just as Frannie spoke up saying, "Frances Denman."

Ned Harris looked from one to the other. Confusion played with amusement on his face. "You two can't agree on her name either?"

As he shifted his cane and looked down at the floor, Maia thought he was about to ask them to leave...or maybe invite them to lunch. She simply couldn't tell. When his face crinkled up and the crow's feet deepened, she grew concerned. When his shoulders began to shake, she stood.

"Mr. Harris, I'm sorry we've disturbed you. I think our information must've been incorrect. We obtained it through a third party and well, you know how that can go." She looked at Juli and Frannie. "I think we should be on our way and leave Mr. Harris in peace."

With one hand still on his cane, he raised the other and held it there. "Hold on. Give me a moment. You've waited this long. I guess you can wait a minute more. Let me gather my thoughts."

Maia sat again. She'd encouraged them in this, hadn't she? Not all mysteries or secrets, had happy endings. Maybe they should've left well enough alone, as Juli had wanted?

A car pulled into the driveway, crunching gravel. A woman was driving. Middle-aged. She cast a quick glance at the gathering on the porch and then climbed out of the car.

"My daughter," Ned said. He nodded. "She lives across the street. Keeps an eagle eye on me."

By then, the daughter had climbed the steps and reached the porch. Her hair was dark and streaked with gray, but her complexion was smooth. A tranquil person, Maia guessed. But watchful of her father who was over here engaging in conversation with three strange women.

Maia stood. "Hello. Mr. Harris said you're his daughter?"

"I'm Shawna Burdette. I noticed he had company."

"Yes, ma'am. Pleased to meet you." She extended her hand.

Shawna hesitated but then accepted it.

"I'd like to explain why we're here."

"Certainly."

"My two friends are searching for their mother's grave. It's a long, involved story, but in short, their mother, Frances Cooke, was married to William Denman. They had two children—these ladies. They never knew what happened to their mother but found out recently that she died many years ago and was buried, as they were told, in a cemetery in New Bern. They were told it was the Harris Cemetery. We didn't realize it was a family cemetery until we arrived here today." Maia shook her head and smiled at Shawna. "Honestly, I don't know for sure if the information was correct, or whether this is the right Harris cemetery. A man at the convenience store gave us directions. Your father was kind enough to speak with us."

"Daddy, do you know if she's buried here? I don't recall seeing that name on the headstones."

Maia said, "She doesn't have a headstone or grave marker, so we were told."

Mr. Harris rapped his cane against the metal leg of the chair. "Yes, she does. I made sure she had a stone." He struggled to rise. "It's come back to me now. I h'ain't been out to the cemetery in a long while. My legs fail me at times. Had to give up farming because of it. But she's got a stone alright."

Shawna put her hand on his shoulder. "Sit down, Daddy. I'll take these gals out there. We'll see what's what. Do you remember about where the grave is?"

He squinted as if seeing the layout of the cemetery. "In the southeast corner."

"I'll get you some water, Daddy." She turned to Maia and the others. "I'll take you in just a minute. Wait here."

The door slammed.

"Mr. Harris, are you okay?"

"I'm fine. Just takes me back a lot of years."

Juli asked, "How did it happen that Frances came here? That she was buried here?"

The emotional undercurrents, the sudden need in Juli's voice, surprised them. Mr. Harris gave her a sharp look just as Shawna returned with a tall glass of ice water.

"You drink this. You look dehydrated." She gestured at them. "I'll walk them out there and then we'll come back. You stay here, Daddy."

He nodded.

Shawna led them around the house and paused at the beginning of the path through the old field. It might've been a warm, but pleasant day down by the water, but here, in the middle of this field, the sun was beating on them. Maia heard scratchy noises of unseen things moving in the dry, dusty weeds. Presumably, those noises were caused by crickets and grasshoppers. The weeds were probably infested with spiders and ticks, too. Her skin itched. Neither Juli or Frannie seemed disturbed or deterred. Maybe they were better at hiding this particular discomfort.

"I remember her now," Shawna said. "I didn't at first. Frances.

Long ago." She shook her head. "She was your mother?" She looked at them all.

"Not mine," Maia said. "Juli and Frannie's mother."

She stared at them. "You do favor each other. It's been a long time since I met Frances and I didn't know her long. I remember she was ill." With that, Shawna started down the path. They followed.

Staring down, watching where she stepped on that path, Maia couldn't help but think of her gentler, shadier path at Bridle Cove and the breeze off the water. She wished for the patches of shade and the sound of the river just out of sight, but instead here they were, broiling and scratching.

A small gate closed off the cemetery. The block wall had been painted in the past, but it was flaking badly. It was quite a large space for a private family cemetery in the country. Quite a few stones, too, but also many unmarked areas.

Someone was keeping the weeds down in here with a weed whacker and probably weed killer spray, too. Effective, but rough and choppy-looking, and any spring wildflowers that might've softened the view were goners.

Several headstones were quite old, the surfaces pitted and all but unreadable. A few were much newer. The southeast corner had no stone at all despite what Mr. Harris had said.

Maia thought of Ben and where he was resting. Much more peaceful. Well-ordered. Perpetual care, right? What was that quote she'd heard? In the midst of life, we are in death?

Was it from the Bible? Where? Regardless, some clever person had said it long ago. She'd look up that quote when they were back in the land of air conditioning, wireless connectivity, and search engines.

Her spine tingled as several droplets of hot sweat rolled down her back. She rubbed her forehead. It felt damp and gritty. The heat was getting to her.

Shawna was speaking to Juli and Frannie. Maia struggled to pay attention.

"She came here with my brother. Ernie. The prodigal son, I guess.

That's how they received him when he came back. Made over him big time. I was resentful back then, but also glad. It meant so much to Mother and Daddy when Ernie came home. He brought with him a scrawny, sad-looking woman. That was Frances. I can see her more clearly now in my memory. It's coming back to me."

Frannie asked, "So, he was helping Frances? Giving her a place to stay? Or?"

Shawna said, "The other way around. He, rather my parents, gave her a place to stay. He came home because of her. They were grateful. They'd been living together for a short while. My parents were very unhappy about that, but they were thrilled when he returned home. Frances wasn't here long—only a few weeks before she died." Shawna looked around at the rough ground and the flaking stone walls. "Here it is."

A thin headstone was standing against the inside of the wall, camouflaged by a bush that had taken root and spread its sprouting limbs like shields. Shawna approached it carefully, shaking the small branches and Maia realized she was checking for snakes or spiders, or warning off other creatures. She leaned the headstone away from the wall and Frannie and Juli rushed forward. The three of them lifted and carried it to that open corner where Frances was buried.

Someone had made it by hand. They'd poured concrete into a form and then wrote her name, and her birth and death years, into the wet concrete. It was clumsy but well-meant.

"I think my brother made this himself. He loved her. Funny how I'd forgotten so much. It was such a brief interlude in our lives. Brief for us, but it meant the world to my parents. It changed their lives, post-return, in ways we'll never know. I hadn't really considered it, but I owe Frances thanks for that."

Frannie said, "You knew her. Your father knew her. I never did."

Shawna frowned. "I'm sorry. I was dealing with my own troubles at the time. I wish I knew more to tell you, but I don't."

Juli said, "What about your brother? He could tell us what she was like and about what happened back then."

"Ernie passed a few years ago. I'm sorry. His lungs."

They stood silently and let that settle in. It was disappointing, no question about it.

Juli persisted, "Is it okay if we ask your father? I don't want to upset him."

Maia glanced at Juli. Her voice held a different tone now. The stressed sound Maia had heard a few minutes ago had changed into something more like hope—hope that her mother had done something good for someone even though she couldn't manage it for her daughters. Maia moved closer, forgetting her itchy skin and the sweat. She put her arm in Juli's. Juli smiled at Maia. Her eyes were teary.

It was a strange place to find hope—in this sad, deteriorating cemetery. But then, Maia supposed hope, or disappointment, depended on the answer, not on where you asked the question. She hugged Juli's arm tighter and Juli smiled at her again, looking grateful.

Frannie was still speaking with Shawna as they walked toward the gate. Shawna was saying something about letting her father say what he wanted, but not to push him. After all, he was elderly, and all this had happened long ago.

Long ago.

In the midst of death, yet we are in life.

Live it or not. It's your choice.

"Are you okay?" Juli asked. "You made an odd noise."

"I'm fine. Just hot." Maia moved away. Those words were still in her head. Like someone had spoken them into her ear and left them behind for consideration.

Juli continued standing and staring down at the grave and at the crude headstone that now leaned face-out against the appropriate section of wall. Her lips were moving but Maia heard no words only soft whispery sounds. She saw Juli had closed her eyes and suspected she was saying a prayer for her mother, and maybe one for herself.

In fact, Maia thought, a prayer wasn't a bad idea for any of them, and she took a moment to close her eyes and bow her head.

ﾂﾂﾂ

Mr. Harris waited for the women to return. The water had done him good and his color was better. He'd put some bottles of water on a nearby table, cool enough that the water was still condensing on the outside of the plastic. Maybe he'd also used the rest as an opportunity to think back, to remember that time when a sick woman had showed up on his doorstep with his son—the lost son.

"Help yourselves, ladies," he said, nodding toward the water.

They drank, glad of the water, before asking their questions.

"What happened, Mr. Harris? What do you recall?"

"My son and I didn't get along. I couldn't see his point of view and he wouldn't see mine. My wife said we were like oil and water. I chose to see it as his fault, but in my heart, I know it takes two. Always takes two. He left one day and vowed never to come back. Broke his mother's heart, just about. A few years later, he turns up. But with a woman he'd been living with.

"Sickly-looking, she was. Ernie said she was at a low time in her life. That she'd had a drug habit but had gotten clean about the time he met her. Ernie said she'd convinced him to come home and made amends while he could.

"She seemed nice enough. Kept to herself mostly. Ernie said she was heartbroken over her kids. That's one reason she pushed him to come home. His mother and I were so glad to see him, we'd of taken in a truckload of people to have him home."

Ned rubbed a handkerchief across his face. "Ended up being pneumonia. It was complicated by some other stuff, I'm guessing, and when she went downhill, it took her fast. I asked whether we shouldn't contact her people. Ernie said no. He said she'd made him promise not to." He shook his head. "I'm sorry, girls. Maybe she would've later, if she'd gotten all the way well. I don't know. I don't reckon Ernie knew who or where anyway. If he did, he didn't tell me."

Frannie said, "I'm grateful you helped her. I'm sorry for your own

233

loss. Your son, and of course, your wife. Shawna said your son had bad lungs."

"We lost him a couple of years ago." He nodded toward the fallow field and the cemetery. "Until then, he kept things up pretty good. But, I'm not up to it myself." He sighed. "How it goes, I guess. You win some; you lose more. Sometimes it's a draw and you just wait for your turn to go."

"Daddy," Shawna said, "I think it's time for your afternoon rest."

"I think it is, daughter." He positioned his cane, and with Shawna's help, he stood. He cast a last look at us and said, "I'm glad you found her. Not sure why it's important, but it still feels important."

Juli spoke first. "It is important, Mr. Harris. Thank you for your time and for taking care of Frances so we could find her."

Maia said, "Is it okay if we make one more trip to the cemetery? I'd like to take some photos of her grave and marker. We didn't while we were there. Didn't think of it, but I'm sure we'll be sorry later if we don't."

Shawna said, "No problem. Watch where you step."

The old man and his daughter went inside. Juli turned to Frannie. "I'm glad we came."

"Me, too."

Frannie stepped forward and Juli opened her arms. The sisters hugged.

The water had helped. Perhaps, also, the gift of Mr. Harris's words. At any rate, Maia's heart felt full. Her throat felt tight. She held up her phone and then turned to walk that path again despite the weeds, the heat and the insects. She might be a mediator or a chaperon, or even one who served, but mostly she was a friend.

As Mr. Harris had said, "You win some, lose many." At least this quest had paid off. Exactly how the pay-off would play out, she couldn't guess, but she felt…successful. When stuff worked out this well, it didn't feel like luck. It just felt right.

She took a bunch of photos. Tomorrow, when she woke up she didn't want to wonder if this had all been a dream.

❦

It was a quiet ride back to Bridle Cove. The silence was occasionally punctuated by voices speaking in short snippets like, "She did a good deed before she died. I'm glad she got herself together." And "She was so close. All this time, a short daytrip away." And "This really doesn't change anything does it? So why do I feel different?" Followed by, "Yeah, me too."

Maia sat in the back seat, not part of the general conversation. Frances Ann Cooke Denman belonged to Juli and Frannie. For her, Frances wasn't much more than an interesting story, except for that common understanding of tragedy every person shared. She kept staring at the photos on her phone, scrolling through them, and enlarging them, and then starting all over again. There was a truth there that she'd almost caught and then it would escape her. She wanted to grab it back and examine it more closely.

It had seemed important. Important to her and her future.

Your choice.

She thought it had nothing to do with Frances or New Bern, but rather about the cemetery and the graves and the deteriorating headstones...and the passing of time. Of their lives. That long or short, lived well or spent in fear, it would all be in the past before you knew it. In the end, each life had an outcome. The reach of the outcome varied, but by then you were gone. What mattered was now. If you wanted something, you should go for it now. The future, and any happiness it might offer, was really nothing more than a bonus.

Juli said, "Are you okay, Maia? You're very quiet."

"I'm fine." She laughed with short, wry sound. "Just soaking in the AC."

"Frannie, did you find what you wanted?" Juli floundered out of that statement. "What I mean is, I hope you weren't disappointed."

"No, not disappointed. What about you? I don't think you brought any real expectations along on this trip. How do you feel now?"

Maia listened now. The words, the tones of their voices...this was a genuine exchange.

Juli said, "I had no idea what to expect, so no expectations. I was apprehensive at first, but no real reason for that. Just that it stirred up some very old, unhappy memories. I'll probably tell you about them one day." She shook her head. "I was very young, and the few memories I might recall won't give you any useful information, so I prefer to leave those in the past for now."

"Agreed."

"All that said, I must admit I feel some closure. Almost a bit of satisfaction. I don't know what I had envisioned for her, the end of her life and all that, but this was definitely better. It had meaning. So, all in all, I think it was good."

"Time to move forward, I think. Brian and I need to have a chat about our plans."

"That sounds almost ominous."

"Well, one can never tell what will happen when Brian and I chat. Pretty much anything is possible."

"You're not thinking of calling off the engagement?"

"Not a chance. It's all about the timing and details."

"Do you two really argue a lot?"

Frannie laughed. "We do, but we don't." Her voice turned serious. "When I was growing up everything was nice and perfect and well-run, and I always felt like I messed up. I opened my mouth and said the wrong thing every time. Stuff I lost. Things I didn't understand. Some of that was Laurel's doing, sabotaging me, but after so many years of feeling like I didn't measure up...it's nice to have someone who is ridiculous and funny and contrary. As if none of that matters. Making a mistake, being too hesitant, or being too bold, it doesn't matter to Brian so long as I'm being me. He blusters and makes mistakes himself, but he doesn't take that as a sign that he's a screw-up and he doesn't allow me to torture myself either. I'm accepted. Regardless. As just myself. Just me. Frannie. Or as Fran, if you listen to Brian. It doesn't matter because Brian loves me however I am. And not only that. He likes me. Me.

"So, as silly as it may sound, I feel a few things have clarified in my head, and this trip, and what we discovered, has all been a part of it."

Juli glanced at the dashboard. "We'll be back by supper time." She glanced up at the rearview mirror and caught sight of Maia. "Thank you."

"Me? Why are you thanking me?"

"For coming along with us on this mad quest. And for forgiving us for our drama yesterday."

"Well, I'll give you that—you gals are never boring."

Chapter Twenty-Eight

Brian said, "We're getting married."

The day after the trip to New Bern, Maia drove home to pick up clean clothing. When the phone rang, she answered it. Brian's words stunned her. Married? Had he really said that?

"I know you're getting married. Everyone knows that. We already had the engagement party. We—" She was busy being annoyed and snarky and then it hit her. She stopped cold.

She said in a voice devoid of all hint of teasing, "Don't kid around like that. It's not funny."

"I can say it again if you need me to."

"Tell me what happened." She shouted, "You aren't there now, are you?"

"Where?"

"Wherever you are about to get married."

"Try not to shout, Sis. And no, of course not. Frannie said I had to warn you first. We aren't going to be needing all those plans after all. She and I are going to the justice of the peace. Keep it simple."

"No."

"What?"

"No. And no. And no." *Breathe, Maia.*

She resumed, but with more control. "You listen to me, Brian Donovan, you aren't going to do this to our parents. They're expecting a ceremony. They are expecting to be present at your wedding."

"No problem. They're welcome. We'll let them know what time and where."

"Not good enough. What about Cathy and Aunt Mags and Paul? What about your nieces and nephews? What about Megan, for heaven's sake?"

"They can be there, too. Everyone can show up as they see fit."

Maia paused to recoup her oxygen and slow her heart rate. Brian was perfectly capable of doing such an outrageous thing. Everyone knew that. But a wedding was important. "How does Frannie feel about that?"

"She likes the idea. She wants to marry me."

"I mean, how does Frannie feel about handling her wedding like an open house? Like a pot-luck supper?"

"I wasn't planning on food, but if anyone wants to bring it, I guess it's okay."

"Stop playing stupid. You're just trying to aggravate me."

"It's easy to do."

"Bully. Beast."

"Maia, in strict honesty, if one of us tends to bully, it's you."

Silence.

Then she said, "Me?"

"Sure. You like things a certain way. You aren't exactly known for your flexibility."

"This isn't about me."

"No?"

"No. This is about you and Frannie and how you two are about to break our parents' hearts."

"Alright, then. What do you recommend?"

"Me?"

"Sure. You know what everyone wants. At least you sound like you think you do."

"Seriously, Brian. What does Frannie want?"

"She wants to marry me like I want to marry her. We don't care about the trimmings. I thought most women did, and maybe they do,

I don't know, but apparently Frannie doesn't. She just wants a quiet, private ceremony. She suggested we invite the immediate family, have a ceremony at the justice of the peace and then host a nice dinner at a restaurant."

"Oh." That sounded pretty good to Maia, too.

"She said I could wear jeans and go barefoot."

"Did she?" Maia's brain was spinning now, more productively. As to jeans, maybe so, maybe not. One had to think of the pictures, for one thing, and how they'd look down the road when people were going through the wedding album...

"This weekend."

"This weekend? No, not possible."

"The thing is, we want to beat Memorial Day with the holiday crowds."

"No, Brian. You have to work with me on this. We can make it work but we need at least another week or two."

"No, Maia. I love you. I appreciate you. You're the best sister a guy could hope for. But no."

"I have an idea."

"Sorry, Maia, but—"

"No, I really, truly do have an idea. We could make this work."

She remembered the *Sea Green Glory* and Juli and Ben's wedding day. They'd been married on the beach, a small almost impromptu party of well-wishers. All strangers to Juli. And then, the dinner Ben had arranged, with a little help from Maia, on the porch. She had a flash memory of the deck, lit with lights and candles, that Joel had dazzled her with, though the memory ended with a stab in her heart. A dinner, then. A special dinner. And she had an idea where, too.

"Where's Frannie? At your house or at *Captain's Walk*?"

"At *Captain's Walk*."

"Excellent. I'll call her. We have some things to discuss."

"Like what?"

"A wedding."

CℛℰᎠ

Will Denman's oceanfront home, *Captain's Walk*, was a modest, one-level house, with adequate parking in front and below. The porch would be perfect for an intimate gathering. If the weather was fine, they could climb to the upper deck. In good weather, it would be a fine view, but less private, and awkward for Mags and Paul, if they attended. The lower porch was the better choice. Possibilities and options were flashing through Maia's head. She called Juli as she was driving over to pick up Frannie.

After Juli's first blustering refusal to accept what was basically an elopement, she said, "We'll hold it here. We have plenty of room at our house, and with the big back yard facing the sound, it will be lovely."

Maia said, "For that matter, Brian's house would work. It's large and fancy and the lawn is nice. Parking might be an issue if the guest list grew. No, *Captain's Walk* feels right. If Frannie disagrees, then I'll offer your house as an alternative." She added, "Whatever you and Luke have on your calendar for this coming weekend, clear it now because we have a wedding to arrange and attend."

A counter was running in her head. Mom, Dad, Cathy and Don, her two kids…. No one would attend from Frannie's side except Juli, Luke and Danny.

Maia sighed. She was sitting in the car waiting for the traffic to pass so she could turn. There would be too many guests for a table on the porch. Maybe a table on the beach?

The beach could work if the weather was good. Her brain ran on, busy and busier. Who would have tables to loan? Could they run an electrical line out from the house? What about music? Was that an option?

CℛℰᎠ

Frannie seemed edgy.

"Are you sure you're okay with this? I want to help." Maia asked.

They were sitting on the sofa. Maia wanted to propose plans, but she needed to be sure Frannie was on board.

"I am. I'm ready. I was worried you'd be disappointed about Brian and me not having a formal wedding. I don't want to disappoint you or hurt your family."

Maia almost laughed in relief. "So, if we can pull this together, are we on for this weekend? Saturday, I guess?"

Frannie nodded. "Brian, Megan and I were planning to go to the justice of the peace."

"Oh. Now that would be disappointing. I mean, if that's what you want, we'd all respect it, of course, but I think we can do better. The Donovan's are very flexible. They just need to know you welcome their help." Suddenly, she realized she was missing an important part and she gasped. Frannie looked alarmed again. Maia dialed Cathy.

"Cathy, I have news. Fun news. Brian and Frannie have decided to elope this weekend."

Frannie's eyes widened and she started to interrupt. Maia squeezed her hand and smiled as she continued to speak into the phone.

"That's what I said, too. But guess what? It's all good. We're going to elope with them. With their permission, of course. I need you to tell Mom and Dad right away. Tell them to keep this Saturday open. If they already have plans, tell them to cancel them."

Juli knocked briskly and let herself in. "Sorry it took me so long to get here. I had to coordinate with Esther and Luke. Danny's napping and these days, it's good not to wake him before he's ready. Besides, I thought we'd do better without the distraction." She dropped her bag on a chair and pulled out a pad of paper and a handful of pens. "I thought we might need these, too." She gave Frannie a long look, probably assuring herself that this was what she wanted, and without reservation. And was apparently satisfied. She made a noise that sounded somewhere between frustrated and triumphant.

Maia said, "So?"

"So, the good news is that the weather forecast is perfect and we're so close to the event that we can be certain the weather will hold."

"True. Excellent point."

"The bad news is that we have to work out decorations and dresses and tuxes. With only a few days, we'll have to take what we can get. Could get interesting." Juli smiled broadly and took them both in with one sweeping glance. "We have a wedding to arrange."

Chapter Twenty-Nine

They divided the essentials list, including things like flowers and bunting for the porch rails and the canopy, between them. Juli was sure Luke or Brian knew someone who'd loan them a canopy at short notice. She'd talk to them about it. As for tables—Juli emphasized the plural—she suggested assigning that to Luke and Brian, too. They knew people, she said. Maia agreed, nodding. Juli took on the linens and dishes. Frannie looked dazed and bemused by the tornadoes spinning around her.

"We forgot the minister," Juli said. They all three fell silent. Juli said, "I'll ask Pastor Herrin. He married me...that is, he officiated at both my weddings." She left the room to make the call.

In the sudden silence, Maia looked at Frannie. She put her hand on Frannie's. "Are you okay with all this?"

Frannie nodded, her eyes bright.

"If those are happy tears, then great. But if we're overstepping or overwhelming you, say so. It's okay to tell us the truth."

"It's good. It's all good. Thank you."

Juli had returned. She said, "He'll do it. Frannie, do you have a likely dress? What had you thought about wearing?"

"Wear? Like a wedding dress? No, we're going to keep it simple. Justice of the peace stuff."

"You can keep it simple, but you're going to have a special dress. For the photos for one thing, and another for having as a keepsake, a special dress to mark a special day."

Juli's face glowed as she explained about the dress. Maia couldn't breathe. Her breath seemed to have caught in her throat and her lungs had turned to iron.

"Maia chose a beautiful dress for me when I married Ben. I wore a different dress when I married Luke. Both of those dresses are simple, but they are my wedding gowns." Juli frowned. "Maia, are you okay?"

Frannie turned toward Maia. She touched her face. Juli came close.

Juli spoke softly, but with warmth. "That dress was perfect for my wedding, Maia. Don't you remember? For that wedding, done in a week, with Ben on the beach—it was a blue dress, like the ocean and the sky and my father's eyes. You couldn't have known how perfectly you'd chosen. It meant so much to me that a stranger would help me like that." She leaned forward and hugged Maia.

Suddenly Maia's lungs eased. She could breathe again.

She looked at Juli. Her voice was hoarse. "I'm sorry. I could've done better. And about the cemetery, too. I'm sorry I tried to control it all. Not giving credit where credit was due."

Frannie asked, "What's she talking about?"

Juli said, with a quick smile at Frannie, but focusing her eyes on Maia, "We all do our parts, sometimes whether we know it or not. We do our best, Maia. That's all anyone can ever do. No more apologies are allowed between us. Only thanks."

Frannie said, "I'm confused. Is everyone okay?"

Juli asked Maia, "Are we okay?"

She nodded. "We are."

"Good. Because we have a lot to do." She smiled.

Maia's phone rang. "It's Cathy," she said. After a few minutes, she put the call on hold and said, "Cathy says she'll handle the decorations for the ceremony and the chairs and such."

Juli said, "Really? That would be great."

Frannie looked blank. Maia gave her an encouraging smile.

"The thing is," Maia said, "you'll have to trust her judgement because we don't have time to coordinate. You can say no if you want. I'll make sure her feelings aren't hurt."

"She'd do all that? She'd help me with my wedding? Why?"

Juli and Maia exchanged glances. Maia said, "Because she wants to. She wants to contribute and be part of it. The best weddings are family events. It's not really about the fancy parts of a wedding, though to be sure fancy can be fun, but it's truly about declaring your heart to your loved ones and having their love and support in return. And when it comes to weddings, frankly, Cathy's good at that stuff, so we're lucky."

Frannie nodded. "Tell her, thank you."

"Do you have any special colors in mind? Pink? Blue? What?"

She shrugged. " I hadn't given it any thought."

Maia bit her lip, then said, "I'm thinking a soft lilac."

"Okay."

Maia spoke to Cathy again and when they disconnected, she moved to sit beside Frannie. "Are you sure you're okay?"

"I'm fine. Really. I can't believe we're doing all this."

"Any regrets about getting married this weekend?"

"No."

She sounded firm about that. Maia heard no doubt in her voice.

"Then let's get busy and have some fun."

They made the list and assigned responsible parties. They informed Luke and Brian what they were responsible for, then the three women drove to the Donovan's house, picked up Mom, and went shopping for a dress.

The requirements were simple—white and not too fancy. They had to guess style and size for Megan who was with her mom.

The upside of a beach wedding was that they didn't have to worry about shoes.

Chapter Thirty

At *Captain's Walk*, on the day of the wedding, Maia thought of Brian and wondered....

The guys had nixed the idea of tuxedos but had promised not to embarrass the bride or her attendants. Maia had had her own full and overflowing task list, so she'd had to trust them. But that day, shortly before the ceremony, her trust faltered, and she sought him out. Brian was alone in the guest room.

She eased open the door. "Brian? Can I come in?"

"Sure, sis. What do you think?"

He was smiling yet looking a little apprehensive.

Maia patted his arm. "You okay?"

"I'm good. Really good. Frannie and I are getting married. I can hardly believe it."

"Any worries?"

He shook his head slowly and deliberately. "Not a one."

Brian was dressed in well-tailored dark gray slacks and a white shirt. A boutonniere, a white rose framed by pale lilac, was pinned to his shirt. She kissed his shaved cheek in relief. No jeans. No stubble. All was well. When she touched his smooth cheek, Brian pretended shock.

"What? You thought I was serious about the jeans?" He added in a low voice, "Luke insisted. He said Juli wouldn't forgive him if I didn't dress up a little. I think I look pretty good, actually."

"You look wonderful."

Pastor Herrin spoke from the doorway, "I understand a wedding is happening here today?" He walked into the room with a big smile and hugged Brian. "Looks like you're getting a second chance today. You're a fortunate man, Brian Donovan."

"I am, Pastor. A very fortunate man."

"Excuse me, Pastor," Maia said, "I have to check on the bride now."

CR&D

Cathy and Juli were in the master bedroom, Will Denman's old bedroom, helping Frannie and Megan with final touches to their flowers and their simple white gowns. Maia walked in and felt her heart soften at the scene.

"You all look lovely. Simply elegant."

Frannie's dress was plain. The only jewelry she wore were the sapphire earrings her father had given her for her sixteenth birthday.

Megan grinned up at her. "See my basket, Aunt Maia? Rose petals," she said. "Don't they smell good? Aunt Cathy put them in my basket."

"They smell lovely. Do you understand what to do with them?"

"Oh, yes." She gave a little, involuntary hop. "Mom explained it to me. We practiced."

Mom? Diane?

Megan tugged her closer, so she could whisper. "She said it was okay to call her that. Do you think so?"

"What do you mean, sweetheart?"

"Instead of calling her by her name. She said it was okay to call her mom when it was just us. When I'm with mommy, I'll call her Fran or Frannie. Is it okay?"

"If it works for the two of you, then it's perfect."

"Thank you, Aunt Maia." She almost vibrated with excitement. "I love today, don't you?"

"It's the best day ever."

Maia turned to Frannie who was standing by the dresser.

"Are you okay?"

Frannie's smile was a lot like Brian's. No doubt was evident. "I'm better than okay. I'm the best I've ever been."

Maia dabbed at her eyes hoping not to mess up her makeup. She tried to laugh politely. "This isn't a good time to cry, is it?"

Juli said, "It's always a good time to cry if the tears come from joy."

Maia met Juli's eyes. "It's always a good time for joy." She spread her arms wide. "Are we ready to move this wedding along? Brian is already outside with Luke and the pastor."

Everyone nodded.

"Then follow me."

Maia had noticed guests arriving earlier, trickling in by ones and twos. She hadn't been surprised. Her family would've spread the word that the invitation was an "open" one. By the time she and the others emerged from Will's bedroom, Maia was stunned by the view through the sliding doors.

Juli said, "Wow. Look at that."

Their first view was of the dining room table and kitchen counter. Both surfaces were laden with covered casseroles, platters of ham biscuits, bowls of all sorts of foods.

Maia gaped. "What's all this?"

Megan giggled. "It's food, Aunt Maia."

Mags was standing in the living room. "This may be the best wedding I've seen in a long while, but I'll cherish this air conditioning 'til the last moment, if you don't mind."

Mom stood next to her sister, Mags, with a wispy smile and misty eyes.

Frannie crossed the room to join Mags and her about-to-be mother-in-law, Irene. "Thank you both so much for coming."

"Well, of course I came, dear," Mags laughed, "I don't know that the wedding would truly count if I didn't attend."

"Well, then, I'm all the happier you're here." Frannie leaned forward and kissed Mags' cheek. Irene Donovan hugged Frannie and then dabbed at her own eyes.

"We'd best get on with it, don't you gals think?" Mags pointed her cane toward the sliding doors.

The oceanfront vista included the usual wooden dunes crossover, the dunes and their grasses, the ocean rolling toward shore, but today it included people, most of them dressed up but barefoot, carrying beach chairs and blankets. Some were crossing the wooden walkway, and many were already on the beach arranging themselves in front of the flower-draped, be-ribboned arbor prepared for the wedding ceremony.

Maia hesitated, experiencing a moment almost like stage fright, but then she smiled, threw her shoulders back, and the feeling passed.

As they moved toward the door, she noticed a group standing at the far end of the crossover. That wouldn't work for the bridal march. They'd block the way. She watched, but they weren't moving. Someone was even holding an oversized umbrella as if for shade, as if they were planning to stay in that spot.

Maia squinted into the sunlight, trying to figure out whether they were family or friends or....

"Frannie, is that your Uncle Will?"

Irene joined Maia. She said, "My goodness. It must be."

They could make out the wheelchair and a woman in a nurse's uniform standing next to it, holding the umbrella.

Frannie said, "I can hardly believe Uncle Will is here. Even though I was hoping, and Brian said he'd try, I didn't believe he'd be able to make it happen."

They stared at the scene.

Juli said softly, "He may have arranged it, but they are here for you, Frannie, and for Brian, to celebrate your commitment to each other. I can't begin to adequately express my heartfelt wishes for the two of you, but I hope you'll allow me to do this. You're wearing the sapphire earrings, so you're covered as to "blue," but I'd like to offer the borrowed part."

Juli held the necklace with its sapphire pendant in her hands. "May I?"

Speechless, Frannie blinked, then turned her back to Juli who fastened the necklace around Frannie's neck. Her hands were steady as she worked the clasp. Frannie turned back to her.

"Perfect," Juli said. "Your father would want this."

"Our father."

Juli smiled.

Maia glanced back outside toward the crowd. It was a crowd, for sure, and a happy one. At that moment, the aide holding the umbrella over Will Denman moved. A second woman was standing there. She was dressed in light colors, a straight skirt and a silky blouse, and had blonde, upswept, hair. A second aide? But the clothing was wrong. Even though she'd never met her, Maia knew it had to be Laurel.

"Frannie," Maia said. "Come here, please." She would've kept her mouth shut, but Frannie would have to walk right past where Laurel was standing. She needed to know before.

"What, Maia?"

Frannie saw. Maia knew she did because her posture stiffened, and her fists clenched. Frannie spoke low and hard, "How dare she show up here? How did she even know?"

Maia was speechless for a moment, but in the silence Juli moved to stand beside Frannie. She put an arm around Frannie, almost deliberately, as if reminding her of their relationship—a relationship Frannie had wanted so badly and now had. A relationship she wouldn't want to sour by hasty actions.

Juli said in a calm voice, "I'll handle it."

"What?"

"I'll handle her. This is your wedding day. What do you want me to do?"

"Tell her to go." Frannie's words rasped through her tight jaw and tense lips. "Tell her she's trespassing and unwanted and if she doesn't leave, I'll call the police and have her arrested."

Maia saw a sudden vision of the woman, her yellow hair perfect and wearing a costly designer suit, being handcuffed and hauled away in front of the guests.

Juli said, "I will tell her she is not invited, but that she may stay where she is if she doesn't approach you or attempt to join the other guests. I'll tell her that when the ceremony is done, she must leave quietly."

"No."

Juli's arm tightened imperceptibly. "That's what I'm going to tell her."

"You talked a lot about forgiveness before, back when I wanted to make her pay for how she treated me and what she did to you, but this is too much. And having her here on my wedding day is too much for anyone to ask of me."

"You misunderstand me, Frannie. Think about it. She can watch but not participate. She can't join us. That's probably the cruelest thing you could do to her today."

"I don't want to be cruel. She just doesn't belong here. She isn't welcome."

"Agreed. I'll go speak to her and when we walk past, except for looking at your uncle, keep your eyes straight ahead. Pretend she's a stranger who wandered in on her own." She held her head high. "You wouldn't be harsh to a stranger, especially one as lost as that woman."

Juli released Frannie and brushed at the wrinkle that had appeared in her sleeve. Cool and businesslike, Juli walked alone down the crossover. Maia and Frannie watched as she spoke first to Will and then the aide. Then she efficiently distanced herself and Laurel a yard or so away from the others and Juli spoke a few more words. Laurel looked toward the house, then nodded and turned away to stare at the ocean.

The Donovan relatives and friends had obviously shared news of the wedding between them, but none of them knew Laurel. They couldn't have told her. How had she found out about the wedding?

A cousin who played the violin at school struck up the wedding march.

Maia stood at the door and listened to the opening chords. She turned to Frannie and said, "It's time."

"Go ahead, Megan," Frannie said. "Remember—not too fast, not too slow."

Maia whispered to Megan as she reached the door, "Don't start scattering the rose petals until you reach the sand."

"Got it, Aunt Maia."

Maia pressed her cheek to Megan's lightly, rather than risk lipstick marks. "You are beautiful, dear Megan. I love you."

Megan smiled, and her dimples bloomed. "I love you, too."

"Go ahead. We'll follow."

Luke escorted Frannie down the crossover. Juli and Maia, as attendants, followed close behind.

At the end of the crossover, Uncle Will smiled up at them. The aide shifted her stance and the umbrella blocked their view of Laurel.

Frannie paused to speak to Will. "I'm so glad you could be here with us."

"I'm proud of you," Uncle Will said. "You invited her. After what Brian said, I didn't expect it, but the ability to rise above anger and to forgive is a great gift."

Now was not the time to argue or explain. Thankfully, Frannie seemed to know that. Maia watched the bride kiss her uncle on the cheek, and then she and Luke turned to the steps and descended, Luke's hand lightly clasping Frannie's arm. Her brother-in-law, Maia thought. At that moment, an ocean breeze caught Frannie's veil and the lace danced in the wind. Juli quickly grabbed the flying ends and smoothed the veil back into place.

It occurred to Maia that Frannie had already gained a sister in Juli, and was now officially gaining a brother-in-law, a daughter and a husband—all people who meant the most in Maia's life.

The more, the merrier, thought Maia.

As Luke escorted Frannie to where Brian and the pastor awaited them, Maia saw Joel standing in the group of guests. Some may have recognized him from the engagement party. They would likely assume Joel was her special guest. He looked her way and caught her staring at him. She fought the instinct to avert her eyes and instead gave him a small smile then turned her attention back to the stars of the event.

Luke and Frannie safely walked the sandy aisle to the pastor with well-wishers thronging both sides. As they came to the arbor, Juli and Maia moved to the side for the duration of the short ceremony.

She was careful to avoid looking at Joel again. Mostly, she succeeded except for a few discreet peeks. He, himself, seemed to be concentrating on the ceremony and his expression was serious. What was he thinking? Might she offer him a penny for his thoughts?

She was fresh out of pennies, she thought, and besides, he was here as Frannie's friend, not for her.

The crowd was sizable and amazingly orderly. They sat on their lawn chairs and blankets. Up close, they were silent and smiling, but even those farther from the action were quiet and respectful during the service. As she listened to the bride and groom speak their vows, Maia focused her attention on the business at hand.

As the pastor pronounced them husband and wife and granted them official permission to kiss, Maia's mind was remembering her own kiss with Joel and their candlelight dance on the river deck. She, Juli and Megan followed the newly married couple back up the sandy aisle.

She kept her eyes down. She wouldn't look at him. She wouldn't.

Maia stepped aside as they approached the crossover and the guests closed around the married couple to offer congratulations. She stared up at the wooden crossover where Will sat in his chair. The aide was still holding the umbrella, providing shade.

Laurel was gone.

Maia felt odd. There was no triumph in the feeling, and no grief either. She felt hope for Frannie though. It seemed to her that what Frannie needed most was lots of loud, supportive extended family...and the Donovans could provide that with heart and gusto.

Chapter Thirty-One

The tables were erected on the porch, covered with white paper, taped to hold it in place, and food was laid out. Along with the food, came the noise and the people as they gravitated toward the enticing smells. Frannie and Brian led the way. This was not the usual wedding, and everyone seemed perfectly happy about that.

One of her older cousins called out, "Everyone! You're welcome to eat where you choose, but please mind your trash! Be kind to the ocean and the shore! Use the recycle cans and the trash cans. They're marked!"

Maia backed out of the main flow of people traffic and stumbled into someone. Strong arms caught her and steadied her.

"Sorry!" she said.

"Don't be."

"Joel."

"I'm glad to see you here. You look amazing. How are you?"

"I'm okay."

"I'm sorry I didn't handle things better. I'm sorry for hurting you."

She looked around and moved to avoid being bumped by a passerby. "Probably not a good place to talk."

"Okay." He looked around them. "We could walk up this way?"

He'd taken her words literally. Not exactly what she'd meant, but she went with him anyway. He sounded subdued. Very low-key. Almost cool. Totally at odds with those looks he'd given her when they were walking down the aisle.

When they found a quiet area, away from the rest, she spoke.

"I was surprised to see you here. I suppose I shouldn't have been. Were you the one who told Laurel?"

"Laurel? No. That's Frannie's business."

"Well, then…." She ran out of words.

"I've been thinking about what happened with us. I hope you believe I was sincere."

"About what exactly?"

He seemed stunned for a second or two. "About us—we were "us" for a while, weren't we?"

"Yes."

"And about breaking if off. I think we both know it wasn't just about work or distance."

"Okay." She felt non-committal and sounded that way, too. "Then what?"

"Memories and responsibilities. Did you and Juli work things out?"

"Juli and I are fine. We have history that involved Ben and things were said that probably should've been said long ago. I thought all that was past. But apparently not. By hiding it, I kept it alive in my heart and head. Sorry you had to hear it, though. It wasn't my best moment."

"I'm glad it's resolved."

"Of course. We're friends. Almost sisters. Even people who love and care about each other have differences and resentments. We probably will again. I hope I'll manage my part better next time."

She waved her hand, emphasizing that was over and done with. "Now, about what concerned us—you and I—I did love Ben. In some ways, I still do." Maia looked at Joel's face trying to read his expression. "Am I crazy? Is it wrong? Do we ever stop loving people to whom we give our hearts? Even when those people are gone? Are we supposed to? Aren't we allowed to cherish their memory?"

His eyes were sad. "Not if it keeps you from loving someone new. From building your life for the future. If that love becomes a wall…if the memory is a haven, a safety net that keeps someone from moving forward—"

"That's not it. Not at all. You think I don't want to let Ben go?" She shrugged. "In a way, I suppose I don't."

He started to turn away.

"But not like you think."

Joel stopped.

"Everyone forgot him." There was quiet anguish in her voice. "How could I do that, too? Everyone else is moving on. Before long Ben won't even be much of a memory in anyone's heart and mind."

Maia clutched her hands. She held them tightly together over her heart. "I know he's gone. He's dead. At least, he's dead to those of us who are left here. And it's wrong to squander our lives. If we have the opportunity to live them, to make mistakes or to try to overcome, to share joy...to do whatever...then it's wrong not to try."

Maia added softly, "I want to live my life. I am living my life."

"Are you happy?"

She stared for a moment and then looked away.

Joel said, "With me or without me, you need to live your life and find your happiness. Don't cherish your memories and hold them so tightly that you can't make newer, better memories."

"I wanted to make those new memories with you." She ignored the way her heart wanted to hijack her calm demeanor. "But there were other things to consider, whether you want to include them or not. Like the long-distance problem and your obligation to your father and the business."

He shook his head. "If we'd wanted to, we could've overcome that. I think the long-distance excuse was just one way of keeping emotional space between us. Same with business. Everyone has business and family obligations."

"You make it sound so simple." She waved her hands. "Don't worry about any of that stuff." This was an argument, a disagreement, in every way that mattered regardless of their courteous words. She moved her hands again, but this time with a shooing motion. "We should just ignore reality and go forth and be happy."

He touched her arms. "Isn't it simple, Maia? It should be. We don't need to create obstacles. Life gives us enough of those." He dropped his hands. "I do care about you. It's hard for me to let go, but I meant what I said. I can't settle for second place in anyone's heart or life. Beyond that, I have responsibilities. I have people who depend on me. And that's reality."

"Then Joel, I have a word of advice for you, too. If you don't want to settle for second place, make yourself available for first place. Be there. And put the other person in first place with you."

Maia walked away, wanting to show dignity while she could. Her control of her temper and emotions felt tenuous. Inside, she was distraught. She left Joel behind, but stood on the fringe of the fun, away from the others and watching. Mags and Paul were on the deck with Will Denman and Maia's parents. Her cousins of all ages were in groups and clumps. Some, especially the younger ones, were running in the edge of the waves and being yelled at by various adults to stay out of the water. Maia laughed, and it helped to dispel some of her angst. They were at the beach. What did the adults expect from the kids?

Maybe that was part of her problem, too. Trying to make events and people match her expectations. Who was she to expect others to meet her expectations? She wasn't God. She couldn't predict her own future, much less theirs.

Frannie and Brian were holding court near the food tables. Frannie laughed loudly. She appeared to be relaxed and having fun. Maia was proud of her. Frannie had cast her expectations aside, including the expectations she thought others had for her. She'd gotten married with only a few days of scrambled arrangements...and barefoot. Barefoot in sapphires. Now, how was that for style?

Maia laughed again and moved toward the steps. She had to admit she'd enjoyed coming to the rescue and getting this wedding whipped into shape so quickly. Maybe she was finally finding her way out of that morass she'd been lost in for so long.

Suddenly, she was ravenous. Her cousin, Lynette, had brought a dish of perogies. Maybe some were left. And cake. She smelled the chocolate well before she reached the tables.

As she navigated the groups of people—all family and friends— she remembered how blessed she was.

ଓଃ୫ଠ

Maia successfully snagged a large piece of chocolate cake. She took it to a quiet part of the deck and leaned against the railing to eat it and enjoy the late afternoon ocean breeze. As the guests left, one of her cousins, Charles Jr., stopped to speak.

"Hi, CJ. What's up? Did you get enough to eat? What about cake?" She raised her plate and fork in salute.

CJ said, "I heard your sister is thinking about selling her place out on the Neuse River. Tell her to let me know first, okay? Before she puts it on the market, will you?" CJ grabbed Maia's arm. "Hey, are you okay? You went awful pale."

Maia shook herself. "I'm fine. Fine. Good."

"Are you sure? It was such a fun wedding, wasn't it? Maybe the most fun wedding I've ever attended, and I didn't even have to dress up. I spoke to Frannie and Brian and told them so. Tell Cathy what I said, okay? I tried to catch her, but it was never a good time. I didn't want anyone to overhear, you know? They may try to outbid me."

"Sure. I will." And she would ask Cathy, without question. But what would she say? Was CJ right? What could she offer Cathy? Not fair market value, that was for sure.

Maia found her sister in the kitchen. She touched her elbow.

"Hey, can I talk to you?"

"In a minute? I'm trying to get this wrapped up." She turned to look at Maia and asked with sudden concern, "Are you okay?"

"One minute, now?"

She frowned. "Sure, honey." She grabbed a hand towel and wiped her hands as they walked away from the others.

"Bridle Cove. Are you going to sell it?"

"Hmm. Eventually. You know that, right?"

Maia breathed to ease her nerves, then said, "Yes. Eventually. CJ asked me to let you know he's interested. Wants first shot. Why does he think it's available? Or close to being available?"

Cathy hugged her, then stepped back. "Don and I are going to get married. It's just short of official. We'll want to make new memories in our own places. I do plan to sell it. The place needs a lot of work. It's not right to let it fall apart, to neglect it. I've been willing to let things go for a while. I know you love the place. But sooner or later..." She smiled encouragement. "Talk to a bank. Maybe you can work something out. Make Bridle Cove your own place."

Maia knew Cathy was right. But she also knew it wasn't meant to be. She couldn't live there, yet work in Beaufort. And she couldn't handle, and couldn't afford, the impracticality and expense of managing two places.

In the real world, some things were meant to be dreams. To stay dreams. Gratitude should be for what a person already had. Maia remembered she was lucky. Fortunate.

"Thanks, Cathy. I don't see that working out, but I realize.... I understand you will sell it someday. Just please let me know first?"

Cathy looked sad now. "Don't sell yourself short, Maia. You deserve so much more than just settling."

"Please let me know first."

"I promise."

"Thanks." Maia walked away. She didn't offer to help with the clean-up. They had plenty of willing hands anyway. She glimpsed Joel standing nearby with a couple of other guys, but she didn't pause. She exited via the sliding door and continued onto the crossover which was mostly deserted now. She was grateful for that, too. Her brain was busy, and she didn't have much conversation to offer anyone. Her smiles seemed to have deserted her again.

Settling. Joel didn't want to settle.

Settling.

Was she settling? She was practical, yes. Surely that was a good thing. She tried to make the most of what she had, to appreciate it and take care of it, and make wise decisions.

She was in her thirties now, and single. She had to be mindful of the present and prepared for the future. Not taking risks. Making wild and crazy choices.

A bird, not much more than a dark, distant shape, skimmed a few feet over the waves, intent only upon wherever he was hurrying to.

And while she was trying so hard to hold onto what she had, perhaps even what was already going or gone, how much time, how much happiness, was slipping through her fingers, almost unnoticed?

Maia wandered down the steps and across the sand to the ocean. A long purple and pink braided streamer still littered the sand. Most of the wedding decorations had been collected and removed. She stopped to pick up the last remnant and as the wind pulled at it, twisting it, she wrapped it around her arm. The sun was setting to her right, to the west, and the fingers of color had wrapped around most of the sky. The colors were bright now but would fade, settling into gray tones—the steely gray of ocean and sky just before the day became night.

They'd been so busy preparing for the wedding that she'd been able to put everything about herself aside. Now, in the aftermath, in the silence and solitude, her mood was changing again. Gratitude was shifting to resentment. Never mind settling. Maia had no idea what she wanted or how to proceed with her life.

The ocean had been unusually polite for the wedding. The offshore breeze had been just enough to cool the day a bit and keep the noise of the waves down to a subtle roar. As the evening drew in, the wind shifted, and the sound of the waves seemed to reassert itself, reclaiming its territory and its natural crashing to shore. People rarely swam at night for a reason, she thought. Aside from the obvious, of course. It was harder to see and harder to be rescued. But it was more than that. It was an instinctive response to nature. To the ocean. Which, at night, cast off whatever invitation the sun-drenched waves offered. At night, the ocean and the waves owned the beach and rejected courtesy, at times with brutality, and for once, Maia's heart beat in sympathy with it.

She sat on the beach, her gauzy dress growing sandy and damp, until Brian told her she had to go home.

"Frannie and I are heading over to my house. Megan left with Mom and Dad ages ago. I can't leave you out here alone. For one thing, I need to lock up *Captain's Walk* before Frannie and I take off. Unless your plan is to interfere with our wedding night, then you need to get up and shake off the sand."

He held out his hand. She took it and rose.

"Sorry."

"Don't Maia. Don't apologize to me ever again. I owe you. I can never repay for what you pulled off today. You're a genius and a nice person, too."

He grabbed her and wrapped his arms around her and squeezed, but not too tightly. "Wish me happiness, Maia. I know you do. And I wish the same for you."

Chapter Thirty-Two

Cathy would sell Bridle Cove. Eventually. And that could mean anything. She and Don weren't officially engaged yet, but Brian and Frannie's ceremony was still fresh in every mind, plus June had arrived. Weddings were in the air. If any month was associated with proposals, engagements, and weddings, it was June.

And speaking of weddings.... Maia did the decent, sensible thing. She called Amelie.

"I'm sorry, truly. Things have been going crazy in my life. I'm not doing my part as far as planning your wedding. The other gals are getting stuck with it all. I'm going to withdraw from the bridal party."

Amelia gasped, and Maia tensed, but when her friend spoke, she said, "I'm the one who's sorry, Maia. I am your friend, yet I had no idea things were going...well, not so good for you. Is there anything I can do? Just tell me and I'm there."

Maia smiled. "It's all straightening out, but I have to focus on other things right now. I hope I'm not leaving you in a lurch."

"Not at all, sweetie. You have to think of yourself. I have a cousin on my father's side that has hurt feelings about not being included. She'll be thrilled, and we have plenty of help."

"I hope I'm still invited. I want to attend the wedding."

"Absolutely. Thanks for letting me know...."

Done. It was a relief for Maia to get off the hook with so few questions, and clearly Amelie was okay with her dropping out. She thought back to that day when Amelie had called and she, Maia, had been upset about not having an escort or a ring. It was an irony of life, that things worth being upset over tended to reprioritize themselves, showing how unimportant they really were.

Not only weddings were in the air. So were vacations and summer sports and everything that buzzed around the Carolina coastal areas when the sun was bright, and the temps were up. It was still peaceful out at Bridle Cove. For now. Maia told herself she'd better go out there and get her head used to the idea of saying goodbye.

It was just dirt, a little grass, and an old house situated near the river, with a moon-sliver beach. Nothing all that special. Not a family history thing, not even a luxury thing. But it was a place where she'd grown accustomed to finding solitude and peace, and enjoying it. A place to find her center.

A place she liked to be. To just be her.

What had Frannie said? That Brian loved her—*her* just as she was.

Maia understood what she meant.

Thinking of Frannie reminded her of that ridiculous ploy she and Juli had tried to pull with the crazy goal of giving Maia something constructive to do, to distract her after the breakup and make her feel needed. If she hadn't been so out of it, she'd have seen through their charade right away. Neither of those gals had a devious bone in their bodies.

It warmed her heart though to know that they'd tried so hard to help her feel better after the mess with Joel.

She took a couple of days off mid-week and made the drive up. With the Memorial Day weekend behind them, the gallery was busy, but Brendan and Lora could handle it all. They could call Luke in, in a pinch.

Ironically, it was the "Not For Sale" painting, BRIDLE COVE, by Juli Winters, that had caused the most stir. It was a gorgeous piece, no question. But there was something about human nature that most wanted what it was told it could not have. She laughed.

Juli was thrilled and embarrassed by the fuss. Maia had told her to settle down and get to work. She had clients to please.

Maia sat on the steps of the porch. She forced herself to think of these trees, this land, this view, belonging to someone else, and insisted her heart accept it. It didn't seem possible. So this visit was important. It was about learning to let go. Gracefully and gratefully. She'd managed it with Ben's memory, hadn't she? She could do it with a few acres of dirt and a rickety house on the water.

There were many ways of saying goodbye, as reasons to say it. And sometimes you had to say it more than once.

When she heard a car coming, her first thought was of Juli or Brian.

Or a realtor. If it was a realtor, she'd die. She'd just flat-out die right here on the spot.

It was Joel. Maia stood.

He exited the car and looked around, then saw her.

"Do you mind that I came out here? I looked for you at the gallery. They told me you might be here."

Maia couldn't help smiling. The gallery. It was more like a way station. First, in that people looked for her there, even before calling, and second, that whoever was on duty directed them here.

"I saw the painting of Bridle Cove. Brendan pointed it out when he told me where to find you. I had no idea that Juli was so talented." He paused. "Am I interrupting?"

Courtesy rose to the fore. "No, of course not." The manners you were raised with were the default, the fallback when you were surprised and couldn't think of what else to say.

"Something you said stuck in my head. About if I didn't want to take second place, then I needed to make myself available and ready for first place."

"Did I say that?"

"Yes. At the wedding."

"Well, it was a busy day, after a busy few days. If I offended you, I...." She remembered what Brian had said about not apologizing, but couldn't help herself. "Then I'm sorry."

"You were exactly right. I'm glad you said it." He shrugged and looked up at the heavy pine boughs overhead and then at the reeds rustling down by the path. When he looked back at her, he said, "I have a question for you, Maia. I don't have the right to ask, but I'd like to anyway. I've felt confused a lot lately. So, if you don't mind...."

"Go ahead."

"What do you want? For yourself? Out of life?"

"What do I want?"

"Not just want. What do you really want? What do you dream of?"

"What do I dream of?" She stepped down to the ground, almost annoyed, and in annoyance she spoke more sharply that she might've otherwise.

"In those moments when I stop to breathe, or when stress is building, and nothing is going right, and the world is closing around me?" She was waving her arms. She reined them in and brought her voice and the tension in it down a notch. "I dream of happiness. Happiness that is more than contentment. I dream of creating something, of embracing something I love and making it even better."

"What about love?"

"Love. It hurts, I know that. I have love. My parents' love. My siblings. The love of my wonderful, if crazy, friends. And I've been *in* love, too, and while there were wonderful moments, it has never brought me more than a temporary happiness." She stared at him. Let him read the truth in her eyes—that he now belonged in the heartbreak category.

Joel asked, "What about Frannie and Brian? Do you think they'll find happiness? Or did they make a huge mistake?"

"Probably a mistake. Their hearts may get broken, and I worry about Megan if that happens. But suppose they make it? Suppose they win that brass ring and one day, five decades from now, we're toasting their golden anniversary? It could happen. And if it doesn't, then I suspect they will be devastated but resilient. More resilient than I am. Maybe that's why they are willing to take the bigger risks, and hope for the bigger win."

Joel was standing so close she could feel his energy, his body's magnetic field moving into her own, meshing with it. She was acutely aware of him and of his power to hurt her, if she allowed that. If she was willing to risk rejection or failure. Another heartbreak. The need for yet one more goodbye.

She moved away and walked toward the ruined dock. She stopped at the edge of the grassy yard where the rotten wood steps led down, vanishing into the overgrown weeds.

Pointless steps to a dock that couldn't be used.

Without looking at him, she asked, "What do you dream of, Joel? What do you want from life?"

"I don't know. I thought I did, but I'm having to rethink it. I do know what I don't want."

"What's that?" she asked, not wanting to.

But he changed the subject.

"I have watched my father, a hard-headed, unromantic businessman fall in love with a woman he didn't even know nine months ago. I watched him get sick, recover, proclaim his love for his nurse—which breaks all laws of common sense and probably ethics, too—ditch the family business, and all the people who depended on it for jobs and income and health care...all of that. For her. For himself."

"Mortality, I guess."

"Yeah."

"Sounds like he had a good dose of it. The reality of his life. And it changed his course. You took over for him. I guess that was inevitable, right? I mean, full-fledged taking over the family business? It was going to happen sooner or later."

"It did feel inevitable. I grew up with it. I didn't mind, generally. But I guess I'd always believed there was some sort of escape clause, that I'd be able to exit when I decided to. All that changed suddenly."

"Now you have the business. I'm sure you'll do fine and get it all sorted out."

He continued as if she hadn't spoken. "The truth is, I was jealous. I didn't mind working in the business as long as it wasn't the only thing in my life, or the most important thing in my life. Or for the rest of my life." He sighed. "When all this started with my father, I thought it would pass, that we'd get back on course. Now that it's not, I'm changing MY course."

Joel shook his head. "I was planning to chart a new course for myself when my father changed all that. And then I thought I was stuck. That I had to see my responsibilities through."

Maia shrugged. "I can understand that."

"I can't. I'm going to break the company up, selling it and trying to protect our people in the bargain. It will be a slow process. It's going to take a while."

"I couldn't go away without telling you that I was wrong. I put too much fault on you while I hid behind the responsibility I thought I had to live with. I'm sorry for that."

Joel caught her eyes and smiled. "Tell me what you see when you look at this place."

"What? A ramshackle house? Overgrown bushes. A dock that's a hazard."

"Well, that's what it is. But my question is what do you see? When you aren't here, and you think of it, what do you see?"

"Beauty. Natural beauty despite neglect. Peace and quiet. Potential. A place that's ready and waiting to soak up attention from someone who cares."

"It's your sister's place?"

"It is. It was her husband's. He died a while ago. She's thinking of remarrying now."

"She's going to sell it, right? She has to or it will fall down eventually."

"Sometimes I think that's what she wants." Maia shook her head and frowned. "What is our problem, Joel?"

He looked surprised.

"It's not Ben. We've already had that discussion anyway. What, then?"

Instead of answering, Joel asked, "Why don't you buy this place if you love it so much?"

Maia groaned. He'd changed the subject again. Seemed like he was as good at avoidance as she was.

"Why don't I buy it? I can't afford it and it's not practical. The upkeep would be costly, and I can't live in two places at one time."

"People do. It's common. They have vacation homes. A place at the ocean, or a cabin at the river or in the mountains, so forget the practicality of it. That's not an issue."

It annoyed her that he could so casually choose what was an issue and dismiss what wasn't. "I can't ignore the money part so easily. That's a reality. Not everyone has a bunch of money sitting around. You're the exception rather the rule." That came out more harshly than she'd intended. "I'm sorry, Joel. I wasn't pointing fingers. I know how hard you work, but the reality for me is different."

"It doesn't have to be. Not if you really want it."

"I don't want your money."

"I wasn't offering it. I'm offering advice. If you see something you really want, then go for it. Move heaven and earth to get it. Life's too short for should'ves and would'ves."

He continued, "I have no doubt that your sister would give you a good price. Luke would loan you the down payment without thinking twice. Your family and friends would be here to help you clean up and restore the place." He paused to look around them. "Once you have it back in shape, you could rent it out to vacationers to help defray the expenses." He looked straight at her. "It's easy, Maia, if you know what you want. Really. Want. But if it's just settling—a place to hide instead of being engaged with life—then let it go. Move on. Because, I repeat, life is too short and while business opportunities are everywhere, the opportunities to find your happiness and grab it, hold it, are rare."

He looked down at his shoes. "You asked what our problem was? We're both good at business and we have an excellent work ethic.

We're good people. Good to our family and to our friends. Somehow, we got to this time in our lives and discovered that while they love us and respect us, most of them can live their lives quite well without us. Oh, they'd miss us, I don't mean that, but somewhere along the way we became more involved in their lives than our own. Now we don't know how to go on. Honestly, Maia, sometimes I feel lost. Disenchanted. I'm trying to figure out what I, myself, want. I do know I don't want my father's business. What I'll end up doing after I divest myself of it, I don't know."

He added, "But Maia, about this house and property, you have to more than want it. Only you can figure that out and make it happen, or one day soon it will be too late. Don't lose an opportunity worth taking because it seemed risky or complicated."

"One last thing, Maia. I won't ask for promises from you. I wouldn't dare presume. But when I'm done, when I'm free of what keeps pulling me away from you, I'll return."

Maia crossed her arms and turned her back to him deliberately. She focused on the water, the grasses, the peace before her, and summoned the words that had to be said. It hurt her to speak them aloud, so she spoke softly. "Don't, Joel. Don't come back. This coming and going is too confusing. I can't allow you to keep breaking my heart over and over again."

She heard a noise and spun around.

He'd walked away. He was getting into his car and shutting the door.

Had he heard her? He must've, right?

She sighed.

She watched him drive away and, despite all logic and good sense, she felt the empty ache his departure left in her heart.

Chapter Thirty-Three

He'd been confused. For how long?
What do you dream of?
He'd asked Maia that, and it was a good question. But he should have directed it squarely at himself.

Talking to her after the wedding had shaken his certainty. He'd had to see her again. Odd how, being out at Bridle Cove with Maia today, his own confusion, stirred up by the weakening of his certainty—the belief that he understood his responsibilities and his motivations—had begun to clear.

What do *I* dream of?

It wasn't the life he'd been leading. He knew that.

He had unofficially inherited his life years before, but he'd thought it was a partnership. Potentially optional, at some point in the future. Now, he suspected his father, perhaps subconsciously, had begun transitioning out of a life he didn't want any more than Joel did, longer ago than either of them knew.

It had taken a near-death experience to show Gerald Sandeford the truth. What about Sharon? He'd found no indication that anything nefarious was going on. Beyond that, was it his business? No.

They'd taken care of the legalities. Now, it was a non-issue for him. Their future was their own. Bon voyage, Dad and Sharon.

He'd been confused for a while and hadn't known why. But he wasn't confused about the impossibility of continuing as he'd been going. He would need a partner, if nothing else. He didn't want to bring a partner in. It would feel like an anchor; not a means to freedom. There were other partnerships, other businesses and opportunities, that appealed to him more.

As he drove away from Bridle Cove, it wasn't the CEO desk he was returning to, but it was the smell of the water and the rustling of the grasses he was leaving. He didn't care about the responsibilities he was returning to, but rather that he was leaving Maia. He didn't need another briefcase or suit, but he desperately wanted new sneakers with some sandals thrown in for good measure.

What stands in my way?

What stood in Maia's way? He suspected it was never Ben. It was fear of risk, of giving up control. Of making a costly decision that would offend her practical nature.

Ben was a rival only in his, Joel's, mind because it was more convenient to blame Maia's divided heart than to take the responsibility on himself.

What stood in his way? It wasn't Ben. It certainly wasn't money. He was fortunate to be able to say that. So, other than legal technicalities and the hassles of divesting, it was only himself, and that sense of responsibility. In the end, though, there were no guarantees for anyone. Not on this earth. He could disappear tomorrow. The business might suffer a few hiccups, but others would step in and it would continue, so he asked himself again, *what stands in my way?*

Only me.

Suddenly, Joel felt free. He meant what he said to Maia about charting a new course.

He had a lot of work to do, but getting it done wouldn't represent loss. It would mean moving on to what he really wanted, instead of always driving away from it and leaving it behind.

Chapter Thirty-Four

August was hot. It always was, especially in eastern North Carolina. Along the coast, the ocean breezes were always welcome in the summer, and if you stood at the water's edge where the waves rushed in from the Atlantic and pounded the sand, it was the freshest, coolest, most beautiful place to be. But that stretch of sand between the wooden crossovers and the water's edge could get hot, so hot a person might have to run right through it, *ouching* all the way, to get it done quickly, so they could reach the paradise part—a lot like making it through life.

It was hot out at Bridle Cove, too. The cove didn't have the ocean wind, but it did have the old, weathered, spreading oaks, the pines, and the smaller trees, too. The breeze off the broad swathe of the river, where river met river, met the shade on land, and made it tolerable on the hottest days. So long as sitting in the shade with a tall glass of iced tea was the only item on your agenda, you were good.

The electrician said the wiring could handle one or two small air conditioning units and she'd had those installed. She'd get the wiring upgraded, but needed to pay attention to the roof and gutters first. Brian showed up with a couple of guys and hauled out that wreck of a dock because he didn't trust Megan to stay off it. He said Maia's housewarming gift would be a new dock because he wanted to be able to bring his boat up the river and dock here. While he was at it, he spruced up the rocks lining the shore and improved the beach area. Megan came with Brian often. Her mom, Diane, was having her own fun this summer and was feeling generous with her daughter's time. Maia appreciate that even if she viewed it rather cynically. Frannie came with Brian, too, and was surprisingly adaptable when it came to the heat, though she did make a lot of trips into the house to stand in front of the AC units.

Luke refused to loan Maia the down payment. Instead, he called it a bonus for a decade of devotion to the Front Street Gallery. Every repair and improvement cost money and she didn't have a lot of extra cash, but she did have a perfect credit history and proven history of employment and was surprised to discover Joel was right—if you wanted something badly enough, if you really wanted it and knew it, then you had to understand the main obstacle. If it was fear, then the only thing to do was to move forward and grab that dream and see if you could hold onto it.

One weekend in mid-August, Maia left the gallery in the hands of Brendan and Lora. Maia prepared a picnic lunch and greeted Luke and Juli and Danny when they arrived at the cove. After their sandwiches were demolished, Luke took a look around while she and Juli sat on the porch with Danny. Danny kept trying to escape.

"I swear he can scent the water. He's determined to get down there."

Danny was determined, even if it meant going head first. In one hand, he held a plastic shovel in a white-knuckled grip and waved it. Maia picked up the bucket from the porch floor as Juli carried him down to the grass. She let him toddle along, her hands only inches from him in case he ran into trouble, but when they reached the path, she scooped him up. He protested briefly but then, from the height of his mama's arms, now with a view over the dunes grasses, he caught the glimmer of the water, the shifting kaleidoscope of sunlight on the moving surface of the river. He waved his arms wildly and they laughed. Bridle Cove was Maia's, but it didn't feel like hers alone, and that felt like a gift.

She understood better now what Joel had been saying. She was grateful for the push he'd given her. And she was glad she'd accomplished it on her own. On her own behalf, as it were, even if she'd had a little help from her friends and family. This was her triumph.

Juli said, "Have you heard from Joel lately?" Juli had said it casually, but there wasn't anything casual about her tone.

"Not since June. I guess we're really done this time. But I owe him. Did I tell you what he said to me?"

"I don't think so. What?"

"He asked me what I dreamed of?" She shook her head. "Without his encouragement, I would never have had the nerve to buy this place."

"Well, sometimes it just takes the right words or the right question. I'm glad you had the answer." Juli said, "I have something interesting to tell you. Believe it or not, Laurel Denman sent me a chatty letter wrapped up in a fancy note card." Juli's lips formed a mysterious little smile. "She has lovely penmanship."

"You're kidding."

"I'm serious. She does." Juli laughed and shoveled a little sand into Danny's bucket, then he reclaimed the shovel. She sat up and said, "She apologized for her actions all those years ago. Pretty meaningless, I guess, but then again, it's better than hearing recriminations and excuses. Probably better if she'd just kept it to herself. It doesn't change history, right? But somehow it feels...I don't know how to say it. It feels like a circuit is complete." She shook her head. "Frannie is still closed to any kind of relationship with her. I don't blame her. One day, she'll feel safe from Laurel, her spell, I guess you could call it. Safe enough to come to terms with it all, and with her."

"Safe enough? Surely Laurel isn't a threat?"

"Not a physical threat. But once someone has that pipeline straight into your head, you never feel quite safe again, not safe from their influence. "

"So, it's cool having a sister, right?"

"It is. It's good. We're getting to know each other and be

comfortable in each other's company. It's kind of a natural fit when you think of it. The connection between us. All of us. But I told you this before—I already have a sister. You. Now I have two."

She spoke softly, but matter-of-factly. She wasn't schmoozing or fishing. That wasn't Juli's style anyway and never had been.

Maia asked, "With all those foster homes you grew up in, and before that, being dependent on Frances with no good memories—was it hard to learn to trust? To give up your self-reliance? To have faith in others?"

Juli smoothed damp hair out of Danny's face and pulled the tube of sunscreen from her bag to add to what was already smeared on his fair skin.

"Yes. And no."

Maia waited.

"I think it all depends on the *who* of it. You know I found Faith—the kind with a capital F—from Ben, but it started smaller. *With* Ben. I trusted him, and the rest followed as naturally as ripples on the lake when a stone is cast. The pastor explained that to me long ago. That was Ben's style. Nice and easy." She laughed. "But that first step can be scary."

"Sometimes that first step to trust, to have faith, requires a push."

Juli laughed and Danny looked up grinning at the joy he felt from his mom. "Sometimes it does. Especially for strong, stubborn people." She gave Maia a pointed look. "For some of us, a push...or gentle, persistent, persuasion is better."

"Like wearing someone down with kindness?"

"Or insisting on helping when they think they don't need help." She smiled. "Remember how you painted Danny's nursery? No one had ever done anything like that for me."

Maia shrugged it off. "It was nothing. I was glad to help."

Juli whispered, "You always are. You're a good person, Maia. Remember what I asked you back then? Back when you were helping me stay sane after losing Ben?"

Maia nodded.

"I said something to you about service, about being a person who was always willing to help others. That I wasn't like that and didn't understand people who were."

"I remember," Maia said. "But now I know the other side of that coin."

"What do you mean?"

Suddenly, Maia shivered. She hugged her arms around herself. "This is going to sound stupid. Stupid and self-serving," she said. "I grew up in the church. I've always been a part of it. I know that I am a child of God. And I love serving others. Loved, that is. Something stopped working in me. Some important part, a light inside me that made me grateful and made my life worthwhile.

"I don't understand why it stopped, but I hate that it did. Like a connection was lost. All that's left behind is anger and resentments. I harbored them in my heart without knowing it. They seem to grow stronger as the light grows weaker and I'm feeling lost."

She waved her hands at their surroundings. "All this helps, and I'm grateful for it, but nothing cures it." She looked again at the ocean, crossed her arms, then released them. Her hands, palms up, settled unmoving on her lap.

"For a while, helping you and Frannie…well, I wasn't always wanting to help, and I thought some very uncharitable thoughts in my head, let me tell you."

"Don't tell me. Please."

"Don't worry. I won't. Some of that emptiness seemed to go away, as if I was changing back, back into me. Maia." She shook her head. "But it didn't last. The negative stuff that moved in in place of the light, seems determined to stay."

"Maybe that light, that love of helping others, didn't leave you."

"It did. I'm telling you, most of the time I feel empty of everything but anger and even a little fear. I want to be happy again."

Juli spoke firmly, her voice clear as she repeated, "Maybe it didn't leave you." She reached toward Maia and touched her arm. "Maybe you pushed it out. Maybe you filled up with grief, regret, and resentments to where there's no room left—no space left for what you'd rather be growing."

A shudder struck Maia. Juli's hand dropped away. Maia rubbed her hands across her face. They sat in silence for a while. Finally, Maia asked, "Do you really think so? That I...I evicted my happiness?"

Juli said, "I don't know how the human heart and brain work, but I know they can be tough and stubborn. I wish you could let the past go. Memories are fine as long as that's all they are."

"Joel said something like that. And I have. I do truly believe that I have."

"As for myself," Juli said, "I've wasted a lot of time trying to avoid bad memories. Wanting to forget they happened. It's exhausting."

"Like with your mother?"

"Yes. But that's done, and I've put it behind me. And now I have a new sister." She groaned. "I have a sister whose stepmother or adoptive mother or whatever she is, wrote me a thank you note. I will *not* be sharing that tidbit with Frannie."

Maia said, "Yes, please don't."

"No worries. You and I are in complete agreement."

In a smaller voice, Maia asked, "We are, right? We're good?"

"We are. We're better than good. We're golden."

Maia smiled. "I like that." She nodded and brushed at the sand in Danny's hair. "I'm going to think about what you said, about what I'd rather be growing in my heart." She shrugged. "I've given up on what I wanted the most. I wanted love. My own true love. Corny. A romantic wedding and my own happily-ever-after." She shook herself. "How foolish that sounds now."

"Not foolish, but we can get so focused on what we think we should want, that we forget God may have other plans. Perhaps better plans."

Maia stared at Juli, then she looked away.

Juli said, "Since I'm all in your business, I'd like to say one more thing about Joel. I don't know what's ahead for you two, but I don't think you're done with each other yet."

Maia let Juli's remarks about Joel go unanswered. Instead, she said, "When you said that you knew I loved Ben, you wondered if you should've told him? I know the answer. You did the right thing. If you'd told him, as kind and caring a man as he was, he would've felt badly, perhaps even felt awkward around me. It would've thoroughly spoiled those last weeks."

Juli nodded. "He said he didn't want to watch himself dying in the eyes of his loved ones." She pointed to herself. "I wasn't one of those loved ones, though I came to be. And in the end, he had regrets because of it. He regretted not fighting the cancer, but it was too late. No do-overs for some things."

Juli said carefully, "There's something else I want to say, if you don't mind. You mentioned a connection. That you couldn't feel it, and what you valued before didn't have the same meaning to you."

"Yes," Maia sighed.

"Have you considered that you are angry with God? Perhaps more so than with me or anyone else? Is it possible that you shut that door? That connection?"

Maia didn't respond. In fact, she was speechless.

Juli added, "In your book and game closet, I saw a Bible. When you have a few quiet minutes, read Matthew 17:20. It was one of Ben's favorites. It may speak to you."

Maia felt resentment, an unpleasant stirring inside, like something hot that wanted to grow and strike out...strike back. Instead, she pressed her fingers to her lips and stared ahead.

They sat in silence for a few minutes while the water lapped at the shore and birds sang in the trees.

Juli clasped her hands, twisted them slightly and then released her fingers. "Since we're having a confessions sort of day...I've been thinking about it awhile...since before Danny's birthday. Maybe now is a good time. I need your opinion."

Maia shook her head. Juli could be such a know-it-all. She

needed Maia's opinion? Not likely. "If this is another Frannie problem, then discuss it with her. You two are getting along fine now. Keep the communication open."

"This isn't about Frannie."

"Is it about Joel, then? Or Brian? No, I don't suppose it would be about Brian." She looked at Juli. "Is it me?" She groaned. "Have I done something else to hurt you or anyone?"

Juli touched Maia's arm. "Relax. It isn't about Joel or Brian or any of that flock of folks you are forever taking care of. Honestly, I don't know how you do it. But this does concern you because I think you'll have thoughts about it."

"I'm listening."

"It's about Danny."

"Danny? Is he okay?" He was at her feet, playing in the sand. "He looks fine. Is there a problem?"

"No and no and no. Danny is fine. It's about his name."

"His name? Benjamin Daniel Bradshaw. Named for his father. You were very clear about wanting that."

Juli added, "And about not marrying Luke until after Danny was born because it was important to me that Danny have his father's name—his full name, including his last name."

"Okay. So?"

"Now that time has passed...and I've been thinking about the future.... I've been thinking about this for a while now, as I said, but it's not something I can decide until I've discussed it with you."

Juli gave a huge sigh. Even Danny looked up. He held out his arms. She picked him up, smoothing his hair.

"In fact, it's already becoming a bit of an issue...the last name. With Luke as his stepfather and my last name being Winters. Everywhere we go people assume his last name is Winters." She planted a quick kiss on the top of his head. "Like mine and Luke's."

That familiar frustration she'd felt over and over recently, grew in Maia's chest and rose, with warmth, to her cheeks. She bit her lower lip delicately, carefully, trying to consider her response.

While Maia was considering, Juli added, "I wanted your opinion. I hope you don't mind me bringing it up with you?"

Bringing it up? That sounded so casual. Juli must realize the emotional impact this subject would have.

Maia rubbed her hands together. "Are you talking about adoption? Luke going from stepfather to... But, Juli, you were the one who was so determined, so certain about Danny keeping Ben's last name. You said you wanted him to keep...to know...."

At the sound of Maia saying his name, Danny held out his arms, reaching for her, crossing the space between her and Juli with laughter and pride at his daring. Maia caressed his cheek and Juli planted him back down in the sand where he returned to shoveling.

"Was that just a gesture, then?" Maia asked. "A gesture called forth by grief? Or was it...."

"Was it what?" Juli said. "Was I sincere?" Juli stared at the far shore. "Was it a bargain so that I didn't feel so guilty about Luke? About loving Luke and wanting to marry him? Was it a decision made to respect Ben's memory? Or to salve my own conscience?"

Aghast, Maia held her breath. Really forgot to breathe altogether. Juli raised a hand and placed it over her face. She drew in a ragged breath.

Maia asked, "I am so sorry. I really didn't mean it to sound that way, or to hurt you. What does Luke say?"

"He doesn't care." She held up her hand. "No, wait. That gives a totally false impression. He said it doesn't matter to him." She frowned and pressed her fingers to her forehead. "I'm getting a tremendous headache."

Juli sighed. "I can do this better. Just give me a minute, Maia." She closed her eyes and concentrated on breathing for about thirty seconds, then she opened them again. "Luke says Danny is Ben's son, but he's also his, Luke's son." Her voice grew thicker, raspier with each word. "That he'll be the best father he can no matter what Danny's last name is...." And Juli devolved into a mess of tears.

Danny looked up, this time in alarm. He dropped his shovel,

pushed up to his knees and tried to climb up his mom's legs, and by that point, he, too, was erupting into tears. Juli grabbed him up and held him close, rocking him. Maia was shedding a few herself and she dashed them away. Lacking a tissue of any kind, she used the hem of her shirt to dab at her nose. Disgusting.

Maia sniffled. "Look at us. This is silly."

Juli glared at her through tear-filled eyes, and then started laughing. Danny, though still looking worried, also began to smile and laugh. Juli hugged him again, but then held him up until his feet were positioned on her knees. She steadied him.

"Look at you, mommy's big boy! Aren't we so silly?"

Danny seemed reassured but wanted to cling a while yet. This craziness was unsettling to him. And no wonder.

Juli found a tissue in her pocket and offered part of it to Maia.

Maia said, "I can't believe all three of us were crying. I haven't seen you cry like this since..." She broke off.

Juli continued pressing the tissue at her eyes, then to Danny's, but playfully, like a distraction.

Maia said, "You are, aren't you?"

Juli kissed Danny's cheek and put him back on the sand where he crawled to his shovel.

"I am what?"

Maia stared.

Juli said, "I am, Maia. No one else knows yet."

Life will out. Life goes on.

What would Ben say about changing Danny's surname and legal status? About Danny legally becoming Luke's son? And becoming a big brother?

Ben would laugh and ask, "Why not? What's the big deal?" That's what Ben would say about it. He'd also say, "Whether it's mustard seeds or ripples from a tossed stone, it all counts."

We are yet in the midst of life. Embrace it. The more, the merrier.

Maia closed her eyes and sent a prayer, one of gratitude.

Juli took a deep, cleansing breath before saying, "I was thinking of keeping Bradshaw, but adding Winter. I don't know if that works legally, but I don't want Danny to ever feel like he doesn't belong, even if it is just a different last name."

Maia felt that idea-shot again, as if it had come straight from the cosmos, and saw the series of foster homes where Juli had never fit in, hadn't belonged. Her heart ached.

"Juli, I don't think Ben would mind at all. As for me, it's none of my business and I'll support you regardless of what you decide. But one thing I do know—you'd better not take too long to tell Luke about the new one on the way because I don't know if I'll be able to keep the news to myself."

She leaned over and put her arms around Juli. "Danny will always belong, just as you do. You had a rough start and some hard years. It took you a while to find us...Ben and Luke and me. Frannie, too. And for us to find you, but we are your family and friends.

"We have you now and you're ours."

Chapter Thirty-Five

After Labor Day weekend things calmed down considerably tourist-wise along the Outer Banks and the Crystal Coast. Not that the season stopped. In fact, many visitors planned their vacations specifically for this time of year because they preferred the quieter beaches and roads. The weather was still warm. A few businesses might have closed for the summer, but most were open, including the Front Street Gallery in Beaufort.

Maia left Brendan to handle the gallery and walked outside to the marina. She sat on the wooden bench. Her palms were damp from clutching her phone. She loosened her grip. She found his number in Contacts and waited as it rang. She was as anxious as a girl with a teenaged crush, so it was probably just as well that he didn't answer. She left a message on his voice mail.

"Hi, Joel. It's me. Maia. I've made some changes Bridle Cove. I thought you might be interested in seeing...if you're home, that is, and not traveling again. Maybe we can get together. That's if you're...interested." She disconnected.

She'd expected him to return before now. To come back to her. To suggest they take another chance to work things out together.

Was she too proud to do the asking? Yes. But the lack of a clear ending bugged her. She would let Joel go, if that's how it turned out, but she wanted an ending that fit, even if it meant risking her pride.

Odd to realize she didn't need Joel, or any particular person, to accomplish her goals. She needed God and faith. Having all the answers would be great, but not essential. She simply needed to understand that it was her choice what to fill herself and her life with.

Her choice.

Today could be fulfilling, too, whatever it offered.

But she wanted Joel. She missed him. It seemed a shame to let what was between them fade into nothingness.

Had he managed to get clear of his father's businesses? He'd said he would return when he was done. Of course, she'd told him not to. Had he heard her say that?

Joel had also said that bit about figuring out what you truly wanted and not taking too long about it, or you'd find you'd missed your chance—or words to that effect.

Amelie's wedding was coming up in two weeks. Bowing out of the bridal attendant's role had been the right thing to do for both her and Amelie. The wedding would be in Emerald Isle, and Maia would attend without reservations. Strange to recall how disturbed she'd been about facing Amelie's wedding as a single gal. In retrospect, she saw she'd been in an upside-down priorities state of mind.

Maybe stripping away obligations and distractions had helped bring her clarity.

Things changed. Lives changed. Time moved on. The status quo was only a picture of the past. You had the choice of falling behind or dancing to keep up. Given those choices, Maia figured she might as well dance, at least a little.

The question seemed to be whether Joel was still interested in dancing with her.

CRILEO

Joel wasn't ready to dance, or he was no longer interested. After a few days, Maia put away her imaginary dancing shoes and returned her focus to her present.

Chapter Thirty-Six

Joel walked in to the gallery shortly before noon. The bell over the door made a clacking noise in addition to the jingle he remembered. He looked up and saw shells had been strung along the bell's chain. Apparently, even overhead door bells could change with the seasons.

He'd hoped to surprise Maia, to catch her free, perhaps entice her to join him for a meal at one of the nearby restaurants, or allow him to join her for takeout in the breakroom. If she was even willing to talk to him, of course.

If he hadn't taken too long with the dismantling of Sandeford Corp.

She'd never know the level of effort required for that deconstruction and divesting, and he hadn't wanted to drag her through that with him. He had this idea that the new re-introduction of them as "us" should start clear and clean of past obstacles.

No one was in sight. Joel stood looking, waiting. Brendan emerged from the office. The customer-greeting smile blooming on his face stalled and changed to uncertainty, and then his expression clouded.

"She isn't here," he said.

"Seriously?"

"Seriously. Don't you ever call first? You could save yourself some miles and hassle, you know."

Joel grinned. Brendan flushed and looked annoyed.

Brendan said, "Sorry. Not my business, I guess."

From what Joel could tell, Brendan didn't seem sorry at all.

"Where is she?"

"Where she always is when she isn't here."

Joel stood there awkwardly, or feeling awkward, in the middle of the gallery floor. He had anticipated some level of ire, perhaps even hostility, from Maia, and he'd rehearsed all the way from Raleigh what to say to defuse it. He just hadn't expected it from her assistant.

Brendan seemed to have grown, not physically, but into the role. Brendan had that in I'm-in-charge posture and voice.

Joel recognized he'd been assessed long before he'd shown up here today and, in Brendan's opinion, he had failed the test miserably.

He tried to sound conciliatory. "Good thing she has you to cover the gallery."

Brendan nodded, but his expression stayed closed.

"I'll be on my way, then."

"Can I tell you something?"

Brendan's hard tone stopped him.

"Sure. What?"

"You've been gone too long. No call. No nothing."

Joel was taken aback. This sounded personal. Like he'd stood Brendan, himself, up. It hit Joel, then, that Brendan was hurt, but on behalf of Maia. He was hurt because Maia was hurt.

"I wouldn't blame her, but has she said that herself?"

"She doesn't have to. I can tell."

"I had business to take care of."

"Everybody does. Some people can do more than one thing at a time."

"Some things are more complicated than others."

Brendan looked at Joel intently.

Joel had run a corporation, traveled extensively, had had the future of many employees, rather former employees, in his hands, but in the face of this young man's regard, he felt compelled to wait for his judgment.

"She deserves the best, Mr. Sandeford. The best. Don't make her

287

settle for less."

"Thank you, Brendan. I agree."

"She left a few minutes ago. You know where she's headed?"

"I do." Joel nodded.

As the door swung closed behind him, he heard the faint jingle-clack of the bell. He paused on the steps, listening, but it had already stopped.

It reminded him of yesterday and today. And he hoped to hear it again soon, in the future, with Maia.

Chapter Thirty-Seven

That morning, shortly before lunchtime, Maia had said to Brendan, "You know how to reach me if you need me," and then she left to go meet the carpenter at Bridle Cove.

Mr. Milner had been checking the porch supports, the fascia boards and all that good stuff for the past two days as he figured out what needed to be replaced. She refused to worry in advance about the cost. The repairs needed to be done. She'd figure it out one step at a time.

It was a fine, blue sky day warmed by the September sun and moderated by the Atlantic breeze. A wonderful day for a drive.

Forty minutes later, she drove through the cluster of houses in Merrimon and soon after, arrived at the metal gate to Bridle Cove. It was open. She wasn't surprised. The carpenter should be there and, sure enough, as she drove along the dirt road to the house, she saw his truck. Bob Milner was up on a ladder. He waved as she parked beside the house.

Maia carried her supplies into the house and was putting the groceries away in the kitchen when she heard footsteps on the porch and a knock on the screen door. She walked into the living room ready to greet Bob, and saw Joel.

She stopped short. He was standing on the porch, waiting.

Because she couldn't think what to say, she asked, "Did you get my message?" She frowned and crossed her arms. "It's been a few days since I left it."

"I wanted to respond in person."

"Phones work."

"So I've been told. Do you mind that I didn't call before coming out here? Is this a bad time?"

"No, the timing is fine. Seems like no one calls first anyway. Maybe the rules of hospitality are different out here."

"May I come in?"

Despite her tightly crossed arms, she tried to sound old-friend casual. "Sure. Come in."

He closed the screen door behind him as he entered. Maia was silent. She couldn't think of anything sensible to say.

He gestured back toward the front door and the yard. "The place is looking good. I see you have a new dock. I'm thinking about getting a boat."

"A boat?"

He shrugged and, in that action, somehow managed to move closer. "I never had the time to sail. Or, rather, boat. I'm not sure what the difference is. Do you know?"

"I think it depends on the size of the craft."

"I guess I need to do some research."

"Luke loves boating. And Brian, of course. I've been out with him a few times, but I'm not much of a sailor myself."

He'd moved another step toward her. She was trying to decide whether she should hold her ground, or…what? She felt more confident, more comfortable with her life now. Did she want to let him shake that up again?

"Why are we discussing boats anyway?"

Joel said, "I want to try on some new habits, hobbies, whatever…now that I have more free time."

"The divesting went well?"

A voice came from the porch. "Ms. Donovan?"

"That's the carpenter. Excuse me." Being summoned outside by Mr. Milner felt like a rescue. Maia went out to the porch. Joel followed.

"Here's my first pass at an estimate. Keep in mind that additional work could be needed once I get into replacing that wood."

"Is it bad?"

"Not as bad as it might be." He smiled. He noticed Joel, gave him a nod, and handed Maia a copy of the estimate.

"I'll call you after I've reviewed it," she said.

He nodded. "Have a nice day, ma'am."

Bob left. His truck kicked up a little dust as he drove away. Then it was back to Joel and her. She decided they could stay on the porch for their…chat.

Joel looked good, she thought. Relaxed, maybe? He wasn't wearing a suit, and not even business casual. His jeans fit him well and his toes, exposed by his sandals, looked like they'd been seeing the sun recently. In fact, his hair was a little longer. But she waited. It was Joel's turn to talk. Since he'd shown up here, he must have something to say.

"You asked about the divesting? It's mostly complete. About as complete as it can be for now. It took longer than expected."

"I see."

"Maia," he said, and reached toward her.

She crossed her arms again. "Not so fast, Joel. I need a little more conversation. Maybe even an explanation or an apology of some kind."

He lowered his voice. "We both had things to work out. To resolve. Our talk on the beach after the wedding brought some truths home to me, but when I came out here to speak with you that last day, so much became clear for me. I never realized how hard-headed I was. In my defense, I did tell you I'd return. I just had to get clear of all that baggage, both business and personal."

"I told you not to come back. Did you hear me say that before you walked away?"

"Maia."

"Seriously."

"I did. I heard you."

"I see." And he'd returned anyway. She nibbled on her lower lip, unsure what to think.

"As time went on…. But when I heard your voicemail, I thought maybe it wasn't too late. Maia, tell me what you want or need to hear from me. I don't want any misunderstandings between us." He touched her cheek. "I'm sorry."

She moved his hand away. "What are you sorry for? Exactly? I need to know."

She watched him struggle with his next words.

"I've been in and out of the country, tied up with negotiations and lawyers. I wanted to get it done, behind me, and then see you in person. To start fresh. To see your face when we spoke, and know I was here, not about to leave, to be on my way to somewhere else."

She eyed him directly. She kept her expression cool. "And is it? All done?"

He shook his head. "Almost, but not quite. I couldn't wait any longer. I was afraid I'd lose you. Even now, if you tell me it's too late, I can't fault you."

"You could've called."

"I could've, but you might've changed your mind. Over the phone it would have been easier to tell me again not to return. I wrapped up what I was working on and came here to see you. Face to face."

"What about Luke?"

He frowned in confusion. "Luke?"

"That day when things blew up with Julie, she mentioned your meeting with Luke. That's part of what angered me and triggered the rest. You met with my boss behind my back, Joel." She paused for a calming breath, then added, "You shouldn't have. Even if there was nothing to it, you should've told me and explained."

He nodded.

"Then, after walking in while I was unloading on Juli, you ditched me. It might not have been my best moment, but it wasn't yours either."

Joel touched the railing, then brushed at a leaf that had settled there. "I admit I was…surprised. Someone, maybe Brian, once said you had a temper hiding beneath your calm, competent, all-business exterior. I knew there was more than business in you, but I didn't expect…the anger."

"It wasn't about temper, though, not for me. I'd been nurturing unhappy things and letting the anger and resentment build and push out the good stuff. For you? I think you were feeling overwhelmed. Maybe uncertain because of everything going on in your life, with your business and your father. But instead of staying to fix it, to work it out together, you left."

She shook her head. "I'm glad we had that conversation after the beach wedding, but it left a lot unanswered, including what your business was with Luke."

"Did you ask him?"

"No."

"We were discussing partnerships. Potential. Nothing firm. I'm sure you know that losing Ben was hard on Luke, more than a personal loss. He wants a new partner."

The small coal of anger, of resistance, of hurt, that was banked inside her, tried to reignite. She did her best to douse it, but still it stirred. "And did he get one?"

"Maia," Joel said softly. "You look like you might strangle me. I promise you, I would never go into business with your friends, much less a friend who's also your employer, without discussing it with you first."

She took a step back. "You told him no?"

"I told him that after I wrapped up my current obligations, and after I'd discussed the possibilities of a partnership, the implications, with you, then he and I could talk again."

"Really?"

He nodded. "I thought I was in partnership with my father. I was wrong about that. He and I worked together, but I had no idea how unhappy he was with his life, and he had no clue I had doubts about my own future involvement. If we were partners and family, how could we have missed that? As for Luke, Luke is interested in a partnership, and I believe I am, too, but the partnership I most want is with you."

Joel paused, then said, "I hope you can forgive me for not being here for you. With you. One day, I hope you can trust me to be here, no matter what." He stared into her eyes. "I'm learning, Maia."

He added, "One more thing. I swear I didn't lie when you asked me about this at the wedding, and even now I'm not sure. I didn't give it any thought until later."

What was he talking about? Just as things were sounding upbeat and full of potential...now what?

"Just say it, please."

"Laurel."

"Laurel?" She tried to re-orient her thinking. "What about Laurel?"

"I told my father about Frannie and Brian rushing into marriage—like he wanted to do with Sharon. It didn't occur to me that he'd tell anyone else, especially Laurel. But he may have."

Maia stared at him for a long moment. "That's possible. We don't know for sure, of course."

"No, we don't. I could ask him when he returns."

"Why don't we just keep it between the two of us? No one has mentioned Laurel recently and sometimes a little mystery is preferable to yesterday's truth. No need to stir things up again."

"Agreed. Just between us. Our secret."

He held out his hand and she offered hers. Together they walked across to the fine, silky dirt and followed it to the beach.

When they stopped at the water's edge, he said, "Can I tell you about my father?"

"Certainly."

"He and Sharon went to the Caribbean for their wedding." He stared out at the water. "I thought of a hundred reasons why they shouldn't marry. My personal preference, and even hopes for my own future, argued against it. In the end, having done due diligence and concluded nothing underhanded was going on, that there were no plots to take advantage of my father or family, then…well, at that point, it wasn't my business and not for me to withhold approval." He nodded as if confirming his decision. "He has to do what he believes is right for him, and I must do the same, and so must you. If you tell me to get lost, I will, but I can't promise that I won't try to win you back."

Maia smiled and found it echoed on his face. He put his arms around her, slowly, cautiously, and when she didn't object, he pulled her close. But he didn't kiss her. She expected him, too, and was a bit annoyed that he didn't try. She looked at him, asking a silent question. He stepped back, but kept her hand captured in his.

"I've missed putting my arms around you. I missed your voice, the scent of your hair, your laughter, but—my arms around you—that's what I've missed the most."

For a long moment, Maia couldn't speak. She hadn't been expecting him to say that. She felt tingling in her toes. It was creeping up her body.

She wanted him to kiss her. Was she crazy?

In that moment, she felt overwhelmed. Could she trust him again? What about herself? She stepped away, wanting some distance between them. She needed to think, to find her center.

Sounding puzzled, Joel asked, "Is that a swing over there? It's practically in the river. You'd get your feet wet when the tide's up."

The swing? Yes, the swing was a safe subject. She could discuss that. She gave a shaky smile.

"I don't swing on it. Too risky."

Joel laughed and raised an eyebrow. "Really? If you swing barefoot, you wouldn't have to worry."

"No," she said. She went over to the swing and yanked on the ropes. "I mean, it might not hold. The ropes or the branch could break."

"Well," he said, "I guess there are risks, and then there are other kinds of risk. As a swing though, if you want to keep it as a swing—your choice, of course—then there are things we can do to make it safer. You could actually use it and enjoy it."

She sat, but gingerly. "I'll add that to my growing list."

"An aspirational list?" Joel asked. "I took the advice I gave you. To go for your dream? I'm almost free of what was not my dream. Beyond that…at this point, the way I see it, our baggage is light and neither of us is settling for second place."

"You sound like you're reviewing a balance sheet," Maia said, hugging the ropes and looking up at him.

Joel flushed.

She'd wanted this. She'd wanted him to return and he had. The decision was hers. And it was already made.

"You're going to have to do better than that, Mr. Joel Sandeford."

Joel grinned ever so slightly. "I'm hoping for the opportunity to try, but I'm still awaiting the go-ahead."

"I was told by someone who seemed very smart about business, not to dally too long over an opportunity or it could become a missed opportunity."

His grin diminished, but his eyes lit. "Am I too late? Is the opportunity gone? I came here hoping to persuade you that taking a chance on us was worth the risk."

Maia said, "That's a good question. The prior opportunity is gone." She shrugged. "But sometimes a missed opportunity leads to a different one…possibly a better one. All the balance sheets in the world, all the best laid plans, can't predict happiness. There's always risk." She leaned forward in the swing, and he put his hand on the rope near her own. "I'm more accepting of risk now. I've gained a little more trust." She added, "I found my heart again. My faith. Without it, nothing worked." "What do you want, Maia?"

She laughed. "My own happily-ever-after, whatever that may be." She shrugged. "I thought I knew what it was before, but now I'm grateful it didn't work out as I thought it should." She paused, sorting her thoughts. "I like being here—in this place, at this time. I'm excited, but patient, taking care of the present while waiting to see what the future has for me."

She said, "It's gorgeous out here, isn't it?"

"It is," he agreed. "You sound different, Maia. More…content."

"I am," she said. "So, you went from having little free time to having lots of free time. What will you do now?"

"Oh, I have a couple of things going on still, but nothing I can't handle from anywhere with Internet. I know I'll never budge you from Beaufort and the gallery." He touched her hair.

She put her hand over his. "Don't be so sure. I'm planning less these days and living more." She rose from the swing and stood close to him. "I'm tired of trying to control everything."

Joel said, "It sounds like we both have potential for adventure. Even nice people get to have fun, right?" He laughed and put his arm around her. "Lots of opportunities, a world full of possibilities, all open to us. If you're with me, I'm ready to take on the future."

She shook her head. "Not the future. There is no better time than this moment. Right here and right now—today—for a fresh start."

This time, when Joel wrapped his arms around her, he did kiss her. Maia returned his kiss. When she drew back, she pressed her cheek to his shirt. They stood for a moment, arms around each other, breathing. She could feel the beat of his heart and sensed when her own aligned with his. She stepped back and looked up into his eyes.

Maia said, "I don't know what's ahead for the two of us, but I'm content to take the future as it comes. For now, for me, it's here at Bridle Cove and at the gallery. What and where it will be this time next year? Only God knows, and I suspect it will be better than anything I could've planned."

"Yes, Joel, I'd love to discover the future with you."

Epilogue

They sat on the porch, leaning back in the wooden chairs and watching the stars arrive one by one over the river, and then suddenly appear in bunches. The crickets scratched their legs in the nearby bushes and gave their song to the night. The occasional splash of a fish in the river meshed with the sound of the water moving, lapping at the dock pilings and the small beach. The soft lights from the citronella pots burned around them to discourage insects, but not so brightly that the flames diminished the star light. And they were content.

Maia asked, "Are you up for a beach wedding next weekend?"

Joel sat up abruptly, startled. She watched him trying to control his expression and she laughed.

"I'm attending the wedding of an old school friend next Saturday. If you'd like to escort me, I'd be pleased. If you're free, of course."

He lifted her hand from the armrest, held it gently and then kissed her fingers. "I'm free and at your disposal." His eyes twinkled, and his smile deepened the lines at the corners. "As a matter of fact, maybe we can get a few ideas for our own wedding."

"Okay," she said, smiling. "So maybe I deserved that. I can dish it out. I can also take it."

"I'm joking, but I'm serious, too. Since you brought it up, I'd like to know. What's your idea of the perfect wedding? Beach? No beach? Small or large?"

"To be clear," she sounded stern. "It's only our fourth date. Or is it our fifth?" She laughed again. "Truly, I won't care where, only who. As to guests…well, for my perfect wedding, I'd keep it to family and friends, and maybe the neighbors, to be neighborly, and then there's a few gallery clients I should consider including."

She looked at his profile in the moonlight. In a softer voice, she said, "Or just the bride and groom and the pastor. Leave the masses behind."

This time, Joel laughed. "No, ma'am. I've seen the Donovans in action. I'll do anything for you, but if they're going to be my family, too, then I'm not risking alienating anyone. Besides, your cousin Lynette's perogies are wonderful. Maybe she'll bring some along," he teased.

Still holding her hand, he rose and drew her to her feet along with him.

"And this Donovan is the most amazing of all, just exactly as you are, wherever you are. From now on, if anything needs to be figured out or resolved, we'll do it together. Wherever you are, that's where I want to be.

THE END

Thank you for reading BEACH WEDDING

BEACH WEDDING is the third full-length novel in The Emerald Isle, NC Stories Series. If you haven't read the other novels and novellas associated with that series, here's the recommended reading order:

BEACH RENTAL is the first novel, followed by the short story BEACH TOWEL. If you missed BEACH TOWEL, no problem. It contains a scene referencing BEACH RENTAL:

BEACH WINDS is the second novel in The Emerald Isle, NC Stories series.

The Christmas novella, BEACH WALK, can be read as a standalone or skipped. It ties into the series just before the third novel in The Emerald Isle, NC Stories Series (BEACH WEDDING).

BEACH WEDDING is the third novel in The Emerald Isle, NC Stories series.

Author's Note

Beach Wedding takes place on the island of Bogue Banks, on the North Carolina mainland in the towns of Morehead City and Beaufort, as well as north of Beaufort around Merrimon and the Neuse River.

I've tried to be true to the geography and beauty of the Crystal Coast and Bogue Banks. For the purposes of this story, certain merchants and locations are fictional, and yet, when I walk along Front Street in Beaufort, I'm always a bit surprised not to see the Front Street Gallery. I have, however, sat on the bench that Maia frequents…or would frequent if she didn't exist only in my mind. And if, from time to time, I speak of Maia and the rest of the folks in the Emerald Isle, NC Stories Series as if they are real and familiar, I hope you will feel free to join the conversation.

Maia's favorite spot, Bridle Cove, is fictional. I wish it was real, but you can only visit it in this book. That said, there are many beautiful areas north of Beaufort, along the Neuse River, and throughout Coastal Carolina. I hope you'll find and enjoy them.

About the Author

Photo © 2018 Amy G Photography

Grace Greene is an award-winning and USA Today bestselling author of women's fiction and contemporary romance set in the countryside of her native Virginia (*The Happiness In Between, The Memory of Butterflies, the Cub Creek Series,* and *The Wildflower House Series*) and on the breezy beaches of Emerald Isle, North Carolina (*The Emerald Isle, NC Stories Series*). Her debut novel, *Beach Rental*, and the sequel, *Beach Winds*, were both Top Picks by RT Book Reviews magazine. Her most recent release (2020) is *A Light Last Seen*.

Visit www.gracegreene.com for more information or to communicate with Grace or sign up for her newsletter. Connect with Grace on Facebook at www.facebook.com/GraceGreeneBooks

OTHER BOOKS BY GRACE GREENE

THE WILDFLOWER HOUSE SERIES

WILDFLOWER HEART (BK 1)

~ Love and hope, like wildflowers, can grow in unexpected places. Kara Hart has been tested repeatedly during her first thirty years. She's recovering, but is she resilient enough to start her life over yet again? When her widowed father suddenly retires intending to restore an aging Victoria mansion, Kara goes with him intending to stay only until the end of wildflower season.

WILDFLOWER HOPE (BK 2)

~ Kara is building a new life at Wildflower House - but will digging in to restore the old mansion not only give her a sense of belonging, but also restore her heart?

WILDFLOWER CHRISTMAS (A NOVELLA)

~ Kara is expecting a quiet Christmas ~ just like she'd always known ~ but if she's lucky she'll have a very different Christmas experience ~ one worth building new traditions to treasure.

A LIGHT LAST SEEN ~ *When Jaynie Was…*

(Another Cub Creek Novel ~ Single Title/Standalone)

Brief Description:

Chasing happiness and finding joy are two very different things—as Jaynie Highsmith has discovered. Can she give up searching for the one and reclaim the other? Or is she fated to repeat the mistakes her mother made?

Jaynie Highsmith grows up in Cub Creek on Hope Road acutely aware of the irony of its name, Hope, because she wants nothing more than to escape from it and the chaos of her childhood. Desperate to leave her past behind and make a new life, she is determined to become the best version of herself she can create. But when she does take off, she also leaves ~ and forgets ~ important parts of her past and herself.

The new life is everything she wants, or so she thinks until she finds herself repeating the same mistakes her mother made. Is Jaynie destined for unhappiness? Is it like mother, like daughter? Did running away only delay the unhappiness she fears she is destined for?

Seventeen years after leaving home, Jaynie needs a new fresh start and returning to Cub Creek is critical, but she promises herself that the visit will be as short as possible and then she'll be out and free again. However, a longer stay may be vital to her future because if she has any hope of changing her destiny, Jaynie must reconcile the past she turned her back on with her present.

Please visit www.GraceGreene.com for a full list of Grace's books, both single titles and series, for descriptions and more information.

BOOKS BY GRACE GREENE

Emerald Isle, North Carolina Stories Series

Beach Rental
Beach Winds
Beach Wedding
"Beach Towel" (A Short Story)
Beach Christmas *(Christmas Novella)*
Beach Walk *(Christmas Novella)*
Clair *(Beach Brides Novella Series)*

Virginia Country Roads Novels

Kincaid's Hope
A Stranger in Wynnedower
Cub Creek (Book One)
Leaving Cub Creek (Book Two)

Stand-Alone Cub Creek Novels

The Happiness In Between
The Memory of Butterflies
A Light Last Seen

Wildflower House Novels

Wildflower Heart
Wildflower Hope
Wildflower Christmas *(A Wildflower House Novella)*

www.GraceGreene.com